# The Untouchable Earl

Amy Sandas

*This series is dedicated to my sisters.*
*For all the late-night whispers and giggles,*
*promises made, and secrets kept.*
*For the dance routines, goofy skits, road trips,*
*and* Charmed *nights.*

Copyright © 2016 by Amy Sandas
Cover and internal design © 2016 by Sourcebooks, Inc.
Cover art by Gregg Gulbronson

Sourcebooks and the colophon are registered trademarks of Sourcebooks, Inc.

All rights reserved. No part of this book may be reproduced in any form or by any electronic or mechanical means including information storage and retrieval systems—except in the case of brief quotations embodied in critical articles or reviews—without permission in writing from its publisher, Sourcebooks, Inc.

The characters and events portrayed in this book are fictitious or are used fictitiously. Any similarity to real persons, living or dead, is purely coincidental and not intended by the author.

Published by Sourcebooks Casablanca, an imprint of Sourcebooks, Inc.
P.O. Box 4410, Naperville, Illinois 60567-4410
(630) 961-3900
Fax: (630) 961-2168
www.sourcebooks.com

Printed and bound in Canada.
MBP 10 9 8 7 6 5 4 3 2 1

# Prologue

*London, 1812*

The young, elegantly dressed gentleman sat in the darkness of his carriage, deftly turning a snuffbox over and over in his fingers. The snuffbox was the only personal item of his father's he had kept, and he carried it with him always. It served as a reminder of a truth he could never allow himself to forget. Every now and then, he looked out the window at the building across the street. This was his third night coming to this spot. On each of the prior evenings, he had not been able to convince himself to leave the vehicle.

Tonight he was resolute.

He had heard much about Madam Pendragon's Pleasure House. It was reputed to offer an extensive array of sexual diversions to anyone with the means to afford the exclusive rate and the proper sponsorship. Aside from the services provided by the ladies of the establishment—and more pertinent to his needs—was the fact that Pendragon was known to enforce strict rules of discretion for her clients' protection.

Discretion was vital to his purpose. Without a guarantee his activities would be kept entirely secret, he would never have considered becoming a client of the high-class bordello.

As he sat slightly hunched forward, maneuvering the snuffbox in a constantly rolling pattern through his fingers, he acknowledged the restlessness traveling through him, like constantly shifting desert sands. It made his skin itch and his blood thrum. The agitation would only continue to increase.

He could not go on in this manner much longer. He understood that much at least, even if he was at a disastrous loss as to how to rectify his situation. But that was why he was here. He intended to seek Pendragon's assistance.

If he could just bring himself to leave his carriage.

With a growl of frustration, he curled his fist around the snuffbox and jammed it into his coat pocket. Allowing no further thought, he unfolded his lean body and pushed through the carriage door to the pavement. He crossed the silent street in long strides and took two steps at a time up to the door. A short, heavy knock prompted its opening.

After producing the required letter of reference, he was immediately shown to a private sitting room. For once, he was grateful for the air of entitlement he had inherited from a long aristocratic line. His wealth and social standing were ever apparent in his manner and bearing. The deference he was afforded had never been as welcome as it was tonight as he waited in solitude for Madam Pendragon. Too agitated to sit, he stood with his back to the velvet-draped window as he watched the door.

The woman arrived within a few minutes.

She was much younger than he had expected—perhaps in her early thirties. Certainly not many years older than that. Blond and rather pretty if not for the assessing way she observed him as she crossed the threshold into the room. She was gowned in flashing red satin. Her figure was lush and rounded, and her smile, when she finally displayed it, held within its curves a wealth of knowledge and mystique.

It was this woman's reported knowledge that had brought him to her door.

"My lord," she said in a velvety tone. "It is a pleasure and delight to have you visit my modest establishment. Please take a seat. Would you like a drink?"

"No, thank you," he replied. "I do not drink in company."

Her laughter was melodious as she crossed to a liquor service. "I insist, my lord. I intend to have a brandy, and it would not be gentlemanly for you to allow me to drink alone."

He watched as she poured the liquor into two snifters and then turned to bring one to him. When she reached his side and extended the glass, he realized what he had initially thought was a bracelet winding around her forearm was in fact a tattoo. A black dragon adorned the pale skin of her inner arm, its serpent-like tail twisting around the delicate bones of her wrist, and the creature's tiny green eyes stared at him as she waited for him to take the brandy.

"Please, my lord. Accept the drink and come sit with me. We shall talk."

There was patience in her voice, as well as an odd note he struggled to identify. Whatever it was, it managed to soothe some of his initial discomfort. He took the snifter and brought his attention back to the woman's face.

Her head was slightly tilted, and her green eyes—much like the dragon's—met his without judgment or expectation. She did not say anything more, just waited calmly for his decision.

He experienced a rush of self-assurance. He had come this far. He had gone years in his current state and had no intention of continuing in the same manner for the rest of his life. It had not been easy to finally acknowledge he needed assistance, especially from a prostitute, however high-class.

As if seeing his acquiescence in his expression, Pendragon allowed her smile to widen before she turned to take a seat in one of the plush chairs. He lowered himself into the chair beside her, holding the brandy snifter balanced on his knee.

The burst of confidence gave way almost immediately to a trickle of uncertainty.

He would need to explain what he wanted.

The heat of his frustration, which never seemed to be very far from the surface lately, began to stir. The old and familiar powerlessness spread through him as he considered his reason for being there. He hated acknowledging it had come to this. He hated knowing he would have to confess his weakness to this stranger if he was to ever find a way past it. He clenched the chair in a death grip.

"My lord," the madam murmured as she leaned forward to rest her hand over his.

He wore gloves only to the most formal affairs, detesting the feel of them against his skin, but he wished he had them now. The moment he felt the warmth of her bare fingers, he flinched away—violently and uncontrollably. "Do not touch me," he muttered through clenched teeth. He lowered his gaze. "I cannot bear it."

He waited tensely for her to denounce him and order him to leave. He had been foolish to come here. What did he expect to gain by coming to a pleasure house when he could not abide even the most casual touch?

"My lord."

Something in the madam's tone had him lifting his gaze to meet hers. She still leaned toward him. Her expression was calm, but he saw in her eyes something he had never observed in anyone else before—acceptance.

She smiled.

"I am beginning to get a sense of why you have come to me, my lord, and I shall endeavor to accommodate your needs. Why don't we start with a few simple questions?"

He gave a short nod, surprised she was willing to go on.

"Excellent." She leaned back in her chair and took a sip of brandy. "What is your age?"

"Twenty-four."

"Are you married?"

"No."

"Your aversion to touch," she began gently. "Is this something you have lived with for long, or is it relatively new?"

His stomach twisted. His breathing spiked. But an iron will developed over years of practice came to his aid as he brought his traitorous body back under control. If he ever wanted to master it, he needed to learn how to talk about his…affliction…without a rush of near-debilitating anxiety. And if he wanted to be able to move about and do his *duty* in society without constant pain, he *needed* that mastery.

He regulated his breath until it returned to a steady rhythm and the cramping in his muscles eased.

Then he looked into the madam's green eyes.

"Since I was young," he answered.

"Interesting."

Madam Pendragon took another sip of her brandy. Her steady gaze never left his. Somehow, her unrelenting focus did not feel invasive. Just the opposite—the assessing nature of her manner, along with her lack of an emotional response, inspired an unusual sort of assurance.

After several long moments, the madam eased the intensity of her regard and released a breath. She gave him a smile, her lips curving in a way that was both light and sensual.

"Tell me, my lord, what do you hope to accomplish in coming to me?"

He hesitated only a moment before giving his answer—it had been a weight in his soul for too long.

"It is time I enter society. As you noticed, I am unable to manage even the most casual of social interactions without difficulty. I cannot allow my personal limitations to become fodder for ridicule and gossip."

The madam nodded, her smile never faltering.

"I understand your establishment provides a wide variety of services to its members," he continued, his voice lowering as he tried to find the right words. "And that you have very strict rules regarding privacy."

"That is quite true, my lord."

"I seek assistance—or perhaps *training* is the more appropriate word—in how to accept the touch, the *proximity*, of another person without the sort of reaction you just witnessed."

"I see." The madam shifted slightly in the chair, stretching her lush body in a way that immediately drew his attention. "Now, my next question is rather prying, but as I am sure you will understand, your answer is also quite necessary for me to know if I am to properly assist you."

Distracted by the curves beneath her red satin gown, he nodded.

"Have you ever been with a woman? In the full sense, of course."

His response came from a choked throat. "No." He had never admitted as much to anyone, yet she barely reacted to the information, simply nodding. He realized this madam was not likely shocked by much of anything.

"Are you able to achieve arousal?"

His muscles tightened, and his fingers curled dangerously around the snifter.

"Yes," he said after a moment.

Pendragon smiled and tipped her head. "Are you attracted to women, my lord, or do you find yourself drawn to other men?"

The question surprised him, but was easy to answer. "I am interested in women."

"Excellent," she replied in a breathy murmur.

He frowned. "I am not certain how such questions are relevant, madam."

"Oh, I think you know." Her gaze then met his with a direct but gentle focus. "You could have gone to a physician for the kind of help you are requesting, but you came to me. Tell me, my lord, what else do you seek?"

He hesitated. Not because he did not understand what she was asking, but because she had seen through to the exact point he had been afraid to admit outright.

Anticipation dosed liberally with trepidation rolled down his spine. His voice was low and thick when he finally answered. "I've known pain almost all my life. I want to know what it is to feel pleasure."

His answer seemed to please the madam. Her smile turned sultry, and a light flickered to life in her eyes.

"And so you shall, my lord."

In a move as subtle as he suspected it was contrived, the madam smoothed a hand over the curve of her hip and down the surface of her thigh as she leaned forward, revealing the deep shadow of her cleavage.

"There is no better way to learn of pleasure than to discover all the ways to give it." Her voice lowered to a husky murmur, and her green eyes stared into his. "If you put yourself into my hands, I promise, my lord, you shall attain both of your goals. You shall learn how to accept a variety of physical stimulation, from the most fleeting and casual to that which is more intimate. You shall have access to beautiful, sensual women. Their bodies will be yours to explore, to command, and to satisfy. When you know what it is to give pleasure to a woman, your own will naturally follow."

At her words, the yearning he had struggled for years to deny surged through him. His heartbeat raced, and his groin tightened. He had lived so long with a sense of powerlessness, believing he would never know what it was to be with *anyone*. The idea that he might finally experience more than pain and panic from the touch of another person was an intoxicating thought.

Pendragon's glance flickered to his lap before lifting again. She smiled, and her expression, which previously had been all business, now contained a hint of playfulness. "I can see the idea appeals to you."

He did not deny it. Her teasing made it easier for him to acknowledge the lust inspired by her suggestion. But still, he knew well his limitations, his total lack of experience.

Meeting her gaze, he clenched his teeth against the apprehension still heavy in his gut. "I should hate to be a disappointment. To anyone."

The woman's green eyes narrowed shrewdly. "You shall do quite well, my lord, have no doubt. I possess a particular sense about these things."

# *One*

*London, May 1817*

Lily Chadwick knew there was something different about the fiercely scowling gentleman the first moment she saw him.

She could feel it.

The instant their gazes met, caught, *held*, something skittered across her skin like a rain of white sparks. It entered her bloodstream, heating her from the inside until her breath became stilted and her knees went alarmingly weak.

He stared at her from beneath a brow drawn low in a forbidding expression. His eyes were so dark, even the light of the glittering ballroom could not be reflected there. The angles of his face were hard, his jaw sharply defined, and he held his mouth in a harsh line that attempted to harden the full curve of his lower lip but didn't quite manage it.

Lily tried to glance away demurely, but she couldn't seem to manage. She felt a flutter that became a tightening in her belly. Her heart stopped, skipped a few beats, then started up again in a frantic rhythm as he just kept *watching* her.

Despite his severe, aloof appearance, something about him reached out to her, touching her with an intrinsic sort of recognition. It left her feeling as though she stood in the heart of a firestorm. She sensed with a certainty beyond rational explanation that his unyielding manner was a facade, as if he were a hero in some gothic novel. There was passion in him. She felt it in every quickened, prey-like breath she took while frozen under his intent stare.

The silent interaction between them was becoming more inappropriate by the minute, yet she could not compel herself to break away. As though caught in an invisible trap, she stared back at him while her hands began to sweat and her stomach trembled.

Finally, the stranger turned toward the gentleman at his side, releasing her.

She sucked in a breath.

Cast adrift, Lily fumbled to control her galloping heart. Desperately wanting to find a quiet place to absorb what she had just experienced, she returned her attention to the young ladies beside her, seeking an opportunity to interrupt their steady conversation so she could excuse herself.

"He quite frankly terrifies me," Lady Anne declared in a thready whisper.

"Do not be so dramatic," Miss Farindon chastised.

"Some say he is a demon."

Miss Farindon laughed. "He is but a man. A moody, rude, and highly arrogant man, but certainly no demon."

Miss Farindon and Lady Anne, out in their first Season, like Lily, were making the most of a short break from the dance floor by gossiping about those still on it. Despite her unease, Lily's attention was caught.

"Look at him. He never smiles."

A wave of awareness rolled through Lily as she realized what, or rather *who*, had become their latest topic.

She followed Lady Anne's furtive glance across the room. Again, she felt the internal rush as she looked upon the black-eyed man still talking with Lord Michaels, their host for the evening.

With the gentleman's attention diverted, she managed to take note of the generalities of his appearance. She estimated he was not quite thirty years old, and though he was above average in height, he did not appear so tall as to completely tower over Lily, who stood just a bit over five feet. He was dressed elegantly in black down to his waistcoat, which put his white shirt and cravat into stark contrast. His hair was thick and black, and he wore it much shorter than the windswept style many gentlemen preferred.

Even in relative stillness, he radiated an intense presence.

Lily forced herself to look away. "Who is he?"

"His name is Avenell Slade, the Earl of Harte," Miss Farindon offered, obviously quite in the know. "He has an estate near ours in Cornwall, though I believe he prefers London these days. I haven't been to the country in many years, but when I was a girl, I used to catch glimpses of him riding his black horse along the cliffs."

Lady Anne gave a visible shudder. "He looks dangerous."

Lily agreed.

"Danger can be fun sometimes, don't you think?" Miss Farindon suggested naughtily, her eyes sparkling as she focused across the room. "Oh, look, he is coming our way."

Lady Anne gasped while Miss Farindon twittered.

Lily resisted as long as she could before she turned to see the two men heading straight for them. The crowd parted for Lord Harte to pass, and Lily noted several downcast glances and quick retreats as the enigmatic gentleman made his way across the ballroom.

If he noticed the odd behavior of those around him, he did not seem the least bit bothered by it.

"*Oh my.*"

Lily wasn't sure which one of the girls next to her whispered the quiet exclamation. But she could guess the reason for it.

The earl's attention was once again focused undeniably on Lily. As he drew nearer, she realized his eyes were not black as she had thought. They were, in fact, a deep midnight blue. And she had been quite right in believing he was not as dispassionate as he appeared, because something else became apparent as he came closer. His expression was not cold as much as it was...*angry*.

Lily stiffened, feeling his animosity like a dousing of iced water. A breath of panic seized her, and she lowered her gaze.

Had she wronged him in some way?

The possibility filled her with distress, even though she knew if she had ever crossed paths with him in the past, she would have remembered it.

Lord Harte and Lord Michaels arrived at their group, and their host began the proper introductions. From beneath her lashes, Lily watched as Lord Harte did not take the ladies' hands to bow over them or press a courtly kiss to their knuckles. Instead, he provided only a simple nod of his head in acknowledgment. He did, however, offer a brief comment to Miss Farindon about remembering her family from Cornwall.

Gooseflesh rose on Lily's skin at the sound of his voice, smooth and rich, like chocolate.

When Lord Michaels gave her name, she lifted her gaze again, but Lord Harte barely flicked a glance in her direction and did not repeat the nod he gave the other girls.

In short, he slighted her.

Harshly, unreasonably, and quite obviously.

Lady Anne gasped at the insult, but Lord Harte was already addressing Miss Farindon again. "Miss Farindon, would you give me the pleasure of a dance?"

The young woman's smile curved coyly as she replied, "Of course, my lord, I would be delighted."

Lily watched the couple glide out onto the dance floor, her cheeks still burning from the insult, the rest of her blessedly numb. The frightened pleasure she'd felt under his earlier regard was now all but gone.

Lord Michaels, who had been a friend of Lily's parents before their deaths, turned to her with an apologetic expression. "My dear, I am sorry. I would not have facilitated the introduction if I had anticipated such rudeness."

Lily forced a smile. She would not have the kind gentleman feeling guilty for the unfortunate interaction. "No need for concern, Lord Michaels. I am quite unscathed."

The older man murmured another uncomfortable apology before turning to take his leave.

Lady Anne started to offer assurances, saying Lily shouldn't take the cut to heart. The man was obviously ill mannered, and Miss Farindon was welcome to him if she had such an affinity for danger, whereas the two of *them* were far too sensible to attract the attention of a man like him and should be grateful for it.

Lily only half listened. Her gaze tracked Lord Harte's position while he escorted his partner through the steps of the country dance. He displayed a predatory grace in the concise manner of his movements. Every step, every gesture, every turn of his head was carefully executed with as much forethought as Lily's older sister, Emma, put into the family budget.

For weeks, Lily and her younger sister, Portia, had been putting their most charming feet forward in desperate attempts to lure proper suitors. At twenty, Lily was older than most of the other debutantes being presented. Still, she had begun her Season with high hopes. Emma worked diligently to see their family through the financial hardship inherited from their father, and Lily was determined to do her part and marry well to relieve as much of the burden as possible.

Gratefully, the Chadwick sisters had managed to claim some modest success with their debuts so far. A good number of gentlemen asked Lily to dance at every ball. Suitors called on her during the day. She was invited to soirees, musicales, and walks through Hyde Park.

But none of the men had actually offered for her hand.

Worse than that, Lily did not want them to.

She had tried. She really had. She did not have high expectations. There was really only one criterion she required in her future husband. She insisted upon at least some indication of mutual attraction. She hadn't expected it to be so difficult to come by. She had done her best to keep an open mind as she had met gentleman after gentleman since her debut. Hoping—expecting—one of them to spark at least a flicker of passion.

Though she was more than willing to do her duty to her family, she would not sacrifice her personal, private yearning for more than a marriage of polite consideration. She wanted to know true desire. She wanted to understand what it was to feel physical yearning for another person.

But it had never happened.

Her suitors were, each of them, of proper social standing, adequate wealth, and pleasant character. It was simply that none of them inspired even a hint of the fire she longed to experience.

Yet tonight, in those short seconds when her eyes had met those of the Earl of Harte, Lily had felt more alive than she had known was possible. The disturbing connection had a visceral, elemental effect upon her.

As Lily watched the earl turning about with Miss Farindon under the glittering lights, an aching unfurled in her chest. She had a horrible suspicion he was *the one.*

And he had rejected her.

# *Two*

"Would you mind terribly, Miss Chadwick, if we did not continue to the dance floor after all?"

The question came from Lord Fallbrook as he led Lily away from where she had been standing beside Emma.

Lord Fallbrook had been an attentive suitor from Lily's very first public engagement of the Season. He was young, handsome, and charming—if not perhaps a bit overly so—and he had enough wealth to make him an ideal prospect for marriage.

Emma had suspected for some time that Lord Fallbrook would be making an offer. Lily was not quite as confident. Despite his winning smile and flirtatious manner, the man did not exude sincerity.

When she glanced at him in response to his question, he smiled in a way she guessed was meant to be self-effacing but didn't quite manage the effect when it layered over his deeply imbedded arrogance.

"I am afraid I find myself in need of some fresh air," he explained. Then his eyes lit up as though he'd just had a wonderful idea. "Perhaps you'd like to join me for a turn outside?"

It would be best to refuse. Though many couples had been drifting in and out through the multiple french doors that opened along the length of the ballroom to the terrace beyond, Emma would not approve of her accepting such an invitation.

At twenty-five and believing herself firmly on the shelf, Emma had become devoted to proper conduct in all things and expected Lily and Portia to do their utmost to avoid any potentially scandalous situations. If Lily hadn't found herself desperately in need of a little respite from the oppressive atmosphere of the ballroom, she never would have considered Fallbrook's suggestion.

But ever since her run-in with the enigmatic Lord Harte earlier in the evening, she had been feeling terribly out of sorts. With the doors thrown wide open, the terrace was in full view of anyone in the ballroom. The starlit sky and the promise of a cool night were alluring.

Surely, a brief stroll would not be so out of the bounds of propriety.

"A moment of fresh air sounds lovely," Lily replied before she changed her mind.

"Wonderful." Lord Fallbrook steered them toward the nearest open doorway.

Stepping into the night, Lily acknowledged it was exactly what she needed to cool the heat of embarrassment and disappointment that still burned beneath her skin. She allowed Lord Fallbrook to lead her along the terrace, smiling as they passed other guests who had chosen to take a moment away from the stuffiness of the crowded ballroom.

"Ah," Lord Fallbrook sighed dramatically. "Is it not a lovely evening, Miss Chadwick?"

"Indeed, it is," Lily replied, distracted.

"And I must declare I am a fortunate man to have such a lovely companion with which to enjoy it."

Lily smiled but did not reply.

It was exactly such flattery that made her question Fallbrook's sincerity. It was not that he said anything so terribly out of the ordinary. Rather, it was the way his flirtatious comments were paired with the light of mischief in his stare and the added discomfiting element of his hand sliding across the low curve of her spine.

That went too far.

Lily stopped and took a step away from him, forcing him to remove his hand.

Too late, she realized they were at the far end of the terrace. There was no one else near them, and the shadows were deeper where the light of the ballroom did not quite reach.

Lord Fallbrook stepped closer. With a flash of panic, she noticed something had changed in his manner. His smile was wicked in the moonlight and his posture more encroaching. He no longer seemed concerned with displaying the fine veneer of a gentleman as he stalked nearer, forcing her to take a step back.

"Miss Chadwick, perhaps you would like to continue with me into the garden. I assure you, there are endless delights to be explored among the heady scent of the blooms."

He reached for her again. His hand slid around her waist as Lily came up against the stone terrace railing behind her. She had nowhere to go.

She felt infinitely foolish for being so trusting and naive.

"My lord, I must insist you return me to my sister." Lily hated how soft her voice sounded. Portia would have managed a blunt and stern set-down at the man's improper behavior.

He curled his arm around her back, and he leaned in close to whisper, "Come now, sweetheart, just a little stroll. I promise you won't be disappointed."

Lily arched back from the smell of liquor on his breath. Panic made her limbs stiff and heavy. "Release me," she murmured, wishing her words had more strength. She lifted her hands to press against his immovable chest. "Please."

When Fallbrook laughed, a low and frightening sound, and forcibly began to lead her toward the stairs at the end of the terrace that led down to the garden, Lily grew angry—with herself.

She knew what he intended. She should have known sooner. The stories she devoured in secret suggested innumerable ways a young woman could be dishonored by a man intent upon ruination. She was innocent but not ignorant of the desires of the flesh.

Hadn't she spent the last weeks craving some sort of passionate experience like those she read of in her books?

How stupid.

She did not want this. Lord Fallbrook's touch felt repugnant. His willful disregard of her wishes was villainous and detestable.

Lily began to struggle in earnest. She tried to twist out of his grip, knowing in the back of her mind that she had to somehow escape him without drawing undue attention to her plight. Should others take notice of her situation, she would be ruined by the gossips. No one would care that Lord Fallbrook had attempted a forced seduction—Lily's reputation would be made to suffer for it.

No matter what she did, she could not free herself as his grip only tightened, his fingers digging painfully into her side as he continued to push her forward.

Then suddenly, she was released and stumbling to catch her balance as Fallbrook was tossed in the opposite direction.

*Tossed* was an entirely appropriate description of how the man ended up falling against the stone wall of the house as *another* man passed like a shadow between Lily and Lord Fallbrook. She straightened, surprised, and lost her breath.

Because in an instant of rushing heat and intricate sensation, Lily recognized who had come to her rescue.

"What in hell is wrong with you, Harte?" Fallbrook growled as he righted himself, squaring his shoulders toward the earl.

"I do not believe the lady wished to accompany you." The earl's tone was dark and disturbingly calm.

"That is none of your bloody business." Fallbrook tugged the collar of his coat back into place and smoothed his waistcoat.

"It would appear I just made it my business."

Lily's heart tumbled into a frantic rhythm. Steeling herself to step forward, she could practically feel the tension emanating from Lord Harte. His back was to her, and the broad strength displayed in his posture was terribly intimidating. She wondered how Fallbrook had the courage to face him down at all.

"You will regret that you did, *Harte*," Fallbrook sneered before he sauntered arrogantly back toward the ballroom. He never even glanced toward Lily where she stood behind the earl, her hands pressed against her stomach to still the wild fluttering there.

"My lord," she said quietly as she stepped up beside him and placed her hand gently on his arm to draw his attention.

The instant her hand made contact, his entire body stiffened sharply, and he looked down at her. His features were more harshly defined beneath the moonlight, and his gaze was far darker than it had been in the ballroom.

This time, she had no doubt it was anger she saw in his eyes. Anger, and revulsion. Her breath caught on a gasp she could not contain.

Lily's hand fell away from his arm while her heart squeezed painfully at his reaction.

"Thank you, my lord," she murmured, wishing she could think of something more eloquent to say.

He glared at her for a moment longer. Long enough for Lily to become acutely aware of all the ways her body reacted to him. The rush of blood, the tingle across her skin. The way he made her breathless and hot and so very uncertain with a single hard stare.

Then, before she could form a clear thought—let alone something she might say in response to his obvious hostility—he turned away from her and strode down the stairs to the garden, where he disappeared in the shadows.

Avenell Slade, the Earl of Harte, stalked through the darkened garden, ensuring each stride took him as far from the young lady on the terrace as he could manage.

His arm still burned where she had touched him. Her touch had been gentle, barely more than the flutter of a butterfly wing, but he felt as though he had been branded.

It had been years since Avenell had experienced such an uncontrollable reaction. What was it about her that nearly erased every bit of self-control he had developed?

Earlier in the evening, when he had glanced up from his conversation with Lord Michaels to find the young woman staring at him from across the ballroom, the poignancy of her gaze had stunned him. Her wide-eyed expression suggested she had been caught off guard, yet when he glared back at her, she did not look away as every other curious debutante had over the past few years.

She was not a striking beauty to assist in setting her apart from the multitude of other ladies in the room. She was small in stature, and though she was in possession of generous feminine curves, she did nothing to put them on display. Her gown was virgin white, her hair was a common brown, and her features, though pleasant, were not exceptional.

Yet in those brief seconds of connection, Avenell had experienced something he could not explain. Something unnameable had surged through him, altering his existence at an elemental level.

Avenell rarely interacted with ladies of his social

circles and certainly never considered an intimate involvement with any of them. Yet, when Lord Michaels had noted the direction of his interest and suggested an introduction, Avenell had been unable to refuse.

It had been a dreadful error on his part.

Miss Lily Chadwick was not for him.

His chest compressed, shortening his breath as he recalled the expression on her face when he had flinched from her touch. She had not been able to conceal the hurt in her dove-gray eyes, or the confusion.

He wished he regretted intervening between her and Fallbrook, but he didn't. Something had come over him when he saw her struggling against the cad's hold. The thought of what Fallbrook likely planned to do if he had succeeded in getting her alone made Avenell ill.

No, he did not regret stepping in.

But he would have to stay clear of the girl in future. She was a danger to him.

Because despite the searing discomfort of her touch, and the fact that he had not been able to manage his reaction to her, the most disturbing aspect of all was that he *wanted* her to touch him again.

And he had no idea what to do with *that*.

# Three

"SHE HAS GOTTEN SO BLASTED SECRETIVE SINCE Father died," Portia Chadwick complained before she flounced back on her pillows.

As had become routine, Lily and Portia had gathered before bed to discuss the evening. The meetings had been Emma's idea; however, in order to continue funding their debuts, Emma had surreptitiously taken a position as the bookkeeper for one of London's most notorious gambling hells and no longer had the time to join them.

Without their eldest sister's focused guidance, Lily and Portia quickly lost their enthusiasm for talk of husband-hunting strategies. Tonight their conversation turned toward Emma and the circumstances that had shoved them headlong into the London Season.

Lily threw her younger sister a disapproving glance as she settled on Portia's bed. "Must you use such terrible language?" she asked. "Emma would be shocked to hear some of the words that fly from your mouth."

"Swearing makes me feel better when I am in a pique," Portia retorted. "They are just words anyway, with no power of their own besides what you give them. And Emma can hardly have issue if she is never around."

"I am here," Lily pointed out. "Must *I* be forced to hear such things?"

Portia arched her brows. "Yes, I think you must. If only to toughen you up a bit." Her smile grew sly. "It amazes me that you can read those torrid novels yet still take issue with a few crude words."

Lily blushed. Portia was the only person in the world who knew of her secret obsession with the kind of novels no pure, innocent young lady should ever get her hands on. She lowered her gaze even as she defended her private little hobby.

"Any…explicit language in my novels is set in a grander context, not simply blurted out for shock and effect. If you would deign to read one, you might understand that."

"No thank you. I prefer to live my adventures out here in the real world rather than between the pages of a book you can only read beneath the privacy of your bedcovers."

*So would I*, Lily thought ruefully.

But a young lady was not supposed to yearn for unrestrained passion with a bold and rakish lover. She was not supposed to admit to wanting to feel overwhelmed by desire.

A young lady was not even supposed to have any understanding of how physical yearning and sexual desire might be experienced.

"I think it is safe to say, at the very least, our financial situation is likely far worse than Emma had led us to believe," Portia declared in an abrupt return to their earlier topic. "I wish she would trust us with the entire truth. The debt Father left behind belongs to all of us, not just Emma."

Lily shook aside her distraction to focus in on the conversation. "I want to help as much as you, but what can we do besides what we are already?"

Portia made a disgusted face. "You mean trying to snag a wealthy husband? I, for one, feel I have more to offer than *that*."

"What do you propose?"

"If Emma is not willing to share the full details of our family finances, how can we know what is at stake? We have to discover what she is hiding."

Portia had a point. If there was more going on than Emma was telling them, they did have a right to know.

"Speaking of the detestable task Emma has set for us…how are things with Mr. Campbell?" Portia asked.

Lily sighed. The gentleman in question was just over forty years in age and possessed a large income from his estate in North Yorkshire, yet had never married. He always made a point to claim a dance and had stopped by more than once during visiting hours.

Lily had momentarily considered him to be a fine prospect, but there was something missing from their interactions. There was not even a flicker of suggestion that any emotion beyond casual consideration existed between them.

There was certainly no passion.

Lily shrugged. "Kind and courteous, as always."

"And Lord Fallbrook?" Portia queried, her focus direct as she narrowed her eyes. They were the same gray shared by all three Chadwicks, but Lily always thought the color was more enigmatic somehow in the eighteen-year-old.

Lily stiffened, and heat bloomed in her cheeks as she recalled the man's ignoble attempt at getting her alone in the garden.

"What did he do?" Portia asked, her fine features suddenly tense with affronted concern.

When Lily did not reply right away, Portia pressed. "Tell me, Lily. I can see by your expression that he did something."

"It is nothing to go on about," Lily replied, trying to defuse Portia's rising anger. Her sister could be very quick to temper. "He tried to lure me into the garden tonight, but he was unsuccessful."

She wasn't sure why she didn't mention Lord Harte's part in saving her from near ruination. She and Portia rarely kept secrets from each other. There was no one she trusted more with even the most personal elements of her life. Yet, she couldn't imagine trying to explain her interactions with the earl.

"I never did trust that man's crafty grin. You are lucky he didn't completely compromise you, Lily."

Lily frowned. She had a tendency to be rather trusting, and as recent events had proven, she was also obviously naive, but she was not stupid. Every young lady knew the dangers of being seduced by a disreputable rogue. Even the suggestion of improper behavior could bring about a girl's absolute ruin. And the Chadwicks could not afford for anything to taint their name. Whether they liked it or not, their dire financial straits required they make the most of their social connections while they had the chance.

"I am well aware of that. Let us both endeavor to stay far from that gentleman in future."

"Agreed," Portia asserted readily.

"And what about you?" Lily asked, turning the subject back on her younger sister. "How fares your progress?"

Portia snorted. "Progress? 'Torture' is a better word. I do not seem to be made for all of this courting business."

Lily felt a wave of compassion. "Portia..." she began but could not think of what exactly to say.

"I am totally in earnest, Lily. I do not think marriage is for me."

"Perhaps you just have not met the right gentleman," Lily suggested.

Portia lowered her gaze and gave a little shrug as she muttered, "More likely, I am not the right lady."

"Of course you are, Portia. You just need to have patience."

Portia lifted her eyes and gave Lily a rueful grin. "Ha! When have I ever possessed such a trait?"

Lily wrinkled her nose. "You are right. You are doomed."

Both girls laughed, and the conversation slid to more innocuous topics after that.

Lily went to bed a short time later. She curled up under her bedcovers and tucked her hands beneath her chin but could not get her eyes to stay closed.

She refused to feel guilty for not talking to Portia about the Earl of Harte. She couldn't discuss what she didn't understand, and she had no idea what to think of the man with the forbidding gaze.

Avenell Slade.

Lily snuggled deeper beneath her blankets.

She loved the way his name felt moving through her mind. It was sharp and smooth at the same time. Dark and light.

Lily knew she was no great beauty. She did not have Portia's dramatic dark hair or flashing eyes. Nor did she have Emma's commanding presence. She did her best to be content with her place among her exceptional sisters.

But now, after experiencing Lord Harte's painful slight, she found herself wishing she stood out more, that she was somehow more attractive, more striking.

She should forget him. Put him completely from her mind. He had made it infinitely clear he did not welcome her interest.

Yet, she wanted to know him. It was that simple and that impossible.

A hollowness spread from Lily's center. It was a sensation she had experienced more than once since she had begun her foray into the marriage market. It was the fear that what she sought might never be found—that the kind of deep passion she yearned for existed only in sordid novels.

As thoughts of Lord Harte continued to agitate her mind and created a growing restlessness in her body, Lily imagined an often-read scene from one of her favorite stories. It was frighteningly easy to cast the enigmatic Lord Harte in the role of dark seducer, but she struggled to envision herself as the intrepid heroine.

Lily did not possess a bold bone in her body. By nature, she had always been rather shy and had never been able to cultivate the kind of self-confidence her sisters possessed. Though she may crave the passionate experiences she read about, she did not possess the courage to explore such things beyond the privacy of her mind.

For the first time since she had discovered the set of erotic novels unintentionally left behind by their last governess, Lily wished she had never read them. What had they done except show her something she was never likely to experience?

Lily woke slowly the next morning and was disappointed to see that the sun had risen long ago. She had always loved waking before the dawn, but the late nights of the social whirl had started to shift her internal clock. Still, she was up long before anyone else and struggled to keep boredom at bay while she waited for the others to awaken.

The Dowager Countess of Chelmsworth kept strict London hours, with the household rarely stirring until after one o'clock in the afternoon. Though their great-aunt lived on a modest allowance from the distant relative who had inherited her husband's title, she had graciously welcomed the Chadwicks into her home and agreed to chaperone them through the Season. Without Angelique, their options would have been severely limited.

Life with the countess had taken some getting used to. The elderly lady rarely censored her words and was occasionally quite outrageous in her speech as she spun fantastical tales of her life as a young woman before her marriage.

Finally hearing movement in the house, Lily left her room to see who had risen. Her surprise when she came upon Emma in the hall had less to do with seeing her sister back from her duties at the gambling club so early than it did with her sister's appearance.

Anyone who knew Emma for ten minutes realized the eldest Chadwick was self-possessed and imperturbable.

The Emma she encountered that morning was so unlike her sister that Lily was instantly alarmed, though she tamed her expression to reveal only light surprise.

"Emma, you are home early. Is everything all right?"

"Everything is fine. I just…developed a headache and came home early."

Lily didn't miss her sister's hesitation, but it was Emma's manner that drew her concern. Her perpetually composed older sister looked *flustered*.

Guilt pierced through Lily's concern. Emma always took far too much on her shoulders. Emma had insisted on being the one to care for their mother during her illness and had done all she could to shield them from their father's destructive behavior.

For weeks, she had been leaving the house early every morning to work the accounts at Bentley's gambling hell.

Though Emma assured them she had no cause to interact in the other activities of the club, there was still the constant strain of knowing a scandal could erupt at any moment should her involvement with such an establishment become known.

And now, clearly, something had happened.

Lily ached with the desire to ease her sister's distress, but she could see by Emma's shuttered expression that her concern would be rebuffed, and Lily was not one to pry or push.

"You do look a little flushed," Lily noted instead. "I hope you are not falling ill, with the hours you have been keeping. You should really try to get more rest."

Emma had turned to open her bedroom door, then looked back over her shoulder. "That is exactly what I hope to do. Would you mind if I forgo visiting hours today? I do not feel quite up to it."

Something was definitely not right. Emma took her role as their guardian quite seriously. Lily could not imagine many things that would cause Emma to be lax in her responsibilities.

"Of course," Lily replied. "We have the Lovells' party tonight. Should I send our regrets?"

"No, I will be fine by tonight. I just need a little rest."

Lily hoped that was all it was, but a kernel of suspicion had been planted. Not wanting to contribute to Emma's stress with her own worry, Lily assured her, "All right. I will make sure you are not disturbed."

"Thank you, Lily. You are a treasure."

Giving her sister a reassuring smile, Lily turned and continued down the hall. As soon as she heard Emma's door click shut behind her, she picked up her skirts in both hands and lengthened her stride, heading straight for Portia's bedroom. The youngest Chadwick had had no problem at all conforming to her new schedule and could be found still abed past noon on most days.

Lily did not bother to knock but slipped into the

darkened room and went straight to her sister's bedside to nudge her awake.

"Portia. Portia!" Lily brought her knee up onto the mattress to bounce it vigorously with her weight.

Portia groaned and tried to draw the covers over her head, but Lily whipped them away.

Her sister's groan turned to an angry growl as she cracked her eyes open in a narrow but fierce glare. "Bloody hell, Lily."

"Language, Portia," Lily admonished, then changed her tone as her sister rolled away from her. "You are right," she offered.

Portia twisted to look over her shoulder. "I know I am. About what this time?"

Lily recalled the harried, flushed look on their oldest sister's face and felt another pang of worry. "Emma. And whatever she is hiding. We need to figure out what is going on—the sooner, the better."

# Four

The Earl of Harte stood at his bedroom window, looking out over the streets of London as he mentally prepared himself for the evening ahead. He never used a valet when he dressed, preferring to accomplish the task in private, but tonight he might have welcomed the distraction of a servant's pointless drone.

A strict and personal rule dictated he spend a certain number of hours mingling with his peers in the drawing rooms, dining rooms, and ballrooms of the *ton*. Only after the requisite hours were fulfilled did he allow himself the freedom of retiring.

Lately, however, the familiar social trial had become nearly unbearable.

Because of Miss Chadwick.

He had no idea by what design the universe had decided to torture him by placing her so frequently in his proximity, but Avenell was determined to stay as far from her as possible. He could not risk a repeat of what had happened on the terrace at the Michaels' ball. It had been the first time in years that he'd experienced a slip in his carefully constructed self-control, and the shocked look in her soft, gray eyes had been enough to convince him he could not allow such a thing to happen again.

Avoiding the woman, however, had so far proven to be more difficult than he anticipated.

Perhaps he should ignore the usual invitations for the rest of the Season and spend his evenings at his club instead. Avenell had been a member of White's since he came of age, but he rarely entered the place. He never imbibed alcohol in the company of others, he did not gamble, he abhorred the cloying smell of tobacco that often filled such clubs, and he preferred to take his meals and read the newspaper in the privacy of his home.

But White's was one place he could be assured he would not find himself passing beneath the attentive gaze of Miss Chadwick.

He turned away from the window, finally feeling some confidence in the evening ahead. He need only stop in at one party at which he had promised to make an appearance, and then he would be free from the possibility of encountering the woman whose demure visage never seemed to leave his thoughts.

"What will we be hearing tonight?" Angelique asked.

The Chadwicks and the dowager countess were in the carriage on their way to a casual gathering at Lord and Lady Mawbry's. Tonight was less about husband hunting and more an opportunity to relax among favorable company. It was a welcome change of pace from the intense socializing they had been focused on for the past few weeks.

Lily especially was looking forward to the informal poetry reading planned for later in the night. It was to be a selection from the work of one of her favorite poets.

"*The Daemon of the World*," she answered. "It is Percy Bysshe Shelley's complete rewriting of *Queen Mab*."

"I hope it does not put me to sleep," Angelique said with a theatrical wave of her hand. Her French accent added another dose to the drama of the statement. "I do not relish the idea of snoring in front of my friends."

"Do not worry," Portia offered with a mischievous smile. "I will give you a jab with my elbow if I see you starting to nod off."

"Ah, you are a generous girl," the elderly lady said with a smile as she reached out to pat Portia's hand.

Portia and Lily exchanged grins.

Lily cast a glance at Emma, seated across from her in the carriage. Her older sister didn't appear to have heard a bit of the conversation since they'd left their great-aunt's house. Emma's distraction was palpable.

Lily looked askance at Portia and saw she had also noticed Emma's uncharacteristic lack of attention.

Despite some aggressive snooping on Portia's part, the girls had not been able to determine what had their sister wound so tight. There had to be more to their situation than Emma was letting on. Lily had suggested earlier in the day that they should just ask Emma what was wrong. But Portia convinced her it would be a useless endeavor. Both girls knew Emma would go to great lengths to protect them and could be infinitely stubborn if she believed it justified. That she had not discussed the cause of her increasing worry already proved she had no intention of disclosing anything.

The carriage rolled to a slow stop at their destination. Emma exited the vehicle first, then assisted the footman in helping Angelique to the ground. Portia followed next.

As Lily attempted to step from the vehicle, her heel caught in the hem of her gown. It took a moment to free herself, and by the time she started toward the house, the others were already up the front steps and nearly to the door.

A light drizzle had begun to fall, and Lily bowed her head and lengthened her stride to catch up. As she reached the bottom of the steps, she felt an unexpected shift in the darkness behind her. A chill seized her breath, but before she could turn, a heavy arm looped around her from behind, pinning her arms to her sides and jerking her to a rough stop. The scent of damp wool and woodsmoke assailed her nostrils.

"Don't be scared, little dove," a rough masculine voice muttered next to Lily's ear.

Every muscle in her body froze. Panic clutched at her heart. Though she wanted to scream, Lily found herself unable to let out even a weak little sound.

"You've got until midnight in two days' time to repay your father's loan. With interest. There is nowhere you can go where I will not find you, so you best pay up." The arm around Lily's shoulders tightened painfully. "I'll have my blunt. Mind my words, little dove."

She was released with a shove that sent her stumbling forward.

Heart racing, Lily brought a hand to her chest and

spun about, instinctively wanting to get a look at the man who had accosted her. But whoever he was, he had already disappeared into the misty shadows.

She stood there a moment in shock, catching her breath. A carriage pulled up in front of the house, but other than that, the street was quiet. Not even a footman stood nearby as witness to what had just occurred.

Her unsteady breath and shaking knees told her she hadn't imagined the swift assault. And the message in his threat had been very real.

Two days left to pay her father's loan. With interest.

Of course she knew Edgar Chadwick had left a mountain of debt upon his unexpected passing. But Emma had never spoken of a loan.

*There is nowhere you can go where I will not find you.*

The stranger's growled warning echoed forebodingly through Lily's head. Spurred into action by another wash of fear, she lifted her skirts in both hands and turned to run up the steps to the Mawbrys' front door. With her gaze lowered and her thoughts in turmoil, she didn't see the gentleman stepping out of the house until he was directly in front of her and it was too late to stop her momentum.

Lily collided full-on into Lord Harte.

With uncanny reflexes, he grasped her upper arms to keep them both from tumbling down the stairs.

And something incredible happened.

In one flashing fraction of a second, Lily felt the explosion of the white-hot awareness she had experienced the first time she had seen him, but this time, it was multiplied a hundredfold. Her arms where he gripped them felt inordinately hot from his touch, sparking a fierce reaction that spread throughout her limbs. The surface of her body where it pressed against him was branded with sensations she barely understood. It was as though she had been ignited in a conflagration of sudden life. Like a phoenix being birthed from flames.

The earl immediately set her away from him with more force than was necessary.

Lily stumbled, fighting for balance after the abrupt loss of support. With a gruff sound of annoyance, he reached out to grasp her elbow again until she reclaimed her equilibrium. As soon as she did, he released her as though even the minimal contact was offensive to him.

She looked up…and sucked in a swift breath at the hostility in his dark eyes. The heat left her body in a sudden whoosh. Her thoughts whirled. She could only gape at him.

"Watch where you are going, Miss Chadwick." His voice, rich and decadent, cut effortlessly through her jumbled senses.

He remembered her name.

For some absurd reason, that acknowledgment ignited a sharp point of pleasure in her chest. Before she could reply—or arrange her thoughts into any sort of organized pattern—he stepped around her and continued down the steps to his waiting carriage.

Lily watched him go.

Since her coming out, Lily had danced with dozens of young gentlemen. She had been annoyed by roaming hands, too-tight grips, and clumsy feet. She had been treated gently, carelessly, and, on occasion, a bit improperly. But she had never experienced the insane rush of sensations she had felt when her body made contact with Lord Harte's.

Now, as before, he seemed to dismiss her completely from his mind as he strode down the Mawbrys' steps to his carriage. But she noticed something interesting.

His hands.

They stretched tensely then curled into tight fists before extending again, the pattern repeating over and over as he walked away. After he climbed into the darkness of the vehicle and waited for the footman to close the door behind him, he looked up at her from the deep shadows.

The angles of his face were hard and forbidding, his mouth set in a firm line, but his eyes… They focused in on her, consuming her despite the distance between them.

Lily's lips parted to draw a swift breath. The flame inside her fanned to a full blaze. She could swear she saw a sort of *hunger* in his eyes.

Hunger, and a poignant suggestion of pain.

Lily's first opportunity to talk to Portia about what had happened did not come until later that night as the sisters met in Portia's bedroom. The younger woman listened with rapt attention to Lily's description of the gruff warning muttered by the unknown assailant.

When Lily finished, Portia stood from the bed and started circling the perimeter of the bedroom as she went over the facts.

"It is obviously in reference to some personal debt Father incurred before his death. Two days," she murmured to herself. Then she glanced up at Lily. "Emma must be aware of it. It would certainly explain her preoccupation."

"I thought the same," Lily agreed. "But I believe she has a plan."

Portia stopped. "You do? Why?"

"Her distraction, if you think about it, seems less uncertain than it does anticipatory. I took the time to observe her tonight, and I swear I could practically see her brain at work, sorting through details and organizing ideas."

"Hmm. You may be right." Portia came back to sit on the edge of the bed. "So what should we do about it? Clearly, this is not a small matter, or the man would not have felt it necessary to issue such a threat."

Lily took a slow breath. "We need to talk to Emma."

After a moment, Portia nodded.

"Agreed. Time for dear sister to fess up about what we are truly facing." Portia bounded up from the bed and marched to the door. Lily followed behind resolutely as they made their way down the hall.

Their oldest sister was dressed in her nightgown, but she was not abed. She was pacing about her bedroom as furiously as Portia ever did.

"We need to talk," Portia announced.

Without waiting for Emma to respond, the young girl mutinously took a seat on Emma's bed, her manner direct and unyielding. Lily sat beside her, folding her hands in her lap.

Emma stood facing them, her calm expression failing to conceal the tension riding her petite frame. After a moment, she nodded. "Yes, we do."

"You can start by telling us about Father's loan. The one we have been notified is due for repayment in two days."

Emma had clearly not been expecting that. She looked at Portia in surprise. "How do know about that?"

"Lily had a rather thrilling encounter this evening."

"What?" Emma's face paled as she rushed forward. "Are you all right? What happened?"

Not wishing to cause unnecessary alarm when Emma already had plenty to worry about, Lily did her best to assure her. "I am fine, really. It was a brief incident outside Lord Mawbry's town house. I never even got a look at the man. He approached me from behind and issued a rather urgent reminder that we have two days remaining to repay Father's loan."

"Tell us, Emma," Portia insisted curtly. "Who is this shady character, and how much do we owe him?"

Emma joined them on the bed. Exhaustion and worry were evident in her expression. "Just before his death, Father accepted a personal loan from a Mr. Mason Hale in the amount of ten thousand pounds."

"My word," Lily whispered. It was a fortune by any standards. There was no way Emma could have managed to come close to accumulating such a sum with her earnings to date. "What do you know of this man? Is he truly dangerous?"

"Good question," Portia agreed. She pinned Emma with an unwavering stare. "Just what would Hale do if he does not get the money?"

Their sister hesitated before replying. "I do not know."

Portia leaned forward. "What is your plan, Emma? We know you have one, and we intend to help."

There was another hesitation as Emma straightened her spine, and Lily had to bite her tongue against the trepidation that flooded her system.

"I am going to gamble for the money."

The declaration was a shock. Emma had often been called upon by their father to play cards with him late into the night. He needed the practice, he had always said, but no manner of practice ever seemed to help him out at the tables.

Emma had come to abhor gambling in any form. They all had. But there was no denying Emma had developed significant skills when it came to card play. Still, there was so much risk. A gambling hell was no place for a lady, even one as pragmatic as the eldest Chadwick. Bentley's club might be relatively safe when the business was closed to its members, but to actually join in on the high-stakes play…

On the other hand, if anyone could succeed in the scheme, it would be Emma.

"It's brilliant," Portia declared confidently after a few moments.

Emma relaxed in palpable relief.

Lily kept her misgivings to herself.

# Five

MASON HALE STOOD BY THE WINDOW OF HIS SECOND-floor office. The day was coming to an end, and the dark of night had begun to take over the sky.

He had not heard from Molly in two days and had no idea where she was.

Last night, after issuing his little warning to the Chadwick chit, Hale had gone straight to the flea-ridden brothel in Covent Garden where Molly had most recently taken up residence. He had wanted to assure her he would be getting the money to help her settle into a different life. A better life for her and their daughter.

But she had moved on again. Just like that, she was gone. He was getting damned sick of chasing the woman from one house of ill repute to the next. At this point, he would do anything to get Molly far away from the world of prostitution and opium use she had gotten twisted up in.

When he had first met her, he never would have suspected she would allow herself to fall so low—and that she would drag their innocent babe along with her.

As he had so many times since his daughter's birth more than two years ago, Hale questioned his decision to leave the girl with her mother. He had never expected to become a father and still didn't think he had it in him to play such a role in someone's life. His father had certainly not given him anything to emulate. Hale had no idea how to care for a child.

If he could just get Molly on a better path, he had to believe she could be a good mother to their girl.

Overwhelmed, Hale gave in to welling rage and fear and smashed his fist into the wall beside him. The plaster crunched and crumbled to the floor, but the destruction gave him no satisfaction. Not when Molly was out there somewhere doing God knows what.

He had to find her before she did anything stupid.

Hale knew London's underworld as well as anyone and had people out searching the most likely spots for her. Still, fear had him by the balls. It was not a feeling Hale managed very well.

He heard the quiet knock at his door but ignored it. He was in no mood to talk to anyone. His anger was too powerful at the moment, too unruly. He knew what he looked like when he was in a rage, what people saw in him.

But the knock came again, more persistent this time.

"Fucking hell," he shouted. "What is it?"

"Someone is here to see you, sir," his annoyingly meek clerk replied.

Before Hale could respond, the door opened, and a familiar voice said caustically, "Oh, for God's sake, just let me in."

Molly pushed past the young clerk and into the

room. Every muscle in Hale's body ached with anger and disgust. If he had his way, he would never have to see the woman ever again. But they shared a connection he could never sever.

At least she looked better than she had when he'd seen her a couple of days ago in Covent Garden. She was dressed properly for one thing, and she looked clean enough. She took a few steps into the room and looked at him with a gentle sneer.

"You just can't keep yourself from destroying things, can you?" she asked, looking pointedly at the dent he had just made in the wall.

Hale did not answer. He glanced at his clerk, who had peeked his small head in through the open door, and gave a nod. The man backed away and closed the door behind him.

Only then did Hale acknowledge Molly's presence.

He eyed her warily, like an opponent in the ring. She may have the general appearance of a proper young woman, but it was easy to detect the glassiness of her stare and the slack movement of her limbs.

"I have been looking for you," he said.

She smiled, and Hale caught a glimpse of the woman she had been a few years ago, before opium addiction had wound its smoky tendrils through her. "Did you need a tup, Mason?" Her voice slid with syrupy sweetness, and she put a deep swing in her hips as she sidled up to him. "Like old times?"

Hale looked into her baby-blue eyes, glazed over and flat. His gut seized with guilt. If things had worked out differently between them, maybe she wouldn't have gotten so lost.

She tipped her head and gave him a coy smile, then boldly cupped him in her hand. She giggled, a grating sound, when she found him soft and unresponsive.

"Well, *that's* not like old times," she cooed as she began to rub her palm against the front of his trousers. "I bet I can still get a rise out of you—but I'll need the coin up front."

Hale felt sick. He grasped her wrist and shoved her away. She stumbled and would have fallen if he hadn't still had her in his grip.

"What do you want?" he growled between clenched teeth.

Giving up her little seduction, Molly tossed her head back to glare at him. "Money, Mason. I need money. Tonight."

Hale released her and walked to his desk, needing space between them. "I will have your money by the end of the day tomorrow. More than enough to set you up in a nice place."

"No. I need money tonight, before dawn."

Something in her voice made him uneasy. "Why so urgent? What have you gotten into, Molly?"

"My life is none of your business. Bring the money to me at the Green Hen by dawn."

Hale shook his head. "I will have it tomorrow night."

"Dawn. Not a minute later," she insisted again, her eyes narrowing to hard slits. "If the sun comes up and you are not there…you will never see your daughter again."

Rage blasted through him. His hands fisted as he took two long strides toward her. "You bloody bitch."

She threw up a hand to stop him and laughed. "You

would not dare to hurt me, Mason, because only I know where Claire is, and I'm not telling you her location until you bring me what I need."

Hale stared at her in disbelief. The violent rage was blown away by a frigid wind. His heart iced over in terror. She couldn't mean it. She wouldn't be so callous, so selfish.

But addiction could make people do terrifying things. Heinous things.

Knowing she had him cornered, she laughed again and sashayed carelessly from the room.

*Oh God.*

His stomach lurched, and he swallowed back the bile pushing up his throat. How was he going to come up with the money in such a short time?

Hale braced his hands on the surface of his desk and dropped his head between his heavily muscled shoulders. He could not give in to the panic making him light-headed. He closed his eyes tightly and focused on his fury, allowing it to well inside him and overtake the feeling of impotence.

Molly would do as she threatened. He couldn't doubt it.

There had to be a way to get the money tonight.

And dammit, he was going to make sure Molly never again had the power to use their daughter as a means of extortion.

# *Six*

The Sherbrooke dinner party was a grand event, with several courses, musicians, and dancing that would likely go far into the morning hours. It was the perfect setting for the younger Chadwick sisters to further the interests of their potential suitors.

But Portia and Lily had something else on their minds.

Tonight was also the night of the anniversary celebration at Bentley's gambling club—a masked event—and Emma was in attendance.

Lily struggled the entire evening to keep evidence of her concern from showing in her outward appearance. After several hours, her fingers began to ache from how tightly she clasped them together, and her back burned with the tension pulling between her shoulder blades.

By the end of the night, Lily was nearly desperate to get home. She could tell by Portia's tight expression that she felt the same. Neither of them were likely to get any sleep until Emma returned safely.

It was not a long drive from the Sherbrooke mansion

to their great-aunt's town house, yet Angelique had found enough time to fall asleep. While Portia turned to wake her, Lily accepted the hand of their driver, who also served as groom. She stepped to the ground and turned to provide another hand to Angelique.

A heavy thud drew her attention, and she turned just in time to see Charles crumple to the ground unconscious as a large, hulking figure swept toward her from the night.

Alarm spread like an icy wave through her system. Terror froze her lungs. The assailant grasped the edge of her cloak and whipped it over her head. Before she could draw another full breath, he wrapped thick, iron-strong arms around her body, pinning her arms to her sides as he hauled her violently off her feet. Her abdomen fell hard across his shoulder, forcing a harsh grunt through her lips.

Lily fought to reclaim her voice to scream, but no sound emerged from her throat. Her limbs were paralyzed in her fear. Though light and sound were muffled by the material of her cloak, Lily was still able to detect the scents of wool and woodsmoke.

Hale.

He was carrying her away.

Portia was shouting with panic and fury, but her sister already sounded a long way off.

Finally reclaiming her wits, she started kicking her legs and thrashing about on his shoulder, hoping to dislodge his hold. But the man was furiously strong, and her efforts had no effect. A moment later, she was dropped to the floor of a carriage. Her cloak had fallen from about her head with her struggles, but the interior of the carriage offered no light to see by. The vehicle rocked violently as Hale climbed in behind her, and the door slammed closed. She caught only another terrifying impression of a broad, hulking form. Hale's feet were heavy on the material of her cloak, keeping her bound in place as the carriage took off at a dangerous pace.

"Stay put, little dove. Do as you're told, and you won't be harmed. Not by me."

Shock and fear held her immobile. Lily closed her eyes against the shadows weighing her down and tightening her chest. Surely, she should do something.

She thought of her sisters.

If Emma were in this situation, she would take no action until she had more information. Then she would consider all options, analyzing them carefully for risk and probable consequence, before making her decision. Likely, Emma would simply reason with her captor, convince him of another way to achieve his purpose.

Portia would do just the opposite. She would be fighting tooth and nail to free herself, regardless of any danger to her person or fear of being thrown from the fiercely rocking carriage.

Lily forced herself to breathe as tears pricked hot in her eyes. Of the three Chadwicks to be taken, Hale had certainly chosen the right one. Lily was the least likely to fight her way free or to devise a crafty escape.

The carriage swung wide around a corner, and Lily was thrown against the bench. The collision knocked her breath from her body in a *whoosh*. After that, Hale braced his feet more securely about her prone figure, effectively cutting off the chance of her tumbling out the door on another reckless turn. Apparently, he didn't intend for her to break her neck. At least not yet.

They had until tomorrow to repay the money. Surely, this was a mistake.

Unless Hale was taking her as added insurance that he would receive payment?

A spark of hope flared. *Do as you're told, and you won't be harmed*, he had said.

Perhaps she could not reason her way out of the situation like Emma, or fight her way free like Portia. But she was not completely helpless. She could be calm and give her abductor no reason to add further restraints. She could be patient and cooperative until an opportunity for action presented itself.

As long as Hale believed his payment would be forthcoming, he would be stupid to risk injuring her while the money was still unpaid.

Lily simply had to trust in Emma to win enough to repay the loan.

And in Hale to set her free when she did.

She held tightly to her hope. As long as she did nothing to tip the scales against herself, she would make it out of this. She had to believe that. It was all she had for the moment.

Finally, the carriage slowed. After another turn, it came to a stop.

When her abductor moved to scoop her up again, she did not resist. Once out of the vehicle, he hoisted her over his shoulder and carried her in long, lumbering strides. Her arms were still pinned in the twisted folds of her cloak, but her head was uncovered for the most part. She was able to determine that they were heading along a narrow alley between two identical brick buildings. Everywhere she looked, the way was lined with dark, encroaching shadows.

Hale made no effort to rush or disguise what he carried, leading Lily to believe he felt secure in their new location, which in turn made her feel distinctly less so.

Coming to a halt, her abductor knocked heavily on a door. Whoever opened to him must have been expecting them. An icy chill swept her blood as no words were spoken, not even to question the body thrown over his shoulder, and Lily was carried inside.

Keeping to her plan, Lily resisted the urge to struggle as she was carried up a narrow flight of stairs. They turned down a wood-paneled hallway lit sparingly by widely spaced candle sconces. The floor, covered in a plush ruby-red carpet, passed swiftly under her gaze as Hale took long strides down the hall. By the time they turned into a room, Lily's ribs were bruised from bouncing about, and her arms had started to go numb from their awkward positioning.

The door closed behind them just before she was dropped onto the floor in an unceremonious heap. With a brief scramble of limbs, Lily twisted her arms free of her cloak and pushed herself to a seated position. Sweeping her tousled hair back from her face, she saw she had been brought to a modest-sized study, well lit by candles. The room was decorated in an excessive baroque style, heavily gilded and swathed in burgundy velvet and gold brocade.

Not at all what Lily would have imagined as the lair of the rough-hewn Mr. Hale.

"Is this the girl?" a woman asked. Though her tone was clipped and impatient, she spoke with a cultured, melodious cadence.

Lily turned to see a woman, surely not much older than Emma, leaning elegantly against a large carved desk. The lady wore a gown of shimmering black silk accented by blood-red beads scattered around the hem like flames licking up from the floor. Her face was artfully painted, though was not overly garish, and her blond hair was piled atop her head in a skillful mass of curls, leaving several glossy ringlets to fall gracefully over her bared collarbone. A fortune in rubies and black pearls swathed her throat.

She gazed narrowly at Lily through a stream of silver smoke that eased from the tip of a thin cigar propped between long fingers. Her eyes were a vibrant green and seared Lily with an impression of calculated intelligence.

The lady in black was stunning in a way that made Lily feel immediately out of her depth. Confusion crept in to join her fear. What role could this dramatic creature have to play in her plight?

"Who else would it be?" Hale snarled in annoyance.

"You may want to mind your tone," the woman admonished mildly, though a note of steel had entered her voice. "I am taking a significant risk for you, Mason. I can still change my mind."

There was a silent pause as the two stared at each other. Lily could not see Hale where he stood behind her, but she could feel the fury and impatience emanating from him. Though the lady in black glanced away first, subtly shifting her attention to where Lily sat prone on the floor, she gave no impression of being cowed by the much larger, gruffer man.

"Release her so I can see what I am getting."

Hale scoffed. "There was no need to tie her up. She's just trussed up in her cloak. She's a timid one."

"Hmm. That may prove to be good or bad," the woman replied thoughtfully. Then she gave a careless wave of her cigar. "Stand her up. I can hardly examine her if she remains in a heap on the floor."

Lily stiffened, resisting the urge to scramble away as Hale stepped in front of her.

No longer concealed by shadows, he was revealed to be as intimidating as Lily had suspected. He was tall and solidly built, with impossibly wide shoulders. His nose was large with a prominent bump, and his eyes were deep set beneath a scowling brow. A short beard darkened his square jaw. He may have been handsome if his features were not so rough and intimidating. Long hair the color of dried hay was pulled back into a queue at his nape, with several loose strands falling across his squarish features. He was much younger than she had expected, but no less frightening, despite the fact that he kept his eyes averted, almost as though reluctant to meet Lily's gaze.

This was the man from whom her father had accepted a loan?

Hale hardly looked to have the means to provide such a hefty sum. Yet, clearly his appearance was deceiving, for ten thousand pounds was a small fortune.

It stunned her to think Edgar Chadwick had been acquainted with this rough character. But then, her father had become a different person after her mother's death.

Hale continued to avoid her gaze as he grasped her upper arms in his large hands, making her cringe at his grip, and hauled her to her feet. He tugged at her cloak and tossed it aside, then brought her around to stand in front of him. The intimidating weight of his hands on her shoulders effectively kept her in place for the lady's view.

Lily was silent throughout Hale's rough handling. Biting her tongue against the urge to resist the direction of his heavy hands, she remained devoted to her plan to give no cause for further restraint or violence. It had worked so far, since she was now free of her cloak's restrictive binding.

Still, she was not so stupid as to think she was safe. Not by any means.

The lady in black brought the cigar to her mouth and drew a long inhalation as she tilted her head and settled her green gaze upon Lily. Then she exhaled a steady stream of smoke from between her lips. Glancing at Hale, she gave a subtle nod. "Leave us. I wish to talk with the girl alone."

"The money. I need it now." His voice was a tight growl.

"You will get it once I verify that she is what you promised." Her tone softened as she gave an added assurance, "No more than an hour."

Hale hesitated a long moment. The tension in his hands transferred through Lily's body. This was a man who did not restrain his physical reactions, and the pure strength in him was enough to frighten anyone.

Anyone but the lady in black, apparently, as she waited patiently for his acquiescence.

"I've got no other options," Hale finally stated. His tone had gone thick and heavy.

"I know," the lady replied. "I will help if I can, but I have a business at stake. Now leave us."

Lily thought for sure he would continue to refuse. There was no denying the man's determination or desperation. But then, with a low, agitated huff, he lumbered from the room. His departure did little, however, to ease the atmosphere.

Once they were alone, the lady in black curved her reddened lips into a smile. Lily detected little true warmth in the expression.

Hale no longer held her in place, but Lily still felt immobile. Insistent fear clouded her brain, making it difficult to wade through the details of her situation. She no longer believed she was to be held as insurance on repayment of the loan. Hale was clearly not planning to wait until tomorrow for Emma to come up with the money. Something had changed. Whatever the cause, it was enough to instigate an abduction off the street. Yet, Lily struggled to comprehend the purpose in Hale bringing her here to this woman.

One thing was blatantly clear—her situation was becoming more sinister than she had first suspected.

Lily quickly scanned the room, looking for any possible means of escape. But there was only the one door through which they had entered and nothing else she could see that might give her the upper hand.

"You are a quiet one, to be sure. But timid?" The lady in black spoke in a soft tone, bringing Lily's attention swiftly back to her.

After stubbing out her cigar in a brass ashtray, she

slowly approached Lily. As she grew nearer, it became clear that she was quite a bit older than Lily had first thought. Fine lines accented the outer corners of her eyes and bracketed her full mouth. Tipping her head to the side, she asked, "Do you speak?"

Lily took a shallow breath. Pride held her chin firm and her gaze steadily forward as she formed the necessary words. "Why am I here?"

The lady smiled. "You shall understand soon, my love."

The endearment was disconcerting.

Then the lady began a slow perusal, walking around Lily first this way, then that, examining the details of her appearance from every angle. Her expression was critical as her gaze swept over Lily's face and hair. But her lips quirked upward at the corners when she boldly passed her glance over the full curves of Lily's bosom and hips.

Lily remained still in the center of the room, her head high and her manner unflinching as she endured the inspection. She had never in her life felt so vulnerable, so violated, though the lady never touched her. It was all she could do to hide the trembling in her limbs as she stood resolute.

Finally, the lady in black came back around to face Lily. "You want to know why you are here?"

"I assume it has something to do with a debt my family owes."

There was a pause before the lady replied. "That is essentially correct."

When she said nothing more, Lily gathered her courage to press further. "Mr. Hale gave us until midnight tomorrow to repay the loan. My sister will have the money," she insisted, hoping to convince this woman there was no need to keep her.

The look she received was almost pitying. A chill of foreboding coursed through Lily's blood.

"Does your sister have the money now?"

Lily's throat tightened. "No."

"Mason can no longer wait until tomorrow. He and I have arranged a way for him to obtain the funds tonight."

Foreboding slid toward panic. "What sort of arrangement?"

The lady in black turned and glided toward a liquor service set against a wall. "Have a seat, my love—there is much to discuss."

Two ornate red-velvet armchairs were set before an unlit fire. An intricately scrolled table stood between them. It was all so very civilized—the epitome of elegance. The juxtaposition between the graceful setting and Lily's perilous situation sparked a flame of anger in her center. Nothing was as it seemed in this place. Despite the lady's glossy manners and smooth tone, the underlying shrewdness she possessed was undeniable.

Lily slid a swift glance toward the closed door. If she bolted for it unexpectedly, she may reach it before the other woman could properly react. Beyond the door was the narrow hall then a flight of stairs to the alley entrance. If she lifted her skirts high in her hands, could she outrun anyone she encountered? But once on the street, which direction would she take? She hadn't the slightest idea where in London they were.

And if she ran and they caught her again…

A sinking feeling claimed her. There were far too many unidentified elements waiting beyond the door. Portia would have run, but Lily could not justify the unknown consequences of such an action.

Praying she might still encounter a better opportunity to secure her safety, Lily approached one of the chairs and took a seat on the edge, folding her hands in her lap. The woman had said they would talk. It certainly would not hurt for Lily to gain a better understanding of what she faced.

The lady returned with two wineglasses and handed one to Lily. "Here." When Lily hesitated, the woman gave an encouraging tip of her perfectly coiffed head. "Take it. You will need it for what is to come."

"Why? What is the purpose in my being brought here?" Lily asked.

A smile curved the woman's painted lips as she lifted her own glass to take a long sip. She offered no reply to Lily's question. She just stood, waiting for Lily to accept the glass she offered.

Taking the wine, Lily nearly gasped at the unexpected sight of a black dragon tattooed on the pale skin of the lady's inner forearm. The serpent's writhing image extended from her inner elbow to where its long tail wrapped her wrist like permanent jewelry.

It was fascinating and unsettling.

To distract herself from the serpent's image, Lily sipped from her glass. The red wine was heavy and acidic on her tongue, but it slid smoothly down her throat, spreading warmth through her chest. There was almost an immediate thaw to her chilled fingers, and her courage bolstered.

"Good girl," the woman said as she settled into the adjacent armchair with the subtle rustle of black silk. "What is your name?"

Lily eyed the woman cautiously, but answered. "Lily."

The lady in black smiled. "Lovely. You may address me as Madam Pendragon." She gestured with an elegant sweep of her hand. "You are currently a guest in my establishment and under my protection." The lady's smooth smile stiffened. It was a subtle shift and may not have been noticed by Lily at all if not for the red paint that accentuated every movement of the woman's lips. "At least…until you come under someone else's protection."

"I do not understand."

Pendragon did not reply at first, but made a graceful gesture of her ringed fingers, indicating Lily was to take another drink of the wine. Lily did so, hoping to encourage further explanation.

Madam Pendragon drank of her own wine before she spoke again.

"I must admit to being at a bit of a loss. Girls do not typically come to me in this way—unknowing, unwilling." Her voice trailed off, and her gaze slipped to the side. After a slow breath, she continued. "But I cannot allow my brother to suffer. You understand I must do what I can to help him. It is unfortunate for you that this is the only milieu I have available."

Lily's brain stumbled over the meaning in the other woman's words. Either Pendragon was being intentionally vague, or the wine was far more potent than anything Lily was accustomed to.

Pendragon went on, almost as though she was talking to herself rather than to Lily. "It is always a shame when a sweet girl must be used in this way"—she sighed—"but it is how the world operates. Men have their needs, and women fulfill them."

"Please," Lily interrupted, pressing her fingertips to the pulse throbbing at her temple. "I am very confused. Can you just explain why I am here?"

Her words dropped strangely from the tip of her tongue, and a new fear encroached upon her awareness. She turned to set her glass on the table beside her and was surprised by how much effort it took to ensure she did not spill. Her fingers felt thick and weighted, and her vision had blurred significantly.

She stared at the other woman, imploring her to answer. As she watched, Pendragon took a long sip of her wine. Lily found herself mesmerized by the way the candlelight reflected off the faceted crystal of the glass in long starbursts of light—so mesmerized, she nearly forgot what they had been discussing.

Then Pendragon leaned forward and took one of Lily's hands in her own. Her touch felt smooth and warm, almost comforting if not for the strange rebellion that seemed to be taking place through Lily's senses.

She fought to regain her mental equilibrium. Her heart beat with an odd, listless quality. Her limbs felt unnaturally awkward, and her mind had slowed to a sluggish crawl.

The woman had drugged her.

As though sensing Lily's inner panic, Pendragon leaned further into Lily's field of vision and smiled.

Her green eyes flashed with light-gold flecks, drawing Lily into her gaze.

"I will tell you the truth, my love, only because the sooner you accept this fate, the better it will go for you."

There was a long pause, during which Lily realized her legs were going numb. She seemed to be observing all that was happening from a distance. Her fear receded farther and farther in the back of her mind, seeming to exist only within a thick haze that Lily could barely penetrate. A strange lethargy was taking over, and she began to wonder what exactly she had been fearful of.

She tried to focus on Pendragon, sensing some extreme importance in what the woman was saying.

"Tonight, your virtue will be sold to a gentleman of the highest caliber."

Lily frowned. What had the lady just said? Surely, Lily had misunderstood. "Excuse me?" The words were horribly slurred, nearly unintelligible.

Pendragon sighed. "Some would see this as a great opportunity."

Lily tried to tug her hand from the woman's gentle hold, but her muscles refused to cooperate. Lily had never in her life felt more vulnerable, more afraid, than she did in that moment, and she could do nothing to help herself. How stupid she had been to fall so easily into this snare.

Tears pricked behind her eyes. Lily fought to gain a mental hold while cloying blackness crowded ominously at the edges of her awareness.

"I will do everything in my power to ensure you go to a worthy man. First, I must confirm your virginity.

This may not be my usual method of business, but my reputation will be on the line. Do not worry, my love—my physician has a gentle hand, and I will be with you."

Lily did not see Pendragon move from her chair, but suddenly the woman was kneeling before her, lifting the potent red wine to her lips again.

"Trust me. You will be well served to drink some more."

Unable to physically resist when the crystal was pressed against her lips, Lily drank from the glass. She felt another wave of intense warmth through her limbs before the numbness in her legs spread through the rest of her body. Her head swam in an intricate sea of shadows and light.

And then, oblivion.

# Seven

Avenell Slade sat completely unmoving in the soft leather armchair set in the shadows at the back of the room. His spine was straight, and one ankle was crossed over the opposite knee. His gaze focused on his snifter of brandy as he swirled its contents, warming the amber liquid in his palm, though he had no intention of sampling the high-end spirits.

After a few curious glances when he had first arrived, the others in the room had directed their attentions elsewhere, leaving him blissfully undisturbed. Everyone knew the Earl of Harte was not a man for casual conversation.

But then, none of them were there to socialize.

An hour ago, Avenell had received a message, notifying him of a singularly exceptional event. The missive indicated it would be a unique experience he would not want to miss but gave no details.

Upon his arrival at the intimate private drawing room, it had been immediately clear Madam Pendragon had invited only the most elite members of her clientele to participate in tonight's entertainment.

The few gentlemen were all from the highest ranks in society, government, and civil operations. Young men and old, but all with generous fortunes lining their pockets.

Avenell acknowledged a thread of unease as he considered the madam's reasons for inviting him. Pendragon never did anything without a specific intention, and he had come to trust her dictates over the years, even if they seemed peculiar at first. She always managed to provide exactly what he needed, which was one reason he had answered her call without much internal debate.

However, the longer he waited in the back of the room, trying to block out the excited murmurs of the others present, the more discomfited he became. It was not his habit to participate in such displays, preferring to conduct himself in a more discreet fashion. Only his trust in Pendragon—and a desperate need for a distraction—kept him waiting as long as he did. But as twenty minutes turned into thirty and then forty, Avenell decided that whatever the proprietress had planned was not worth the aggravation.

He shifted, uncrossing his legs in preparation to rise, when the madam swept into the room, her trademark cigar held lightly between her ringed fingers.

"Gentlemen," she said in greeting to the room as a whole. A generous smile and teasing gaze lit up her features as she sashayed through the small crowd. Those present ceased their conversations and angled their heads to follow her progression. The previously restless atmosphere settled into a subtle hum of anticipation.

Madam Pendragon knew her business well, as each of these men would likely attest. They all were waiting at the edges of their seats. Avenell scoffed inwardly at their eager curiosity even as he acknowledged his own. He settled back into his chair, deciding he may as well stay long enough to find out why she had called them to her establishment so unexpectedly and at such a late hour.

Coming to stand in an elegant silhouette before the flickering light of the fireplace, the proprietress turned to the gathered gentlemen. She paused, as though measuring the interest of the room. When her gaze swept the shadows occupied by Avenell, her lips curved, and she offered a nod in acknowledgment of his attendance.

The madam's lengthening silence triggered a renewal of agitation. Finally, one man interrupted the quiet.

"What have you called us here for, then? I haven't got all night, love."

Avenell tensed as he recognized the speaker as Lord Fallbrook. The man had nothing but time. He was the son of a marquess, and his family had more wealth than intelligence. With his father still alive, Fallbrook had very little social or political obligation and a disproportionate sense of entitlement.

Not to mention a proclivity for dishonorable behavior, as Avenell had witnessed the other night.

Fallbrook's dissonance encouraged others to speak up as well.

"Tell us what you've got for us tonight."

"Let's get this done so I can go enjoy one of the girls downstairs."

Pendragon smiled as though her guests were a group of unruly boys anxious for a new toy. And really, wasn't that exactly the case?

Avenell's stomach tightened with discontent. They were just a bunch of dissolute men aching for the next grand distraction from the hollowness of their useless lives.

Damn, he was in a mood tonight.

In an effort to ease his growing disquiet, Avenell focused his eyes hard on where Pendragon stood. She appeared as though she was finally ready to address the reason for having called them together.

"Gentlemen. My honored friends." Her green eyes danced with the suggestion of pleasure as she waved a graceful hand through the air. "You have each received an invitation from me because I hold you in the highest esteem. I would consider only the best of my clients for the unique and wonderful gift I am about to offer tonight." She smiled with a kind of innate feminine mystique that reminded every man present just how she had come to be so successful in her chosen occupation. "I will not torment you any longer."

She turned to the silent footman standing much like a guard beside an inner door and gave a small gesture with her cigar.

The footman opened the door, and three women entered the room.

Two of them were dressed in diaphanous gowns in the pleasure house's Grecian theme, designed to tantalize and tease. The pastel silk draping their bodies only suggested modesty while revealing more than enough to incite the lust of the men avidly observing their movements. Between these sensual nymph-like creatures walked a third woman. Her slim arms were linked with the other two as they came forward to take their places before the fireplace.

This third woman was young and dressed in a modest gown of white with a pale-blue sash cinched beneath full breasts well covered by a pleated bodice. Whereas her two companions looked boldly out at the small crowd with flashing, inviting gazes and knowing smiles, the woman standing between them kept her chin lowered shyly. Her features were obscured by a curtain of brunette tresses falling in silken waves over her shoulders and down to her waist.

Avenell's blood ignited in a furious storm of awareness, and his stomach clenched violently. His fingers tightened around the brandy snifter as he studied the details of the third woman's appearance, uncertain if he could believe what his eyes were suggesting.

But there was no doubt. It was her.

What the bloody hell was the demure and very proper Miss Lily Chadwick doing in the middle of a notorious brothel?

Murmurs of conjecture spread through the room. Some men rose to their feet to get a better look.

Avenell was frozen to stone.

"Now, gentlemen," Pendragon said, bringing the attention of the room at least partially back to her. "It is my unbelievable pleasure to present to you a sweet and lovely maiden. Untouched. Unsullied by the hand of any man. And all yours, if you are willing to be generous for the honor."

Avenell barely noticed as the madam went on to describe the girl's physical charms and graces. His focus was fixed on the woman herself.

What hellish fate set her before him?

He had done all he could to avoid her over the last couple of weeks, though the effort was more challenging than he had expected, especially when thoughts of her never left his consciousness. Then came the night they collided outside the Mawbrys' town house. For a brief and painful moment, he had held her warm body against him, and the elemental shift she had caused in his core had spread like a shock wave through his system.

Now, here she was, dressed again in modest white, her brunette hair falling in loose waves, the red glow of the fire behind her casting her figure into a decadent display of shadow and light.

As his hungry gaze soaked up every detail of the woman who had been haunting his thoughts, he noticed something odd in her manner.

Her lovely gray eyes were lowered, and with her hair shielding much of her face, she presented a perfect example of shy modesty. The posture struck Avenell as wrong. Despite Miss Chadwick's innocence and quiet manner, she was not one to avert her gaze. He had observed her enough in the preceding weeks to know she had an unnerving tendency to view her surroundings with direct, consuming attention.

The girls on either side of her were clearly meant to highlight Miss Chadwick's virginal appearance by contrasting it against their more obvious sexual lures. But Avenell noted they served another purpose as well. Keeping their arms linked with the young woman, they were able to subtly keep her in place as she swayed on her feet.

An icy chill swept through his blood.

Miss Chadwick had been drugged. Laudanum perhaps. Enough to relax her muscles and dull her brain. The girl was not there of her own free will. She was a virgin sacrifice being offered to the debauchery of the men before her.

A sickening dread rushed through him with such force that he thought he might be physically ill. His hands froze into fists, and his head throbbed.

Avenell looked away from the gross display at the front of the room and set his snifter of brandy on the table beside him as he rose abruptly from his chair.

His cool gaze swept over the other men in the room who had already started to shout their bids for the privilege of claiming Miss Chadwick for their own. It was difficult to tell if anyone else had recognized her, but it was obvious that no one intended to step forward and stop the proceedings.

Avenell stood locked in place, knowing that if he made a scene by dashing forward to interrupt, he would only provide more cause for scandal and her ruination should she be recognized. His body tensed to granite as he considered the best way to intervene.

Madam Pendragon laughed at the enthusiasm of some while teasing others to go higher in their bids. Avenell scowled in her direction and noticed that she sent him a sly glance in return.

As if waiting for—no, imploring—him to join in on the bidding war.

He looked away from the madam, for the first time not trusting the woman's direction. He sent his gaze out over the other patrons.

The gentlemen were practically salivating as they competed for the opportunity to purchase the hapless Miss Chadwick. On any other night, these men may have faced the same girl in their own drawing rooms and would have been compelled to treat her with the highest degree of respect. But here, she deserved nothing but their lust.

Another wave of disgust rolled through him.

He turned a hard glare toward Madam Pendragon as he heard the bid spike into an astronomical range. Anger clawed at him, along with an unexpected sense of betrayal. She should have known he would not be able to stand for this type of diversion, that he would be compelled to find a way to act and save the young girl from a ruinous fate.

Of course, she would be pleased by the income she would garner from the spectacle, but as he watched her, he noticed signs of tension in the supremely self-possessed woman. At that moment, the madam glanced his way again. Her brows lifted a minute fraction of an inch as she subtly tipped her head toward the prize.

Avenell clenched his jaw tight but finally looked back to Miss Chadwick. There was the expected twist in his gut, the stumbling in his chest, the thudding in his ears he had been experiencing the last couple of weeks whenever he looked upon this particular woman.

The laudanum appeared to be wearing off. She had managed to lift her chin, and she stared out at the room with confusion and wariness in her eyes. She tried ineffectually to pull her arms away from the girls on either side of her, but they held fast, making a play of rubbing their bodies against her to disguise their forceful detainment.

Their ploy was effective, and the other men in the room reacted to the show.

But Avenell was not fooled. He saw the fear in Miss Chadwick's unfocused eyes and the bright spark of rebellion.

In the next moment, Miss Chadwick's wavering gray gaze found him in the far reaches of the room. And when her eyes locked with his, she refused to let go. He could no more look away from her than he could unleash the moon from its orbit.

There was only one thing he could do.

Speaking in a loud, clear tone, he entered the fray with a firmly stated offer that nearly tripled the last bid.

His competition turned to glare at him for how suddenly he had brought an end to the entertainment. No one was willing to top such an exorbitant price.

Avenell ignored them all.

He was far too busy battling an intense internal war between disgust at what she had been subjected to and an alarming thread of *triumph*.

Because no matter how they had both ended up here, no matter how wrong this all was…the woman who had been tormenting him for weeks now belonged to him.

# Eight

Lily pushed up through the layers of a distorting mental fog. A strange sort of exhaustion clung to the edges of her awareness and weighed down her limbs. At first, the struggle to simply open her eyes consumed enough of her thoughts that she could not acknowledge anything else.

When she did manage to peek them open a crack, what she saw confused her. The violet-colored ceiling of her bedroom at her aunt's home was gone. Illuminated overhead by flickering candlelight was a damask canopy of the darkest blue draped across a four-poster bed frame.

She closed her eyes again and sifted patiently through her memory, trying to reclaim whatever details she had forgotten that would explain where she was and why. Much of what flitted through her mind was so baffling and convoluted that she could barely make sense of the distorted impressions.

Thick unease encroached upon her awareness. She tamped it down and tried harder, reaching farther back into her memory.

She remembered being in the carriage with Portia and Angelique. They had just gotten home from the Sherbrooke dinner party. Emma was—

Anxiety laced through her as she recalled Emma's plan to attend the masked celebration at Bentley's club in an effort to win the money they owed Mason Hale.

At the thought of the moneylender, another stab of recollection shot through her. Her body tightened with the fear delayed by the muddle of her brain.

Hale had snatched her off the street.

And then there was the woman in black. What had been her name?

Lily went painfully still. She remembered talking with the elegant woman, but she could not pull up the details of their conversation. She opened her eyes again and tried to sit up. Her overwhelming physical weakness made the effort it took to resist the weight of the lush bedcoverings nearly enough to exhaust her.

With a burst of fearful determination, she pushed herself to a seated position. A wave of dizziness made her stomach roil as she looked around the room. She was alone.

The bedchamber was large and luxurious. It was easily thrice the size of her room at Angelique's. Wood paneling gleamed with polish, a plush carpet in the same dark blue as the bedcoverings spanned the floors, and a gentle fire lit the room from a marble fireplace carved with neoclassical accents.

Lily noted a set of large windows stretching from floor to ceiling and saw they had been left uncovered. The haze of London streetlights against a black sky indicated it was still night.

Fear and confusion pulsed through her veins, making her hands tremble with more than weakness. Her head ached from the effort of trying to remember and understand how she had come to be in such a place, but immovable shadows remained in her mind, concealing too much of the recent past.

Accepting the futility of reaching for lost memory—and refusing to acknowledge the very disturbing fact that she was in the residence of someone as yet unknown—Lily focused instead on what she needed to do.

She needed to get home.

She needed to assure Portia and Angelique she was all right and find out if Emma had safely returned from the gambling hell. It seemed likely she had been gone at least a few hours. Her family would be frantic.

She was very nearly frantic herself.

But releasing the chaotic emotions swirling in her center and allowing them to take over would not help her. Scooting through the cool bedsheets, Lily made her way to the edge of the expansive mattress. She pushed the coverings aside and swung her legs to the floor.

Lily gasped as she realized she had been stripped down to nothing more than her thin muslin shift. The sight of her near nakedness filled her with an intense vulnerability.

Starting to panic, she looked around for her clothes and saw them laid out tidily on an armchair nearby. Keeping a litany of frightened questions from coming to the fore, Lily retained a firm grip on herself. Pushing her palms against the mattress on either side of her hips, she tried to rise to her feet but collapsed back to the bed with a whimper. Her legs felt as though they were made of water.

Lily took long, steadying breaths and stared at her neatly folded clothes set significantly out of reach. After several minutes, she tried again to stand. Another wave of dizziness assailed her, and her knees wobbled uncontrollably. Biting her lips to fight off tears, she stumbled forward, then pitched herself against one of the bedposts. Wrapping her arms around the smooth wood column, she used it to stabilize her balance while she fought to dispel her unnatural vertigo and shore up more strength.

Then she heard the sharp click of a door latch being released. In her weakness, she could do nothing but stare wide-eyed at the bedroom door as it opened.

Avenell Slade, the Earl of Harte, walked in.

At the sight of the ominously handsome lord, Lily's first thought was not a thought at all, but an intense flare of tingling awareness. It started in her belly and rushed down to her toes before bouncing up again through her chest and out to her fingertips.

Her second thought was that she had been rescued.

But her relief was painfully brief as she noticed his expression in the flickering light of the fire. The same dark emotions she had seen before seemed intensified now as he stopped in the doorway to stare hard across the room at her.

Lily fought against the impulse to cover herself. If she released the bedpost, she would crumple to the floor. An instinct for self-preservation urged her not to reveal the full extent of her vulnerability. Not now. Not with him glaring at her so harshly.

Tears burned behind her eyelids and clogged her throat.

She wanted to believe she was caught in a nightmare, but there was no denying that whatever was happening was frighteningly real. The appearance of Lord Harte made it all the more confusing. What connection could he possibly have to her abduction?

Oh, how she wished she could remember more of what had happened after Hale had left her with the lady in black.

She stared back at the earl's hard, forbidding features and gathered all of her strength to push her fear aside long enough to speak. "Where am I?"

He did not answer immediately.

Since entering the room, he had kept his focus locked on her face. But Lily watched as the direction of his gaze slid down her body. His perusal was slow and comprehensive, sliding over her breasts and continuing past the curve of her hips and down her bare legs beyond the short hem of her shift.

Though he revealed nothing in his stony expression, there was something in the gleam of his blue-black eyes that brought a delicate quiver to Lily's belly.

She glanced at his hands where they fell at his sides. He held them tensely extended, his long fingers spreading wide, before he clenched them into tight fists as he finished his slow review of her body. By the time the path of his perusal made its way back to her face, Lily was breathless and hot with a different kind of fear and…something else.

"You are in my bedroom."

The intimate depth of his voice struck Lily with an

acute force. Her head spun, and her legs collapsed. As she tensed for a collision with the floor, she was swept up in strong arms.

The fire raging beneath her skin flared with bright intensity as Lord Harte scooped his arms beneath her legs and around her back to lift her high against his chest. It took only a few short moments for him to set her back on the bed.

He released her abruptly to flip the bedcovers over her, then turned and strode away.

Lily was left with the striking impressions of his body's warmth, the strength of his arms around her, the woodsy scent of his skin, the brush of his embroidered waistcoat felt through the muslin of her shift, and then the sight of his broad back as he walked away, putting the entire distance of the room between them.

Before she could figure out what to say or think or do, Lord Harte returned to her side, a glass of water extended in his hand.

"Drink this. I had hoped you would sleep off the worst effects of the laudanum, but it seems to be lingering in your system."

Lily stared at the water, refusing to raise her gaze to his face, not wanting him to see the frustration and uncertainty filling her eyes.

"Drink it," he said again, more sternly.

Lily still did not move. As if understanding the reason for her resistance, he lifted the glass and took a drink before offering the water to her again. This time she took it in a tenuous grip.

Something about knowing his mouth had touched the rim of the same glass made her belly tremble, but the clean water was heavenly on her parched tongue and slipped gracefully down her throat. She took a long drink and then another before lowering the glass.

She thought she heard him give a sound of approval before he turned and claimed a seat in one of the chairs. Her courage strengthened, Lily lifted her chin to look at him only a few feet away and swallowed hard past the knot of doubt lodged in her throat.

Dressed in elegant evening wear, he sat with his back stiff and straight despite the plush cushion of the chair. His knees were spread and his feet braced squarely on the floor. His hands, with his long masculine fingers, splayed on the surface of strong thighs. He was the epitome of masculine sophistication and mystery.

Dark, enigmatic, handsome, and intense.

Her heart raced as he stared back at her, and she fell headlong into the deep draw of his gaze.

She could not crumble with weakness again. Her pride, if nothing else, would not allow it. Drawing her uncertainty inward, she straightened the muscles along her spine.

"Why am I here?"

"What do you remember?" His voice rolled through her, smooth and penetrating.

Lily sifted through the vague images swirling in her brain. Some of the fog had lifted, and various impressions were becoming clearer. She remembered again the lady in black…what *was* her name? There had been a glass of heady wine…the sense of growing numbness through her limbs…a strange softness invading her mind…

There were so many shadows. She closed her eyes,

and more images floated past. More women, talking in soft voices but holding her arms with relentless grips. The lady in black again. A room of men with wicked grins and blatant lust.

And then him. The Earl of Harte. Standing beyond the farthest reaches of the light, staring at her as though she belonged to him.

She remembered surrendering to his gaze. Falling into it as though it were a dark and secret corner where she could hide.

Opening her eyes, she drew in long, deep breaths. A chaotic whirl of unsettling emotions and physical sensations fought for purchase. She gathered enough strength to meet his penetrating focus.

"Tell me," she said.

His expression seemed to harden even more, and his eyes darkened. When he spoke, it was in a low, even tone.

"You were auctioned off in a pleasure house. Your virtue, a prize for the highest bidder."

Though his words rang true and fit with everything she was slowly coming to remember, she still rejected the statement. Such things simply did not happen. It was too fantastic. Too horrible.

More than that, she wanted to believe the earl's role in the night's events were that of savior, but it was difficult to hold on to that hope when he stared at her like he did now, with that deep, unfathomable focus.

"Were you the highest bidder?" she asked in a whisper.

He gave a shallow nod. "I was."

Heat spread out to her fingertips. A strange breathlessness claimed her. It was a sensation completely unlike her earlier fear.

"Why?"

His frown was fierce as he stared at her. She saw the small tick in his jaw as he clenched his teeth. Then he tipped his head just the slightest amount to the side as he asked, "Do you think me a beast, Miss Chadwick, to leave an innocent girl at the mercy of lustful men?"

Lily met his gaze, doing her best to show him she was not afraid of him.

"*You* were one of those men."

"I was," he agreed darkly without elaborating further.

He implied that his purpose in claiming her had been to save her from a ruinous fate, but something in his manner had her wondering if there was some other motivation behind his actions.

From the moment Lord Harte had entered the bedroom, she had begun to experience everything differently. Her thoughts, feelings, and reactions originated from a deeper source. Her fear and confusion had made way for other, more urgent sensations. The longer she sat under the earl's harsh and heady regard, the further she slipped into a state of expectancy.

She felt on the verge of something, but she had no idea what.

As the weakness in her mind and limbs continued to dissipate, she acknowledged that she could not blame her odd reactions on the aftereffects of the drug.

He was the cause of her heightened responses.

It was more than the wealth of secrets and mystery contained behind his midnight eyes. It was how he made her feel. Intrinsically. Viscerally. When he looked at her with his hooded gaze, she experienced something in the marrow of her bones, in the blood flowing through her veins, in the ether of her mind.

Lily lowered her chin to stare at the glass of water cradled in her hands. She struggled to organize her thoughts. Something he had just said repeated through her mind until she was able to acknowledge its full meaning.

*...at the mercy of lustful men.*

*Oh no.*

"The others," she said, lifting her gaze again though her hands had begun to tremble, "did they recognize me as you did?"

"One gentleman aside from myself was likely aware of your identity."

Lily's hands began to shake in earnest.

No young lady's reputation could survive her having been in a brothel, let alone on an auction block for the sale of her virtue. If word got out, her entire family would be affected by the scandal. The Chadwicks' position in society would be forfeit. Her sisters would drown in the scandal alongside her.

"Who?"

"Lord Fallbrook."

Lily's heart stumbled and fell. Her eyes remained locked with his as all she could manage was a low, whispered reply. "I am ruined."

"Not necessarily," he replied in a quiet undertone.

"Of course I am," Lily countered, forcing the words through her tight throat. "Fallbrook has already proven himself to be severely lacking in honor. Tales of my presence in that...place are likely already spreading across town."

"Pendragon's establishment runs under very strict rules of confidentiality," he replied confidently. "No man would dare speak of what happened without facing dire consequences."

She so badly wished she could rely on such an assurance, but she knew better.

Even if Fallbrook did not spread tales, what was to stop him from furthering his ignoble pursuit of her now that he knew of her disgrace? And the other men who were there tonight? There was no certainty she hadn't been recognized by more of them. And if not tonight, who was to say they might not see her at some point in the future and realize she was the girl who had been up on that auction block?

In the eyes of those gentlemen, she would no longer be a lady deserving of protection and esteem. Even if she retained her innocence after this night, she would still be labeled damaged goods.

"But there is no guarantee," she stated quietly.

He lowered his chin. "There is not."

She paused, gathering all of the dignity she still possessed to stiffen the length of her spine and meet his shadowed gaze directly. She could not afford to be passive in the face of this wretched disaster.

He had brought her here to his home. He had said he was no beast, but would he do what was necessary to safeguard her future?

"What is *your* intention, my lord?"

There was a long pause before he answered, during which his manner appeared to harden even further, proving he understood the nature of her inquiry. She had thought him forbidding before, but this went beyond angry scowls and terse glances.

Lily held her breath.

"I cannot marry you."

Such a simple phrase, but when spoken with the quiet control the earl displayed, it cut straight through Lily's center. Hurt pride and more forced a lift of her chin. "Cannot, or will not?"

He did not answer, just stared back at her. There was not a drop of empathy in his expression, not a hint of concern.

Lily experienced an uncharacteristic burst of temper. It was not like Lily to speak in anger, but she suddenly couldn't bring herself to care what he might think of her. His opinion of her was obviously quite low already. She stared at him with her manner unwavering, finding courage when she hadn't expected it.

"Of course," she muttered with a rough laugh that was far from humorous, "how foolish of me to consider such a thing when I have seen the evidence of your loathing myself."

"Loathing? Oh yes, I despise you," Avenell murmured darkly. The sarcasm dripping from his harsh words sent a shiver down her spine. He lowered his chin but did not break eye contact. "I would love to show you in a thousand ways just how much I *loathe* you, Miss Chadwick."

As he spoke, his expression slowly shifted. It felt as though he allowed his facade to fall away, giving her a glimpse of the truth beneath before he shuttered his features again. For a brief moment, she again detected that hunger she had first seen the night they had collided outside the Mawbrys' town house.

It left her breathless. In a blast of heat and trembling awareness, she understood that what she had been seeing in him all along had never been anger or revulsion.

It was desire, possibly as deep and complex as her own.

The revelation stunned her.

The harsh mask was back in place, but he continued to stare at her across the shadowed room, holding her gaze with silent command.

Lily could only stare back. Her fingers encircled the crystal glass so tightly that her knuckles began to ache.

"I shall never take a wife," he stated quietly in the lengthening silence.

She could not resist asking, "Why not?"

There was a long pause before he replied. "Marriage to me would bring only disappointment."

Her chest squeezed tight, and though she wished to urge him for more of an explanation, she could not force anything more from her throat. She could not believe his words, but it was clear that *he* believed them, and for some reason, that made her terribly sad.

Lily tried to tell herself not to pity him. Though he had taken her from the brothel to save her from a wretched fate at the hands of another man, he would not save her from ruination.

Yet he had brought her here to his home, his bed.

What, then, did he want?

Warmth spread out to her toes and fingertips. There was an unfurling inside her. The boldness and daring she had long since given up on possessing suddenly seemed within reach. She forced herself to speak plainly. "What *do* you intend to do with me, my lord?"

She watched his expression tense before he replied, "Once you are recovered, I will see you home."

The cool finality of his words sent a jolt through her system.

Home.

What awaited her there? And after?

If by some miracle her involvement never made it to the gossips' lips, she would eventually have to accept a proposal of marriage from one of her passionless suitors. She would become devoted to her husband, despite the fact that no one but the earl had ever made her feel such a wild rush of sensations. Had ever made her feel *alive*.

And if tonight's events ultimately led to her ruin, she would receive no honorable offers, from passionless gentlemen or otherwise. She would become a spinster and live out the rest of her days a virgin, destitute from the lack of funds a good marriage would provide.

Either way, she would be forever unknowing.

Resistance claimed her. She could not accept such an end.

She had often imagined what it would feel like to be the object of a worthy man's passion. To experience that physical yearning for another person, which all the heroines in her books led her to believe could be real. She had never been so close to those imaginings becoming a reality as she was when she looked into Lord Harte's eyes.

How would it feel to have such a man state passionately that he intended to have her as his own, despite his honor and her reputation, despite whatever good intentions he may have had? How would it feel to know that even if she did end up recognized and ruined, she wouldn't be doomed to a desperate, penniless life, never having known what it felt like to be so consumed? Lily had never held any power, and she never would again—but she did *now*, in this, if she were only willing to take her own gamble.

Overwhelmed—and shocked—by what she was honestly contemplating, she dipped her chin to stare at the glass she cradled in her lap. But only for a moment. She did not want to risk losing this urging inside her.

From the moment she had been snatched off the street and tossed to the floor of Hale's carriage, her life had been inexorably set along a new course. This evening had taken her through a whirlwind of emotions: fear, confusion, uncertainty, longing, despair, and disappointment. And had brought her to this moment of breathless anticipation.

Lily did not have Emma's confidence or Portia's audacity. But perhaps she did not have to live vicariously through her sisters or her novels. Perhaps she had just enough courage. She would never be able to forgive herself if she did not at least try.

With a small toss of her head to clear the wisps of hair that had fallen against her face, she looked up again to meet his hard gaze. "What if you did not?" she asked, her tone strong and clear.

His body tensed. His hands curled into tight fists

on his thighs. When he spoke, his voice was low and fiercely controlled. "Did not what?"

"What if you did not take me home?" she clarified. "At least…not right away."

Lily's heart raced. She had never been more terrified in her life.

But it was a beautiful, exhilarating sort of terror as she waited for him to understand what she was asking. Her entire body felt tight, as though every part of her held its breath in wait for his response.

"Miss Chadwick." The earl's voice was low and heavy. "Do you know what you are saying?"

A tremor ran through her. Her mouth went dry even as her palms began to sweat. "I believe I do."

His eyes burned black in the darkness, but he said nothing more.

She dropped her gaze briefly to where his hands fisted and extended in a rhythm already becoming familiar to her.

"Lord Harte."

"Yes, Miss Chadwick." The melted warmth of his voice sent shivers of anticipation across her skin.

There was no going back.

"I would like for you to claim me," she said softly.

# Nine

Every nerve ending in Avenell's body sparked with life. Sensations skittered across his skin in varying degrees of intensity. His fingers curled into fists so tight it made the muscles of his forearms cramp.

Her gaze had been locked with his, but now it fell again to watch his hands as he forced them to relax. Just that slightest bit of her attention sent liquid fire through his veins, and he wondered what it would feel like for her to watch him while he placed his hands on her body.

To let her touch him in return…

His skin buzzed violently at the thought.

Since first laying eyes on Miss Chadwick, he had been disturbed by his fierce attraction. She had gotten into his blood. The very depths of him. This girl who stared at him so candidly and made him yearn for the slide of her fingers over his skin despite what he knew would follow.

This gentle young woman who told him so guilelessly that she wanted him to *claim her.*

His hands fisted again, and he clenched his teeth.

Dear God, he had never wanted anything so much in his life, but he knew intimately the challenge such a thing presented. Simply wanting something did not make the impossible possible.

Despite the intensity of his attraction to her, he'd never intended to have this woman in his bed. He would have gone on indefinitely avoiding her, denying his attraction forever if necessary. But the idea of her falling into the hands of one of the others present at Pendragon's had been inconceivable. A few hours ago, his only thought had been to get her out of the brothel. He had not considered the ramifications of bringing her to his town house, had only wanted to get her someplace safe while the effects of the drug left her system.

He would have left her to sleep fully clothed, but the wrinkled and disheveled state of her clothing stood as stark evidence of what she had endured. Her gown needed pressing, and the rigidity of her confining stays convinced him she would be more comfortable without them.

He had stripped away her clothes himself. He was no stranger to the female body, but the vulnerability inherent in her innocent form as the shadows of her figure were revealed through the thin material of her shift had struck him acutely. Desire had burgeoned beneath his skin until he recalled that it very easily could have been another man stripping her at that moment and for another reason altogether.

Fury had tempered the lust in his blood.

He had left her there, her thick brown hair spreading out over his pillows, while he had retreated to the silent sanctuary of his study. He had not returned to his bedroom until a couple of hours had passed and he could be certain of his physical reactions. When he had walked through the door to find her awake, the sight of her thinly clad body and the way her gray eyes met his with stunned disbelief had brought to mind only one stark thought.

She belonged to him.

He had felt the truth of it down to his marrow.

Just as he had known he would never claim her.

*I would like for you to claim me.*

Desire flared hot beneath his skin, making him burn.

Avenell had learned a great deal from Pendragon about managing his reactions while in society so no one would suspect his aversion to even the briefest touch. And as she had promised him when he first came to her, he also learned all the ways a man could touch a woman—pleasure a woman.

What Lily Chadwick had just suggested was something else entirely.

She waited for his response.

The gentle directness of her stare suggested deeply hidden strengths the likes of which Avenell was desperate to explore. He was suddenly filled with a powerful sense of anticipation, a primal desire to possess.

Could he take this girl as his own? Claim her? Pleasure her in all the ways he had imagined doing from the first time he had seen her staring so opening across the ballroom?

Could he take it further?

He imagined what it might feel like to have her soft eyes watching the path of her hands as she caressed his body. His skin lit with sensations akin to pain but that were at the same time so very different. It was an unfamiliar intensity—a sharp longing for something he had never expected to have.

He took a steadying breath, and when he spoke, his words sounded harsher and colder than he had intended. "You want me to…claim you." He felt compelled to understand. "Why?"

He had noticed before that when he spoke, her eyes would widen fractionally in an involuntary reaction to the sound of his voice. He saw the reaction again, and it fanned the flames already growing inside him.

He sensed something hidden behind her gaze, something he couldn't quite access as she stared at him. Her quiet focus was like a tether of white lightning connecting them, and he realized as he watched the shadows move through her quiet gaze that she revealed only a portion of what went on beneath the surface.

This woman had secrets.

That, at least, was something he understood quite well.

After a moment, she lowered her chin and gave a subtle shrug. The gesture was innocent enough, but it shifted the bedcovering partially covering her near-naked form, causing it to reveal one thinly clad breast and the luxurious curve of her hip and thigh.

Avenell soaked in the sight of her. Heat blasted through him.

She took a long breath before she lifted her gaze again. As their eyes met, he did nothing to hide the dark yearning. Even though he knew his desire must be reflected in his eyes, she did not glance away. He might have suspected she did not understand the full depth of his hunger for her, if not for the way her breath became shallow and swift through her parted lips and the pulse at the base of her throat fluttered.

"That is why, my lord," she answered in a husky whisper. "When you look at me like that I feel…alive inside. It makes me desperate to know what else I might feel if…"

"If I touched you," Avenell murmured when she did not finish her thought.

Her eyes widened again, the gray rings narrowing as her pupils dilated.

"Yes." Her reply was issued on a sigh before she licked her lips and continued. "Am I wrong in believing you feel something of the same nature for me?"

His palms buzzed at the thought of sliding them over her skin. The hunger would not be easily appeased. It would come with its own challenges.

Challenges that would take time and patience. She would not understand…

"You are not mistaken," he replied in a tone far more raw than he expected. He cleared his throat. "Miss Chadwick, I cannot agree to your request."

Her body tensed at his reply. Her embarrassment was evident in the heightened color in her cheeks and the way her eyelashes fluttered as though she wished to look away.

Avenell forcefully held her gaze with his, demanding she see the truth.

"If I took you as my own, one night would not be nearly enough."

Her gray eyes darkened, and her voice was a thick murmur. "Then take more."

There was no hesitation in her reply, no coy flirtation. The words were a perfect blend of plea and command. Just as her manner was equal parts vulnerability and strength, courage and beauty.

Avenell's chest tightened with a feeling he could not identify. He could do nothing beyond acknowledging it was something more than lust and so much more than the desire to possess. He was helpless to resist the sensation as it traveled through his bloodstream, leaving him in a state of heightened anticipation.

There were so many reasons to refuse her.

Lily Chadwick was meant to be a noble gentleman's wife, not the lover of a damaged man.

He studied the woman seated on his bed. Her brunette hair fell in soft waves down to her hips, and her skin was nearly luminescent beneath the thin material of her shift. Her focus never wavered from him as she waited with parted lips and bated breath for his response.

She was temptation incarnate.

His body tensed painfully at the thought of making her his.

He had never wanted anything more.

He forced his tense jaw to relax as he took a steadying breath. "Miss Chadwick, are you offering to become my mistress?"

---

His mistress.

The idea triggered a wealth of feelings in Lily.

Excitement, desire, a twinge of uncertainty, and an exhilarating kind of fear.

Strange how the word resonated so deeply.

Mistress.

She knew she was staring at him wide-eyed and breathless. She suspected she looked nothing at all like a mistress. She had always assumed the ladies who held such positions to be sophisticated and confident. Alluring.

She was none of those things.

But she wanted to be.

When she did not reply, he lowered his chin, and his expression seemed to harden even more.

"I have never kept a mistress," he stated simply, his voice deep and intimate. "I am not an easy man to get along with. Relationships of a personal nature have always been difficult for me."

Lily did not speak. There was something in his manner that reached a deep place inside her. As though he was sharing a long-held secret he had never revealed to anyone else. She waited, still and silent, for him to continue.

"If you were to claim such a position"—he paused again, just long enough for his gaze to flicker over her body, making her skin heat instantly, before his eyes met and held hers again—"your time, your body, your every gasp and sigh would be mine to exploit and command. You would belong to me, Miss Chadwick, and only me, for as long as I wanted you. Is this what you are offering? You would give yourself to me completely?"

He was trying to shock her, perhaps frighten her a little.

But everything he said only made her blood run faster.

Yes. She wanted all of those things. With him.

She had no guarantee that her name was not already being tossed about town on the waves of scandal. Her sisters would be drowned in social ruin along with her. Their whole family would be disgraced. All opportunity to reverse the damage their father had wrought would be crushed by the first whisper of Lily's presence at a brothel.

Even if Pendragon's rules managed to stem the tide of gossip, Lily would always be wondering, fearful of the day the truth would come out and she would be unable to protect her sisters from the devastation of scandal.

But a man like the earl certainly possessed the type of influence to prevent the events of last night from becoming common knowledge. As his mistress, she would be under his protection.

It was truly stunning how swiftly the course of one's life could change. With her decision made, a new boldness breathed life into her—a whisper of power and sensuality that left her wanting more.

He waited for her response, his expression stony, his body taut and unmoving. Aloof and unapproachable. But that was not all there was to see. Lily's heart tripped dangerously at the subtleties she detected in him.

His eyes sparked with white heat. The seething tension in his expression—in his entire body—sent a wave of powerful sensations through her. A familiar thrill raced along her nerves as she resisted a fierce urge to stand and go to him.

She knew what she wanted.

She wanted to be his lover. For reasons far more personal than for the protection and security of her family. Though she need not admit as much.

"Yes, my lord, I wish to be your mistress," she said softly.

An unholy light flashed in the depths of his eyes, and Lily's heart skipped several beats. For just a split second she felt a moment of the apprehension he had tried to inspire in her.

"On one condition," she added. "Our arrangement must be held secret. And if you are to become my…protector, I will need your help in keeping the events of tonight from becoming known among the *ton*. I cannot have my family harmed by my…change in circumstances."

He was silent for a long moment. To the point that Lily worried he may not accept her terms. But when he finally spoke, she realized he had been considering what it would take to accommodate her wishes.

"As I said earlier, the discretion of the others present at the auction is likely assured. But if I am to be thorough, I must know how you came to be at Pendragon's in the first place."

The urge to hold her tongue was stronger than Lily expected. It had been a long time that the Chadwick sisters, each in their own way, had had to look out for one another. Portia had been so right when she had once declared that keeping secrets was a family trait. To reveal the vulnerability they had been so determined to protect went against the grain.

The earl lowered his chin. "It will be vital as we go

along, Miss Chadwick, that you learn to trust me. I cannot shield you from threats if I do not know what they are."

It was a delicate risk to put her faith in him, but he was right.

"My family owed a significant debt to a man named Mason Hale. I understand last night was his way of collecting."

"How much was the debt?"

Lily swallowed. Despite everything, there may still be a reason to fear Hale. What if he had not gotten the full amount from Pendragon?

"How much?" the earl prompted.

"Ten thousand pounds," Lily muttered thickly.

He gave a low harrumph. "Though I am sure Hale was more than compensated for his trouble, I will pay the man a visit to ensure he is no longer a concern. Will that do?"

Lily nodded past her astonishment. He had barely blinked at the amount. Just how much had he bid for her?

"We have an agreement?" he asked, his voice lowering.

Hot sparks rained through her. "Yes."

Nothing changed in his expression. He continued to stare at her with a gleam in his eyes and an unforgiving angle to his jaw.

Then she saw the barely perceptible curve of his mouth—a shadow of a smile—and she wondered if he might be the demon Lady Anne had claimed him to be after all.

Her stomach fluttered. The thought left her more excited than wary.

He lifted one hand from the arm of the chair and turned it palm up. "Come here." His voice was dark and commanding.

The physical numbness she had experienced upon waking was completely gone, leaving Lily's senses in an acute state of awareness. She felt...everything. Warmth from the fire bathed her skin, soothing her sensitized nerves. Her fingers and toes tingled, as though she were suspended over a great open chasm. Her stomach was tight and her breath thin, but her heart beat a powerful rhythm against her ribs.

Staring into the earl's eyes, Lily felt a distinct sense of inevitability, as though her life had been laid out by fate long before tonight.

With only a slight hesitation, she lowered her bare feet to the floor and stood.

He immediately swept his gaze in a scorching path over her body, barely concealed by the shift. Her insides melted. Though she acknowledged the thread of vulnerability still present in her core, Lily was amazed to feel something else as well. There was something empowering in choosing to accept his desire. And her own.

Lifting his eyes again to hers, he repeated, "Come to me."

Lily walked toward him. Each step increased the buzzing along her nerves and heightened the hum in her blood. She felt as though she were coming to life for the first time.

She was not a tall woman, and as she came to stand before him seated in his chair, she noted with a sharp inhale that her breasts were level with his gaze. A flush spread across her cheeks, but he did not seem to take notice. His eyes were locked upon hers, his focus penetrating.

After a long moment, he straightened in the chair and reached for her. The slow intention in his movements was riveting. Lily tensed in anticipation of the first touch of his hand on her body.

When he carefully took the glass she had forgotten she was still holding, a heavy sigh slid from her lips.

He set the glass on the floor before selecting an article of her clothing from the chair beside him.

It was one of her stockings.

She watched him pull the delicate bit of silk slowly through his fingers. Then he took one of her hands in his. The moment their fingers touched, sparks ran through her.

He paused, as if he too felt the rush of sensation.

Recovering after a long breath, he drew her a step closer. A flood of heat pooled low in her body. Her knees wobbled, and her fingers tightened on his hand.

Giving no attention to her obvious moment of weakness, he released her hand and bent forward to slide his fingers around the delicate bones of her right ankle, but did not touch her anywhere else. Every movement was carefully controlled and measured. Clearly, he had a specific intent, and he was not in any hurry.

Lily tried telling herself to relax, but every nerve was at full alert. The simple pressure of his large hand curved around her ankle created a wealth of reactions through her body.

He encouraged her to lift her foot, and she obliged, balancing carefully.

He slid the stocking over her toes, around her heel, then slowly up her leg, awakening her to the realization of just how sensitive the arch of her foot was and how luxurious it felt to have silk smoothed over the curve of her calf by a masculine hand. When he eased the silk higher, the brush of his fingertips tickled the skin behind her knee, sending shivers coursing through her. Finally, he drew the stocking up around her thigh and secured it with the garter.

As he reached for the second stocking, Lily fought to rein in the light-headedness crowding her awareness. Her entire body was alive and tingling with a unique kind of heat. He kept his head bowed, and she was grateful for that, knowing if she looked into his eyes, she would likely stop breathing altogether.

This was what she had craved from the first moment she'd seen this man. The breathlessness, the hunger, the yearning to understand all of the things he made her feel with his dark gaze and intense demeanor.

She had crossed a threshold in allowing him the liberties of touching her in such a way. No gentleman would dare to force such intimacies upon an innocent debutante, but he would dare that and more with his mistress.

The acknowledgment of her new circumstance, the untold delights she was likely to experience under the direction of the enigmatic man before her, sent another surge of heat through her body.

By the time he finished easing the second stocking up to her thigh, she was convinced he had magic in his hands. Delicate impressions danced along her nerves, tightening her belly. She could hear the slow and heavy rhythm of his breath moving in and out.

Without speaking, he took both of her wrists, his fingers pressing against her fluttering pulse. He pinned her hands against her thighs. Then he leaned forward.

The warmth of his breath heated her skin a second before he pressed his lips to the inner curve of one breast. It was a brief kiss. The shift kept his lips from touching her bare skin, but within that moment, Lily felt more than just the pressure of his mouth on her body. There was the rough texture of his jaw brushing across the soft cotton. The point of his high, starched collar pressed into her belly, and his fingertips tightened over the pulse in her wrists, assuring that she did not move.

Lily bit down hard on her lower lip. Her insides erupted. She felt hot and jittery and aching all at once.

From a kiss. A simple, brief press of his mouth.

He drew back and reached for her stays.

"Turn around." His voice was rough and low.

Lily did as he directed, turning to stare across the room at the bed she had recently vacated.

He rose to his feet behind her and brought the stiff garment around her body. The corset pressed flat to her abdomen and fitted beneath the heavy weight of her breasts, lifting them. Lily brought her hands up to hold the stays in place as he swept the length of her hair over her shoulder, then began tightening the laces down her back. His warm and even breath swept across the back of her neck, sending delightful shivers down her spine, making her ache for the press of his mouth at her nape.

But he kept his focus on the mundane but intimate task, while the stays tightened around her like a piece of feminine armor and her breath grew shallower with every exhale.

It was then Lily finally realized something that should have occurred to her much sooner: he was not going to claim her virtue tonight.

Keen disappointment stabbed through her. Having made the unbelievable decision to become his lover, she was quite ready for it to begin. More so now that he had teased her body with the tantalizing caress of his fingertips and the single fleeting press of his lips.

Agitation and confusion gripped her. Had she misunderstood something?

After securing her stays, he assisted with her petticoat and then her gown. When he finished fastening her dress, he turned his attention to her hair, securing the thick tresses at her nape with a length of ribbon he removed from the trim of her gown, allowing her hair to fall down the center of her back to her hips.

The gentle but insistent direction of his hands at her shoulders turned her back around to face him. She tried to discern his intention by the expression on his face, but she caught only a glimpse of a severely drawn mouth and heavy brow before he lowered himself to one knee before her. Lifting first one foot then the other, he placed her shoes on her feet.

There was tenderness in his touch, but more than that, she detected a strained edginess to his actions. A hint of conflict in his manner that made her anxious.

"My lord..." she began, hearing the uncertainty in her tone and wishing she could have disguised it. "I thought..."

He rose to his full height and finally met her cautious gaze.

Her chest tightened, and her breath caught in her throat.

"You have chosen to give yourself to me, Miss Chadwick." The words were low and clear. "I do not take it lightly, this gift you've bestowed. But as I said, it will take far more than one night to make you mine."

Lily released her breath on a soft sigh.

Something flickered in his impenetrable stare, and he added in a murmur, "There will be no going back."

The sentiment echoed her own from earlier, and Lily experienced a sense of rightness in that moment that overcame any lingering question or concern. They would be lovers.

As they stood facing each other in silence, barely an inch separating them yet not touching at all, she wanted so badly to lift her hand and press it to the side of his face. She wanted to feel the hard angle of his jaw against her palm and the roughness of his skin where the shadowed start of a beard darkened his cheeks.

Something held her back.

She touched him with her studied gaze instead, observing the harsh lines of his face as a frown hardened his visage. She slid her attention briefly to the pulse beating at his temple, then across his oppressive eyebrows, down the slope of his strong nose. His mouth was pressed into a stern, unforgiving line, but it could not disguise the elegant upper arches or the generous lower curve of his bottom lip.

His mouth was beautiful, she thought.

Lifting her gaze again to meet his eyes, she was struck by the raw need she saw there. The fierce and weighted denial.

"It is time to take you home," he said. His voice was gruff and deep.

Lily did not move. She focused on trying to analyze her conflicting emotions. She was frightened and exhilarated. Calm yet restless. And deep down, beneath all the rest, was a sense of self-assurance she had never before experienced.

"If it had not been me at the brothel tonight, but another woman, would you have bid on her?"

The small muscles at the corners of his jaw flexed and bunched.

"I do not know," he murmured thickly.

"I am glad you were there."

A shadow crossed his expression while a flicker of something unnameable ignited in his gaze. "You may yet change your mind on that, Miss Chadwick."

# Ten

THE EARL BROUGHT HER HOME IN A NONDESCRIPT carriage displaying no livery to give away his identity. He did not live far away, and they made the short trip in silence. Dawn had arrived, but it was a quiet, slow dawn, and the city still hovered in that long breath before action. The atmosphere was pregnant with the anticipation of things yet to come.

Seated across from him, Lily could not keep herself from studying his face. He looked cold and hostile. But some instinct already knew it to be a facade. A wealth of rich emotion seethed beneath his stony surface.

He watched her as well.

Typically, Lily would be supremely uncomfortable under such an intense regard. But with him, she didn't mind the vulnerability he incited. She wanted him to see her.

When the carriage reached its destination, he leaned forward to offer her a hand from the vehicle but did not descend, remaining instead within the anonymous interior.

"I will send word," he said.

That was all.

Lily looked at him for a moment, then gave a nod before turning away.

Lily did not glance back as she made her way to Angelique's front door—not even when she heard his carriage roll away after she stepped inside. There were further challenges to face before this night came to an end, and she needed to train her focus forward.

Everything inside was quiet but not fully darkened. A dim light burned in the entrance hall, and a glow spilled out from the parlor.

Guilt washed through her at the thought of how worried her family must be. She had no idea what she would say to them. Something as close to the truth as possible seemed the best course. Lily had never been much of a liar—there had rarely been cause in her life to practice the skill—but she had no intention of disclosing the arrangement she had entered into with Lord Harte.

Stepping into the parlor doorway, Lily noted with a mix of relief and anxiety that everyone was present. Angelique sat in her favorite chair while Portia and Emma sat close together on the sofa, deep in debate. Emma was still dressed in the revealing turquoise gown she had worn to Bentley's club. The visceral tension in the room crushed Lily with remorse.

"Lily!" Portia shouted, having noticed her in the doorway. The girl leapt to her feet and rushed forward to enfold Lily in a fierce hug.

Lily closed her eyes for a moment as she allowed herself to feel the welcoming comfort of being back with her family. Though her night had ended in a way she never could have anticipated, it did not change how close Lily had come to a terrifying fate. She still did not fully understand what her future would hold, but her decision to enter into an illicit relationship with the earl had at least brought her home.

Pulling back from Portia, Lily looked to Emma, who had also risen to her feet and was intently scanning Lily for signs of injury or distress.

"Tell me you are unhurt," Emma demanded tightly, seeking confirmation in Lily's eyes.

Lily detected the thickness of tears in her sister's tone and smiled in an attempt to ease her worry.

"I am fine, Emma."

"Thank God," Emma breathed as she closed the distance between them and took Lily into her arms.

She held Lily tight for several breaths. Lily could feel Emma's fear in that embrace. She closed her eyes, hoping her decision to accept Lord Harte's offer would not bring more distress to this sister who already shouldered so many burdens.

Emma released her and drew back, her sharp, assessing gaze intent upon her face. Lily smiled to assure Emma all was well. But after a moment, her sister's stare began to feel too shrewd, and she glanced aside.

"Come sit, *ma petite*," Angelique called out almost joyfully. "Have some tea. It may still be warm."

Grateful for the shift in focus, Lily removed her cloak. Portia tugged at her hand, drawing her down on the sofa. Within moments, she had a warm cup of tea in her hand and realized she still had no idea what she would tell her family.

After taking a bracing sip of tea, she looked up to

see three pairs of eyes studying her intently. It was far too much to hope that they might accept her return without an explanation. She would have to think of something fast.

"Tell us what happened, Lily," Portia insisted as she grasped Lily's hand in both of hers, practically bouncing on the cushions next to her. "You must. I have been frantic with worry all night and cannot wait another moment to learn how you managed to get home."

"Give her a few more moments, Portia," Emma interjected. "She has likely been through quite an ordeal. We can be patient."

Portia slumped back into the sofa with a gentle huff. "Maybe *you* can."

Emma took a seat across from them, and Lily carefully kept her gaze averted, worried that Emma may see the anxiety that still rippled beneath the surface.

Just as everyone was finally settled, Angelique rose to her feet. "I am off to bed, darlings."

"How can you leave now?" Portia argued. "We are finally going to learn what happened to Lily."

"When you have had as many adventures as I have, one becomes much like the last. You girls catch up. I need my beauty rest. *Bonsoir.*"

"I will walk you up." Emma stood to follow their great-aunt, but the lady waved her off.

"*Non*, you stay—I shall find my bedroom. I assume it is where I left it this morning."

While Angelique made her way from the room, Lily took a few more sips of tea. As the warmth from the brew spread through her system, she felt a rush of confidence. She had made it through some undeniably harrowing experiences over the last several hours—surely she could make it through this conversation.

"Now, let us get to it, shall we?" Portia insisted as she leaned forward expectantly. "What in bloody hell happened? How did you escape the brothel?"

"How do you know about that?" Lily asked in shock.

Portia's expression was just a touch smug. "Angelique and I have been on a mission to find you all night."

"You have?" Lily had not expected that. A flash of panic ignited. If they already knew about the brothel, what else had they discovered? Did they know of Lord Harte?

"Of course, did you think I would just watch you get carried away and not do anything to save you?" Portia's eyes shone as she explained her part in the night's adventure. "It so happens Angelique knows of this mysterious man in the East End they call Nightshade. We hired him to help us. He tracked down Hale and learned the despicable monster had you auctioned off at a brothel. But he lost you after that. Nightshade is even now still trying to learn what happened to you—"

"You have to stop him," Lily interrupted. The more people who knew where she had ended up, the more likely a scandal would erupt. No one else could know she had been won in an auction by the Earl of Harte and then taken to his home—especially not her sisters.

The path she was on was hers alone to traverse. They would not understand what had provoked her to the decision she had made in the earl's bedroom. Portia might perhaps, but she would demand information. Lily's desire to become the earl's lover was an intimate and personal one. It was hers alone, and she wished to keep it that way.

"What? Why?" Portia argued, her eyes wide and stunned.

Even Emma seemed concerned by Lily's sudden declaration. "Are you certain you are unharmed, Lily?"

"I cannot say I wasn't frightened. I was, terribly so." Lily had to come up with a reasonable explanation and quickly. She reminded herself that the best lies contained mostly truth. "There was a woman at the brothel. I thought maybe she would help me. Instead, she gave me something to drink that made me feel quite strange."

She paused. Details of that time frame were still unclear.

"I do not know much of what followed. It is all muddled and foggy in my head. I remember a room... with men. Laughter and talking. It wasn't until later, after the drug started to wear off, that I learned what had happened."

Portia scooted closer and put her arm around her.

Lily wanted only to set her sisters at ease. "I am fine, really. One of the gentlemen recognized me. He knew I should not have been there, and he rescued me."

This was going to be tricky. She could not allow Emma's astute perception to detect the lie in her tone. And if she created too much mystery, Portia would never let the matter drop.

"His only request was that his identity remain entirely

unknown." Lily steadied her voice, hoping her sisters would accept her words at face value. "His reputation—his family—would suffer if anyone knew he had been present at such an establishment."

Lily turned to her younger sister, pleading with her gaze. "Please, Portia, you must stop any further investigation. I would not betray this gentleman after he saved me from what could have been a disastrous fate."

Portia was clearly confused. And rebellious. "But the information would be revealed only to us. We could keep it from becoming known any further."

"No," Lily replied sternly. "I would betray this man to no one. Not even you."

Lily could see the refusal in Portia's eyes. She would not easily understand. Lily met her sister's incredulous gaze and silently pleaded for her acceptance.

After a tense moment, Emma spoke. "I think we must honor Lily's wishes, Portia. Can you send a message to this Nightshade to call off any further investigation?"

Portia hesitated, still staring at Lily. "If that is what Lily wants, yes, I can contact him."

"Thank you," Lily replied, hoping she had evaded the worst of the inquiry. Shifting her attention to Emma, she added, "Now, I wonder if I might retire. I feel like I could sleep for a week."

"I think we could all use some sleep," Emma agreed. "Come, I will walk you up to your room."

Lily was extremely grateful for Emma's practical nature just then. She knew that if given the opportunity, Portia would very likely press for more information. Lily had done all the lying she was capable of for one day. If she was to maintain the secret of her agreement with Lord Harte, she would need to be more mentally alert than she was at present.

"Perhaps you should send off the note to Nightshade before you retire," Emma suggested to Portia.

It was clear Portia still would have liked to refuse but did not. "Yes. I will do it right away. Good night. Or should I say, good morning?" she added. The front window revealed the light of morning spreading through the city.

"I am so proud of how both of you handled the events of last night." Emma's tone turned somber. "I will never forgive myself for not being here."

"You could not have known Hale would preempt his deadline."

"Speaking of…how did you fare last night?" Portia inquired with an arched brow.

Lily tensed at Emma's heavy sigh.

"I won more than enough to pay Hale. If he had just waited until today as he had indicated he would…"

"Please, Emma," Lily entreated, "there is no changing what happened. I am home safe. Can we not put this all behind us and move forward?"

"I agree," Portia said. "Once Hale is in custody, facing the full consequences of his crimes, we need never think of it again."

"No," Lily interjected with some force. "We shall not report Hale to the magistrate."

"You must be joking," Portia exclaimed, her eyes wide. "He deserves to be hanged for this. Kidnapping is a capital offense. He sold you to a brothel, Lily."

"I know. I was there," Lily replied. "What do you think will happen once the *ton* discovers this little tale? The minute we report this, everyone will know where I was tonight. There will be no coming back from that."

Lily glanced at Emma, pleading for her sister to see the sense in keeping everything quiet. Her older sister studied her carefully, her expression set with concern, but she said nothing.

Lily looked back at Portia.

"Please, Portia, I do not fear Hale. He has his money and no further cause to threaten us. But I do not think I could bear it if this ignoble adventure were to become common knowledge. I am home. I am unharmed. Can we please let the rest of this go?"

Finally, Emma offered her support. "Of course, Lily. We can talk more about what we plan to do after we have had a chance to restore ourselves." As they left the room, Emma added in a stern tone to Portia, "Do not forget to send that note."

"Go on to bed," Portia called after them. "I will take care of it."

The two sisters made their way upstairs in silence, neither of them particularly inclined toward discussion. Emma, at least, had always honored Lily's tendency to keep things to herself.

Their shared appreciation for silence was perhaps one of the few ways they were alike. Even so, Lily did not fully relax until she was alone in her bedroom.

She undressed slowly. As she did, she couldn't help but recall what it had felt like to have Lord Harte's strong, masculine hands smoothing each article of clothing over her body. By the time she drew her nightgown on and curled up beneath the cool sheets, her skin felt heated and sensitive from the inside out. She might have thought it another aftereffect of the drug if not for the way the mental image of Lord Harte's tortured gaze consumed her thoughts.

Despite the tumult swirling through her mind, she fell quickly into a deep sleep.

# *Eleven*

Avenell Slade lounged back against the padded seat of the carriage, but he was not relaxed.

He withdrew a snuffbox from his coat pocket. It was an antique, made of gold and inlaid with onyx, mother-of-pearl, and lapis lazuli in a flowered motif.

He didn't take snuff, but the box was a treasured possession. It had once belonged to his grandfather, a man Avenell remembered from his early youth as being noble and good. The snuffbox served as a vital reminder of how the traits of the father did not inevitably pass down to the son.

He rotated the box in his long fingers, flipping it this way and that, sliding his thumb over the textured lid, testing the hinges and clasp. The movements had long ago become habitual and were often performed when he was contemplating something of importance.

Tonight, his manipulation of the snuffbox felt awkward, and Avenell realized his hands were shaking. He closed his fist around the heirloom to cease the trembling of his muscles. But the quaking went too deep. It infused his entire body and had from the moment he had stepped forward in Pendragon's drawing room to claim Lily as his own.

He slammed his fist down hard on his thigh. What the hell was he thinking? He knew nothing about keeping a mistress and even less about innocent young ladies.

His visits to Pendragon's had been sufficient. There had been no reason to desire anything else. It had taken him a long time to learn how to manage the sensations he could not control. He accepted that he may never be able to withstand the intimate touch of another human being—would likely never experience pleasurable responses to a lover's hands on his skin.

He had found ways around his limitations. He had discovered how to give pleasure and, by extension, how to enhance his own experience, though indirectly.

It had been enough.

But then, one look into soft gray eyes and his careful existence had been blown to hell. His unprecedented desire for Lily Chadwick was stronger than anything he had ever known. It was as if he suddenly felt everything, all at once. He experienced a primitive need to protect her even as he suspected she was in possession of an inherent strength that she seemed unaware of. The mysterious shadows in her eyes suggested a wealth of secrets he was dying to discover. He wanted to know every quiet part of her and uncover what she kept hidden from the rest of the world.

She made him yearn for pleasures previously unexplored. And for that reason, he had to be careful.

The depth of his reaction to her overwhelmed him. It terrified him.

He had to be mad to consider an intimate arrangement with a woman like her.

And she more so to have agreed to it.

Before he could question his sanity any further, the carriage reached its destination. It was time to question someone else.

Sliding the snuffbox back into his pocket, Avenell stepped from the vehicle and ascended the steps of Pendragon's pleasure house. It was very late—or quite early, as morning was already approaching—and most revelers had gone. A footman still manned the door and, with a subtle bow, allowed Avenell to enter.

"Where is Madam Pendragon?" Avenell asked. "I wish to speak with her privately."

Without any change in expression, the footman gestured toward the stairs. "Allow me to show you to a room where you can wait while I see if Madam is available."

Avenell nodded and followed the footman up to the second floor and down a hallway to a small sitting room. He recalled having been in this room only once before, the first time he came here more than five years ago. He took a seat and waited.

Less than ten minutes later, the madam glided through the doorway.

"My apologies for keeping you, my lord." She smiled as she entered the room but did not approach him. Instead, she swept past him in her shimmering black skirts to the liquor service in the corner. "What an unexpected pleasure to receive you twice in the same evening."

He did not respond but watched as she poured

them both a glass of wine and brought one to him. Avenell sensed the woman's tension, though she hid it well beneath her smooth and graceful veneer.

"Are virgin auctions to become a new feature of Pendragon's?"

Nothing changed in her expression, but Avenell saw the tightening of her irises as he took the wineglass from her elegant hand.

"Last night's entertainment was a singular event," she replied smoothly as she turned to take a seat on the narrow sofa across from him, stretching her body in a way to accentuate her deep feminine curves.

Avenell's voice hardened. "You do not appear concerned with the potential repercussions from your part in the abduction of a noble-bred lady."

She did not answer right away. Her gaze was narrow and as sharp as flint. As Avenell continued to stare back, she finally replied, "In certain situations, great risks become necessary, my lord."

"And what prompted last night's aberration?"

She arched her brows. "This is a curious line of questioning, my lord. Was your prize not to your liking?"

Ignoring her question, Avenell said, "You know I am a careful man. I expect to be apprised of the circumstances in which I am involved."

Pendragon stared at him with flashing green eyes. There was a wealth of intelligence and experience in her gaze. She was not a foolish woman, nor was she likely to be intimidated by any man.

Still, Avenell fully expected her to tell him what he wanted to know.

But first she took a sip of her wine. Then lifting the glass to swirl the red liquid in the light, she replied causally, "The girl's family owed a debt, which has now been repaid."

"She told me as much," he said. "What power does Hale have to force your cooperation?"

Pendragon laughed, but it was a tight sound. "No man can force me to do anything, my lord. Especially not my hotheaded brother."

Avenell was surprised by how easily she admitted to the familial connection. As far as he knew, it was not common knowledge.

He had done significant research on the madam before stepping foot in her establishment five years ago. He knew all there was to know of her path from being a gin shop girl who made it to the theater as an understudy to more talented actresses, to her time in a brothel similar to the one she now ran, through the bedrooms of several influential men, to the day she opened her own place. Any lovers she had ever had had been disposable. Her family was dead or had never been around in the first place—except for a half brother eleven years her junior.

The brother's name was Mason Hale, a celebrated bare-knuckle fighter turned money man who handled the stakes for the fights in which he used to participate. When Miss Chadwick had mentioned his name, Avenell had immediately recalled Pendragon's connection to him.

"Yet, you assumed a great risk on his behalf," he pointed out.

"I did," she acknowledged with a dip of her chin,

"but even I will do things I swore I never would to help someone I love."

Avenell could not understand her sentiment, but clearly she meant it. He saw no other reason for her to have gone to such an extreme to help her half brother. And he could see by her shuttered expression that she was not going to say any more on the topic. She was not going to betray Hale's motivations to Avenell.

Catching her wary gaze, he changed the subject, asking something that had been bothering him all night.

"Why include me on your guest list?"

The shrug of her slim shoulders was innately sensual. It was easy to see how she had reached such an elevated level of success in her profession. Pendragon was as exceptional a courtesan as the pleasures her business offered. But she had not made it as far as she had by being stupid.

"I invited those of my clients who I thought would most appreciate the uniqueness of the opportunity I presented."

Avenell forced himself not to give in to the tension rising in his shoulders at the thought of the other men who had been present for the auction. "What made you think I would have any interest in an innocent young woman who clearly was not here of her own volition?"

She smiled again, and her face became ageless. "But you did, my lord. Your bid ensured no further competition. It seems I was quite accurate in assessing your interest."

A realization made his gut twist painfully. "You intended me to have her all along."

Pendragon laughed then, a lovely melodious sound as she rose gracefully to her feet. "Of course I did, Lord Harte."

The madam circled around him, close enough that he tensed against the potential brush of her skirts against his legs. Of course, she was far too good to make such a mistake. He heard her moving behind him, and when she didn't speak or reappear, he turned in place. She stood beside a table, taking her time choosing a thin cigar. After running it under her nose, she placed the cigar between her lips and leaned forward to light the end in the flame of a candle.

Avenell waited while she took several puffs of the tobacco. The smell of the stuff made him ill, but he concealed his reaction as he waited for the woman to explain herself.

Watching the smoke trail from the end of her cigar in a wavering pattern, she finally spoke. Her tone was at once casual and meaningful.

"I had an opportunity to talk with the girl before..." The madam smiled and cast an almost apologetic look toward Avenell. "Well, shall we just say, before she had to be readied."

Avenell's chest tightened painfully as he imagined what Pendragon might have done to prepare Lily for the auction.

"It is my business to understand people, Lord Harte. Not only my gracious clients, but the girls who would entertain them. Not everyone is compatible. Lust is not always enough. It is my responsibility to ensure my clients are matched with just the right woman"—she shrugged a slim shoulder—"or man, as the case may be, who can provide what they need most in their sensual exploits."

Avenell took a slow breath in an attempt to smooth out his rising discomfort. He marveled at his ability to keep his tone civil when he replied. "And you thought I needed a damned virgin?"

She tipped her chin and peered at him with a look in her eyes that suggested disappointment. "Come now, my lord, she is more than her maidenhead. You know that," she added in a knowing murmur.

He did not reply. Surely, she could not have detected his obsession with the girl.

Pendragon continued. "Despite her virginal glow and pristine facade, your young lady possesses hidden depths. Who better than you to tend to her intimate darkness?" She paused before adding in a suggestive tone, "Perhaps she will tend to yours as well."

Pendragon walked toward him then, holding his gaze with hers. Her poise and confidence was unwavering as she added, "You came to me more than five years ago seeking my assistance."

"And I have become adept at managing my reactions while out in society. What does that have to do with the lady in question?" Avenell asked, growing annoyed with the madam's lack of true explanation.

"That is not all you asked of me, my lord. Do you remember?" Her voice lowered to a sultry tenor. "You asked for pleasure. And though I understand you have learned a great deal about the giving of pleasure—my girls have assured me of that—I also know you have yet to demand the same in return."

Avenell did not speak. Every muscle in his body

tensed. Of course she would know every detail of the time he spent within the walls of her establishment; he just hated having the truth acknowledged so plainly.

"I have noticed that your visits have become fewer and farther between, my lord. I have no intention of reneging on my agreement."

"Again," he said finally through clenched teeth, "what does the woman have to do with any of this?"

The madam's green eyes flashed as her smile grew practically smug. "It occurred to me that perhaps it would serve you to experience a switch in roles. Rather than remaining the pupil, you would become the master, tutoring an untried girl in how to experience sensual fulfillment. How to provide it in the specific ways you would require. Tell me the idea does not appeal to you, my lord."

When he did not reply, she added confidently, "I believe the young lady you claimed tonight will prove to be a treasure you cannot imagine."

Avenell thought of the many fantasies he had conjured involving the lovely Miss Chadwick over the last few weeks. He could imagine quite a bit.

To conceal his rising tension, he replied in a cold monotone, "You place a frightening amount of trust in me."

Pendragon did not falter. "It is my business to know my clients better than they know themselves, my lord. I have faith that the gift you received tonight will not go undervalued."

Avenell's eyes narrowed.

"Which brings me back to my original question," she continued with a sideways glance as she turned away from him to retake her seat on the sofa. "I expected you to be rather occupied tonight. And though I adore your company, my lord, I am curious to know what brought you back here?"

He had promised Lily the security of her reputation.

"I need the names and addresses of each of the men who were at the auction."

Pendragon laughed. "I cannot give you that information. I run this house on a strict policy of discretion. You know that well enough, as you yourself benefit from such a policy."

"Discretion is exactly my purpose."

"My lord." She sighed heavily, as though distressed at having to deny him the request. "Though I suspect your query is due to an honorable desire to protect the young lady from harm, I am afraid I simply cannot disclose such information."

Avenell stared hard at the madam. "How much?"

Laughing again, she shook her head. "Lord Harte, there is not a bribe large enough to risk my livelihood. But I can assure you with everything I hold dear that none of the men present last night would dare to breathe a word of what happened in my parlor. Each of them understands the consequences of such a blatant disregard for my rules."

It was what he was hoping she would say. Pendragon had proven to be as guarded as he had expected. Her reputation for protecting her clients' privacy was well earned. He had no doubt she had the power to keep the events of last night from becoming common knowledge.

"Trust me, my lord," Pendragon said. "I would never have forced such indignities upon the girl if it hadn't been necessary. I have no intention of allowing further damage. What happened here will remain within these walls. Going forward, she belongs to you, Lord Harte. I trust you will take care of her." Her final words carried a hint of challenge. Then she added, "If, despite all precautions, word should get out...well, then you may just have to do the right thing by the young lady."

Avenell sent the woman a deep scowl, finding no humor in her jest. He rose to his feet and gave a shallow bow. "It has been a long night. I shall leave you to the remainder of yours."

A sly smile widened Pendragon's reddened lips. With a sideways glance from beneath her thick lashes, she asked, "Is there nothing else I can do for you, my lord?"

Avenell stared back at her, knowing her offer was not a personal one. As far as he knew, Pendragon never involved herself with any of her clients. But she did have an uncanny knack for reading people.

"There is something you could do for me," he admitted.

"Anything, my lord."

He had never had a woman in his home before Lily, and the intimacy of it was not something he had been prepared for. The pleasure house suited his purposes far better than anywhere else.

"I will need a private suite, reserved for my explicit use. I will send you advance notice when I need use of it, but no one is to use the room in the interim." He reached for the slip of paper he had tucked into the pocket and handed it to her. "My required specifications."

Pendragon read through the list and smiled. "I believe I have exactly what you need, my lord, but it will cost dearly to keep a room reserved for you alone."

"Cost is irrelevant." He lowered his chin. "There shall be no interruptions and no questions. I expect complete confidentiality."

With a graceful tilt of her head, the madam acknowledged his request. "Of course, my lord. There is a private entrance from the alley along the east side of the building. It will bypass most of the house and will ensure your comings and goings are kept in confidence."

Avenell gave a nod. "Have the room ready for Friday night."

"That shall be fine." She smiled smoothly. "Is there a particular girl you would like available to you, my lord?"

"No. I will not be arriving alone."

"I understand," she said with a confident smile. "It shall be done, my lord."

Avenell set his wineglass on the table, not having taken a single sip. Then he turned and strode from the room.

Dawn had topped the horizon as Avenell stepped out onto the street and got back into his carriage. Returning home, he bathed and changed his clothes, trying to ignore the fact that an intrusive feminine scent still lingered in the shadows of his bedroom. He did not try to sleep. His mind was too alert, too focused on tying up loose ends to allow him any rest.

Once the sun had reached a more reasonable height above the skyline, Avenell called for his carriage again.

He knew roughly the area where Mason Hale had his office. Still, it took some time to find the exact location. A thin, ragged-looking servant opened the door to the narrow brownstone. The poor man looked like he had slept in his clothes and was not fully awake. Worse, it appeared his nose had been recently broken—the area was swollen and had taken on a grotesque purple color.

The man took one look at Avenell and backed away skittishly as he pointed up a narrow staircase. "Hale's up there," he grumbled. "He's not much for company right now, but I'm sure that don't matter to ya."

Then the servant slipped back into a shadowed hallway, leaving Avenell to make his way on his own.

Avenell dismissed the servant from his thoughts as he ascended the stairs. A closed door met him on the top landing. He did not bother to knock but opened the door wide. He entered a room that essentially took up the entire second floor of the building. A desk sat at the far end, and an old sofa was pushed up along an adjacent wall. A few chairs and a couple of odd tables were scattered here and there but still left a great deal of open space.

Another glance around showed various pieces of training equipment, not unlike what Avenell had seen at Gentleman Jack's boxing club, shoved out of the way. And the bare wood floor spanning the center of the room showed a significant number of scuffs and scrapes.

Clearly, the former prizefighter turned bookmaker still found time with his new business to continue some degree of training. The assumption was further evidenced by the sight of the man himself.

Mason Hale was a brute. His large, muscled frame dwarfed the spindled chair he occupied in the far corner of the room as he stared out the window, an empty bottle cradled in his arms.

Hale did not turn around to acknowledge Avenell's presence. Not even when Avenell cleared his throat. Annoyance colored his tone as he finally spoke.

"Mr. Hale—"

"Do you have any idea how frigging frustrating it is when you drink all the liquor at your disposal and still can't get drunk?"

At Hale's thickly slurred interruption, Avenell stopped his advance into the room. He suspected the man was deeper in his cups than he realized, but he wasn't about to argue the point.

"Mr. Hale, I have a matter to discuss with you."

Hale turned then to look across the room at him as though he'd just realized he wasn't alone. His long hair was drawn back in a messy queue at his nape, with strands falling haphazardly across his face. Confusion warred with irritation in the man's rough features. When Hale continued to stare with bloodshot eyes and an unfocused gaze, Avenell continued.

"I must speak with you about a debt."

The chair he was sitting in scraped across the floor as Hale rose to his feet with a deep, rumbling growl. "Can't I get any blasted peace tonight? I don't give two fucks about any debts right now, mate. Can't you see I'm busy? Come back tomorrow, or next year for all I care."

Avenell's brow tensed with irritation. He had no patience for drunks.

"This will be settled now, Mr. Hale. My concern is with the Chadwicks," he clarified. "One of them in particular, whom I understand you had dealings with this evening."

"Damn the Chadwicks," he mumbled under his breath. "I wish I'd never heard the name." Hale swayed in his widespread stance. Despite the bleariness of his eyes, he managed to jut out his square jaw and level a hard glare at Avenell.

Keeping a level tone, Avenell replied, "Kidnapping is a crime, Mr. Hale."

Defiance rolled through the man like a wave, straightening his spine, bunching the muscles in his arms, and tightening his jaw. "Then call in the bloody magistrate. They owed me money," Hale said through clenched teeth. "If they'da paid me what I was entitled to, I wouldn'a had to—"

His words cut off abruptly. His shoulders slumped, and he lifted a hand to run it over his face before he swung his attention back to Avenell with another angry glare. "I ain't got to explain nothing to you. And I don't take kindly to threats. Get yourself gone, or I'll do it for ya."

"Not yet, Mr. Hale. Miss Chadwick—and by extension, her family—are now under my protection." Avenell spoke slowly and clearly to ensure that the man understood the change in the Chadwicks' circumstances. "The authorities will not be advised of your criminal activities tonight if you vow to stay away from the Chadwicks going forward."

Hale's face scrunched up as though in pain as he took heavy, lurching steps toward his desk. The empty liquor bottle was still clutched in his fist, and he set it on the cluttered surface. It teetered dangerously before tipping over and rolling off the edge. It did not shatter when it hit the floor but simply rolled into the shadows at Hale's feet.

"I don't give a bloody goddamn about those chits. The matter is finished. None of it fucking matters anymore. It's all gone to shite."

Hale's muttered ramblings had gradually grown more morose until this last was choked out on a raw sob. He lifted his hand to his face again, pressing his fingers and thumb hard against his eyes as he asked mournfully, "Where could she be?"

Avenell tensed at the man's emotional disintegration, regretting that he had to be witness to such a devastating loss of control. He wanted nothing more than to leave the man to his misery, but first, he needed to be assured of Lily's safety.

"Mr. Hale, I insist you have no further contact with Miss Lily Chadwick or any of her family."

The large man dropped his hand from his face and looked at Avenell in surprise. It looked as though he had forgotten he wasn't alone. Then he twisted his mouth into a mocking sneer.

"What? And you think you can somehow make me?"

Avenell stepped forward, his gaze hard and steady on the other man's face. "You have no idea what I am capable of, Mr. Hale."

The two men stared at each other for a moment before Hale glanced down at the paperwork scattered across the surface of his desk. Avenell was too far away to identify what the man saw there, but whatever it was, it caused a change in him. Hale released a heavy breath before he spoke again in a tone more defeated than defiant. "As I said, my business with that family is done."

Avenell was silent for several moments. He would have liked more concrete assurance, but was not likely to get it from the man in his current state. The brute should be arrested and hanged for kidnapping a lady and selling her to a brothel. But that would not serve Lily's best interest, when she would need to testify as to her involvement.

In the end, what mattered most to Avenell was Lily's future security.

"If I am informed of anything to the contrary, you will regret it, Mr. Hale."

Hale lifted his bullish head to pin him with a look that carried far more weight than Avenell suspected even his fist possessed.

"You've no idea of the depth of my regret, mate."

# Twelve

Lily watched debutantes floating past on the arms of handsome admirers, or in giggling groups of three or four, and realized how much had changed. Of course, no one would notice anything by the look of her. But inside, she felt like an entirely different person.

And she was, wasn't she?

The prior Lily Chadwick had always been a modest and contented creature—at least on the outside. A middle sister with no greater expectation for her future than to marry, have children, and live a simple, secure life.

The Lily standing there tonight had boldly agreed to become the secret mistress of a lord with more mystery and sensual allure in the furrow of his brow than any man in existence.

It was stunning. And whenever Lily considered it, her breathing sped up and her palms began to sweat.

The new Lily had finally acknowledged the flame of wickedness burning inside her. And she rather enjoyed it. She liked the tingling anticipation she felt low in her belly whenever she envisioned Lord Harte's dark image. She liked wondering what was to come next. She appreciated the delicate and intricate sense of expectation that filled her at the thought of their next meeting.

If only she knew when it would be.

Two days had passed since the night of her abduction.

The Chadwick sisters seemed to follow an undeclared agreement not to speak of the events of that night. Lily was the least inclined to broach the subject. She'd spent much of the last two days in her room, claiming she needed to rest. In truth, she mostly wanted to avoid any lingering scrutiny from her sisters.

She suspected they would be watching her carefully for a while, to ensure she suffered no lasting damage from her escapade, and she did not want to endure the inevitable questioning glances or anxious hovering.

Tonight, however, there was no escaping the Duchess of Beresford's annual ball. The Chadwicks had accepted the invitation weeks ago, and no one cried off on the duchess.

Lily glanced at Portia. Her sister stood beside her, staring, much as she was, out over the drawing room still filling with arriving guests.

Lily tilted her chin to look at her sister more fully.

Portia looked…pensive.

Portia never looked pensive. On occasion, she brooded and pouted, but this appeared to be a deeper, more internal sort of pondering.

Noticing Lily's attention, Portia turned her head to stare back.

When Lily said nothing, Portia arched her black brows. "Is there a problem?"

"I do not know. What has your thoughts so occupied?"

"Nothing. What has *your* thoughts so occupied?"

"Nothing," Lily replied just as evasively, knowing it would irritate her sister.

Portia shrugged and glanced back out at the crowd. It was not the reaction Lily had expected, but she waited patiently, knowing her sister would not hold her thoughts secret to herself.

"It feels different, somehow, don't you think?" Portia said after a few minutes. "I mean, with Hale no longer a threat and Emma having won enough to save us from the financial pit of ruin…for this Season at least."

It was a rather exaggerated description, but Lily had to agree with Portia's general sentiment.

Yesterday morning, a messenger had delivered the original signed loan agreement between their father and Hale with the words *Paid in Full* written across it. Being released from the debt should have resulted in significant relief for the eldest Chadwick sister. But Emma did not give the appearance of someone who had just been freed from an impossible obligation.

Lily leaned forward to gaze past Portia to where their older sister stood, holding her place at Angelique's side. Emma, typically so well contained, appeared to be taking her severity to a new level tonight. Her shoulders were straight and unbowed, her gray eyes were fixed forward, and her features were practically frozen into an expression of non-emotion.

"I wouldn't stare too long if I were you," Portia warned. "You may get turned to stone like she has been."

"Portia," Lily automatically admonished.

"Honestly," Portia continued in her defense, "have you ever seen a harder expression anywhere?"

Lily could think of one particular gentleman whose harsh expression could rival Emma's, but Portia was right. Their sister was looking exceptionally unyielding, almost as if she were afraid to express anything lest it crack her rigid composure and send it crumbling into dust.

Lily felt a rush of sympathy. Portia had explained to her how Emma had been brought home by Mr. Bentley the night of Lily's abduction. She went into detail on the tension she had witnessed between the two of them. Emma had resigned from her position as Bentley's bookkeeper that night, since she had won enough money at his celebration to no longer require the employment, and she hadn't uttered a word about the man since.

Lily wondered if her older sister's continued distress, subtle though it was, had to do with her former employer. A weight pulled at Lily's heartstrings.

"At least she hasn't been pressuring me to make nice with all the eligible bachelors tonight," Portia noted in a rare expression of positivity.

"And you are bored out of your mind, aren't you?" Lily challenged.

Lily understood Portia's dissatisfaction with her debut season had less to do with the fact that she was expected to find a husband and more to do with the lack of men Portia would reasonably consider for herself. Her younger sister was intelligent, independent, and ferociously determined to live by her own rules.

Lily doubted there were many men in London—no, the world—who would be a proper match for her.

"An understatement, I think," Portia replied dryly, then muttered in a more aggressive tone, "I cannot wait for this bloody Season to be over."

Lily would have said something about her sister's language in a place where she could easily be overheard, but the sentiment was so sincere, she hadn't the heart to criticize.

Besides, it felt terribly hypocritical to continue preaching decorum considering her change in circumstances.

"I am going to get some air," Portia declared suddenly. Before Lily could respond, she slipped through the crowd toward the doors thrown open to the balcony. Lily watched her go, understanding her sister's desire to escape.

She would have returned to Emma's side then, but some flash of intuition urged her to glance to her left. And then she couldn't move, even if she'd wanted to.

The sight of Lord Harte making his way through the crowd in his slow, reserved manner secured her to the spot. A tingling blast of exhilaration seized Lily's system, awakening every nerve, sharpening every sense.

He was resplendent in a dark-blue coat, the exact color of his eyes, over a champagne-colored silk waistcoat. His nearly black eyes looked out over the drawing room, assessing and dismissive at once.

Lily held her breath.

Moments later, his attention swept past her. The touch of his gaze was so brief, she might have missed it if not for the sudden spike in her body temperature.

She stared after him, helpless to do anything else, as

he continued on until he was obscured again by the growing crowd.

Lily glanced around. He must have seen her. She stood alone, in full view despite the steady flow of guests. The subtle weight of disappointment and uncertainty settled in her stomach. She wondered at his ability to so completely disregard her existence.

She certainly couldn't do the same. Goodness, she had deteriorated to a trembling mess from a single sweeping glance. She was a dreadful ninny and so entirely out of her depth.

Was it possible he did not feel the same intense reactions she experienced?

She feared it was.

But then she remembered the way he had looked at her in his bedroom. Even though he had sat so stern and cold, fire had burned fierce in his eyes.

Reclaiming her breath, she pressed her hand to her abdomen just below her sternum.

Was this part of their agreement?

Was she to expect avoidance—or worse, animosity—whenever she encountered him in society?

She had requested their relationship be kept secret, but surely that should not mean they could not interact as acquaintances, at least.

The sound of music from the ballroom next door signaled a start to the dancing. Lily looked up to see her first partner for the evening coming toward her.

It was Mr. Campbell, a gentleman who could not be further from the earl in nature and character. Mr. Campbell was open, friendly, and charming without being insincere. Lily was reminded that despite the twenty-years-plus separating them in age, this man had been at the top of her list of prospective suitors.

Odd, how easily her interest had faded once she had seen the earl. A frown threatened at the thought. Lily did not like to consider herself a fickle sort, but there simply was no comparison between the two men. Even if she still thought to consider Mr. Campbell as a possible future husband, such an option was no longer available. At least, it wouldn't be once she was the earl's mistress in truth.

The thought of her arrangement with Lord Harte sent a flush of heat across her skin. She hoped it did not show in the pink of her cheeks.

Mr. Campbell reached her side and performed a small bow, displaying just the right amount of respect and courtesy. His smile was pleasant. "Good evening, Miss Chadwick. You are looking lovely as ever."

Lily smiled back. "Good evening, Mr. Campbell, and thank you."

"I believe I have claimed this dance, though if you would prefer not to move to the ballroom just yet, I can take you around for some refreshment."

Lily shook off her discomfort and the lingering effects of having seen Lord Harte. Regardless of her altered circumstances, no one could suspect anything had changed. She would do what she could to protect her family from potential scandal, and that meant continuing to play the part of hopeful debutante.

"I would be delighted to dance, Mr. Campbell."

With an agreeable nod, the gentleman offered his arm, then led her through the milling guests toward the wide archway opening to the ballroom. Before passing through into the next room, Lily caught a glimpse of midnight blue from the corner of her eye. She turned her head—just a slight repositioning of her chin—and saw Lord Harte standing in the shadow of a marble pillar. His gaze was steady and intense as it followed her progress on Mr. Campbell's arm.

She nearly tripped over her skirts. Her nerves tingled. It was a wonderful sensation to experience such a delicate, intrinsic loss of control.

Thank goodness Mr. Campbell was an accomplished escort. He offered no comment on her sudden clumsiness, and by the time Lily regained her composure, they had passed into the ballroom, leaving Lord Harte behind.

The dance was a simple quadrille, allowing Lily far too much opportunity to glance about the room in hopes of seeing Lord Harte watching her. Aside from that one time he had escorted Miss Farindon onto the floor, she had never seen him dance. She hoped he might have followed her into the ballroom, but as the quadrille went on and she was forced to engage in light conversation with Mr. Campbell, she realized the earl had remained in the drawing room.

When the dance ended, Mr. Campbell escorted her to where Angelique and Emma were seated among the other chaperones, having moved to the ballroom once the dancing had started. Lily had only a moment to catch her breath before she was claimed by her next partner.

Hours passed, and still Lily had no further glimpse of Lord Harte.

Perhaps he had left. But how could that be? They

had never discussed how they would go about the logistics of their relationship. Surely, they had to find time to be alone together.

Oh, she was so ignorant of such things.

The night continued steadily on. Lily's feet began to ache, and her cheeks grew sore from the constant smiling. It was unbelievably difficult to participate in all the niceties necessary for polite socializing when your heart simply wasn't in it.

Was this how Portia had been feeling all Season? She would have to be more sympathetic to her sister's complaints.

It was well after midnight, and though the musicians were claiming a break, they would soon return to play for another set. The party was still in full swing, yet Lily wished only to go home. Glancing at the dowager countess, she saw Angelique's eyes drooping. The lady would soon be sleeping in her seat. Though anyone who did not know her well would have missed it, to Lily, Emma also looked drawn and tired. Perhaps it would not be so difficult to convince them to make it an early night.

Just as she was about to suggest it, Portia approached on the arm of her last dance partner, who deposited her gratefully into her family's fold. As soon as the stiff young man walked away, Portia turned to her sisters.

"I am quite ready for this night to be over," she declared in her blunt manner.

Emma sighed. "It does seem to be dragging on rather painfully, doesn't it?"

Lily had expected her older sister to argue for them to stay at least another couple of hours. That she didn't showed more than anything else how things had changed in the last two days.

"What is that, darlings?" Angelique perked up momentarily. "Is it time to depart?"

Lily said nothing, but waited patiently as Emma paused and looked at each of them in turn, assessing and calculating which course to take.

"Yes," she said finally, which resulted in a heartfelt "Thank goodness" from Portia. "I think we can all stand for an early night," Emma added. "Shall we?"

Portia stepped around to offer her support to Angelique while the older lady rose to her feet.

The Chadwicks and the dowager countess said their good-byes to their hostess, then left the ballroom as a group to make their way through the drawing room. That was when Lily finally saw him again.

The sight of him was so unexpected that an audible gasp slid from her lips. Thankfully, her family had not heard it.

The Earl of Harte stood speaking with several older gentlemen near the doorway to the front hall, as always looking elegant, remote, and handsome in his harsh, untouchable way.

Her stomach tightened. He *had* been present the whole night and hadn't once tried to seek her out, or speak with her, or request a dance. And now she would have to pass right by him to leave.

Her steps had slowed when she noticed him, and she trailed behind the others. She tried—she truly did—to keep her eyes focused on Emma's back. But as she passed his position, her gaze involuntarily slid sideways, craving just one more glimpse of him before she left.

He was speaking to the others in his company, and Lily found her attention arrested by the sight of his lips forming each word and the way his eyes focused intently forward. In less than two seconds, she would be past him, but before she was, he flicked a casual glance in her direction. Buried within the blue of his eyes, she saw evidence of a deeper awareness. She used to believe it was anger, but she now understood it to be far more complicated.

And then she was past him. A poignant sense of loss filled her. Tonight suddenly felt like a terrible missed opportunity.

She lowered her chin, intending to quicken her steps to catch up to her family, who had already gone out into the front hall. Before she could reach them, a footman came up beside her, halting her progress. The servant presented a neatly folded missive, and Lily took the note instinctively. Opening the folded paper, she read its contents, then quickly concealed it in her glove as she glanced back over her shoulder toward the earl.

Another brief flick of his gaze sent a swift rise of exhilaration through her blood.

The note had not been signed, but it was from him. She knew it as certainly as she knew there were stars in the sky. With a trembling breath, she hurried to catch up with her family.

Her night was not over yet.

# Thirteen

One hour and twenty minutes later, Lily slid through the deep shadows of Angelique's town house, heading toward the kitchen and the door leading out to the gardens. Breathless excitement kept her alert for anyone else who may be about at the late hour. But her great-aunt kept only a minimal staff, who retired early. Lily did not encounter a single soul as she made her way.

Stepping into the fragrant garden, she noted even the moon assisted with her mission as it hid its full silver light behind a passing black cloud.

*The mews beyond your garden. 2 a.m.*

That was all his message had said. No words of breathless anticipation. Not even the hint of a suggestion that he might be looking forward to their first engagement.

None of it detracted from Lily's own excitement.

What did it say about her that she was so eager to meet a gentleman in secret for the purpose of initiating an illicit relationship?

Defiance flared inside her. Oh, if her sisters could see her now.

Then she glanced back over her shoulder at the windows of the house, realizing that was still a possibility.

She drew her cloak more securely around her as she ran forward along the twisting lane. She made her way through the plots of vegetables and herbs, then past the roses and the willows that framed the back of the walled garden. She sought out a gate tucked into one corner, though in the full darkness, it was harder to locate than she had expected. By the time she found the latch and pulled it open—silently, thank goodness—the moon had started to glide beyond the cloud, illuminating the narrow lane beyond.

She passed through the gate and stepped hesitantly to the side, pressing her back against the stone wall as the gate swung quietly closed beside her. The hood of her cloak cast much of her face in shadow but did not hinder her view as she scanned the darkness.

She saw the carriage almost immediately. It stood beneath the reaching branches of one of the willows no more than thirty feet away. The horses were well trained and did not even bother to nicker at her sudden presence.

*He* sat in that carriage. Waiting in the shadows. For her.

Lily held her breath and pressed both hands firmly against the rioting flutters in her stomach. She sensed danger and excitement. Both urged her forward.

Becoming the earl's mistress would afford her protection against an uncertain future. But that was not the true reason she stood there.

The earl had promised pleasure. His eyes had touched upon some deep yearning within Lily that she simply had not wanted to deny. There was something powerful in her reaction to him. She experienced something in his presence she wanted to explore. The heat, the tingling awareness, the whoosh of energy that made her feel like she could dance on treetops. He made her feel…daring.

While she stood there, her back still pressed to the stone wall, the carriage door swung open, and the earl descended from the vehicle to stand facing her in the lane. He wore a greatcoat but no hat, and the hard angles of his features were evident, even at the distance still separating them. He stood silent and resolute under the silver light of the moon—watching her, waiting for her.

With a flutter in her belly, she started toward him. With each step that brought her closer, rising anticipation washed away any lingering questions about her motivation. She was here now, and nothing seemed as important as getting to him.

The closer she came, the more she was able to detect in his person. He was so rigid in his bearing, so cold and…resistant. His expression was hard and aloof. But still, she sensed the fire he kept contained behind his forbidding stare. What caused such a dichotomy in his manner?

Fear crept in.

But it was a fear unlike any she had ever experienced.

As a child, Lily had been afraid of thunderstorms. She used to worry when her parents would go out at night, leaving her and her sisters to the care of their nurse. Then as she grew older, after her mother died, Lily feared the uncertainty of life. She feared having any part in causing distress for those she loved. Especially when Emma already had so much to worry about with Portia's rebelliousness and their father's descent into the twin vices of drinking and gambling.

But she had never known the kind of deep disquiet she felt in that moment as she considered how she would be changed once she climbed into the earl's carriage. Yet, it was not an unpleasant sensation. Intense and personal, but not alarming. It was not a reaction to him or the unusual context in which she stood. It was a direct response to everything she felt inside.

It was herself she feared. She could not deny, as she looked upon the earl, the exhilaration burgeoning inside her.

She hadn't realized she had stopped in her approach until he shifted. Not much, just a slight angling of his shoulders as he lifted his hand and held it out to her, palm up.

His fingers were long and elegant in a way that exuded strength and competence. The intrinsic desire to touch him overruled all other thought. Lily took the last couple of steps to reach him and brought her hand out from beneath the heavy fall of her cloak to place it in his. He wore no gloves, and his hand was smooth and warm, and his touch sent a jolt of lightning through her system. His hand seemed to twitch, just a subtle tightening of his fingers as her palm slid across his, and she wondered if he felt the jolt as well.

She climbed into the carriage. The vehicle swayed as he climbed in behind her, taking the seat across from her. Then the door closed, and with a gentle jingle of the reins, they started off.

She had done it.

The curtains were drawn over the windows, preventing any relief to the darkness enveloping them. The atmosphere was surreal and painfully quiet despite the sound of the horses' hooves and the creaking movement of the carriage.

A kind and thoughtful gentleman would say something to put her at ease.

The earl was not such a man.

Typically, Lily appreciated quiet moments, but tonight was not typical, and her nerves forced words to tumble from her lips without conscious choice. "You were at the Beresford ball tonight," she said inanely.

He replied, "I was."

Two small, insignificant words, yet spoken in his rich, velvet tone, they had a visceral effect in the darkness.

"I would have danced with you." Again, she wished she could take it back as a blush warmed her cheeks. It sounded like a complaint. And hadn't she already acknowledged to herself that she had never seen him dance but that one time?

He did not say anything right away, and Lily hastily muttered, "I am sorry," then felt even more ridiculous for apologizing when she had no apparent reason.

Goodness, she was a disaster.

There was another long moment of silence during which she could hear his breath, long and even. Then he spoke.

"There is more than one reason I could not dance with you."

Lily was surprised he had decided to provide an explanation. He did not seem the type to explain himself.

"I dance only once per Season, and only with a lady of innocuous charm. It is a rule I have followed for years. Any deviation could be noticed." His voice lowered. "You demanded a condition of discretion in our relationship. Not only would a second dance this year be noted, Miss Chadwick, but discretion may have become impossible if I had been in a position to touch you earlier tonight."

He paused then, and Lily sensed a slow shift in the atmosphere around them. Her muscles tensed.

"Why is that?" she whispered and was amazed at her own boldness.

She heard the subtle sounds of him shifting his position on the seat. The sound of soft fabric sliding against leather lingered in her senses. Her skin grew hot beneath her cloak.

"I am in unfamiliar territory," he murmured. "There is an intensity to my desire for you I have not experienced before. I do not yet know how that will manifest, so I must proceed with caution."

Lily trembled from head to toe. His explanation swirled through her brain. She was still terribly confused, but her body lit up again with the fire he had sparked with a glance.

Before she could reply—before she could think straight—the carriage came to a rocking halt. The footman opened the door, and the yellow glow of streetlights stretched into the interior of the vehicle.

Lily was provided with the breath-stealing sight of Lord Harte, sitting stern and handsome across from her. His expression was coldly emotionless, but in his eyes burned a hunger that curled her toes.

With slow, elegant movements, he leaned forward in his seat.

Lily sat stunned while he reached for the edges of her cloak, which had fallen open. The midnight depth of his eyes held her captive as he clasped the material between his long fingers and brought it together in front of her. It seemed he made a deliberate effort not to touch her body, not even with an accidental brush of his knuckles as he covered her exposed gown. Then he drew her hood more fully over her face.

"For your protection," he explained. He withdrew his hands and turned to exit the carriage.

Lily exhaled slowly to quell the jittery feeling in her belly. She glanced out through the door to see that they had pulled up in front of a large brownstone building. The wide front windows were dark, but Lily thought she heard the muted sounds of music coming from within.

From her brief view of the earl's mansion, she knew he had not brought her back to his home. While she wondered where they were, he stepped into the doorway of the carriage. The streetlights cast his features into sharp, contrasting shadows as he offered assistance.

Lily set her hand in his, again feeling the shock of contact, and stepped down to the pavement beside him. She was careful to keep her chin lowered and her cloak secure around her.

After taking exceptional care in settling her hand

into the bend of his elbow, the earl led her down along a narrow drive beside the building.

Something uneasy pricked at Lily's awareness. Since the night of her abduction, memories had continued to filter back. More details had been retrieved and vague impressions clarified. The alley they continued down was disturbingly familiar.

Her steps stuttered, and tightness squeezed at her chest.

The earl said in a whisper, "I am with you this time. You are under my protection."

His words confirmed her suspicion. He had brought her back to the brothel. Why?

They reached the side door where Hale had carried her into the building over his shoulder. Tension stiffened the muscles along her spine. She considered refusing to enter. She turned to look up at the earl from beneath the shadow of her hood.

His angled his head to meet her gaze. It was far too dark to read his expression.

"Trust me," he said quietly, then lifted his hand to knock on the door.

It was opened immediately by an intimidatingly large young man in footman's garb. Once they stepped into the hall and the door closed behind them, Lily acknowledged that there was no going back. She focused on the heat radiating from the earl's body despite his distant manner. She was his mistress now, not a frightened girl with no knowledge of what was to come.

She had chosen this. She had chosen him.

"Follow me, my lord," the footman said as he turned to lead them down the hall.

"No," the earl said in a clipped tone. "We will make our way without escort."

Lily wondered at the obvious strain, not only in the earl's voice but in his demeanor as well. If it were not a ridiculous notion, she may have thought he was as nervous as she was.

The footman gave a brief nod and extended his hand toward the earl. "A key, my lord. Madam said you may keep it for your personal use." Then he stepped back to allow them to pass. "Up two flights. Your room is the last door at the end of the hall."

They took the same narrow stairs she had been carried up by Hale. But instead of turning down the hall of the second level, they continued upward. Though the sounds of a party she had first heard on the street were louder inside the building, they remained muffled and distant, telling her they were somewhat removed from the main part of the house.

With each step they ascended, it seemed to Lily as though they had entered a private world made just for them. The long shadows extending from the sparsely lit candle sconces created an atmosphere of mystery and anticipation.

Thick scarlet-colored carpeting cushioned their steps along the third-level hallway, and closed doors interrupted the wood-paneled walls. It was far more modest than she would have imagined for a brothel. No risqué paintings or scandalous decor. Perhaps such things were more prominent down below. They had clearly bypassed the main part of the building by entering through the side door.

She realized she could no longer hear the sounds

from the main level. They were entirely alone in the deepening silence. Again, she experienced an odd sort of fear that wasn't fear.

The earl seemed intent upon ensuring a proper distance between them, not even allowing for a casual brush of their bodies against each other as they made their way. Lily risked tipping her chin up to glance at the earl's face. Though he surely had to know she was looking at him, he kept his focus forward so she could see only his profile.

But what a handsome profile it was.

His forehead was wide and swept regally upward. His thick black hair was trimmed much closer than the current style, but it worked well with his angular features. Heavy black eyebrows were drawn low over his eyes.

The unforgiving line of his jaw was more evident from the side, and Lily noticed a shadow of beard spreading from his sideburns to his chin. The shadow hovered over his mouth as well. Lily's attention snagged there for a moment. His lips fascinated her. The harsh expression he donned worked so well to eliminate any sign of softness, but not there. His lower lip was too full, too gentle to be affected by his stern manner.

Lily experienced an urge to test the resilience of that lip with her teeth.

The thought came so unexpectedly it startled her, then filled her belly with a spreading warmth that angled down between her thighs.

She glanced away quickly, worried that her reaction might be apparent.

At the same time, Lord Harte brought them to a halt. They had reached the very end of the hall and a solid wood door.

"We are here," he said.

Withdrawing the key from his coat pocket, he released Lily's hand to unlock the door. He pushed it open and stepped into the room beyond then turned back to look at Lily.

His expression was unreadable, but his eyes were compelling in a way she felt down to her toes.

Her rising nerves, rather than holding her back, increased her newfound boldness, and she stepped forward without hesitation. With her body relentlessly craving his nearness, she reveled in the small pleasure of having to pass close by where he stood holding the door.

Looking around, she was astounded by the luxury of the room. The plush carpeting was the same scarlet color as the hallway. An enormous gilded mirror spanned the wall between two small windows that were covered in heavy curtains of gold brocade. There was a dining table big enough to serve two, with gold-painted chairs cushioned in velvet. An elegant settee sat facing the fireplace already glowing with steady flames.

Two doors opened off the sitting room. She thought she caught the shadowed image of a large four-poster bed through one of them, but the room was unlit, and she may have been mistaken. Her nerves went wild at the thought of a bed so close, reminding her why she was there. But before the idea had a chance to sink in, her attention was claimed by the sound of the door closing behind her.

She looked over her shoulder to see the earl turn the key in the lock. The jolt of a different sort of anxiety pierced through her.

He turned back to face the room and his eyes locked with hers. His jaw clenched, and he set the key in the center of a small table beside the door.

"To secure our privacy only."

Seeing the key so easily accessible helped to ease her sudden alarm, but only just.

He did not move from the door, but stood watching her, a possessive gleam in his eyes.

Licks of flame danced through her blood, and the boldness she had momentarily possessed left her in a long exhale. He wanted her. It was an amazing thought. And though the forbidden novels she had read had given more insight into what happened between a man and woman in the bedroom than any young lady should have, there was simply no way to feel prepared for what was to come.

Even though this moment was inevitable and had been from the first time she had seen him.

As she stared back at him, his brows lowered even farther over his eyes, intensifying the delicate anticipation roaring through Lily's body.

His rich voice, when he spoke, flowed through her like fine wine.

"Remove your cloak."

# Fourteen

Avenell waited, governing the rush of need that coursed through his body by focusing on his hands. He curled them into fists before extending his fingers again. Exerting his will over even that small measure of movement reminded him that he was in control.

He noticed that her gaze dropped to watch the repetitious movement, and he wondered what she must think of him.

But after a moment, she pushed the hood of her cloak off her head. The light from the fireplace danced over her creamy complexion and caressed the burnished brown silk of her hair. Lifting her eyes to his face, she released the ties beneath her chin. One graceful sweep of her arms and the voluminous cloak lifted and spun away from her lovely figure.

His heart jolted at the sight of her.

Earlier in the evening at Beresford's ball, he had made a serious effort not to study her too closely. It had been unbelievably difficult to see her with other men. It was a stark reminder of how commonplace a thing it was for a gentleman to lead a lady about on the dance floor, when for Avenell, it was anything but simple. Seeing her triggered old frustrations he thought he had learned to manage.

At least now he finally had her to himself. He slid an intent gaze over the vision she presented.

The pure white of her gown was cinched tightly beneath her breasts before falling gently past the generous curves of her waist and hips. Her bodice was overlaid with lace and fitted securely over her bosom, suggesting the lushness there but revealing only a modest expanse of bare skin.

Her slim neck was arched proudly as she endured his perusal. Her gloved hands were clasped in front of her, and her lips, a perfect rosy pink, were shaped into a gentle bow as her gray eyes stared back at him. There was caution in her gaze.

She was the epitome of the sweet and modest maiden.

And she had agreed to be his.

Deep disquiet rolled through him. He had begun something that went way beyond his capabilities. He knew it, but he couldn't stop his forward progression.

He wanted her.

He could never have expected the intense sensuality in the act of drawing her clothing onto her body that night in his bedroom. The lightest brush of his fingers over her smooth skin had fired his blood in a way he had barely been able to contain. For a moment, he had given in when he had pressed a kiss to her heated body.

The experience had left him shaken and convinced he would have to advance carefully. Taking them out of the intimate spaces of his personal bedroom was a start. But tonight would be the true challenge to his control. His desire for the untutored woman before him was unprecedented, and she had placed herself in his hands. He had yet to prove worthy of her confidence.

Neither of them had spoken for several long minutes. In fact, she hadn't said a single thing from the moment they had arrived at the brothel. Yet, the silence between them was not uneasy.

He lowered his chin to study her expression more carefully.

Steady gray eyes returned his gaze. The firm angle of her head revealed a hint of determination in her manner. The subtle parting of her lovely lips suggested…anticipation.

"Make yourself comfortable, Miss Chadwick," he instructed a bit more sternly than he had intended as he crossed the room toward a bottle of champagne he had requested be waiting for them.

He was not about to rush things.

"Are you hungry? There is fruit and other light fare." He tipped his head toward a sideboard holding silver-covered trays.

"No. Thank you."

Taking the time to pour two glasses of the sparkling wine allowed for a slight easing of his heightened senses. But not much.

"Did you have trouble getting away?" he asked.

Turning back to the room, he saw she had taken a seat on the delicate settee facing the fireplace. He approached her from behind, and his attention was drawn to the graceful line of her neck and the way light wisps of brown hair had escaped her coiffure to curl against her nape.

She turned to look up at him, and the softness of her eyes reached into the innermost parts of him. He handed her the glass of champagne before stalking toward the fireplace. The fire burned hot in the grate, but it was not nearly as heated as the blood in his veins.

"No. The house was quiet and still when I slipped out." She paused then asked, "Why did you bring me here?"

Avenell tensed. He had not expected the direct question. But she deserved an answer. He turned back to meet her steady gaze. Her eyes were calm but certainly not relaxed. Focused but not contentious.

"Considering your desire to keep our association a secret," he began, "it seemed appropriate to arrange our meetings at a location with no specific ties to our identities. Even the best servants will gossip. Here, we have some assurance of anonymity."

She remained silent, as though considering his reasoning.

"We are in a private wing of the building and are quite removed from the house's public activities." He lowered his voice, hoping to assure her in case she still had any misgivings. "I will always be with you."

Avenell's chest constricted as he waited to see if she would balk further.

And if she did? How could he explain that having her in his home, in his bedroom, was distressing to him personally when he did not fully understand it himself?

An odd light flared in her eyes. With a graceful turn of her head, she slowly scanned the room. "I never could have expected the path of my life would lead to a brothel," she said softly, "and more than once." She brought her gaze back to meet his, and a curious little smile curled the corners of her lips. "It is interesting how a single event can so dramatically alter one's existence."

She astounded him. He wondered at the nature of someone who could face such a dramatic alteration in circumstances with the sort of serenity and gentle acceptance this young woman possessed.

A slow blush lit her cheeks while she sat under his regard. "You look at me as though you do not know quite what to make of me," she said.

"That is because I do not," he admitted.

The way she stared back at him gave him the oddest sense that she was challenging him. It was in the way she held a subtle curve to her lips as she tilted her head. And in the direct focus of her gaze that darkened as he watched. It seemed as though she was keeping herself just out of his reach while silently daring him to come closer at the same time.

Then with a gentle flutter of her lashes, she lowered her eyes, and the moment passed. She lifted her glass of champagne, and Avenell's attention was drawn to the purse of her lips over the rim of the narrow glass as she took a sip. By the time she lowered the glass again, the muscles in his stomach had drawn taut.

"Are you going to try the champagne?" she asked.

He looked at the elegant glass in his hand. The act had become such an ingrained habit that he never even thought about it anymore. But then, no one else seemed to notice when he did not actually raise his glass to drink.

"I prefer not to have my judgment clouded."

In truth, he never consumed anything that might promote a loss of control while among society. He had to be ever diligent if he was to successfully maintain his composure.

Perhaps tonight more than ever.

"Then why pour yourself a glass?"

"It has become habit, I suppose. A way to blend with my peers and avoid drawing attention."

She tilted her head. A smile played about the corners of her mouth. "You do what you can to blend in, whereas I've always secretly wished I possessed some quality that might help me to stand out. We make an odd pair, my lord."

Avenell's lips curved upward involuntarily. "We do indeed, Miss Chadwick."

He hadn't intended the intimate tone that had crept into his words, but in seeing her eyes widen with that barely perceptible reaction she had to him, he was glad for it. Knowing he could cause the involuntary response made him feel as though they were on a bit more equal ground.

"Will you call me Lily?" she asked with a modest dip of her chin. "It feels odd to be so formal, considering our…association," she added hesitantly.

It took him a moment to gather himself enough to respond. "Would you like me to call you Lily?"

"Yes. I think so."

He nodded.

"Shall I call you Avenell?"

Hearing his name on her lips created a fine point of pressure in his chest. He instinctively squared his shoulders in defense. Although he was pleased she would allow him the intimacy of using her given name—in fact, he intended for her to share far more intimacies with him—he could not do the same in return.

"I prefer you address me as Lord Harte." He knew his words sounded cold, but there was no help for it. "Or my lord."

A shadow slid across her expression at this response. Her mouth curved softly downward in a way he found intensely alluring. A tiny line formed above her brow, then quickly disappeared. He could see his refusal bothered her. For a moment it appeared she might dispute him, but she held her tongue.

While she remained silent, Avenell felt an unusual desire to provide some sort of explanation. Not all of the truth, perhaps, but something to help her understand that the denial was not a personal rejection.

"I have never kept a mistress," he began, carefully easing into what he needed to say.

"I recall you telling me as much," she replied. "And of course, you know I have never been one before."

Her tone was gentle, and her features were set in a perfect expression of serenity, but he could have sworn he detected a note of dry humor in her tone. Her composure despite the subject matter astounded him. She was so unlike the typical modest young lady.

Something in the steadiness of her gaze urged him to glance away, to look anywhere but at her. He resisted the temptation and began again. "I never entered into such an arrangement because I knew there would be an expectation of certain liberties that I cannot allow."

There was a long pause, during which the point of pressure in his chest spread outward. Then she tilted her head in a subtle gesture.

"What sort of liberties?" she asked softly.

Her voice had changed. It was difficult to identify exactly what it was, but it warmed him. Made him feel a burst of impatience, a wave of deeper desire. He took a moment before he replied.

"You will understand more fully soon enough. But I promise, I will not allow my limitations to lessen the pleasure you experience during our association."

A blush pinked her cheeks. But she did not look away.

"And what of your pleasure, my lord?" Her voice was soft and low. Smoky, like her eyes.

It weaved through Avenell's senses and hit him hard in the gut. Heat scored through his insides on a direct path to his loins. He had suspected from the start that her gentle manner had lured him so strongly. But the unexpected boldness in her query had an intense effect on him.

His arousal roughened his tone as he answered, "My pleasure is assured. Do not doubt that."

The pink in her cheeks spread down across her chest and the upper swells of her breasts, but still she held his gaze. He wondered what she might be thinking. Her stillness was disconcerting when he sensed so much going on inside her.

After a few moments, her lashes swept low as she looked down at the glass of champagne held lightly in her hands.

Avenell set his own glass on the mantel over the

fireplace and turned to face her more fully. It was time to begin.

"Come here, Lily."

---

A waterfall of tingling sensations flowed through Lily at his quiet command. It was a similar directive to the one he had given that first night in his bedroom.

This time he used her name. Hearing it in his deep voice made it sound erotic somehow, and sparks ignited deep inside her. From the moment they had entered this room together, she had felt his growing tension, and she wondered again if he might be just as uncertain as she was.

No. It wasn't possible. Her uncertainty filled her nearly to overflowing. Yet it did not stop her from following his low-spoken command. In fact, it was her uncertainty that urged her to proceed. She wanted to know what came next.

She set her slim-stemmed glass on the table beside the gloves she had taken off when she first sat down. Smoothing her hands down the front of her gown, she rose slowly to her feet then walked toward him. His body remained rigid, and his brows were heavy over his gaze as she approached. When she came within arm's reach, she stopped.

His eyes flashed with dark fire. "Before we begin, I must ask you to promise to do exactly as I say. I intend to go about things differently than you may expect, but I assure you everything has a purpose."

Something twisted low in her belly. It was an unusual sensation and not unpleasant.

"Can you promise me?"

She would likely promise anything just then. "Yes."

He said nothing in response, not even to acknowledge her acquiescence. He just stared at her with his fathomless eyes.

She sensed these silent moments were important to him. In truth, she appreciated them as well. They allowed her to sink more deeply into herself, to fully acknowledge her new reality. Soon she would understand more of the feelings that ran through her every time she was with the earl—she would actually experience the things she had read about—and it thrilled her from head to toe.

Goodness, she had wickedness in her. She had suspected its existence for some time but had not fully recognized it until she had first encountered this man. In the years since her mother's death, she had learned to suppress so many contrary aspects of her nature. This reckless longing may be just another element she had always possessed.

"Tell me what you are thinking when you look at me like that."

There was iron and ice in his voice. Not even a hint of tenderness. For some reason, his harsh manner did not bother her. She sensed something beautiful and elusive existed behind his daunting facade. The possibility of discovering what it was filled her with delicate anticipation.

She looked into his eyes and answered truthfully. "I am thinking about how you make me feel."

The muscles along his jaw tensed, and his eyelids lowered just the barest fraction. He brought his hands around to clasp them behind his back.

To keep from reaching for her?

"How do I make you feel?"

Her skin tingled in reaction to the raw note in his voice. Lily took a moment as she thought about how to put it into words. It was a difficult thing to explain, and she wanted it to come out right.

"I feel..." she began, then hesitated. Her breath caught in her chest, and she had to force it out on a heavy sigh. "I feel strong and weak at the same time. When you look at me, I feel exposed, as if you can see my most private thoughts. And though it frightens me—*you* frighten me—it is such an exquisite sensation that I do not want it to end. Because I want you to know me, to see the deepest parts of me."

At first he did not respond beyond a fierce clenching of his teeth, and Lily wondered if he wanted to hear something else. Had she revealed too much of her inexperience? Should she have said something more provocative, more sophisticated?

"Do you desire me?" he asked finally.

The molten heat running through his words curled around her, heating her breath, her skin, her blood. She looked into his eyes and felt a swirling deep within. It tingled like white fire and spread to the most intimate places in her body.

"I believe so," she replied in a whisper.

His answer was a curt demand. "Show me."

"How?"

He stepped toward her until he stood close enough that she would have had to tip her head back to look into his eyes. Instead, she focused her attention on the full curve of his lower lip as he spoke.

"I am going to touch you, Lily, but I require that you remain completely still while I do so. You must not reach for me or touch me in return. You will keep your hands at your sides. Do you understand?"

She managed another nod.

She could smell his scent—something subtle, rich, and male—and she could practically feel the expectation humming through his taut body. Or was it her body that trembled so acutely? She couldn't be sure and didn't care.

"I want you to show me your desire in your responses." His voice lowered as he continued. His words felt like a caress flowing through Lily's awareness. "I want to see it in the way your body reacts to my touch, hear it in the way your breath changes, and know it in the darkening of your eyes. If you find something I do to be unpleasant or distasteful, I expect you to tell me." Lily shook her head, intending to deny that possibility, but he spoke first. "I insist upon your complete honesty. In everything."

She looked up to meet his harsh stare. There was only a brief hesitation as she noted the intense set of his features, the forbidding scowl and tense jaw, before she replied, "Yes, my lord."

The strength of his gaze held her captive as he said, "I am going to touch you now."

Lily's lips parted. Anticipation made her pulse flutter and her stomach tighten.

Pressing his lips into a firm line, he breathed in slowly through his nose. The muscles in his jaw tensed as he lifted his hand to drift the backs of two fingers along the side of her throat. Starting just below her ear, his barely there caress smoothed down her neck then out to where the edge of her gown caught over the crest of her shoulder. Tingling gooseflesh rose up in the wake of his gentle touch even as a fire stirred deep in Lily's center.

He released his breath in a low rush of air before he breathed in deeply again.

Turning his hand, he traced the upper edge of her bodice with the lightest brush of his fingertips. Across her chest, over the tops of her breasts, sending tiny frissons of sensation toward her nipples.

He slowly stepped around her and continued to trace the edge of her gown around to her back.

Without him standing in her line of sight, his image serving as an anchor, she felt his touch more acutely. The whisper of his fingertips across her upper back incited more gooseflesh and an awakening of the nerves along her spine.

His fingers began to work on the buttons running down the back of her gown. Did he intend to strip her down right there in the middle of the sitting room? She brought a hand up to press to the front of her bodice as she turned her head, trying to look over her shoulder toward the darkened bedroom.

"Shouldn't we—"

He interrupted. "I have reasons for the things I do. You must trust me," he added.

"Trust is not a thing to be commanded, my lord," Lily replied gently, bringing her gaze forward again.

"But it is necessary if we are to proceed. I need for you to remain still."

She heard the strain in his voice and noticed he

hadn't moved his fingers since she had spoken. She realized then how badly she wanted him to continue.

She lowered her hand back to her side.

Her gown quickly loosened around her body. Staying behind her, the earl eased his hands beneath her gown, gliding them over her shoulders until the garment slid down her arms to catch briefly at her hips. A gentle tug had it falling the rest of the way to the floor.

Lily stood still as he had directed, though sensations swirled more insistently through her as he loosened the laces of her short stays. Tossing the stiff undergarment aside, he then untied her petticoat, allowing it to pool at her feet as well.

There was a moment of silence while Lily held her breath.

She stood in nothing but her whisper-thin shift, stockings, and shoes. The earl did not touch her for several long seconds, though she could hear the even sound of his breath behind her.

Her skin tingled with a contradictory mixture of chills and heat. Her muscles were tense as she waited for him to touch her. Her nerves sparked when she finally sensed him move. Slowly, he came around to stand before her again.

She risked a tentative glance at his face.

His features were as hard as granite. His lips were pressed firmly together, and he had that dark, angry look in his eyes.

Her heart jolted. She was starting to understand what caused such a look.

"Would you remove your shoes and stockings?"

Lily tipped her head to the side, a smile rising unexpectedly to her lips. "You are asking, my lord?"

She was not sure what had inspired her to tease him. An attempt at lightening his tension, perhaps, or her own.

His eyes met hers, and his voice had a gravelly quality when he replied, "It would give me pleasure to see you—all of you."

Her belly fluttered. All thoughts of teasing left her. Lowering her gaze, she slid her feet from her shoes and then rolled her stockings off one at a time. In nothing but her shift, she straightened and waited for what would come next.

Without touching her, he swept his gaze over her barely clad form. When his attention fell across her breasts, her nipples hardened and peaked beneath the gentle weight of her transparent shift.

Lily could see that he had noticed her body's reaction. His eyes flickered with something dangerous. Something that made her breath turn shallow. Her short inhalations caused the material to shift over her breasts with delicate friction.

Sensation speared through her belly and down between her legs.

As if he knew what she had experienced, he dipped his chin and continued to stare at her from beneath heavy brows. "Your breasts are very sensitive."

Lily knew it must be so, because his very mention of them made her nipples tighten even more, her breasts heavy and aching. She loved the way his rich, masculine voice made her body melt and her thoughts go languid.

"I promise to discover just how sensitive they can be," he added thickly. "You are very beautiful."

Something squeezed tight in her chest. "I am… quite ordinary."

A new darkness shadowed his features, and it was unlike the hunger with which she was becoming familiar. "You are far from ordinary."

The way he said it actually made her believe it.

His gaze swept down her body again. "Remove your shift."

Lily released the ties, then slid the narrow sleeves off her shoulders. The undergarment drifted to the floor like a sigh.

She watched him as he looked at her, expecting to feel some shyness, a need to cover up. She did not. There was intense vulnerability in standing naked and wanting, but Lily reveled in the power and pleasure of feeling his gaze travel over her skin, from shoulder to wrist, chin to navel, and hip to toe. Everywhere his focus fell, she felt it.

And in that moment, she felt beautiful.

"My lord?" She spoke in a thready whisper, but at the words, he lifted his eyes back to hers. Her belly tightened deliciously at the heat she saw there. "What would you like me to do?"

# Fifteen

Avenell's gut clenched viciously.

It was everything he had feared. He wanted her too badly. His body strained with a sensual craving stronger than anything he had ever known. She was perfection. From her soft and open gaze, to the lush curves of her breasts and hips, to the dimples in her knees and the delicate arches of her feet. Her body was flushed and her eyes needful.

Her modestly uttered question brought to mind so many ways he could answer. But he replied with only one.

"I want you to enjoy this."

It sounded simple. Avenell knew it was anything but.

The intensity of his reaction to her stunned him. No matter what he had done to avoid her, to deny the feelings she invoked, it had all led her to him anyway. And he had never wanted anything as much as he craved the feel of her touch.

His chest burned. His muscles trembled with the amount of effort it took to maintain his composure as she stared at him. Her steady focus revealed new facets of light and shadow. There was too much mystery there, too much temptation. He suspected it would take hours to explore the depth and complexity of her gaze. But such pleasure was not for tonight.

"Close your eyes."

She did as he asked with a flutter of her lashes as they swept down against her cheeks.

Avenell stepped closer to her and took a long breath, detecting the clean, pure scent emanating from her skin. Fresh and sweet.

"Remember," he said in a rough murmur, "remain still and keep your hands at your sides."

Her reply was an incoherent sound from the back of her throat that shifted to a soft inhale through parted lips as Avenell stroked his fingertips up the length of her arm. He teased the sensitive skin at her inner elbow before he lifted his hand, and with deliberate care, brushed the backs of his knuckles over the outer curve of her breast. Heat lit across his skin where it met hers. As his drifting touch circled nearer the rosy peak, her nipple tightened beautifully.

He heard her quiet gasp but did not look up to see the pleasure in her face. Instead, he turned his hand to touch her creamy, silken skin with his fingertips, skimming first over her collarbone, then down her sternum, between her lovely full breasts. With a touch as light as a breath, he drew a path to her navel, circling over the skin of her low belly until the muscles of her abdomen tightened and he heard another quiet gasp.

Avenell concentrated on keeping the rhythm of his pulse steady as he continued the gentle exploration of her body. She was exquisite to touch, her skin unbelievably soft, the dips and valleys of her body enticing and mysterious. He wanted to learn every bit of her.

He brought his hand back up to curve his palm around her rib cage, so the heel of his hand rested against the outside fullness of her breast. Then he smoothed his hand down her side, learning the bend of her waist and the swell of her hip before gliding back over the feminine lushness of her buttocks.

The sound of her breath coming swiftly between her lips caused a spike in his awareness. Blood pulsed heavily through his veins. She was so receptive to the first touches of his hand. He pressed his tongue hard against the back of his teeth as his fingers curled into the bare flesh of her buttocks. He ached with the desire to pull her body in to his.

He resisted.

Tonight was a test of his tolerance and aptitude. Tonight, he would touch her.

Learn what she liked and what she didn't. Gauge her reactions.

Gauge his own.

He circled around her again, taking the opportunity to breathe in her scent as the air stirred across her skin.

Standing behind her, he teased the soft tendrils of brown hair curling against her nape with the barest brush of his fingertips. Gooseflesh rose on her skin. He traced his fingers down the hollow of her spine, feeling the tension in the muscles that held her resolutely in place.

From behind, her waist appeared impossibly narrow above the generous flare of her buttocks. He brought both hands to rest on her hips and took a moment to press his thumbs into the dimples on each side at the very base of her spine.

He was impressed by her stillness. Her calm willingness to allow him such liberties.

To reward her, he leaned forward, just enough so he could press his lips to her shoulder. Touching the tip of his tongue to her skin, he reveled in the sound of her breath catching with pleasure. She tasted salty and sweet. Innocent. Pure.

A delicate shudder passed through her, and she turned her head toward him. Her lips were parted and swollen, as though she'd been worrying them with her teeth. The thick drift of her lashes was still lowered over her gaze.

"My lord?" she said in a whispered plea.

"Do you enjoy the feel of my hands on your body?"

"Yes."

He kept one hand pressed to her lower back as he stepped around to her side, where he could better observe her full reactions. His other hand slid over her hip and across the gentle curve of her belly. Her body quivered.

"Are you afraid?" he asked as he moved to cup her full breast in his hand.

"Yes," she replied in a weakened voice. Her spine softened, and her chin lowered by a fraction. "But I love the way you frighten me."

Her confession reached deep inside him and grabbed hold to twist painfully. Avenell reacted to the invasion by squeezing her breast, pinching her hardened nipple between his fingers.

She arched abruptly, and a silent gasp passed between her lips. Her breasts were as sensitive as he had suspected. The sight of his hands covering her lovely flesh caused a jolt of need to arc painfully through his system.

Watching her face intently, Avenell shifted his attention to her other breast. Drawing his fingertips in ever-tightening circles toward the peak, he noted the shortening of her breath. When the pad of his thumb first brushed across her nipple, she stiffened, and her teeth closed over her bottom lip.

Avenell clenched his teeth hard against the urge to take her breast with his mouth.

What would her reaction be if it was his tongue flicking over that peaked flesh?

He was determined to find out. But not tonight.

He released her breast to trail his fingers up to the delicate line of her jaw. Pressing his thumb lightly to her bottom lip, he drew it away from her teeth. Her soft breath puffed between her lips, and her eyelashes fluttered.

"Eyes closed," he muttered roughly. He could not withstand the force of her gaze just then.

Assured she would obey, he continued to explore the sensitivity of her body—touching her breasts, her belly—sliding his fingers along her inner thighs, her buttocks, and the length of her spine. She seemed to receive pleasure from everything he did.

Her response was torturous and lovely.

Avenell's yearning rose inexorably inside him. The rushing of his blood to his groin made him dizzy, and his jaw ached from how tightly he clenched it in his determination to maintain a certain detachment as he learned the subtleties in her response.

She started to undulate beneath his hands. It began as a gentle arching of her spine, then a small roll of her hips. Her breath was fast and short, and her hands were fisted fiercely at her sides as she moved.

Sensing the time was right, Avenell skimmed his hand down her belly toward the dark curls at the apex of her thighs.

With a raw gasp, she stiffened at the first touch.

He continued until he cupped her secret flesh, then he held still.

She was hot. Receptive.

As he felt her begin to relax, he shifted to ease his middle finger along her cleft. The warmth of her body coated his finger, easing its path to the bud that waited for his touch. With delicate focus, Avenell circled the pad of his finger, urging her body to soften, willing her to accept more.

A beautiful moan slid from her throat, and she started to move against his hand.

Avenell stared hard at her face, enraptured by the way her pleasure played across her soft features. Her full lips glistened, and her eyes were tightly closed as a furrow creased her brow.

She was soon writhing.

He had never been so caught up in a woman's reaction. He whispered dark, wicked words into the gasping quiet of the room. Demanding her surrender, declaring her *his* from this point forward.

He desperately wanted to press his fingers into her virgin body, feel the heat inside her as she drew him in. But he would not introduce even that gentle invasion until she first understood what it was to experience the pleasure he wanted to give her.

He stroked her sensitive flesh. Teasing, coaxing, awakening her to the sensations he could create.

She released another heady moan, and her legs trembled. With a gasp, she reached for him, grasping hard at his arm just above his elbow.

Searing pain shot across his skin. He jerked free of her grip, pulling his hand from her as his breath caught sharply in his throat. He stepped back, regret and self-directed anger coursing through him.

He had gone too far, too fast. He had lost himself in her expression of pleasure.

She made a soft sound of protest, and her eyes swept open to look at him. Confusion was already overcrowding the desire in her gaze.

He knew he must look a beast, standing there practically panting as he struggled to control the rioting in his body. The pleasure and the pain. The need and the fear.

Avenell turned away before he saw the disgust, the accusation he knew would come to replace her gentle expression. He would not withstand the revulsion. Not from her. Not now.

"My lord?"

"Once you have dressed, I will see you home," he said, hating the strangled sound of his voice.

He clenched his teeth as he strode swiftly to the adjacent room, seeking the farthest shadows, craving distance and solitude as he focused on settling the painful fire that spread across his nerves.

He knew his retreat had likely upset her, but it was better she understood the truth from the beginning.

He was broken in a real and vital way, and nothing would change that.

# Sixteen

Lily sat in the darkness of the gently rocking carriage. She was shocked, confused, and growing increasingly frustrated as the earl continued to hold his silence.

He sat stiff and rigid, his only movement the subtle manipulation of a small snuffbox with his deft fingers. He barely seemed aware of the object in his hand, his actions apparently originating more from habit than any particular intention.

At least she was regaining some of her composure. Trying to dress herself with shaking hands and wobbly knees had been difficult. But not as difficult as trying to understand what had happened—what had gone wrong.

He had created so many wonderful sensations with the sweep of his hands over her skin…and the slide of his fingers between her legs…only to bring it all to a sudden, heart-wrenching halt. He had left her standing there in the middle of the private sitting room. Naked and shaking from head to toe, on the verge of some inexplicable revelation. She was sure of it. She had been close to something astounding when he had pulled away from her.

She did not know why he had stopped touching her, and she suspected an explanation would not be forthcoming.

After leaving her shaking and stunned, the earl had not returned to her side until she was completely dressed. Without a word, he had assisted her with her cloak, bringing the hood up to shield her face. They had left the brothel as they had arrived, having stayed for barely more than a couple of hours.

The carriage made a wide turn, and she was reminded that the drive to Angelique's town house was not a long one. Lord Harte was obviously not inclined to provide any sort of explanation for his abrupt behavior. Of course, she knew it had to do with the fact that she had broken her promise when she touched him. But it seemed far more complex than she could decipher.

Lily was not one to force conversation or to pry into another person's thoughts, but she was never going to learn how to be his mistress if she could not bring herself to be bold.

Shifting in her seat, she clasped her hands together in her lap and stared across the carriage to his shadowed form. Taking a swift breath, she broke the silence. "My lord, have I displeased you tonight?"

He did not move or make any sound to indicate that he had heard her. She struggled to decide between settling back in silence or clearing her throat to try to gain his attention. Then she heard him exhale heavily, as though he had been holding his breath.

"No, you did not."

His words did not reassure her. There was too much rigidity in his tone, too much conflict. "Tonight was a test of sorts," he added after a moment.

Lily lifted her chin. "You were testing me?"

Her tone was made sharp by her injured pride and her confusion. She wished he would be more forthcoming with what he wanted from her. She hated feeling as though she had somehow let him down.

"You were not the one being tested."

The tenor of his voice was strained, as though it had been difficult for him to say the words.

"I do not understand," she murmured. Her internal frustration warred with a sudden urge to comfort him.

"I know. I am sorry for that."

He was not going to say more. Her stomach tightened, and she fell back into silence. There was so much to learn about the man who held himself detached even as he explored her body with such gentle intimacy. So much he was unwilling to reveal.

She could feel his resistance. And it made her ache.

After another lull, he spoke again. His words were a rough murmur. "All I can do is ask you to trust me."

Lily took a long breath. "I trust you, my lord."

He stared at her. His attention was harsh and direct, allowing no retreat from his gaze.

"You understand there will be pain…the first time?"

Her heart skipped a few beats, and she had to swallow hard before she could answer. He still intended to become her lover. She had not realized how fearful she was that he had changed his mind until she received confirmation to the contrary. Her body ignited swiftly with renewed anticipation.

"Yes," she answered.

"Do you know what happens between a man and a woman?"

Lily blushed as she thought of the scenes explicitly described in her novels. "Yes," she answered, trying to keep her voice from wavering.

He nodded, then leaned forward. She braced for his touch. But he was only reaching to unlatch the door. She hadn't even noticed the carriage had come to a stop.

"I will let you know when I plan to come for you again," he stated.

Lily nodded. She should have known not to expect sweet words of tenderness. Though she was disappointed when he did not even offer his hand as she moved to exit the vehicle, she said nothing.

Accepting the groom's assistance, she stepped to the ground. It was difficult not to look back, but she managed it. With her head high and her hands trembling beneath the fall of her cloak, she walked to the gate and slipped into Angelique's garden.

She wasn't sure she breathed again until she had closed her bedroom door behind her. Then she fell onto her bed with a heavy sigh.

Her night with the earl had been more amazing than she ever could have anticipated. Never would she have been able to imagine the things he had made her feel. Not only the physical pleasure, but also the aching stab of frustration once she had realized he was not going to allow her to touch him. He had stayed completely clothed, entirely unmoved, while she had been reduced to a trembling wanton.

The enigma he presented was all the more difficult to unravel because the mystery was deeply intertwined with his sensuality. There was darkness associated with his desire. Behind the forbidding gaze resided his passion—and he was fiercely determined to keep it confined.

It had been glorious to experience her body's awakening under his careful ministrations, but before she had reached the veiled heights of what could be discovered under a lover's caress, he had abandoned her. Abruptly and intentionally.

Because she had broken her promise to remain still and, in her mindless desire, had touched him.

It worried her and confused her.

He had given her the pleasure of his hands on her body but refused the same for himself.

He had said tonight had been a test. She hoped it would not need to be repeated.

She longed to explore his body the way he had hers. The thought of discovering every crest and angle of his masculine strength with the slide of her fingertips made her ache with renewed longing.

Surely, at their next meeting, he would allow her the pleasure of a simple touch.

Lily spent the next four days pondering the details of her first experience as a mistress. Four days of waiting and wondering when he would pass another message while her patience steadily wore thin.

She began to feel desperate with the anticipation of seeing him again. Even if it had to be in silent acknowledgment or in a too-brief glimpse across a ballroom. Even if he did not touch her again. Even if she had to find a way to contact him herself.

Unfortunately, he had not given her any way to reach him. And he had not implied in any way that he would want her to.

These concerns occupied most of her attention as she accompanied Angelique on a brief shopping excursion. The dowager countess had used the last of the rose and juniper perfume she always wore and needed to purchase another bottle.

The shop where she procured the precious scent was tucked along a narrow alley that extended off the southern end of Bond Street. The curved little lane was rather dank, with piles of refuse gathering in corners. Lily tensed at the sight of what possibly could have been a small cat or a large rat skittering between doorways up ahead.

Angelique, however, glided along as though they were strolling through St. James's Park, the opera glasses she carried with her everywhere lifted to give her a better view of the path before them. She was chatting away about the first time she had discovered the little scent shop and how she had managed to convince the proprietor to create a scent all for her.

Lily smiled at the old lady's declarations. Though the story could be true, it was just as likely to be another of her great-aunt's grand fabrications. The lady told so many fantastical tales, it was difficult to ascertain when anything she said had any bit of truth.

Their destination was nestled between a musty old antique book shop and the offices of someone whose sign boasted services to assist in personal legal matters. Certainly, it was not the most fashionable part of the shopping district.

They entered the tiny shop, and the silence that greeted them suggested that they were the only patrons. In fact, the atmosphere was so oddly serene, Lily wondered if anyone had been in the place for quite some time. It felt as though the air, heady with an array of mixed scents, had not been stirred in ages.

Still, the shop was enchanting. Everywhere she looked there was something unusual catching her eye. Tables and cabinets of various shapes and sizes held an infinite array of scented delights. There were slim bottles made of crystal embedded with colored glass, hand-painted porcelain jars, larger decanters of polished silver, and everything in between.

And as the gentle afternoon sunlight streamed into the shop, it reflected and refracted between the crystal and glass, creating a hazy miasma of rainbow-colored light.

"Hello," Angelique crooned. She swept confidently forward, sashaying past a glass-topped display containing a crowded jumble of perfume bottles.

Lily followed behind at a much slower and more careful pace. Even a small bump against one of the spindle-legged tables could send a wave of crystal and porcelain crashing to the floor.

"Hell-llo?" Angelique called out again from somewhere up ahead.

Lily reined in her fascination and stepped around a

display of large wooden bowls containing collections of dried flowers. The deep red of her aunt's gown became muted to a darker shade by the dim shadows at the back of the store.

Then she heard the wavering voice of a very old man finally reply, "My lovely Lady of the Garden, how I cherish these rare visits."

A small man dressed in deep forest green with a shock of white hair came scuttling from a back room to grasp both of Angelique's hands and bring them to his lips, one at a time.

Lily hid her smile and turned away.

*Lady of the Garden?*

She resisted a small giggle.

Intentionally diverting her focus from the disturbingly flirtatious reunion at the back of the store, Lily wandered toward a shelf containing scents to sample.

She reached first for one labeled *The Glory of Gardenia* and quickly set it down after a brief sniff. The flowery scent was fiercely overwhelming. She continued down the row, trying several more: one scented with orange blossoms and juniper, one laced with lavender, one that contained an interesting blend of rose and mint, and one that was crisp with the scent of lemon and some exotic spice.

As she perused the scents, she did not realize that someone else had entered the little shop until she felt a presence come up behind her. The sudden awareness of another person startled her into fumbling dangerously with the slim glass bottle stopper she was holding.

The stopper tumbled from her fingers. Lily gasped

in dismay and tensed for the inevitable sound of shattering glass. At the last moment, a man swooped in, catching the stopper before it hit the floor.

Lily's breath expelled from her body as she looked down to see Lord Harte crouched elegantly beside her, looking up at her from beneath the shadow of his brow.

Her heart gave a wild flip as he straightened again to his full height. She had been foolish to think her reaction to him would ever ease. His effect on her seemed only to intensify with each encounter.

"You dropped this." His tone was intimate and private.

She drew a slow breath. Delicate tingles raced over her skin. Though he did not wear gloves, she did, yet she could feel his warmth when he handed the stopper back to her. She cradled it in her palm.

"Thank you," she replied in a whisper.

He stood so close. The intensity of his nature emanated from him and infused her blood. She swayed gently toward him.

He stiffened and glanced aside to the row of perfume bottles on the shelves.

"Have you found a scent you like?" His words were conversational, but the underlying tone spoke of so many other things.

Light-headed from his unexpected appearance, Lily discovered the act of finding a proper response took more effort than expected.

"No," she finally murmured, "I am afraid I have not found one I feel would suit me." There was an intrinsic sense of urgency in the moment. Lily did not wish to waste time with idle small talk. She gathered her courage to ask pointedly, "Why are you here?"

He looked back to her, his gaze intense.

"I was driving past and saw you turn down the alley."

"My great-aunt is in the back of the store."

"I know."

"She may finish her business at any moment."

"I know," he said, continuing to stare at her.

His expression was so hard, so closed off, but still Lily saw something that seized her breath. It was there in the infinite depth of his dark-blue eyes. It was in the unforgiving line of his mouth, the tension of his jaw, the weight of his brow. Though he did not touch her, she felt him. Everywhere, she felt him.

And despite the coldness of his manner, it was heat she felt.

Unable to take the silence any longer, she whispered, "My lord?"

There was a swift and sudden flash of light in his eyes. "Tomorrow," he said deeply. "I will come for you at midnight."

"I—"

The sound of Angelique's voice filtered toward her from the back of the store. Lily turned her head. At the same time, he backed away. Within a second, Lily was left standing alone before the sample display, her hands shaking and her stomach aquiver.

"Come along, *ma petite*. If we hurry, we may have time to stop for sweets before heading home."

Lily watched her great-aunt sweep toward her, holding a small brown-wrapped parcel.

Angelique tilted her head and gave her an odd look. "Darling? Are you feeling ill?"

Lily resisted the urge to glance around for a glimpse of the earl. She carefully replaced the stopper she still held in its bottle. "No. I am fine. Just a bit light-headed from all the perfume, perhaps."

"Come along, then," the lady replied, linking her arm through Lily's. "We will get you into the fresh air. *À tout à l'heure*," she called out with a little finger wave toward the back of the store.

"My heart stops until your return, my lady," the shopkeeper declared from the hazy depths of the back room.

"What a foolish old man," Angelique cooed with a girlish smile as she guided them back out onto the narrow street.

Lily finally risked a glance over her shoulder. Though she thought she saw a shadow pass behind the window, she couldn't be sure.

The next evening, Lily was in her bedroom, preparing to ready herself for the dinner party they were attending that evening. She had just finished her bath and sat at her dressing table in her robe as she ran a brush through the still-damp length of her hair. Her aunt's personal maid dressed their hair for formal events, and Lily knew she had some time before it was her turn.

She stared critically at her reflection in the mirror above her dressing table, studying her features in a way she had never done before. Lifting her chin, she looked first this way then that, trying to identify what it was Lord Harte saw in her as desirable.

She was so dreadfully ordinary.

Medium brown hair parted in the middle. Muted gray eyes that did not snap with determination and intelligence like Emma's or glitter with mystery and excitement like Portia's. A straight nose with a base she always thought was a bit too wide. A common enough chin, cheekbones that were nicely defined, and rather straight brown eyebrows beneath a high forehead.

Lily made a face at herself before glancing over at the gown laid out on her bed.

It was an elegant pink batiste, so pale it appeared white in certain lighting. It was one of the new gowns purchased with Emma's winnings from the club. The gown was simple and beautiful, but very clearly denoted Lily as a debutante, one of the many young ladies scouring London drawing rooms for a husband.

Lily scowled, worrying at her bottom lip with her teeth. Her gaze traveled critically over the delicate flounces layering the hem and the flowered embroidery that decorated the bodice.

The dress was all wrong for a midnight tryst. She wished she had something more daring. More alluring. Something in red perhaps, or a vivid blue.

Her contemplation was interrupted by a quiet knock at her door.

She startled, not having expected to have her hair done for at least another half hour. She would need to dress quickly. She rose to her feet and called for the maid to enter.

It was not her aunt's maid but a girl from downstairs

who peeked her head in the door. "Excuse me, miss, are you alone?"

"Yes, please come in," Lily replied, curious at the unexpected interruption.

The young maid came forward quickly after securing the door behind her. She brought a small wrapped parcel around from behind her back.

"The courier insisted specifically that I deliver this to you when you were alone."

Lily eyed the package, feeling a delicate twist in her belly. She took the parcel from the maid with a muttered "thank you." She barely made notice of the girl departing until the door clicked shut, leaving Lily alone once again.

Taking the small package with her, she went to sit on the edge of her bed. She turned the box over in her hands several times, looking for a means of identifying where it had come from. There was none, which managed to solidify her suspicion of who had sent it.

With a flutter of excitement, she carefully unwrapped the brown paper to reveal a simple wooden box. Aside from a gentle scroll pattern carved into the top, it was unadorned. Lily set the box on her lap and released the latch to open the hinged lid. Inside, on a bed of black velvet, lay an exquisite perfume bottle designed from rose-colored glass caged in a silver overlay that twined about the glass like living vines. In the very center of the oval shaped bottle, the silver was formed into the image of a lily in full bloom.

It was likely the most precious and expensive gift Lily had ever been given. She ran her fingertips over the delicate silver work before lifting the bottle from its velvet bed to allow the candlelight to shine through the rose-colored glass.

She noticed then a folded slip of paper still in the box. Setting the perfume bottle in the valley of her lap, she lifted the paper and broke the tiny wax seal.

In his precise, slanted script, Lord Harte had written:

> *I was unforgivably remiss in not having a gift for you the other night. I chose the elements for this blend myself. It made me think of you.*

Lily brushed her thumb over the ink before setting the note back into the box. Then she lifted the bottle and removed the glass stopper. The scent wafting from the bottle was light, but heady. She noticed first the rich notes of clove and honey before her senses were claimed by the smooth, velvety scent of jasmine. Lily closed her eyes, allowing the aromatic infusion to settle into her awareness. There was another element hidden deep within the perfume. A layer of earthiness that warmed her blood. Sandalwood.

Lily was enthralled. It was a complex and lovely scent. Floral and exotic, light and dark. Impossibly sensual.

And it made him think of her.

Something deep and fundamental spread through her core, and she understood why young ladies were warned so often not to accept gifts from gentlemen. It was a personal and intimate thing to acknowledge how he had wanted her to have something he chose himself.

She would have to keep the gift a secret from her sisters. Just one more secret among many Lily knew she would be harboring before her relationship with the earl ran its course.

There was a twinge of guilt at the thought. But only a twinge.

Even without the scandalous circumstances of their arrangement, her feelings for Lord Harte were far too personal to consider sharing. Even with Portia, who had been privy to more of Lily's private thoughts and wishes than anyone.

Lily lifted the bottle again to her nose and drew a long breath. As she imagined what it would feel like to have him place the scent on her skin with the gentle brush of his fingers, the muscles of her thighs tightened, and heat gathered between her legs.

Glancing at the clock, she realized she had only a short time to dress before her great-aunt's maid arrived. She had already planted the seeds for escaping from the dinner early by mentioning a burgeoning headache earlier in the day. It should be an easy thing to request the use of Angelique's carriage to bring her home ahead of the others. When they arrived home, they would assume Lily was sleeping.

If all went well, she would be with the earl again in just a few hours. And she intended to be wearing his scent.

# Seventeen

"Damn."

The earl's curse was muttered so quietly under his breath, Lily almost did not hear it.

He was looking out the carriage window as they slowly made their way through a spot of unexpected traffic to the narrow drive that ran alongside the building that housed Pendragon's Pleasure House.

He turned to look at her, and she could tell by the fierce lines of displeasure on his face that something was wrong. Curious, she shifted on her seat, leaning toward the window in an attempt to see what had irritated him. She managed just a glimpse of the brothel, but it was enough to note that every window in the place appeared to be lit up.

"What is it?" she asked.

"Pendragon is throwing one of her parties tonight. If I had known..."

He did not need to finish. She understood that he would not have chosen to bring her to the brothel on a night when it was clearly very active.

"I will take you home."

"No." His eyebrows arched at her swift denial. "Please, there is no need to change our plans."

The carriage had made it up the drive and stopped near the rear of the brothel.

"There will be guests everywhere. Wandering the hallways, seeking diversions. Pendragon's parties get very wild."

Her curiosity spiked. "How wild? Are there orgies?"

He inhaled a swift breath at her words, then coughed a little.

Lily couldn't be sure if he was choking on shock or amusement. Either way, she felt her cheeks heat.

The groom opened the carriage door, but the earl did not move to get out. He sat staring at her in the dark of the vehicle.

"What do you know of orgies?"

Lily's blush spread. An innocent should not even know the word, let alone find herself curious how such a thing might manifest. And she *was* curious. Exceptionally so.

She considered how much she wanted to reveal about her unusual cache of knowledge. He would likely be shocked to discover that she knew certain things, by description if not by actual experience.

"I...ah, understand it is a sort of party," she replied.

"There is a bit more to it than that."

She was completely incapable of keeping the breathlessness from her voice when she asked, "Like what?"

He remained silent, staring at her intently by the dim light flowing into the carriage from the open door.

Lily stared back. The growing tension between them was not an unpleasant feeling.

Finally, he asked, "Do you wish to attend Pendragon's party?"

Excitement flared at the possibility. But before she replied, she tried to determine if there was any hint of shock or censure in his tone. All she heard was a thread of dark sensuality that resonated acutely with the tingling expectation flowing through her.

When she did not answer right away, he added, "I would like you to feel that you can be honest with me, Lily. I would never pass judgment on anything that might bring you pleasure, just as I would honor your wishes in regard to whatever you find abhorrent."

Lily was warmed by his words in a way that had nothing to do with physical desire. For the first time in her life, she felt free to be fully truthful about what she wanted.

"I am rather curious," she admitted. "It is not likely I will have many opportunities to experience such an event. Perhaps we could make a brief pass through the party. Just to observe," she clarified.

This time, there was a definite note of humor in his tone as he replied, "You wish to *observe* an orgy?"

"*Is* it an orgy?" she asked, her eyes widening.

"Likely not yet. It is still early."

His answer eased her shock to some degree, but it also stabbed her awareness with an uncomfortable realization.

"You have attended such parties in the past?"

"Only once," he replied, his voice very low. Very dark. "To observe."

"Oh." She didn't know what else to say.

More silence as he continued to stare at her.

"Wait here," he said just before he slipped out of the carriage and disappeared through the side door of the brothel.

She waited with strained patience, listening to the sounds of revelry filtering from the brownstone into the night.

Why had he gone in without her?

Had she succeeded in shocking him after all? Would he insist upon returning her to Angelique's?

Disappointment swept through her at the thought.

She was still trying to come up with a sound argument for them to stay when he returned. One moment he was simply there again, standing in the doorway of the carriage.

Lily's breath hesitated at the forbiddingly handsome image he presented. It amazed her that he could look so stern and hard when he possessed such trembling gentleness in the drift of his fingers.

"Put this on," he said as he handed something to her.

She looked at the object in her hands and was surprised to see a heavily bejeweled half mask.

She looked up in surprise. "We are going in?"

"To observe. And only for a brief pass through before heading upstairs. You are to remain at my side the entire time. You cannot say a word to anyone or risk being identified. Do you understand?"

"I do."

Tingling anticipation ran through her limbs as she secured the mask to her face. It covered her features from just above her mouth to mid-forehead. She would be completely anonymous.

The thought was thrilling.

The earl held out his hand to help her from the carriage. Then he carefully drew the deep hood of her cloak forward, further shielding her from view.

"I must be mad," he muttered before taking her hand in one of his and carefully setting it in the crook of his arm.

She felt the muscles of his arm twitch and tense under her fingers. Then he took a long, even breath before leading her into the building. Clearly, he was unnerved by the prospect of escorting her. That he chose to do it anyway inspired a wealth of gratitude.

The pleasure house was filled with the sounds of revelry. Instead of going up the back stairway, they continued down the hall on the main floor. After passing through a narrow door, the hall widened, then turned a few corners before opening to a sort of general receiving area.

Lily gaped at the scene before her.

Gentlemen of all ages—and a few elegantly gowned ladies—stood about in their most resplendent evening wear, chatting with one another as though they were in the finest drawing room. If not for the obvious gender imbalance of those in attendance, they looked for all the world like guests at any party of the beau monde. But it was not the sight of the guests that caused Lily's eyes to widen behind her mask. It was the fact that all around, women walked about completely nude. Some of the naked women carried trays of champagne flutes, others offered pipes or cigars to the guests, and still others appeared to have no true purpose other than to smile and be seen.

She was so stunned by the unexpected sight that Lily barely noticed the earl leading her around the perimeter of the room. A few guests glanced their way, but most didn't appear particularly curious about their swift passing. She had guessed there would be an obvious salacious element to the party—they were in a brothel, after all—but she just hadn't expected it to be so blatant.

Or so casually displayed.

It surprised her.

And intrigued her.

How interesting that people could be so comfortable with a woman's completely bared flesh that they barely seemed to notice it so prevalently displayed in their midst.

As she and the earl neared the other end of the room, she was given cause to swiftly reevaluate that assessment as a tall gentleman with distinguished streaks of gray in his brown hair accepted a glass of champagne from one of the women while simultaneously reaching out to fondle her bared breast.

The woman laughed—a coy sort of throaty sound—before she turned around and offered the groping gentleman her rounded buttocks, which he promptly spanked.

Lily gasped. Her fingers curled into the earl's forearm.

She thought he may have made a sound as well, but she was too quickly distracted. The tall gentleman's friend, a more portly fellow with significant balding, stepped toward the woman and slid his hand into her artfully coiffed hair as he leaned toward her to whisper something in her ear.

With another laugh, the woman set her tray on a nearby table and reached for the second gentleman, her hands sliding seductively down his chest.

Lily and the earl passed through a doorway into a short corridor leading to the next room.

Curiosity flashed as Lily wondered what would happen next between the pair. She had a strong urge to look over her shoulder.

"Do not look back," the earl muttered fiercely.

Lily glanced up at him through the narrow slits of her mask. He stared straight ahead. His chin was set at a sharp angle, and his lips were drawn painfully thin.

She experienced an urgent need to push him a little. To see if she might crack his hardened veneer. "Why not? I thought our purpose was to observe."

They entered the next room. This one was much smaller. The lighting was lower, casting everything into a burgundy haze. The result reminded Lily of the dreamlike drama inherent in baroque paintings.

A solo violinist played in a corner while various spectators gathered around a sofa across the room. Lily caught only glimpses of what they were watching. She saw a lady in a silk-threaded gown and a mask held in a gentleman's passionate embrace. Then the flash of her bare leg as the lady's skirts were raised.

She heard the low moans and quiet gasps of the two lovers and the murmurs of those who watched.

As Lily and the earl continued past the scene, she angled her head, trying to see the couple on the sofa better through the shifting crowd. The whole tableau amazed her.

Not the nature of the act they performed—she had

read of its description many times—but at the lack of care the couple exhibited for the fact that a small audience had gathered around them.

"Observe. Not watch," the earl stated beside her as he continued to lead her through the room.

A thrill ran through her center. "Is there a difference?"

"Quite."

She considered the crowd of people watching the couple as though they were players on a stage. It was obvious that they were deriving a certain pleasure from watching the scene.

In truth, the sight of the almost frantic coupling did speed up Lily's pulse and brought a fine sheen of heightened awareness to the nerves running through her body. But it also made her want to escape with the earl to a place more secluded.

She glanced away from the couple to see that he was looking down at her. His eyes were dark and entirely unreadable. She forgot all about the couple and their friends. Her attention became engrossed in the fine tension of the earl's features. She was disappointed when he redirected his gaze forward to navigate their passage through another doorway.

"Does this make you nervous, my lord?" she asked, sensing his reaction was about more than simply protecting her innocent eyes from illicit scenes of debauchery.

"Infinitely," came his stark reply.

"Then why did you agree to escort me?"

"It is what you wanted."

His simple answer made her stomach tighten. "I only thought that having an opportunity to view such things might assist me in my role as your mistress. I wish to learn."

He glanced down at her again, his eyes sharp. Penetrating.

"I will be the one to teach you, Lily. Not these men and women, strangers who have no place between us."

The next room was even darker than the last—so dark, it took a moment for Lily's eyes to adjust. When they did, she began to see various forms around her. Men and women of all shapes and sizes grouped in twos, threes, or more. Another violinist played in the corner, but the music was not enough to cover the gasps from those occupying the space.

"Bloody hell," the earl growled beside her before he slipped his arm around her waist to rush her through the room. Once in the corridor beyond, with the door secured behind them, he stopped and released her, stepping back to put as much space between them as possible in the narrow hall.

Lily stood facing him, her breath unnaturally shallow as she considered what she had seen. So many bodies. Such a lack of discretion. Sex in its most primal, physical form.

"It would seem it was not too early for an orgy after all," Lily whispered.

Several beats of silence followed her words.

"I should never have agreed to this."

"I am glad you did," she replied, still feeling the aftereffects of such blatant carnality in the pounding of her heart. Though it had been dark, and the images had been more impressions than actual details, there was no denying the raw sexual energy contained in that room. "I acquired a new understanding I had not expected."

"What do you understand, Lily?" His tone was deeply reserved, as though he held back everything he was thinking to keep it from being revealed in his voice.

Lily deliberately did the opposite.

"There is a distinct difference between acts of the nature we just witnessed and what I experienced with you the other night."

"What difference?" he asked when she paused.

The strain in his voice reached into her center. Lily thought about how to put into words something that was more an instinctive sense than specific knowledge.

"It seems to me that the people we observed through those rooms were intent upon their pleasure for the sake of pleasure itself. I almost wonder if it would have mattered a great deal with whom they engaged in such acts. I imagine the anonymity itself adds to the excitement of it."

"That is likely true," he replied.

The heat beneath Lily's skin deepened. It was strange how much easier it was to discuss such things when it was about someone else. Speaking of her desire was still so challenging.

But she was a mistress now. She needed to practice her boldness.

"What happened between us..." she began again with a bit more hesitation, not because she was uncertain of what she wanted to say, but because she wanted to be sure she was explaining herself properly, "was quite the opposite, I think. For me, anyway," she added with a sigh.

"How do you mean?" he prompted stiffly when she did not continue right away.

Lily tried to meet his eyes in the darkness of the closed corridor. She was disappointed to find the shadows went too deep.

"I could not imagine feeling the kind of pleasure I experienced from your touch if it had been with anyone but you, my lord."

"Why do you think that is?" he asked, and Lily could hear a shift in his tone, though she was not sure what it indicated.

She thought for a moment before she answered, trying to understand the truth of it herself. "When I am with you, I feel safe. Safe to express myself in a way I have never had the courage to do before. I feel…like you might understand me as no one else can."

He did not reply, and they lapsed into silence. The only sound was of their breath and Lily's pulse beating heavy in her ears.

He stood so still, his hands fisting at his sides, his chin lowered. Saying nothing. Though she could not see his eyes, she could feel his focus. Observing her.

Finally, she could bear it no longer.

"Will you take me upstairs now?"

---

He shouldn't.

He should take her home and try to forget he had ever agreed to become her lover.

He was certain he would never be able to get out of his head the breathless sound of her voice when she had asked him to take her upstairs.

He could not possibly fathom all of the thoughts that must be going through her mind after what she'd observed. They had just traversed through one of the wickedest, most dissipated scenes she was ever likely to encounter.

He was still affected by it. Of course, he had been viewing everything as he imagined she would see it—through the eyes of an innocent.

He glanced at her from the corner of his eye as he led her through the servant hallways to the back stairs. Her head was bowed as she kept pace beside him. Fiery sensations danced over his arm where she rested her hand, and only the stiff rhythm of his stride kept her from brushing against his shoulder with each step.

He was wound so tight, that slight contact would be more than he could tolerate.

When they reached the private suite on the third floor, she strode ahead of him into the room.

He turned the key in the lock to ensure that there would be no interruptions from guests wandering too far from the party.

Then he watched with tension in every inch of his body as she pushed back the hood of her cloak and loosened the ties beneath her chin. Removing the encompassing outer garment, she draped it over the back of the settee before reaching up to untie her mask. Her manner was unhurried, though he noted a trembling in her hands.

Her calm composure was as much a facade as his aloof demeanor.

He was discovering a complexity to her nature that had not been evident in their earliest interactions. She was far more than she appeared to be: reserved, yet fearless in a way he could not have anticipated. Modest and sensual at once. In possession of a quiet confidence that was layered within everything she did.

Admiration flowed through him, followed quickly by a dose of doubt.

Things had not ended well at their last encounter.

Getting swept away in her response had been… astounding—and far more potent than he had anticipated. His desire had overwhelmed him, and he had forgotten himself.

He could still see the astonishment in her face when he had abruptly pulled away, leaving her bereft and unfulfilled.

It would not happen again.

She turned in place, and their eyes met for a moment. Her smile was shy and uncertain, sending a jolt of awareness through his chest before he glanced away.

"Would you like a glass of wine?" he asked.

She released a shallow breath. "Yes, thank you."

Avenell strode toward the bottle and glasses set in wait on the side table.

"Perhaps you would enjoy some as well, my lord."

Avenell hesitated in the act of pouring the bordeaux.

Though he never consumed alcohol in public, he occasionally enjoyed a glass of wine when dining alone. Just enough to set him at ease when there was no one else about.

He would like to feel at ease with her.

It shocked him that he would even consider it. He had spent years learning how to maintain his self-control around others. Yet now, when he would need his self-possession more than ever, he was tempted to relax his near-constant vigilance.

Turning back to the room, he noted that she had not moved from her spot, but stood with her hands clasped lightly at her waist. Her head was set at an almost imperceptible tilt as she waited.

Avenell acknowledged a rush of exhilaration as he approached her with the wine.

He passed the glass to her in a way that avoided any chance of contact with her fingers. He didn't even have to think of the act, it was so ingrained.

"Thank you, my lord." Her voice was soft and melodious. She brought the glass to her lips and took a sip of the deep red wine.

"It's lovely," she said, then flicked a glance toward the glass in his hand. "Won't you try it, my lord?"

Was that a hint of challenge in her tone?

In that moment, his desire to share the heady wine with her was stronger than his anxiety. He lifted his glass.

The wine was full-bodied and velvety. He should have suspected that Pendragon would stock only the best. He took a moment to savor it, knowing Lily had tasted the same flavors on her tongue. It was an intoxicating thought.

"Shall we sit?" he asked, gesturing toward the settee.

She blinked and glanced aside. He could see that she had not expected the suggestion, but he was determined to proceed more carefully tonight.

"Of course," Lily murmured politely as she lowered herself to the settee.

Avenell took a seat beside her. The piece of furniture was small, and his knee bumped against hers as he turned a bit to face her. She did not withdraw from the contact. Neither did he.

A gentle silence fell as Avenell took another drink of his wine. The alcohol slowly eased into his bloodstream, warming him if not actually relaxing him.

After several minutes, she straightened her spine and turned toward him, her expression earnest.

"I want to thank you, my lord, for your part in making sure my name has not been whispered among the gossips of town."

"As I've explained, there are strict rules governing Pendragon's clients."

She made a small gesture with her hand. "Yes, but I would hazard a guess that you added your influence to the matter."

His chest tightened at the sight of the gratitude in her eyes. "It is a small thing."

"But it is not," she argued. "It is important to me. I would hate for my recent activities—those I had no control over and those I chose willingly," she clarified with a subtle dip of her chin, "to have an adverse effect on my sisters."

"You are very protective of them," he observed.

A smile quirked the corner of her mouth. "I would say we are all quite protective of one another. Each in our own way."

Avenell marveled at the kind of family she described. It was difficult to imagine.

As though sensing his train of thought, she asked, "Have you any family you worry about, my lord?"

"No."

Her eyes widened. "None at all?"

"I suppose there may be some distant cousins somewhere. I have no siblings. My mother died giving birth to me, and my father passed when I was twenty."

"I am sorry."

He shrugged off her sympathy. "I no longer mourn for them." He paused, then continued, "I understand you lost your father recently?"

She dropped her gaze to her lap as she replied, "Yes. He died unexpectedly from a weak heart." She sighed. "Life had been challenging for him—for all of us—after my mother passed away from illness several years ago. I like to think my father has finally found some peace."

"Do you do that often?" he asked quietly.

"What?" She brought her gaze back up to his. Her expression was open and unguarded, though shadows remained in the gray of her eyes.

"Seek the good in tragic situations?"

She smiled. "I am afraid so. My sister Portia teases me dreadfully for my optimism. But I cannot see a reason to dwell on the things we cannot change. It is better, I think, to find the reasons to continue on with hope."

"Though you lost your parents, I suppose it helps to have your sisters," he observed.

She gave him a rueful smile. "When I was young, I used to wonder what life would be like if I had been born an only child. It is easy to fade away between my sisters. They each have such strong personalities. One so confident and self-assured. The other bold and fiercely independent."

Avenell heard the pride in her voice as she spoke of

her family, but he also detected something she worked hard at concealing.

Dissatisfaction.

"You said you used to wonder. You don't anymore?"

A gentle shrug, a brief downward glance. "I suppose I have come to understand myself better as I have gotten older. I do not truly crave outward attention. It was only in juxtaposition to my sisters that I felt lacking. I discovered ways to find contentment in other things." She smiled. "I am very grateful for the life I have."

"Yet you risk your reputation and your position in society to continue our intimate association," he noted in a low murmur.

Her eyes darkened. "I do."

He stared back at her, his muscles tense and his chest tight with the awareness of how much she risked in being there with him in the private suite of a brothel.

"My lord," she began softly, "I can see that you do not understand my motivation, and I suppose it must have been a shock when I…propositioned you the way I did."

She glanced down at the wineglass in her hand as a blush rose on her cheeks. But after a moment, she lifted her gaze again.

"Considering the nature of our…relationship, I feel I must confess something rather personal." She paused before she leaned slightly toward him. "I am not so innocent as most ladies my age. I have read novels in which love and passion are explained in explicit detail."

"Do you mean erotic novels?" he asked in surprise.

His question brought another wave of pink to

her cheeks, and her eyelashes fluttered as though she would glance away, but she resisted and held his gaze as she nodded.

It certainly explained how she was able to take in the scenes below with the amount of poise she had displayed. This woman stunned him in so many ways.

"I know I shouldn't admit to it, my lord, but you have asked me to be honest with you. The truth is that I have long been…curious about the more passionate aspects of human existence. I do not want to live my entire life huddled beneath my bedcovers, imagining what desire must feel like. I want to experience it. I *do* experience it with you."

Her words stole his breath.

"From the first moment I saw you, my lord, I felt something ignite inside me. Something powerful. It is important to me that you know I would never have considered becoming the mistress of anyone but you."

Avenell's heart stopped.

He knew he should say something to help put her at ease, but he found his chest too tight to form words, his brain incapable of an appropriate reply. Finally, he cleared his throat and managed a rough, "I am honored."

The sentiment was horridly inadequate, but it was all he could manage.

She smiled gently. No judgment. No demand for more. Her soft gaze swept over him as he sat stiffly in the corner of the small settee.

Heat coursed through him, but it was not the burn of too much sensation on his skin. It was the heady warmth of longing that captured him when she looked at him as she did then.

"The room is warm, my lord," she said into the lengthening silence. "May I remove your coat?"

Her request gave him pause as trepidation clutched at his insides.

Memories of being dressed and undressed as a child rose unbidden to his mind. The rough handling by impatient nurses, the curses and slaps as he struggled in their hold, which only brought on more pain and terror.

He fisted his hand tight against his thigh before extending it again, then repeated the action.

What she wanted would be difficult.

But he wanted it as well, more than his fear, more than anything.

He lifted his glass for another sip of the silky red wine. He welcomed the warmth of it spreading through his center and out to his limbs, though in that moment, he wished it were something more potent.

Setting the glass aside, he rose stiffly to his feet.

She stood as well and turned toward him. She moved slowly, as though sensing his uneasiness. He kept his gaze trained over her head, not wanting her to see the level of concentration in his eyes.

She kept a subtle distance between them. Still, he tensed when she reached for the buttons of his coat.

This time he was prepared for the heightened sensation across his skin as her gentle movements translated through his clothing. He clenched his teeth and breathed long and deep through his nose.

"Will you look at me, my lord?" There was as much command as there was question in her tone.

Avenell obeyed, lowering his gaze back to her face.

He knew how he must appear—his features tense and harsh with concentration. He could feel the heavy pull of his brow over his eyes and knew his lips were pressed firmly together as he fought to contain his flinch.

By direct contrast, she looked up at him with such patience. Her features were so serene, he almost missed the subtle sort of breathlessness in her expression, nearly concealed beneath her steady composure.

Anticipation.

Avenell's pulse jumped.

Her lashes swept briefly over her gaze, but not before he detected the flame of desire and curiosity in the depths of her eyes.

Very carefully, she began to ease his coat back over his shoulders and down his arms.

He held his breath. His body stiffened as he fought his instinct for self-preservation and held himself still beneath her ministrations.

Removing the coat completely, she set it aside. With the same slow, careful movements, she repeated the same with his waistcoat.

He focused on maintaining his control despite the searing flicks of fire igniting across his skin.

"My lord."

Her whispered words drew his attention, and Avenell opened his eyes, not having realized when he had closed them.

Her gaze was lit with inquiry and compassion. Surely she had noticed his discomfort, but he could see that she did not intend to press for an explanation.

She glanced to the side, and the tip of her tongue

moistened her lips before she spoke. "Shall we retire to the next room?"

Avenell was immediately reminded of how young and inexperienced she was. For all of her quiet self-assurance, she was a maiden still.

The sense of possession that followed that thought added fuel to the steady blaze growing within him. She had chosen him.

He would do everything in his power to prove himself worthy.

He held his hand out toward her, palm up.

She slowly placed her hand in his, sending a tingle of sensation up his arm and across his nape. It was a pleasant sensation.

No. More than that.

It was exhilarating and triggered more of the same deep within. He was suddenly impatient to move his hands over her while she gasped and tensed in reaction.

And this time, he would not cease until she experienced the full depth of pleasure she craved.

# Eighteen

Lily walked with him toward the bedroom, her heart pounding wildly.

There was something different about him tonight. It was not obvious, but it was there in his quiet intensity. If their last encounter had been a test of sorts, tonight felt like an initiation.

Just inside the door of the bedroom, he released her hand and strode ahead of her toward a row of candles set in a gothic wrought iron stand. His shoulders were broad and strong beneath the white of his shirt. She had noticed when she had removed his coat and waistcoat that his shirt was made of silk rather than cotton or linen. It was not a common choice, and each time her fingers had brushed the decadent material, a thrill had passed through her.

As he lit the candles one by one, the room became gently illuminated by the flickering golden light.

The bedroom was smaller than the sitting room, but it was far more dramatic in its decor. The walls were covered in black and silver brocade. The bed was large and imposing, with a high, scrolled headboard that gleamed a cherry red in the candlelight. Black velvets, silks, and satins mingled on its surface.

Her gaze swung away from the bed to the center of the room, where a chaise was placed conspicuously by itself in the open space. Something about the odd piece of furniture gave Lily pause, and she found herself staring at it. It stood on elegantly curved legs and was upholstered in a sleek red leather that made her want to run her hand over its surface. Unlike most chaises, it did not have a raised end for reclining, and aside from two rolled pillows on either end, it did not possess any sort of head or arm rests. In truth, it was nothing more than a large cushioned bench.

A low-standing chest containing dozens of little drawers was set against the far wall. Beside the chest was a large captain's chair upholstered in the same cherry-red leather as the bench.

"Lily."

Her gaze swung back to him at the sound of her name in his rich-toned voice.

He stood stiffly in front of the candelabra. The light at his back cast his features into severe shadow.

"I am sorry for the way I left you at our last encounter."

Lily's body heated at the memory of being on the verge of something beautiful and stunning, only to fall short.

"I was not properly prepared," he continued. "It will not happen again."

Lily was not sure she understood. "Prepared for what, my lord?"

There was a long pause during which she wondered if he would answer.

"How you made me feel."

His reply sent a rush of longing through her, filling the hollowness at her center.

"Are you prepared now, my lord?"

Instead of answering her question, he asked one of his own. "Do you recall your promise to do as I say?"

His tone had become cold and distant, but Lily believed she knew what that meant. The more rigid and icy his demeanor, the more intensely his passions burned beneath.

"Yes, I remember."

"Do you regret that promise?"

She felt only the slightest hesitation before she replied. "No."

The tension in him was palpable and had been from the moment she had joined him in his carriage. It reached out to Lily, causing a pleasant twist in her belly. He said nothing as she stared at him. She wished she could see the details of his expression, but the shadows were too deep. It was clear he wanted something, and she waited with bated breath and heated skin to discover what it was.

"Undress for me."

The harshness of his tone pierced her like a fire-tipped arrow. If his voice had been soft and gentle, it could not have affected her as intensely as when he spoke with such a hard edge.

Though he was giving the commands, she realized it was she who held the power to keep or renege on her promise. At any moment, she could refuse to do as he said. As understanding of the power she held dawned, she felt a surge of confidence and daring.

Suddenly, the thought of undressing while he watched from a distance took on an unexpected appeal.

The last time she had disrobed in his presence, the pleasure from his touch had allowed her a heady distraction. This would be altogether different.

The idea inspired her.

On a deep exhale, she stepped forward, leaving the light of the sitting room behind to merge with the uncertain glow that danced about as the candles flickered in their stand. She continued only as far at the chaise in the center of the room before she stopped.

"Please, my lord, won't you make yourself comfortable?" she said with a gesture toward the red leather chair.

Following her suggestion, he crossed to the corner of the room where the candlelight did little to illuminate the shadows and lowered himself to the chair. He sat with his spine straight and his feet flat on the floor and braced wide apart. His fingers curled tensely over the arms of the chair. Though the light was dim and wavering, it was enough to see the hard intensity of his expression, the silent assessment in his heavy gaze.

He had become so still that he may have been made of stone.

She wondered what it would take to soften the hard edge of his self-control.

Though she lowered her gaze modestly, every particle of her awareness stretched toward him. His silent focus ignited a slow burn throughout her body, and she tried to recall the descriptions she had read of women undressing for their lovers. It was always depicted as such a sensual act.

In reality, it was not so easy.

She reached behind her for the buttons running along the back of her gown. She had to arch deeply to accomplish the task, which pressed her breasts against her bodice and created a twinge of discomfort in the muscles of her arms. It was not a simple task, but the Chadwicks had gone without a maid for years, and Lily was accustomed to the effort.

After a few minutes, she was able to slide the material off her shoulders. She withdrew her arms, then eased the gown down her body until she could step free. Lifting the gown, she turned to drape it over the chaise beside her, the pale pink contrasting sharply with the sleek red leather. The stiffness of her gown's embroidered bodice had made stays unnecessary. It was quick work to remove her petticoat, and within moments, she was left with only the fine lawn shift to cover her nakedness.

She risked a glance then in his direction.

His expression had grown even more severe in the last minutes. His slashing brows were drawn low, and his eyes were black as he watched her. She noted the steady sound of his breath and instinctively deepened the rhythm of her breathing to match his. His hands extended and fisted in what she was coming to understand was a reflex of self-control.

Again, she felt an inexplicable flow of power.

With her nerves aflame and her belly tightening to a sweet ache, she slipped free of her shoes then bent forward to reach beneath the hem of her shift and release the garters secured above her knees. She removed her stockings and dropped them one at a time onto the chaise. The last item to go was her shift.

Standing entirely naked before him, Lily could feel the hot possession of his gaze as it roamed over her body, though he remained unmoving in the chair.

Tension squeezed her chest at his restraint.

His need was evident. His desire palpable.

Why did he not claim her?

The longer she stood waiting, the more intensely Lily felt the tingle of anticipation across her nerves. The heat spreading outward from her core swirled through her limbs and pooled low in her body. An ache weighted her breasts. The pulse of her blood set a rhythm to her desire, a steady, rushing need.

Looking at him, she felt every second pass like an hour. The open neck of his shirt revealed just a peek of the hard planes of his chest. His black breeches strained over the taut muscles of his thighs. His hands gripped the arms of the chair.

She would give anything to feel his hands on her again. Anywhere. It didn't matter. Even the most innocuous touch sent intricate sensations spiraling to the deepest reaches of her body.

Just as the lack of such left her feeling distinctly bereft.

Bereft and unfulfilled.

"Tell me what you want, Lily."

The velvet tenor of his voice caused a deeper pulse of sensation between her legs.

Taking a few steadying breaths, Lily bravely met his hooded stare. "I want you to touch me," she confessed in a soft murmur.

Without saying more, he lifted one hand and turned his palm upward in a gesture indicating he wanted her to come to him.

Enjoying the conflicting mixture of strength and vulnerability coursing through her, Lily approached slowly. It was a heady thing to have his gaze follow her movements so intently as she came to stand between his spread knees.

Yet he did not reach out to her.

She stood trembling as he perused every shadow and curve of her naked figure. When his attention settled briefly on the fullness of her breasts, her nipples puckered in reaction. She thought she heard him utter a low hum of appreciation, but she could not be sure. Next, he swept his gaze over the flare of her hips and thighs, brushing hotly over her feminine mound.

Lily clenched her muscles to prevent her knees from wobbling.

As if finally acknowledging her silent yearning, he shifted toward her. The soft leather made no sound as he leaned forward.

Lily held her breath.

He settled one hand possessively on the curve of her hip. He pressed his fingers into the soft flesh of her buttocks and brushed his thumb back and forth over her belly. With a smooth, unhurried caress, he slid his other hand up the back of her thigh.

She stared down at his bent head, her breath releasing on an involuntary puff as she felt his fingertips only a sigh away from her heated core.

"Remember to keep your hands at your sides," he instructed. The raw nature of his voice revealed his tension.

"But—"

"I would not insist if it was not important."

Lily contained the rush of disappointment that threatened at his harsh interruption. She understood that it was her hand on his arm that had ended things the last time they were together. But she had hoped he would allow her to touch him this time.

"I promise," she replied in a whisper.

He took a few slow, deep breaths through his nose then tipped his dark head back to look up at her. The intense light in his eyes sent sparks flying through her blood.

"You are wearing my gift," he said.

A blush of heat rose on her skin. "Yes."

He lifted his hand from her hip to claim her fingers in his and brought her wrist to his nose. He inhaled, then released her hand to look at her in question.

"I had to apply it where it would not be easily detected by my family," she explained.

The muscles in his jaw clenched. Lily was tempted to place her hand along the side of his face to feel that tension more intimately against her palm. She resisted with difficulty.

"Where?" he asked. The one word was weighted with something that sounded suspiciously like fear.

Instead of touching him as she wanted, Lily lifted her hand to drift her fingertips over her sternum. "Here," she whispered.

His intense regard fell to the hollow between her breasts. He did not move for a moment as he stared at her pale skin. Then he grasped her hips in both hands, as though to keep her in place.

Lily almost smiled at that. She had no intention of going anywhere.

He leaned forward until his hot breath fanned across her belly and the rough texture of his jaw brushed against the inner curves of her breasts.

When he first swept his lips across the spot she had indicated, Lily caught her breath sharply behind her teeth. Her skin tingled at the light and reverent kiss.

He drew back and waited.

She drifted her fingers over the gentle swell of her belly. "Here," she whispered again.

He curved his spine and lowered his head to press a hot kiss just below her navel.

Her legs shook beneath her, and she closed her eyes.

"Where else?" he asked in a low murmur.

Lily slowly turned in place, feeling his hands drop away from her body. When she faced away from him, she reached around to press her fingers to the small of her back.

The touch of his mouth there was more intense than she expected—the wet and warmth and intimate pressure. She shivered as delicious, tingling chills sped up and down her spine then spread out to her fingertips and toes in a delicate, rippling wave. But it was over too quickly.

She turned around again and looked into his eyes, her heart beating so fast she wondered how she could sustain such a pace without fainting.

Because she was already thinking of the last place she had applied the heady perfume.

At the time, she had felt wicked and daring. Now, she feared she might dissolve into a trembling mess should he continue along the same path.

His eyes met hers. His jawline was hard, and his firm, masculine lips were slightly parted, making the curve of his bottom lip look all the more sensual. Yet, there was so much strain in his expression.

She ached deep inside for what she sensed hidden beneath his iron control.

"Where else, Lily?"

Hearing her name murmured in that decadent voice turned gruff with need nearly made her legs collapse beneath her. But she was not about to turn coward now. Holding his gaze, she acknowledged her wantonness—and embraced it.

Slowly, she reached down and slid her fingers along the soft skin of her inner thighs.

She wouldn't have thought it possible, but his eyes darkened even more. He did not move, except for the muscles along his jaw tensing and a quickening of his breath. Then he broke his gaze away from hers, sliding it down the length of her body. With deliberate care, he curled his fingers around the back of her leg. Applying the barest amount of pressure, he urged her to lift her knee until he could fit her foot onto the chair beside his thigh.

Lily's breath became fitful as she stood there, open to him, exposed. Her pulse was frantic, and the muscles along her spine ached in her effort to remain composed despite the sensations running rampant through her body. She focused her attention on keeping her hands at her sides, though she would have loved to slide them into the cool silk of his hair.

In a whisper-light caress, he drifted his hand along the back of her thigh. His fingertips again came frightfully close to where her flesh throbbed gently with heat, making Lily catch her bottom lip in her teeth.

But he did not touch her there.

First, he lowered his head toward her inner thigh, a couple of inches above her knee. She heard his slowly drawn breath, felt his hand beneath her thigh, holding her steady. Then his lips.

So light at first. Just barely tracing a wandering path over the sensitive skin of her thigh. Lily held her breath in an attempt to eliminate any distraction from the delicate feel of his kiss.

The first unexpected touch of his tongue was wet and hot and sent a tingling jolt of fire through her core. She would have fallen to the floor if he hadn't splayed his hand over her hip to keep her steady while he teased her by easing his mouth ever closer toward her mound.

Lily panted. Her hands fisted against her outer thighs.

It seemed his intention was to torture her. Every time he got near enough for her to feel his hair brush against her belly, or the warmth of his breath bathe her heated folds, he would retreat again, sliding his lips back toward her knee.

Tension and frustration built upon itself. She knew what she wanted, had read about it with shock and amazement. But she didn't know if it was a common thing outside the realm of novels. Would he be stunned by her overwhelming desire to feel his mouth on her? The longer he teased and tempted her with the proximity of his kisses, the more she suspected she might die if she did not experience that exact wicked pleasure.

It seemed her boldness had gone beyond anything she could have expected.

Finally, as he trailed his tongue along her inner thigh, again coming breathlessly close, Lily spoke without thinking. A single word, expressed on a tremulous sigh. "*Please.*"

He complied immediately, as though he had been waiting for just that entreaty. His hands tightened on her body, and his mouth covered her in a hot, open-mouthed kiss.

Her knees trembled, and her chin fell forward against her chest. The focus of every nerve in her body shot toward the apex of her thighs. Pleasure rippled through her as his tongue slid over her folds. Languid at first, then with increasing demand. Her legs tensed, and her back arched. She rocked her hips against his mouth, seeking that pinnacle he had brought her so close to once before. She sensed it was near and craved it with every ounce of her being.

Then, as he flicked his tongue relentlessly over the most sensitive spot, he slid his hand up to cup her breast. One more long stroke of his tongue and a delicate pinch on her nipple, and her pleasure burst free. It pulsed from her center in a wave of sensation that reached out to her fingers and toes and slid up the back of her scalp.

Before the stunning sensation completely left her, she was brought abruptly back to reality as the earl pulled away roughly. He released her hips and leaned back, as though to put as much distance between them as possible. He grasped the arms of the chair in a white-knuckled grip and had lowered his chin to his chest. His breath was fast and ragged like hers.

Too late, she realized that in her mindlessness she had brought her hand up to grasp his shoulder. She could still feel the smooth texture of his silk shirt and the heat of his skin beneath burning her palm, though he had retreated out of her reach.

Lily caught her bottom lip between her teeth and took a step back. Her hands fisted at her sides, and tears burned in her eyes. Her body still pulsed with receding pleasure.

"I am sorry," she whispered, hating that once again it was her broken promise that brought the beautiful experience to a crashing halt.

He did not reply.

The rigidity of his posture and the harsh pass of his breath implied that he was in pain and distress. Her heart stuttered at the turmoil she sensed in him. Lily wanted desperately to reach out to him, soothe him. She backed away instead. How could she think to ease his discomfort when it was clearly she who had caused it?

Dejected and confused, she returned to the chaise and quickly slipped her shift back over her head. She recalled his reaction the last time they had been together, and earlier, when she had touched his arm after he'd saved her from Fallbrook.

"Lily, I..."

Her entire body jolted at the sound of her name in his rough tone. There was a deep plea in his voice.

With her emotions thick in her throat, she turned to look at him.

He had risen to his feet and stood there so strong and stern. The rhythm of his breath had slowed, and the strength of his body was undeniable. But it was his vulnerability of spirit that struck her in that moment.

He pressed his mouth into a hard line before he cleared his throat and began again. "Believe me, Lily, I *want* you to touch me."

His words were heavy with need. Yes. He desired her—she knew that much to be true. He had seemed to find enjoyment in moving his hands over her naked body, in kissing her intimately.

Yet a simple touch of her hand to his shoulder managed to bring it all to a crashing halt.

"Please, my lord," she said, trying to keep the emotion from her voice. "If you want me to touch you, why do you forbid it? Why does it seem as though my touch pains you?"

"Because it does."

The simple statement, spoken so plainly, caused her breath to catch. "Why? What happened to cause this? Has it always been thus?"

"Enough, Lily." The exhaustion in his tone halted her curiosity.

Her chest ached. "I just want to understand. I have no wish to cause you pain, my lord."

The way his eyes held hers, with such darkness and weight, filled her with sadness.

"Such is inevitable, I am afraid."

Silence fell, and Avenell suspected she was trying to make sense of what he had said. He held himself rigid, waiting for her expression to shift into one of disgust or pity before she walked away.

He should have known taking a lover was an impossible endeavor. He should have called it off after that first night, should have accepted his failing as unavoidable.

What in hell had convinced him he could do this?

He stared at her as she stood in her shift and nothing else. Innocent, vulnerable, and so beautiful it made him ache.

*She* had convinced him he could do this. It was the way she looked at him, as though she truly saw him, not just his hard veneer. It was the softness of her mouth, her tranquil demeanor, and the fact that somehow, deep down he believed—he hoped—she would not be the same as the others in his life had been.

Avenell had experienced righteous cruelty and callous intolerance in his youth from those he had loved. His father had blamed him for his affliction, claiming Avenell possessed some moral or intrinsic defect. Others believed he was making it up—a spoiled child determined to be difficult in order to get attention.

Pendragon had been the first person to accept his condition without judgment, but Avenell wanted so much more than acceptance from Lily.

The feel of her body in his hands, her skin like warmed silk under his lips, had been intense. He had never experienced a woman's body the way he had Lily's, as though every bit of her was magic. Her softness and quiet strength had inspired him to a tenderness he had not known he possessed. The scent of the sweet jasmine and earthy sandalwood of his perfume mingled flawlessly on her body. On every inhale he had drawn her essence in with his breath, and his blood had heated dangerously.

And the taste of her…

Every quiver in her muscles, every hitch in her breath had sent shocks of sensation through him. He had never derived such delicate satisfaction from anything before. His lust had distracted his every sense, so when he felt the pressure of her hand on his shoulder, he had reacted out of pure instinct for self-preservation.

And hated himself for the distress he had seen on her face, her breath still heavy and her eyes glazed with pleasure.

Craving her nearness like an intrinsic pull, he slowly approached her.

She drew a long, even breath as he came to a stop within arm's reach of her. He could not resist the urge to touch her, even though in so doing, it brought the imbalance of their situation back into stark awareness.

She remained still as he lifted his hand to slide his fingers over the curve of her shoulder and around to support her nape.

Tipping her head back, she looked up at him. Her dove-gray eyes were filled with compassion, uncertainty, and the lingering evidence of her sensual release. The sight of it sent subtle rippling waves of desire through his system, despite his current tension.

He brushed his thumb along the line of her jaw, clenching his teeth when her lips softened in reaction.

"I cannot…" he began, then stopped.

She tilted her head to the side, and a small furrow formed between her brows. She wanted to understand.

He could see it in her features—a hint of determination. After she took several breaths, her gaze slid from his to glance aside.

His chest tightened as he prepared for her rejection.

"Do you still want this?" she asked quietly. "Me?"

"With every breath," he replied.

She brought her gaze back to his, and what he saw there stalled his heart.

"I can be patient, my lord," she whispered.

He swallowed hard against the emotion pressing in his throat. His attention lowered again to her lips. He ached to taste them, to test their softness with his tongue.

Instead, he released her and turned away. "I have something for you."

# Nineteen

Lily released a shaky breath as she watched him stride from the bedroom. An overwhelming wealth of emotions swirled about inside her. Her whole body tingled in the aftermath of what she had just experienced. She was weak and unsteady from all the things he had made her feel.

But as powerful as their encounter had been, it had not affected her nearly as much as the quiet fear she had sensed in him as he struggled to explain. What could have caused such fear?

He reentered the room, and she watched his approach with a new kind of longing. He strode with such strength, yet she had seen the evidence of so much more within him. She wanted so badly to know everything.

"Please, sit," he said as he came to stand before her.

She lowered herself to the red leather chaise. She had not even noticed that he carried something in his hands until he crouched in front of her and set the small white box on the bench beside her hip.

His gaze captured hers, sending sparks of renewed

awareness through her body even as her heart clenched tightly at the hint of apology in the rueful pull of his lips.

"Since you prefer to keep our association secret, I cannot clothe you in gowns of the finest silks and satins, or shower you with jewels as I would wish to."

He opened the box and withdrew something white and fine, drawing the silken contents across her lap.

"It will please me to know you wear these beneath your gown, as it pleases me more than you could possibly imagine to know you wear my scent."

Lily's gaze fluttered down to see the most delicate and beautiful pair of stockings she had ever seen. Tentatively, she ran her fingers along the embroidered silk, so soft and fine it felt like water beneath her touch. Stunned by the beauty of the artistry, the delicacy of the intricate embroidery, she could barely breathe. She had never touched anything so exquisite.

She swallowed hard, fighting the unreasonable prick of tears.

"They are unbelievably lovely," she finally replied in a whisper. "How can I thank you?"

"You do not have to."

She looked into his eyes, feeling so many things she feared putting a name to. "But I have nothing for you."

An awkward curve shaped his lips. It was the first time he had smiled at her, and it stopped her breath. The subtle smile was all the more poignant in its tentativeness than it would have been if he had expressed it more freely.

"You give of yourself, Lily. That is a far more precious gift than anything I could give you."

Lily bit her lip against the obvious comment that a more equal gift would be if he gave of himself in return.

"You will wear them?" he asked.

She nodded, and he swept the stockings up in his hands. One at a time, he smoothed them up her legs. They felt like rose petals against her skin, soft and luxurious.

He reached for the box again and withdrew garters of light-blue satin, embellished with tiny gems: sapphires, rubies, emeralds, and onyx in an intricate geometric design.

Lily gasped at the sight of them. A fortune was sewn into the decorative garters.

He secured the garters over the stockings above her knees, then braced his hands on the edge of the bench. His body hovered close to hers, his arms caged her, his chest was a breath away, but he did not touch her.

"When you wear these, think of me. Think of how I am counting the hours until I can see you again." He bent to brush his mouth across the top of her thigh just above the garter. She fisted her hands against the leather to keep from sliding her fingers through his hair. "Know that I am dreaming of your softness and your smile."

Lily could barely breathe. Her chest was tight, and her body hummed with awareness.

After placing another light kiss to the top of her thigh, he rose to his feet.

"I have also opened a spending account for you. I will give you the information you need to access the money. It is yours to spend as you wish. At any time, for any reason."

Lily stiffened and looked down at her lap. It was difficult to process what he had said in practical terms just then. The thought of him giving her gifts, specifically those chosen by him with her in mind, was one thing. To know he had set aside funds in an account… was something entirely different.

She chided herself. This was what she had agreed to. She was a mistress.

Though Emma had won enough at Bentley's party to get them through the Season, and Hale had relinquished any further claim against their family, life was still an uncertain thing. Lily could not deny it was reassuring to know she had her own means of financial security.

Still, she would prefer never to have cause to touch the account. Then she would not have to think on its existence and what it meant.

"We should be on our way," he added. "Dawn will be coming soon."

He left her there to finish dressing.

She was quiet and pensive when she entered the sitting room to see that he had also re-dressed in his waistcoat and coat. He held her cloak for her, and after setting it around her shoulders, he led her from the room. His movements had once again become stiff and efficient, his manner distant. They left their private sanctuary as they had arrived—in silence.

Lily knew what kept her from speaking; her consciousness was quite overwhelmed with the process of incorporating tonight's revelations into her existence.

He had pleasured her with his touch—with his mouth—bringing her to a trembling peak of sensation so intense it shocked her to her toes.

How could a man so generous and tender one moment so forcefully close himself off in the next?

Lily had heard the raw tone lingering in his voice and knew by the sharp angle of his gaze that he had not been unaffected. She wanted to acknowledge it somehow, challenge the return of his cold facade. But as she glanced at him walking beside her and noted the stern lines of his profile, she knew she would not.

She was not so daring after all.

The earl was the first to break the silence. "I will be unavailable for a few days. I will come for you again in three nights."

She frowned. There was something vital she needed to tell him, some bit of information she was forgetting that seemed pertinent to the conversation.

They had just reached the bottom of the narrow stair, and Lily turned to start down the hall to their exit when she abruptly came up against an enormous wall.

No, not a wall. A man. A large man who smelled faintly of woodsmoke.

Alarm spread through her in a violent wave, and she tried to step back, but Hale had already grasped her upper arms in his hands. It had likely been a reflex to keep from plowing her over, but to Lily it was far too reminiscent of when he had held her still for Pendragon's inspection.

"Oh-ho," Hale said in mild surprise as he looked down at her. Lily suddenly realized that they had left her mask in the room. Her cloak hood had fallen back, and she could see that he recognized her. "What are you doing here, little dove?"

"Hale." The earl spoke quietly, but his tone was deathly cold.

In her shock at coming face-to-face with the man who had abducted her, Lily nearly forgot the earl was behind her, but after that single word, there was no denying his presence. She had never heard such icy malice in a man's voice.

Hale lifted his chin to glance over her head at the earl. His eyes flickered cautiously, but he said nothing.

"Release her. Immediately."

Again, the steel in the earl's voice startled Lily. It had an effect on Hale as well as wariness crossed his expression. But instead of letting her go, he drew her an inch closer in defiance. She resisted, and his hands tightened around her arms. Not painfully, but enough to keep her in place.

She looked up into the brute's face, trying to gauge his intention. This appeared to be a random encounter. Surely, he had no purpose in detaining her. Hale's manner was confrontational, but his focus was directed over her head toward the earl. Her initial fear slid to concern. But not for herself.

The animosity in his glare was clearly not directed at her.

"I remember you," Hale said as his eyes narrowed above a slightly disfigured nose.

"Then you also recall that this woman is under my protection."

"And you will recall that I don't take lightly to threats."

"I do not issue threats, Mr. Hale."

Hale drew himself taut. His shoulders nearly spanned

the width of the hall, and his square jaw lifted. "You think you can best me, do you?" He rolled his head on his thick neck, then stretched his lips in a menacing grin. "I've been aching for a good fight for more than a week. You would be doing me a favor, mate."

"Do I look like a man who fights with his fists, Mr. Hale?" The earl's response was given in a calm and even tone, but the intensity running beneath his words could not be misunderstood. "Release her, or you will regret it."

Hale hesitated once he realized he would not get the fight he obviously wanted. His features shifted to something Lily suspected he rarely revealed. Obviously a man of violence, he appeared at a loss with how to respond to the earl's controlled challenge.

"Now," the earl demanded, still in that deathly calm voice.

As soon as Hale loosened his grip, Lily stepped back until she came up against the earl. He slid his arm around her waist, drawing her against his side with stiff movements.

His entire body was rigid and motionless.

Though he had let her go, Hale did not move aside to let them pass. He kept his focus locked on Lily as he spoke. "You've got nothing to fear from me, little dove." He paused, and his expression tightened fiercely. Lily found herself wondering what this man concealed beneath his bullish exterior. "I regret what I had to do." He shifted his attention back to the earl and gave an irreverent grin. "But it seems you're doing all right."

The earl's hand flexed over her hip. "Good evening, Mr. Hale," he replied, his voice hostile.

The large man gave a tug at his forelock, then turned and sauntered down the hall and out into the night.

The earl released the tension of his arm around her, allowing space to come between them. "That should not have happened. I am sorry."

Lily shook her head. "It is all right. You could not have known he would be here."

He did not reply, and Lily sensed his self-recrimination. But after another moment, he gently guided her forward. "I will see you home."

# Twenty

The Griffiths' country estate possessed an enormous gothic-style manor and was located in the Cotswolds of Warwickshire. The manor was surrounded by several hundred acres and contained miles of walking trails, a flourishing trout stream, and some of the best hunting in the area. For guests who did not wish to wander too far afield, the house was adjacent to an extensive garden complete with a maze, various fountains, and several gazebos. The house itself contained two-dozen guest rooms, no less than seven public sitting rooms, a large music room, armory, library, game room with two billiard tables, a theater complete with a stage and seating for up to fifty, and a grand conservatory filled with citrus trees and windows overlooking the garden.

It was the perfect setting for a weekend party, perhaps the most idyllic location Lily had ever visited. Yet she could not enjoy it.

They had been there for two days. Two long days of endless socializing, fresh air, and diverting activities. Tonight was the night Lord Harte would be coming for her in his carriage. He would wait under the willow tree behind Angelique's house.

And Lily would not come.

Because she was stuck in the Cotswolds until Monday.

With a very uncharacteristic growl of annoyance, Lily swung away from the window and paced across the room. She had retired early to the bedroom she shared with Portia, hoping to be asleep before her sister came up, so she could avoid the conversation she knew was coming. Portia had been sending her meaningful glances all day. Her sister had something she was burning to discuss.

But so far, Lily had been unable to sleep.

Her thoughts continually flew to the earl. She imagined him sitting in the silence of his carriage, waiting for her to join him. Would he think she did not want to see him? Would he worry that something had gone wrong? The idea of letting him down filled her with regret.

When she had first recalled that they would be going out of town for the weekend, she had nearly panicked. She would have tried to send him a note, but she had no idea how to address it. To inquire on the address of the Earl of Harte would have raised any number of questions she was not about to answer. And she certainly couldn't send a message to Pendragon.

Lily wrapped her arms around herself, but it did nothing to ease her anxiety.

Then the bedroom door opened, and Portia swept in with a dramatic harrumph.

"I knew you would still be awake," she declared.

"You could have at least found a way to include me in your excuse to retire. Once you were gone, Emma insisted I stay until the charades had finished. It was dreadful."

Lily realized too late she should have at least stayed in bed to have the option of feigning sleep.

"I am sorry, Portia. I was not feeling well." It was essentially the truth, since her anxiety was causing a certain degree of physical distress.

"Hmm," her sister replied with a sidelong glance as she strode forward to begin changing into the nightgown laid across her side of the bed. "Are you going to tell me what is going on with you, or shall I have to pry it out of you?"

Lily knew there was little point in denying it. She had not been herself the last couple of days. Her mood had been nearly as morose and anxious as Portia could get at times. She considered what she would say. Portia had always been her confidante. Only a bit more than a year apart in age, they had grown up side by side. They had shared everything.

What would Portia think if Lily told her about the earl?

"I hate this sense that we have been growing apart since our debuts. We used to be inseparable, Lily. I miss that," Portia muttered in a glum tone.

She had finished changing into her nightgown and strode to sit at the vanity. Looking at Lily through the oval mirror, Portia began taking down her coiffure. Out of habit, Lily walked over to help her unravel the long sable tresses. Then she picked up the brush to run it through the remaining tangles.

"We are not growing apart, Portia, we are growing up," Lily replied, trying to put another perspective on something she did not want to examine fully. "It is inevitable that we begin to lead more independent lives."

Portia lowered her gaze with a deep frown as she began to fidget idly with the bric-a-brac on the vanity. "Independence is one thing, but you seem to be keeping secrets lately when such a thing never used to exist between us. I wish you could trust me, Lily."

"I do trust you," she replied after a few moments. "But there are some things too private to talk about."

"Nonsense," Portia exclaimed. "I tell you everything. Always have."

Lily flicked her gaze up to meet her sister's in the mirror. "Everything, Portia?"

Her younger sister stared mutinously back at her before she rolled her eyes in dramatic fashion. "Fine. Not everything. I suppose everyone has a few secrets." She spun around in her seat to face Lily, grasping her hand. "But, Lily, I know when you are upset. I can see something is disturbing you, and I feel I should be given an opportunity to help."

Lily smiled. Portia could not stand being inert when there might be something she could do.

"Is it Fallbrook again?" Portia asked.

Shaking her head, Lily nudged her sister's shoulder to turn her around again so she could plait her hair into a neat braid.

"I saw you dancing with him earlier tonight," Portia noted when Lily did not reply quickly enough. "What did he say to make you look so distressed?"

Lily had experienced a moment of sheer panic when Lord Fallbrook first joined the country party earlier that day. But he had barely acknowledged her presence, let alone behaved in a way suggestive of the last time she had seen him—or rather, the last time she recalled seeing him.

The earl had assured her that Pendragon had consequences for those who broke her rules of discretion, but that did not mean Fallbrook would follow them. He could call her out at any moment and denounce her. He could ruin her with a few choicely used words, and there would be nothing she could do about it.

Gratefully, he had basically ignored her, and she did her best to return the favor.

That is, until the dancing started after dinner. Fallbrook had approached her for a dance while she stood in the company of their hosts. She had been unable to refuse without appearing rude.

There was nothing untoward in his conversation at first. Just a gleam in his eye, a sort of speculative curiosity. Then as the dance took them to the far end of the ballroom, he claimed the opportunity to lean toward her and whisper dramatically, "I have been warned to stay away from you, you know."

The dread that had weighted Lily's stomach from the moment she had seen him walking toward her sharpened to a near panic.

"Perhaps you should. Your behavior in Hawksworth's garden was unforgivable," she stated sternly, hoping he would focus on that incident and not bring up the other.

He laughed at her attempt at evasion.

"It is no matter. I do not intend to risk future diversions by being impatient," he confided before he guided her in a turn that allowed him to slide his palm down over her buttocks before he took her gloved hand again. "I can wait until Harte tires of you," he said. "Then nothing will keep you from being mine."

The song came to an end. Fallbrook flashed her a charming grin, and then he bowed and walked off as though nothing had happened.

Recalling the incident, Lily again experienced a sharp stab of trepidation. The rest of the night, she hadn't been able to keep from scanning every gentleman present, wondering if anyone else at the country party had been privy to her disgrace in Pendragon's Pleasure House. It was supremely disturbing to know she might be recognized at any time.

It was another reason Lily had claimed the first available excuse to retire for the night.

Portia was still waiting for a response. Meeting her gaze in the mirror as she tied off the end of her long braid, Lily replied earnestly, "Fallbrook is no gentleman. Promise me you will avoid the man at all costs."

Portia gave a snorting sort of laugh. "Oh, that is not necessary. The man already avoids *me* like the plague. I danced with him only once after the time he tried to lure you into the garden. I made it clear in no uncertain terms what I thought of his behavior. He was rather annoyed and took me back to Angelique before the dance was even halfway through."

Lily smothered her own laugh. She could imagine

Portia's burning set-down. "I so admire your audacity, Portia."

"You could do the same, Lily." She rose to her feet to face Lily with an impassioned expression.

"No, I cannot." Lily turned away to extinguish the few candles that were still lit.

"That is a terrible lie, Lily Imogene Chadwick," Portia stated, setting her hands on her hips. "You have a deeply hidden vein of wickedness in your soul, and someday you will have to explore it. If you haven't already."

Lily tensed at the knowing tone in her sister's voice.

"You know I have never had your courage or Emma's confidence to do anything other than exactly what is expected of me."

"Bollocks."

"Portia!"

The younger girl arched her fine black brows. "Oh yes, how silly of me. I forgot that all of the young ladies I know keep a collection of sinful, erotic novels and daydream of being ravished."

Lily's eyes widened. "Not ravished, exactly."

"Then what?" Portia pressed. "What do you dream of? And do not dare tell me it is to marry one of those dull suitors who have latched on to you. Not one of those gentlemen would know how to make you happy if it were spelled out in an instruction manual."

Lily ignored Portia's rising tone and turned away to flip down the bedcovers.

"What would you have me do, Portia?"

There was a pause.

"I want you to be happy. Are you happy?"

Lily did not answer. Sitting on the edge of the bed, she bent her head to look down at her hands folded in her lap. Was she happy? No, but she believed she could be.

Portia came forward to kneel in front of her. Her voice softened as she continued. "All I am trying to say is that we all deserve to seek our happiness, wherever that leads us. And we should support each other in that endeavor."

The youngest Chadwick's expression turned bullish. "You should know I have decided I may never marry." Lily opened her mouth to argue, but Portia shook her head. "I am not willing to sacrifice the kind of life I want for myself in order to satisfy some man's idea of what behavior is or is not appropriate. I cannot be what these people"—she swept her arm out in a gesture to encompass their surroundings—"or Emma want me to be."

Lily arched her brows. "What? You mean obedient, reverent, contented?"

Portia made a face of disgust. "Exactly."

"I know, Portia," Lily replied. "You were always meant for other things, and I promise I will support your endeavors to find happiness along whatever path you choose."

"Even if it causes scandal?"

Lily narrowed her eyes. "Why? Are you contemplating causing a scandal?"

Portia shrugged as she took a seat on the bed beside Lily.

"One doesn't always plan such things. Sometimes they simply happen, and I want you to know that I would stand by you in the same circumstances."

Panic swept through Lily as she once again thought of Fallbrook. "Have you heard any whispers about… that night?"

"No," Portia answered quickly. "I was speaking hypothetically, in case you wished to engage in some outrageous behavior."

Lily gave a weak laugh. "I cannot imagine what that might be."

"Oh, I don't know. Considering your reading habits, I would think you could imagine far more than I could."

"Portia!"

The youngest Chadwick laughed and gave a saucy shrug. "I just think it is far past time for *you* to be a little daring. Take a risk. Explore a bit of that wickedness buried within you before Emma has you settled down with a perfectly boring old country gentleman."

Lily glanced aside to evade the intensity in Portia's quicksilver gaze. She couldn't help but wonder if sneaking off to a brothel to make love with a sensual and enigmatic lord would be daring enough in Portia's opinion.

The thought filled her with the sudden urge to laugh. She rolled her lips in to hold it back, but Portia had noted her expression.

"What? What is so amusing?"

Lily rubbed her hands over her face before meeting Portia's gaze.

"I am sorry, but this is one secret I cannot share. Even with you. Not yet."

Portia's eyes narrowed, and her lips pursed. Lily could see her sister resisting the urge to argue. Then she appeared to reconsider. Her expression softened, and she sighed.

"Just promise me something, Lily."

"Of course."

"I swear I cannot withstand the sight of another sister descending into self-inflicted misery. If you have the opportunity to be happy—truly happy—promise me you will take it. No matter the consequences."

Lily felt the sincerity in her sister's words down to her marrow. The earl's image encroached upon the back of her mind, but she shoved it away.

"I promise, if you do the same."

Portia nodded and gave a wink. "I never had any intention otherwise. Now, how the hell do we get Emma to make such a vow?" Portia asked as she dropped onto the bed and rolled over to tuck herself in on her side.

It was on the tip of Lily's tongue to chastise Portia for her language, but she realized it was more out of habit than any true objection.

She sighed as she also climbed beneath the covers. "An excellent question."

Emma had not been the same since the night of Lily's abduction. She was distracted, distant, as though her thoughts were always somewhere else. Of course, she no longer had the urgent motivation of getting her sisters settled into matrimony, but still, Emma had become practically aimless over the last weeks. It was entirely outside her nature to be so unfocused.

Lily had a suspicion as to the cause of her older sister's altered manner. And for that reason, she was reluctant to interfere.

"I do not know it is our business to pry."

"Nonsense." Portia snorted. "You know as well as I what has her out of sorts, just as you know what is holding her back. If we do nothing, she will continue to martyr herself for our sake."

Portia had a point. Emma would never consider acting on her feelings for Mr. Bentley. An association with the proprietor of a gambling hell would cause a scandal that would reflect on all of them. It was the reason Emma's employment at the club had to be covert.

Rolling onto her side, Lily tucked her hands beneath her cheek as she met Portia's wily gaze. Memories rushed to mind of when they had been young and would crawl into each other's beds to whisper secrets and giggle into the night.

"What do you propose we do?"

Portia grinned in the darkness. "We will have to wait for the right opportunity. Emma is not going to get away with dooming herself to a life of loneliness on our account. If it requires drastic measures to make that happen, that is what we shall do."

Lily smiled back. "More scandal, Sister?"

"Emma may need the excitement as much as you do."

Lily narrowed her eyes dangerously, but a moment later the sisters added in unison, "*More*," then broke into the kind of laughter they hadn't shared since they were young.

# Twenty-one

The theater was stifling and noisy as everyone crowded to their seats in preparation for the performance to begin.

The Chadwicks had been offered the use of a box by one of Angelique's old acquaintances, and they were taking full advantage. Attending the theater was not a luxury they would otherwise have an opportunity to indulge in, and the ladies were quite looking forward to it.

Angelique took her seat and lifted her trusty opera glasses to watch the crowds below. Portia sat next to her, and the two of them took turns trading commentary over the inevitable social dramas playing out in the audience.

As the lights dimmed, indicating the performance was about to commence, a hush fell over the theater, and the excess noise faded away.

Lily was swept up in the drama playing out on the stage. For at least a little while, she allowed herself to be carried away. Her anxiety over being gone for days in the country, and her disappointment in arriving home yesterday to find not a single message had been left for her, faded to the back of her mind. She was so entranced by the performance that she did not once take her eyes from the stage until the curtains closed and the lights came up to indicate intermission.

"La! What a lovely bit of drama," Angelique exclaimed as she turned in her seat. The lady delicately dabbed at her eyes with a handkerchief.

Lily thought she saw Portia lift the back of her hand to her eyes as well. Even Emma, who was always so much in control of her emotions, had to blink back the suspicious glistening of tears.

All four ladies looked at one another. Portia was the first to issue a snort of laughter.

"Well, aren't we all a bunch of silly sops?"

Lily smiled.

"We are not the only ones," Emma said as she gestured out to the theater.

Looking down from their box, Lily could see dozens of ladies dabbing at their eyes.

"There is nothing so cleansing as a good cry, no?"

Portia linked her arm through Angelique's. "Shall we stretch our legs and seek some refreshment?"

"Yes, darling, my joints are creaking from sitting so long."

"We shall all go," Emma suggested.

As Angelique stood to lead the way, she glanced down at Lily with a smile. "Lily, darling, I believe the strap on your shoe has come loose."

"Oh, thank you." While the others continued on from the box, Lily sat to check her shoes. By the time she remembered her shoes did not have straps, the curtain had dropped into place, leaving Lily alone in the shadows. A small frown tensed her brow. What had Angelique been thinking? The dowager was eccentric to be sure, and was often rather flighty, but Lily had never known her to see things that did not exist.

With a shake of her head, Lily stood and glanced out over the rapidly emptying theater. Some internal instinct encouraged her to lift her gaze, and a gasp slid from her lips.

In a grand box overlooking the stage stood the solitary and striking figure of Lord Harte. And he was staring straight at her.

It was too far to truly see the look in his eyes, but Lily *felt* it.

Across every nerve, deep in the marrow of her bones—from the tingling along her scalp to the curling of her toes—she experienced the intensity of his focus. She was suddenly reminded that she wore his stockings beneath her skirts. The thought made her feel deliciously wanton as she considered the possibility that she was a better mistress than she realized. It was far easier to be wicked than she had ever expected.

Her heart fell headlong into a frantic rhythm. All her worry and fear over being unable to advise him of her absence from town coalesced into a dense point in her center. It was all she could do not to fly to him.

Instead, she remained in place, willingly trapped by his gaze.

Time slowed. It may have been a moment or forever when, without any gesture or shift in his expression, he turned and left his box.

Lily gasped for breath, lifting her hand to her chest

as she filled her lungs. During those moments when she had been caught in his gaze, he had literally stolen her breath. She fought to reclaim it, along with her scattered thoughts.

Goodness. She had been worrying for days about what he might have thought when she was unable to meet him. She should have been more concerned with what he had felt. In that brief, distant connection, despite his rigid presentation and harsh stare, she had sensed a tumultuous mixture of emotions.

Before she fully had herself under control, Portia stuck her head back through the curtain.

"Are you coming, Lily? There is quite a crowd out here. You wouldn't want to become separated."

"Yes, I am sorry. I will be right behind you."

Portia had not been exaggerating. The crowd thickened the closer they got to the main hall, where the doors had been opened to allow the night air to cool overheated bodies. Emma and Angelique led the way through the crowd toward the refreshment room, with Portia close behind and Lily trailing after.

A few times, Lily lost sight of them and had to hurry to catch up. She couldn't help it that she kept scanning the crowd, desperate for another glimpse of the earl, even though she knew he would not acknowledge her with more than a passing glance in such a public venue.

In her distraction, it was only a matter of time before she tripped over someone's foot and found herself plunging toward the floor. Panic raced through her at the thought of falling beneath the crush of people. She would be trampled.

She flung her hands out to grasp hold of anything that would keep her upright, but it was unnecessary. Suddenly the earl was there, grasping her upper arms in a firm grip as he drew her in against his chest.

"I have you."

Lily's body hummed in reaction to the vibration of Lord Harte's voice, and her skin warmed to the feel of his body pressing along hers. His fingers tensed then relaxed before he smoothed them slowly around her upper back to further protect her from the jostling crowd, which did not seem to notice at all the couple embracing in their midst.

All sound fell away—the world fell away—as Lily tipped her head back to meet his glowering gaze. She had so many things she wanted to say to him, but as she stared into the deep blue of his eyes, all that escaped from her parted lips was her rapid breath.

She realized in a quiet corner of her awareness that the moment could not last. Time did not actually slow for them alone. The world still existed. At any moment, their intimate encounter could be noticed. But Lily didn't care just then. More than anything, she needed his closeness, craved it with everything in her.

"You did not meet me," he accused in a thick murmur.

"There was a party in Warwickshire," she whispered hastily, fearing their opportunity for conversation may not last long. "I could not beg off, and I did not know how to get a message to you."

She saw the muscles of his jaw tense; she wasn't sure if it was in response to her answer or something else, but the movement drew her eyes down to his lips. Her stomach swirled as she wondered what it would feel like to have his firm and sensual mouth on hers. Without thinking, she pressed the tip of her tongue to the center of her bottom lip.

His arms tightened around her, and the muscles in his jaw bunched just before he looked up to scan the area around them.

"Can you meet me tonight?" he asked, still glancing about the crowd.

"I think so. It may be quite late."

He looked down at her again, his stare hard and fathomless. "The carriage will be waiting."

He slowly eased his arms from around her. Lily didn't realize she had been clutching his coat in her hands until she was forced to release her grip. Something in his eyes spoke clearly of his intention to make up for the time they had lost. Then he stepped back and melted into the crowd.

She stood where he had left her. As the full faculty of her senses returned, she realized the crowd was thinning rapidly. A moment later, Emma came up beside her and linked an arm through hers.

"There you are," Emma said with obvious relief. "I thought we had lost you. We must make our way back to our seats. The show is about to recommence."

Lily blinked. She did her best to behave as though nothing untoward had happened, though her heart still raced beneath her breast. She looked around as they started toward the stairs leading back up to their box. "Where are Portia and Angelique?"

"They should be quite a ways ahead of us." Emma smiled. "Angelique has a special talent for parting crowds."

Lily lifted her brows. "What did she do?"

Emma's lips quivered suspiciously. "She quite loudly declared that the heat was making her woozy, and she thought she might be ill."

Lily resisted her own laughter. It would not be ladylike to find humor in something so crude. "Yes, I can see how such an announcement would do the trick."

They reached the stairs, and just before losing sight of the hall below, Lily glanced over her shoulder. The earl was nowhere to be seen.

Nor did he return to his box for the second half. It seemed he had left the theater altogether. Her disappointment at not catching at least one more fleeting glimpse of him was tempered by the knowledge that she would be with him later that night. A deep thrill sped through her blood at the thought.

As it was, she did not manage to get away for several more hours. After the theater, they attended a dinner party, which went quite late. By the time they returned to Angelique's town house, it was well into the morning hours.

Another hour slipped away as Lily waited for the household to quiet down before making her way out. Even so, she had to hide for several minutes in a kitchen cupboard when she heard someone else moving about—most likely a servant who had forgotten to complete some task before retiring.

When she finally stepped through the garden gate into the mews beyond, Lily held her breath in fear that the earl might not have waited so long for her to appear. But the carriage was there in its usual spot. She rushed toward it eagerly, anticipation giving her wings. It had been five days since their last private encounter, several hours since their brief run-in at the theater, and a lifetime of yearning had built within her.

Their private suite was cast in darkness. No romantic candlelight awaited their arrival. No opened bottle of wine or champagne on the sideboard. Only the glow of the fireplace lit the room.

Lily stopped when she heard the door close behind her. Her heart raced. She sensed the earl a second before he came up behind her. Without a word, he reached around her shoulders to release the ties of her cloak and sweep the heavy garment away from her body.

His aloof detachment and rigid manner were more pronounced tonight. There had been very little said on the drive from Angelique's.

She was coming to understand his need to do things in his own time, at his own pace. She could wait for him to speak, to instruct her on what he wanted. She took a moment to smooth her hair back and took a few steadying breaths before she turned in place to face him.

He had retreated to stand before the fire. He said nothing and did not move from where he stood to close the distance between them. He just stared at her with a heavy gaze. He was hard and forbidding. So still he appeared to be made of stone.

There was longing in him as well.

She felt a desperate desire to press her fingertip to the center of his lower lip. She wanted to feel the sensuality and softness possessed in that generous curve. She wanted to taste it with her tongue. Her stomach erupted in a series of breath-stealing flutters at the thought, and she realized with no small measure of surprise that he had never kissed her on the mouth.

The ache in her chest expanded, and she smiled as she started toward him.

"Lily."

The harshness in his voice, suddenly breaking through the silence, brought her to an abrupt halt.

Her smile wavered.

"There is something I must tell you," he added roughly.

Lily tensed at the gravitas in his words. When he did not go on, she clasped her hands together in front of her and waited. Her emotions wavered between compassion for his obvious distress and fear over what he might say.

She focused on her calming breath to keep her apprehension from showing.

"You amaze me." He spoke the words on a low, shuddering breath. Lily was certain she misunderstood. "Even now I can sense the peace within you—your quiet acceptance of whatever may come. Does nothing disturb you, Lily?"

"Only the thought that you might send me away."

Her answer drew a ragged sigh from his chest, and he bowed his head for a moment. "I could no more do that than I could stop my own breath. But you may wish otherwise after I have told you what you must know."

The fear spread farther through her, but Lily refused to allow it to take over.

"Trust me, my lord," she whispered.

His gaze met hers through the uncertain glow of the room. He stared at her, as though he sought an answer in her eyes to a question he hadn't asked.

"I have never lain with a woman."

The phrase confused her.

Then sent a jolt of shock to the base of her brain as she considered the meaning in his words.

How could that be?

Words tumbled from her lips unheeded. "But you frequent a brothel…the way you touch me…I do not understand."

As she spoke, she noticed his hands at his sides, fisting and extending, over and over.

She took a breath and spoke again, lifting her hands in supplication. "Please, my lord, I wish to understand."

"As you know, I struggle with being touched. I came to Pendragon's years ago for assistance in learning how to tolerate the types of casual and unexpected physical exchanges I would expect to encounter while out in society. I could not have the *ton* speculating as to the nature and depth of my…affliction." His tone was strictly modulated as he explained. "You have witnessed my unguarded reactions to the touch of another person. I have never been able to retain control around you."

He paused. His entire body was rigid with tension.

Lily wished in the depths of her soul that she could go to him, soothe him somehow.

She remained where she was.

"Yet I have felt your hands on me," Lily said. "How is it that you can touch, but not be touched in return?"

He sighed. It was a rough sound that came from deep in his center. "It is not an easy thing to explain. My affliction primarily affects the areas of my upper body and my arms." He looked down at his hands, holding the palms up as he extended his fingers then curled them into tight fists before he continued. "When I touch you, I am in control. I am able to anticipate the sensation and can manage it."

Lily considered that for a moment. It made sense when she thought of the few times she had reached for him without thinking. His reaction to her unexpected touch had been swift and involuntary.

"Madam Pendragon has helped you with this?" she asked.

"Yes." His eyes lifted, and Lily felt as though he looked for something within her that she wasn't sure she possessed but desperately hoped she did. "I also wished to understand the notion of pleasure," he continued matter-of-factly. "It was not a concept with which I had any familiarity. In that, Pendragon's girls were very accommodating."

Jealousy burned acidic in Lily's stomach, but she ignored it. "You learned how to give pleasure, but not to receive it?"

His features hardened even more, like a warrior preparing for battle. He cleared his throat, and Lily could see how difficult it was for him to reveal so much to her. It pained Lily to think he might see her as someone he needed to protect himself against.

"I learned about lust and how to pleasure myself. But I never..." He stopped with a low sound before he pinned her with a stare so intense that she felt it down to the marrow of her bones. "I never wanted that kind of intimacy with any other woman. I want it with you, Lily."

Her heart broke at the vulnerability threaded deep in his voice even as her body lit up in response to the need he could not hide.

"And I want it with you. More than anything," she replied.

His reply was a ragged breath. She could still see the tautness of his frame, the unrelenting uncertainty that had him in its clutches. She wanted so badly to dispel it, to finally have the opportunity to give him what he had given her—liberation, passion, and truth.

She took a step toward him, but before she could take another, he glanced to the side, breaking the connection of their gazes. His broad shoulders curved inward, and his chin dropped as he held up his hand to halt her progress.

"Lily, I cannot… I am…"

The tone of his voice was broken and harsh. Lily ached deep inside for what she saw in him—the emotional strain of his confession…and the fear.

He was not ready.

Her stomach clenched, and she took a long breath to steady her inner turmoil. She could be patient. If she wanted him—and she did, quite desperately—she would have to be patient and allow him his terms. But that did not mean she would not try to show him she was worthy of his trust.

Taking it slow, she started toward him again.

He did not move this time to stop her, but stood rigid and silent.

Coming to a halt in front of him, close but not touching, Lily tipped her head back and looked into his shuttered gaze.

"Kiss me," she said.

~

Avenell sucked in a tight breath as Lily's words hit deep in his core. He had told her of his shameful inexperience, and she still wanted him. He tried to force the air out again in a slow exhale, but a bloom of hope expanded in his chest. It caused his breath to catch somewhere between his lungs and his throat.

Hope was a painful sensation.

"Kiss me," she said again, imploring and commanding at once. Her gaze held his and wouldn't let go. The power she held over him with barely even trying was frightening.

He couldn't resist her. He didn't want to.

In torturously slow degrees, he lowered his head toward hers. Every sense, every nerve in his body was focused on the next few moments. He knew he would want to savor the memory of this, the first time he had kissed Lily.

He pressed his lips to hers gently at first, not knowing what to expect. But even such a light touch sent a swift rush of sensation through him. It was unlike anything he had ever known. Delicate and passionate at once. The silken texture of her lips, her pliant softness, the little moan that caught in her throat.

It stunned him. Stopped his breath and jolted his heart.

Intent upon exploring this new experience, he

shifted the pressure of his mouth, brushing his lips across hers before he flicked his tongue out to touch just the center of her bottom lip. Her lips parted on a sudden exhale. Her warm breath mingled with his. Something more than desire coursed through his blood.

He lifted his hands to grasp her shoulders, and with a groan, he crushed her mouth with his.

A voice in his head demanded he slow down, relish the sensations. But he was too desperate to know more. He tilted his head, craving the taste of her as though it could save his soul. He swept his tongue past her teeth, sliding into the recesses of her mouth. She tasted of innocence and shadows, and he was ravenous for her.

It shocked him—that desperate, obsessive need to consume her, to take all that she was into himself. To make what was hers, his. Her breath, her taste, her softness, and her need.

She arched her body toward him, bending her spine in a luscious curve as she returned the kiss with increasing fervor. Though she kept her arms faithfully at her sides, he swept his hands down to catch her wrists in his fingers. Even in his growing desire, he feared her touch as much as he craved it.

She accepted the restraint as he had known she would.

In fact, it seemed as though his hold on her emboldened her.

Rising to her toes, she swept her tongue over his. Her teeth scraped his lower lip. He didn't know if it was by accident or by design, but it had an intense effect on him. She did it again. This time her teeth gently closed.

A shock of pleasure shot through him.

She released him to bathe the spot with her soft tongue.

It was teasing and torturous.

Avenell released one of her wrists to grasp her nape, intending to hold her steady as he took her mouth in a deeper kiss. But before he could, he caught sight of her face. Her chin was tipped up, her lips parted, her lashes resting on the translucent skin below her eyes. Those lashes, thick and lush, fluttered and lifted as he continued to stare at her.

So beautiful. So trusting and generous as she waited for him to show her what he wanted. He could see her desire, her yearning, and more. An impulse claimed him.

Lifting her hand, he brought it up between them. On a carefully controlled breath, he turned her palm toward him and pressed it to the center of his chest.

The familiar pain lit across his skin, but he focused on her eyes and the pink of her lips and the gentle courage that was Lily.

Then suddenly the pain dove deep, tightening his chest and fisting in his stomach.

That damnable hope again.

# *Twenty-two*

Lily was not able to get away again until two nights later. Two nights interrupted by two long days during which she repeatedly relived their last conversation.

And the kiss.

The wondrous, enlightening kiss.

She hadn't expected to feel so many new and delightful things when his mouth had moved over hers. Her books had never explained how intimate the act could be, but it had affected her in ways their previous interactions had not.

She knew he could bring her pleasure with his hands upon her body, but his kiss… His kiss brought forth yearnings from her very heart. It was the first time she and the earl had been on equal footing, both of them giving and taking of each other with similar greed and abandon.

He had felt it too. She knew it when he'd drawn his mouth away and she'd seen the raw ache of longing in his eyes. And when he'd brought her hand to his chest, she'd been overwhelmed with emotion. Because she understood.

He may not have been ready to accept the extent of what she wished to share with him, but he was willing to try.

It had been a beautiful moment.

But that was where it had ended.

Two more days had passed, and she was finally going to be with him again.

Surprisingly, the earl was not waiting in the carriage when she got out to the mews. The groom explained that he was already at the destination.

It was odd and unexpected, but she rode to Pendragon's with a mix of acute anxiety and titillation building within her. Tonight, she fully expected to become the earl's lover in its fullest definition.

The groom insisted upon escorting her to the door of the brothel, where the familiar footman then took over and accompanied her up the stairs and down the hallway. She considered saying it was unnecessary, that she knew the way well enough, but she suspected that the earl had arranged the escort. Of course, he would know that despite her familiarity with the long back hallways, she would feel some trepidation in traversing them alone, considering her first experience at the establishment.

His consideration warmed her, though she was already quite heated with anticipation of the evening ahead.

Her body fairly hummed as she entered their rooms. Though the fire in the grate had died down to red glowing coals, the room was cozy and warm. The gaslights had been turned down as well, leaving only a handful of candles placed about the room to illuminate the space. She immediately scanned for the sight of the earl, but he was not present in the sitting room.

Pacing farther into the room, she glanced toward the shadows of the attached bedroom. Through the open doorway, she could see the earl's dark form beside the imposing outline of the bed as he lit more candles there.

A moment later, without looking back in her direction, though she suspected he had heard her enter, he stepped away and crossed out of her limited view.

She would go to him, without a trace of doubt. She just needed a moment first to breathe. To acknowledge all she was feeling—the blooming expectation, her growing desire, and that subtle ache of deeper emotion pulsing in the center of her chest.

She welcomed it.

That quiet ache of longing felt right. It felt beautiful.

Lily removed her cloak and smoothed her hands down the front of her gown, acknowledging the flutter of excitement in her belly. Then sensing his presence, she looked up to find him standing in the doorway of the bedroom. He had already divested himself of his coat and waistcoat. His white silk shirt had been opened at the throat and glowed softly in the candlelight.

He was beautiful—so masculine and strong—in his state of half-undress. Her breath caught around a thickness in her throat. She wasn't sure if it was her painful longing that triggered the emotion or the fact that she could so acutely sense his tension and disquiet.

The longer they stared at each other, the more breathless Lily became, until finally the earl tipped his head as he said, "I have arranged for us to dine tonight. Nothing too extravagant. Just a few delicacies I thought you might enjoy."

Lily looked to the table set with elegant dishware and covered trays. In truth, she was starving, having been far too focused on the night ahead to enjoy the supper she'd attended earlier with Angelique and her sisters.

Despite her hunger, she was not interested in food.

She glanced back to the earl and tried to smile as she replied, "I am sure it is wonderful, my lord, but at this moment, I doubt I could eat a thing."

His jaw tightened, and as she watched, his chest rose and fell with a heavy breath before he held out his hand to her.

"Will you come with me into the bedroom?"

Lily eagerly crossed the room to him. Her gaze never left his dark visage as she placed her hand in his. His palm was warm against hers. The solid feel of his hand closing around her fingers grounded her to him as he led her deeper into the bedroom.

Rather than draw her toward the bed as she expected, he brought her forward to the center of the room. Then he stopped, releasing her hand as he turned to face her.

His intent gaze traveled slowly over her face, then down the length of her body.

She was suddenly grateful for the gown she had chosen to wear that night. Though it was not so bold a color as red or sapphire blue, Lily believed the shimmery lavender complemented her skin tone and made her hair look darker, her eyes brighter.

She could sense the earl's rising tension even as he

continued to hold himself stoic and silent. It was all there to see in the familiar lines and angles of his fiercely handsome face.

There was no way she could have missed the same intense anticipation, the uncertainty, and the longing that she felt herself. The fear and the lovely, breath-stealing desire.

Desire that felt overwhelming in the quiet, flickering darkness. Desire that burned hot despite the instinctive need to tread with caution and care. Desire that felt so right, so unbelievably perfect.

It was all there, dancing in the air between them, racing over her skin, and trickling a path of fire through her veins. She wasn't sure she could bear much more of it.

But he did not reach for her.

A moment of panic gripped her.

Surely, she had not misunderstood his intention for tonight. Surely, they would finally make love as she had dreamed of for so long.

She noted his stiff, unyielding posture, and in a swift flash of insight, Lily knew what she needed to do.

Catching his weighted gaze, she smiled. His only response was to fist his hands at his sides.

Without a word, she took three steps back, lengthening the distance between them, urging him to trust her with her eyes and her smile and the heavy beat of her heart.

Then she slowly began to undress.

As she did so, she made note of how his intent focus followed her every movement, how his hands stretched open as a wide swath of skin was revealed.

The catch in his breath when she released the jeweled garters and slowly rolled the stockings he had given her down her legs.

She came alive under his focused attention. Her nerves were alight, her belly trembled, and heat swirled everywhere.

In attempting to seduce him, she was the one being seduced. By the time she stood naked, her clothing draped alongside his coat and waistcoat on the chair, she was breathless and hungry for him.

He stared at her from the shadows, his features harsh in the muted reach of the candlelight. He swept his gaze down the length of her bared body before looking into her eyes.

"I will do what I can to ease your experience," he said.

Lily bit her lip. His concern was for her when all she could think of was him. They would be exploring this new experience together.

Acknowledging the magic of that sent a heady wealth of emotion through her.

"Go lie on the bed, Lily."

The commanding nature of his tone empowered her. Lily's body warmed with anticipation, and there was no hesitation as she turned to walk naked to the bed, feeling the heat of his gaze on her backside with every step. Stretching out on top of the black bedcovering, she breathed a trembling sigh. The contrasting textures of velvet, silk, and satin against her sensitive skin gave rise to a new wealth of sensations.

Surrounded by black shadows and golden expectation, Lily felt as though she existed in a dream. Not only in the atmosphere of the room and the prospect of what was to come, but also in the intense depth of her need, and the hope that tonight he might finally join her in a mutual exploration of desire.

⁂

Avenell removed his boots and stockings, then stripped his shirt off over his head. Tossing the shirt aside, he reached for the fastening of his breeches. All the while he stared at the image of Lily lying in wait for him on the bed.

Everything about her was exquisite in a way more painful than he ever could have imagined. The silken glow of her skin, the lushness of her hips and breasts, the way her lips parted with her shallow breath. The quiet hunger in her eyes.

Still dressed in his breeches, he stalked toward the bed. She lay on her back, her body pale against the black bedcovering. She had one foot flat on the mattress with her knee slightly bent, revealing the shapely lines of her thigh and calf. Her arms rested elegantly at her sides, and the peaks of her generous breasts were puckered and waiting for attention.

His stomach clenched when she turned her head to watch his approach. Her smoky gaze held his intently, as though silently demanding something of him. Stopping at the side of the bed, he studied the stretch of her body. She so eloquently displayed both shameless sensuality and innocent anticipation. She was maiden and courtesan together. Bold and modest.

So many sumptuous curves and mysterious shadows. Beautiful and all his.

Hot desire stabbed his chest and sent a fine jolt straight to his groin. Avenell clenched his stomach against the possessive craving that pressed inexorably outward from his center. Going too fast could lead to disaster, and this was far too important.

Holding her smoldering gaze, he trailed his fingertips up the length of her outstretched leg, teasing the sensitive skin of her inner thigh before sweeping his hand over her hip and across the creamy plane of her belly. He continued his caress higher over the shallow bumps of her ribs, easing closer to where her breath lifted and lowered her full breasts. He drew lazy swirls around her peaked nipples.

Her eyelids lowered over her eyes as she bowed her spine and shifted her legs. Her body was heaven beneath his fingers. Her reactions were honest and unadulterated.

He wanted more.

Holding his breath, he slid his palm over her navel. Then lower.

As if anticipating his touch, she gave a gentle buck of her hips. At the exact same moment, he eased his hand between her thighs, pressing his palm intimately against her core.

She stilled. Rough gasps puffed through her lips. The sound of it tightened his loins. He shifted his hand to draw the wide pad of his thumb along the seam of her folds. Moisture coated her flesh, and when he made a second pass, he deliberately added more pressure as he slid his thumb over her tightly swollen bud.

A muffled sound caught in her throat, and Avenell risked a glance at her face.

Beautiful tension rode her features. Her eyes were closed, and her lips were rolled in between her teeth.

The warmth that flooded Avenell's system was different from the heat of desire he fought to contain. Different from the need and hunger that consumed him. Nothing at all like the fear he kept tucked deep beneath it all.

It was something altogether new.

He steadied his breath.

Withdrawing his hand from her heat, he ignored her quiet sound of protest and walked around to the foot of the bed and stripped off his breeches. He grasped her slim ankles in his hands and drew her legs apart so he could kneel on the mattress between them. The sight of her body all soft and needful on the bed sent a sharp arc of lust through him.

He knew he should take another moment to manage the riot inside him, but he could not keep his hands off her. He smoothed his palms over the surface of her legs and noted the way she crushed the velvet coverlet in her fists. He looked up along the length of her body to her face, and his heart stuttered.

She stared back at him from beneath sultry lashes. Her lips glistened, and her tongue pressed against the edge of her teeth. She radiated passion and sexual anticipation.

"Do you trust me?"

She nodded and replied readily, "I do."

Avenell leaned forward over her and bent down to press his open mouth over her navel. He darted his tongue into the sensitive well.

She closed her eyes with a sweep of her lashes and a tremulous sigh. A torturous, lovely sound.

Avenell sensed her touch a moment before he felt it, yet still he stiffened when her hand lifted to his shoulder. His breath burned in his lungs. He forced himself to slowly inhale and exhale as he clenched his teeth against the urge to pull away.

"Lily," he warned softly.

Her lashes fluttered as she opened her eyes. A small sound issued from her lips, and she quickly lifted her hand away.

"I did not mean to," she muttered weakly.

Avenell regulated his breath, forcing himself to relax before he replied, "I know." He stared into her eyes, darkened with desire, and felt a long and languid pull in his center. It was like a gravitational attraction. Something he could not deny. "But I cannot allow it to happen again. I want nothing to interrupt us tonight. Do you understand?"

Her answer came out on a sigh. "Yes."

"Reach your hands up over your head."

Her expression was impossible to read, but she did as he said. Her willingness to please him triggered an ache deep inside.

He pressed another kiss to her belly just to see her eyelashes flutter. As he rose up on his hands and knees over her prone form, his body cast hers into mysterious shadow. He took a moment to smooth his hand up along her side, brushing his thumb over her pebbled nipple and eliciting a sharp gasp. Then he stretched out to reach toward the head of the bed. It took only a moment to find what he sought beneath the pillows. He looped the velvet rope loosely over her joined hands, circling it twice around her wrists.

He did not tighten it, sensing just the suggestion of the binding would be enough. Looking down into her flushed face, he asked, "Are you all right?"

"Yes."

There was no hesitation in her answer. No hint of alarm. Her gray eyes met his boldly as she waited with parted lips for whatever might come next.

He continually underestimated her.

He held her gaze as he trailed his fingers along the sensitive skin of her inner arm. He covered one of her breasts, loving its weighty fullness and the press of its hardened peak against his palm.

Her eyes closed, and she arched her back, pressing herself more fully into his hand. He knew her breasts were sensitive, and he wanted nothing more than to ease her silent yearning.

Curving his spine, he lowered his head and drew the exposed nipple of her other breast harshly into his mouth, allowing his teeth to scrape the peak.

The sound of her desperate moan stopped his breath for several seconds. Not interested in giving her quarter, he sucked hard while molding the other soft globe with his fingers. Her gasps and moans grew more fitful with each sweep of his tongue. But it was when he hollowed his cheeks to pull her deep into his mouth that she began to circle her hips beneath him.

Her passion was intoxicating, and Avenell needed to keep a clear head.

Planting his hands on the bed and straightening his

arms, he put a necessary distance between her hot skin and his.

She opened her eyes to look up at him with a low sound of protest. Her desire swirled like a storm in her gaze. The vulnerability and strength revealed in her eyes reached into his gut and squeezed the breath from him.

"Tell me what you feel," he demanded. "Right now, in this moment."

Her arms flexed as she pulled against the rope around her wrists, stopping just shy of loosening the restraint. She licked her lips, and her gaze fell to travel hotly over his bared chest and abdomen. And then lower to where his painful erection jutted fiercely from the shadow of his groin.

His entire body tensed when her attention seemed to lock on that part of his body.

"I am on fire from the inside out," she whispered in a husky tone. "I feel desperate and frantic. As though I am fighting for my life." She brought her gaze back to his face. "And only you have the power to save me."

She arched her body, lifting her breasts and rolling her hips. "Please, my lord. Kiss me," she sighed in a quiet demand.

Kiss her? He wanted to consume her.

In that breathless moment, her gaze seemed to contain all the mysteries of life and death. Mysteries he wanted desperately to explore…until he acknowledged with an intense stab of regret that a woman like Lily would not reveal the depths of her heart unless she could expect reciprocation in kind.

Avenell would never know the beautiful secrets she kept. But he could know this.

The sigh she breathed as he lowered his head toward hers.

The silken texture and lush softness of her lips beneath his.

The sweetness of her tongue, the sharp edge of her teeth.

The way he so quickly and easily lost himself in the languid exploration of her mouth.

She arched more deeply toward him. The peaks of her breasts pressed into his chest. He tensed at the rise in sensations but did not pull away. The kiss took priority over all else.

Her tongue played fiercely against his, and her teeth scraped along his lower lip, demanding more of him. Her body melted as her moans and sweet whimpers fanned the fire burning hot inside him. She strained beneath him, arching deeper, pressing harder toward him.

It was the deepest pleasure.

And the harshest pain.

He reached between them to slide his hand between her legs. Her outer folds were slick with her need as he caressed her. She moaned into his mouth. He responded by dipping two fingers into her silken passage. He stroked inside her while thrusting his tongue past her lips, desperate to taste every gasp of pleasure.

Her response was perfection. Uninhibited, passionate, and pure.

She tangled her tongue with his and drew him deeper

into her mouth until he began to wonder who was possessing whom.

He burned for her, inside and out.

Lowering his mouth again to her plump breast, he swirled his tongue over her distended nipple while she writhed and gasped her rising pleasure. Her legs trembled as she rolled her hips urgently against his hand. Her body grew taut. She made a gorgeous sound in the back of her throat before her breath caught and her head pressed back into the pillow.

Her surrender was evident in her gasping breath and fluttering eyelashes. But most poignantly of all, he felt it in the first pulses deep inside her body.

Releasing her breast, he slid down to lower his head between her lovely thighs. As he continued to move his fingers, he covered her with his mouth, suckling her sensitive flesh.

Her body stiffened with a strangled moan as her climax overtook her completely.

Once she began to relax, Avenell pushed himself away from her to sit back on his heels. His chest was tight, and his body still surged with need. He pressed his hands on the top of his thighs as he consumed the sight of her—languid and weak and distracted by her receding pleasure.

He had never seen anything more beautiful.

Until she opened her eyes and the stunning light in her gaze speared him like a dagger.

"Come to me."

Three small words, but when issued from her lovely lips, they nearly decimated him.

He was already feeling far too much. But the intensity

of the sensations across his skin could not compete with the depth of craving that stretched inside him.

Aching and harder than he had ever been, Avenell rose up and carefully lowered his hips between her spread thighs until he pressed intimately to the entrance of her body, which still pulsed subtly with her release. His breath hissed out between clenched teeth.

Propping himself on his elbows, he looked down into her heavy-lidded eyes. The depth and intensity of her climax was evident in her gaze, and for a second, Avenell believed he could feel the pulse of her pleasure in his own body.

His chest tight and skin on fire, he pressed forward. Entering her by slow, torturous degrees. Her softness and heat caressed him. Her silvery gaze beseeched him and bewitched him.

She bent her knees, bringing them up alongside his hips, drawing him in.

The muscles of his arms, shoulders, and back were tight with the effort to keep his upper body apart from hers as he propped himself on his bent arms. He did not want any pain to distract from the pleasure that spread like fire through his body. He trembled from head to toe, and he knew it was not all from his determination to go slow when he wanted nothing more than to take possession of her with one reckless plunge. It was wonder tainted with fear that challenged his composure.

There was so much heat. So much tenderness in the way her body accepted his. Encompassing, consuming, drawing on his final reserves. It was a sensation unlike anything he could have imagined.

Finally, he could take no more. Tensing his buttocks, he gave one long thrust and drove deeply into her core. His jaw clenched, and a guttural moan caught in his throat. He nearly closed his eyes in an instinctive urge to contain the fierce rush of pleasure, but he could not look away from Lily's face.

The tip of her tongue pressed delicately against the top row of her parted teeth as she gasped for breath.

It was the only reaction she gave to the rending of her maidenhead.

While he felt as though he had trespassed into nirvana. Being inside her, fully encased in her warmth, was more powerful a feeling than he had expected. It was possession and surrender at once.

Each ragged breath he drew as he remained still and focused on managing the overwhelming stimulation only made his body crave more. As stunning and intimate as it was to feel so connected with Lily, there was an undeniable force within him, demanding he take them both to the limit of what they could endure.

He knew he should wait, allow her body to adjust to his intrusion, but he couldn't. He had been reduced to nothing but a primitive urge to finally, *finally* explore the bone-deep pleasure of being joined with this woman.

And it was pleasure, he realized in awe. Full, encompassing, undeniable pleasure.

The flashes of pain across his affected nerves were not nearly enough to distract from the beauty of everything else he felt.

He held her gaze—or she held his—as he slowly began to guide himself in and out of her body.

They discovered the wonder of it together as every movement sent rippling waves of sensation on top of sensation expanding outward from where they were joined.

Her passion was stunning as she moved with him, taking him deeper and deeper with each thrust.

Being inside her with the taste of her still on his tongue was an experience he never wanted to end. He measured each stroke, trying to prolong every nerve-screaming sensation. He fought to contain it and control it even as the temptation to submit rose higher and higher.

Avenell's chest squeezed painfully as he fought off his approach to the edge.

There would only ever be this one first time that he made love to Lily. If he could, he would make it last forever—the consuming fire, the overwhelming sensations that lit every nerve and flowed unheeded through his bloodstream, obliterating fear and pain. The sense of being joined with her in a way he had never wanted with anyone else.

She belonged to him.

It was an undeniable truth.

And in that moment, he acknowledged another truth—he belonged to her as well.

Staring into her face, he was enraptured by the pink flush on her cheeks and the glistening moisture on her lips. As he watched, a tiny frown line appeared between her eyebrows, and a lovely tension began to claim her features.

He intentionally slowed his pace, and after a few more languorous thrusts, she broke eye contact. A soft sound caught in the back of her throat as she arched. Clenching her lower lip in her teeth, she clutched at the velvet rope overhead.

His every sense focused in on her as he thrust as far as he could go, wishing he had the power to touch her soul.

Her inner muscles tightened around him, and she gasped his name.

Not *my lord.*

*Avenell.*

It was too much. The hot, tight pulse of her body around him as she achieved another climax. The heady sound of her stuttered breath. The scent of his perfume on her damp skin. The sound of his name on her lips.

Avenell shook from deep within. His climax was coming before he was ready. Before he had a chance to stop it. Before he could withdraw from her tight sheath. He achieved release in a hot rush, his shoulders and neck muscles cording tight.

It was intense and swift. Decimating his reserve. Eradicating fear and pain.

# Twenty-three

LILY SLOWLY UNCURLED HER FINGERS FROM THEIR fierce grip on the velvet binding her wrists. They ached from how tightly she had been clutching at the rope. In truth, everything ached. Her arms, her legs, the muscles along her spine all the way up to her skull. Even her jaw ached a little bit.

And deep inside…

There was a tenderness that was beautiful and raw and perfect.

She felt sated, yes, but so much more than that—she felt awakened. As though she had finally discovered some secret treasure.

She gave a subtle stretch, loving the changes she felt in her body.

Her movement disturbed the man on top of her. Though his hips still pressed intimately between her thighs, his upper body was levered away from her as he held himself on his elbows. His head hung heavily between wide shoulders covered in a sheen of sweat, and his breath fanned over her damp skin.

Feeling oddly shy after the depth of what they

had shared, Lily kept her eyes closed. She was not sure she could keep everything she was feeling from reflecting in her gaze, and she was not ready to reveal so much.

He shifted, reaching up to unwind the rope and release her wrists. Lily bent her elbows, relaxing her reach, but she did not feel a need to bring her arms down just yet. She had known the binding had not been tight enough to hold her if she had wanted to be freed, but there had been something terribly exciting in submitting to the restraint.

The earl lifted away from between her spread thighs and lowered himself to lay beside her. He no longer touched her physically, but she could still feel him—his breath, his heartbeat, his heat—as though he had become a permanent part of her.

And she felt the languid relaxation slowly ebb away from his body as tension returned.

"Are you hurt?" The sound of his low murmur was like the shadows flickering around them—warm and dark, secret and sensual.

"No," she answered simply.

How could she express the soul-deep tenderness she felt, the aching vulnerability, the steady, searing need that still ran through her blood?

Finally, she opened her eyes to look at him. He lay on his side, propped up on an elbow as he observed her. The candles had burned low, and his face was heavily distorted by shadow, but what she saw gave her a pang of concern. She wondered at his rigid expression. Tension rode high in his frame. His brows remained heavy over his midnight gaze. And his lips, which had been both so demanding and generous on her body, were drawn into a stern line.

Before she could consider what it might indicate, he shifted and rose from the bed in a swift and fluid motion.

Lily's disappointment weighed her down for a long moment as she listened to him moving about the room. She heard the water in the basin as he washed himself and then his footsteps as he returned to the bed.

His movements were adept and gentle as he used a damp cloth to wash away what had been left behind by their lovemaking. Lily shivered when he walked away again, though it was not from any chill touching her skin.

He was avoiding her gaze.

No matter how much she wished to remain in the euphoric aftermath of what she had experienced, the lovely haze was sliding away. She pushed herself to a seated position and swung her legs over the edge of the bed. Her hair fell about her shoulders in a tangled mess. The pins had been lost somewhere in the bedcovers.

Pushing her hair back over her shoulders, she looked up to see the earl standing at the washstand. He was turned away from her, and his hands were braced on the surface. He wore his breeches, but they rested low on his narrow hips. Lily's attention was captured by the sight of his muscled back, his broad shoulders, and the strong bulge of muscle in his arms. Her gaze slid down over his firm buttocks and solid thighs, wishing they had not already been covered. She had gotten only a shadowed glimpse at the part of him that had been inside her body, but as she recalled that image, her mouth went a little dry, and her stomach quivered delightfully.

It was astounding that she could still feel such a sensual pull after the pleasure she had just experienced. She suspected that pull would always be there.

She was no longer a virgin. They had become lovers in truth, and this time, he had claimed his release as well. She had felt the sudden tautness of his body over hers, had felt him pulsing deep inside her.

It had been a moment of pure elation. Infinite rightness.

Yet now that it had passed, she felt him once again retreating from her, closing himself off.

His confession earlier rang through her mind. It had been his first time, as well.

Alarm trickled through her. Perhaps it had not been as...wondrous for him.

The thought that she may have disappointed him filled her with dismay.

Rising from the bed, she gathered her courage. She could not allow this weight and distance to remain between them. Not after the depth of connection she had felt. Her steps were silent on the thick carpet as she walked toward him.

Her trepidation grew the closer she got. There was a subtle harshness to his measured breath. The tautness of the muscles running along either side of his spine and the stiffness of his arms as he held on to the edge of the washstand revealed his physical distress.

Lily's chest squeezed tight. He had told her once that pain would be inevitable.

She could feel him hurting as certainly as her own heart ached.

Avenell did not realize she had left the bed until he felt her presence directly behind him. His back and his chin came up sharply as a familiar dread washed through him.

His gaze found hers in the long, oval mirror above the washstand. She stood just beyond his shoulder, her dove-gray eyes looking at his reflection with undisguised concern. Her nude body made a beautiful contrast to the shadows surrounding them.

"My lord?" she asked softly. The kindness in her voice increased his panic. He was terrified of what she might be seeing in his reflection. "Did you…did you not experience pleasure?"

Deep inside, he still shook with the aftermath of the most intense climax of his life. Being with Lily—being inside her—had shattered him to pieces. The pure, unadulterated sensations had broken every bond of control he possessed and had left him like this. Trembling and too weak to manage the fire crackling across his skin.

"More than I ever thought possible."

"But now?" she asked.

He could not answer. His throat had closed up, and his tongue was stiff against his teeth.

While deep in the throes of passion, the sexual need within him had overtaken all else. But with his mindfulness returning, all he felt was the pain.

He hadn't felt so at the mercy of his affliction

since he had been a confused and frightened child in the hands of people with no tenderness and even less empathy.

Frozen in place, unable to speak, he watched as she lifted her hand, as though she intended to place her slender fingers against his back.

The panic inside him condensed to a single searing point in the center of his chest.

"Don't."

Though the word screamed like fire inside his head, it came out sounding clipped and stone cold.

Her hand stilled instantly, and her eyes widened. She slowly lowered her hand to her side.

"I wish only to offer comfort," she said softly. "What can I do?"

"Nothing."

Something akin to regret flickered across her features, and the sight of it, even as fleeting as it was, hurt far worse than all the years of emotional degradation and physical torment he had endured in his life.

Her eyes met his. Soft and resilient. "Won't you let me try?" she asked.

His skin prickled fiercely at the thought, but he said nothing.

Making love to her had been an experience he would never forget. The fire and passion. The melding of two bodies. The sensations roused and fed by his desire had grown until they had overwhelmed all else.

But this would be something entirely different. Allowing her to touch him in his current weakened state terrified him. He did not have the strength to manage the inevitable pain.

Yet, he could not bring himself to refuse her.

Taking his silence as acquiescence, she took a step toward him. Not so close that she touched him yet, but he could feel the warmth coming from her bared skin, her kind heart. Holding his gaze in the mirror, she slowly slid her hand around his waist to press her palm low against his abdomen, where his body was undamaged.

Avenell could barely breathe. Sensations slid swiftly across his nerves, but they were not unpleasant, not there where she touched him. The other pain was still present across his shoulders, chest, and down his arms, but he also experienced the odd impression of her touch distracting him from other sensations as his focus centered in on her and what she was doing.

Then she shifted behind him, easing closer. Her belly curved against his buttocks, her full breasts pressed to his back, and most distressing of all, she rested her cheek against the back of his shoulder.

He could not move. His body turned to stone while frantic, uncontrolled sensations claimed the nerves of his upper back. He closed his eyes to focus on the effort of drawing breath into his lungs and forcing it out again. He could endure this.

He tried, but his body was too weakened, his soul vulnerable, and the pressure was too much. She was too much.

With a rough exhale, he grasped her wrist and turned to face her, gently pushing her arm behind her back to prevent further torment. His breath was fast and uneven, matching the tumult of thoughts and emotions tumbling through him.

Though she had stilled at his abrupt movement, she

did not pull away. Her gray eyes were wide beneath the thick sweep of her eyelashes.

How could she look at him that way, so quietly confident and hopeful?

It angered him.

Did she not see the truth? He was not like other men. Inside, he was as damaged as the nerves that burned like a thousand flames beneath his skin.

He did not deserve her gentle regard, her sweetness. Why could she not see him for what he was?

She tried to release her hand from where he held it behind her back, but ceased when he did not loosen his grip.

"I want so badly to touch you." Her voice was an intimate whisper. "To make you feel the things I feel beneath your hands."

He clenched his teeth so hard his jaw throbbed. "That will never happen."

A small line formed between her brows, and her chin tilted. "Given time, perhaps—"

"No, Lily," he growled angrily.

She did not understand. How could she? No one knew the fear, self-loathing, and powerlessness he had lived with. She had never experienced a parent's abject rejection and disgust. The sense that something was broken inside of him—that he didn't, couldn't, belong anywhere. She could not know how far he would go to protect himself from ever feeling that again. Especially from her.

"It will *never* happen," he continued, hating how cold and distant his voice sounded in the darkness. "Accept it now, or this cannot continue."

He watched the effect of his refusal roll gently but inexorably through her body as she lowered her lashes over her gaze. He wished he could see into her eyes, know what she was thinking. But she hid it from him.

After another moment, she took a deep breath that lifted her breasts before she released it in a slow exhale. Then she took a step back and turned away from him.

Avenell nearly shouted for her to come back, to wrap her arms about him despite the pain and the denial. He watched her in silence instead, while his stomach tightened with regret, and his heart thudded painfully against his ribs.

Before he could sink even further into the encroaching distress within him, Lily paused to smile at him over her shoulder. Her gray eyes were soft. Her expression was once again generous and open.

"Shall we dine, my lord?" she asked lightly. "I find myself rather famished."

Avenell released his breath and gave a nod that felt wooden and stiff. "Of course."

He glanced at his shirt where it lay on the chair, tensing at the thought of having to put it on over his still-rioting nerves. Though silk was much easier to bear than linen or cotton, during his current state, it was guaranteed to cause significant distress.

"Don't put it on."

Avenell looked up in surprise to see Lily standing in her shift with her lovely hair falling in tangled waves down her back as she watched him. She had obviously rightfully identified his reluctance.

She lifted one shoulder and tipped her head to the

side. "There is no reason we cannot be comfortable while we eat. It is rather warm in here anyway."

The heat that spread through Avenell's chest had nothing to do with the room and everything to do with the woman who stood patiently waiting for his response to her casual suggestion.

With a rueful curl of his lips, he walked toward her, enjoying the way her gaze flickered over his bared torso with admiration. The desire that never quite went away when he was in her presence flared bright in response. Tightly reining in his physical reaction, he executed a formal bow before reaching for her hand to bring it to the bend of his elbow.

Her fingers fluttered in his hold before resting warmly on his bare skin. The stimulation of her touch challenged his control. Not only due to the painful prickling that raced beneath his skin, but more so due to the craving her touch ignited deeper within. When she glanced upward with a lush sweep of her lashes and curved her lovely mouth into a smile, Avenell's heart fell.

Unexpectedly, irrevocably.

It took him a moment to recover, and he nearly stuttered over his words as he said, "Miss Chadwick, would you honor me by joining me for supper?"

She performed a graceful curtsy as a pink blush colored her cheeks. "My lord, I would love to."

The exchange was fanciful and light, and their meal followed through in the same tone as Lily kept up a steady stream of conversation. Her eyes sparkled with laughter as she told stories of her sisters. He heard much in her voice when she spoke of her family.

Not only the obvious love and regard she held for her sisters, but her sadness over the loss of her mother when she had been on the very cusp of womanhood. And her confusion and regret over her father's gradual dissipation and ultimate death from a weak heart.

He was well aware that she spoke as a means of distracting him from the pain he'd been unable to conceal from her. What surprised him was that it worked. By the time they finished their meal and decided to move to the sofa to finish their wine, he was more relaxed and content than he had been in years, perhaps in his entire life.

After stoking the fire back to life, Avenell turned to find Lily resting sideways against the back of the sofa, with her legs curled up beneath her and her lips parted in sleep. Her innocence was palpable. Her softness a stark contrast to the hardness he felt in himself.

Moving silently to her side, he eased the wineglass from her hand and set it on the end table before lowering himself onto the sofa beside her. Taking care not to awaken her, he gently traced his fingertip across the crest of her cheek, then along her jaw to the point of her chin.

With a murmured sound, she shifted in her sleep until she nestled along his side with her head against his bare shoulder.

Avenell held his breath, afraid to move. Pain seared the surface of his skin and burned through the sudden tightness of his lungs. It angered him that he could still feel the intense adverse reaction even while holding something so precious. Despite the distress it caused, he deliberately wrapped his arm around her curved form and drew her in closer to his chest. Her unconscious sigh fanned across his burning skin, soothing and destroying him all at once.

He forced himself to focus on her. The warmth of her body, the silken texture of her skin, her complete, yielding trust. The longer he held her, the easier it became.

After a while, he was able to regulate his breath to match her deep and quiet rhythm.

After a little while more, Avenell allowed himself to wonder…

And as he wondered, that clenching hope claimed him in its grip once again and wouldn't let go.

# Twenty-four

"*Mon dieu*," Angelique exclaimed with a dramatic sigh. "I cannot recall if we are attending a dinner party, a ball, a rout, or a soiree tonight."

Emma turned to reply over her shoulder. "It is a ball to celebrate the engagement of Miss Farindon to Mr. Pinkman."

They were in line to enter yet another grand London home, and Lily honestly couldn't blame her great-aunt for her confusion. As they finally reached the receiving line to be greeted by their hosts, Lily had to stifle a yawn behind her gloved hand.

She had spent five out of the last eight nights with the earl. A naturally early riser, even when she stayed up until dawn, Lily was not getting the amount of sleep her body needed, which should have made the many social events they attended a torment to get through. On the contrary, despite her exhaustion, Lily was enjoying herself far more than she had at the start of the season.

Though Emma still insisted they attend social functions in their efforts to obtain an honorable proposal, she no longer put such urgency on the issue. Her winnings from Bentley's ensured that they would have the whole Season to find husbands.

And since even that motivation was gone for Lily, she found she had much more freedom to simply enjoy herself now that she did not have to worry about impressing suitors. She loved dancing and had made several friends over the weeks.

Miss Farindon, the girl celebrating her engagement tonight being one of them.

The only thing that could make evenings such as this better was if Lily could share them with Lord Harte. Every now and then, when her brain was soft with lack of sleep, she would entertain the fantasy that they might somehow manage to continue their relationship indefinitely.

A foolish dream. Gentlemen did not marry their mistresses.

Especially not the secret ones they purchased at a brothel auction.

Oh, but she wished they did. Somewhere along the way, her near-obsessive infatuation with her lover had turned into something much more complicated.

She had fallen in love with him.

And though the feeling, in acknowledging it fully to herself, gave her such a wealth of hope and happiness, in full context it was frightfully depressing.

She did not often think about it in full context.

As she followed Angelique and her sisters up the wide and curving staircase to the second-floor ballroom, she pressed her hand to her abdomen, trying to contain the swirling feeling that came to life whenever she thought of Avenell. Since the night of the theater, a new layer had been added to their time together.

She never reached for him unexpectedly, never wrapped her arms around him as she wished to do. His admission that night had touched her with a helpless sort of sadness. Though she wanted to honor the restrictions he demanded in regard to their physical interaction, she also wished there was something more she could do, some way she could help him.

She understood that he experienced pain from stimulation on his skin, but the why of it was still unclear.

She was loath to cause him more discomfort by pressing him to accept what she was so desperate to give him. Though he was not demonstrative in the common ways of affection, his generosity was unmatched. He was intense, passionate, and tender.

Her time with the earl had liberated her passion, but he had also opened her up to life in a thousand subtle ways. She wanted to share it all with him. But as long as she was his mistress, what they did—what they could *be* to each other—was frightfully limited. She ached with subtle longing for what she could not have. The more time Lily spent with the earl and came to appreciate the full depth of his rich, giving nature, the more she saw a possibility for a more profound connection.

And also couldn't help but notice the heartrending absence of it.

As his mistress, she was free to make love to him, but not to love him.

It was a cruel design.

Though she found herself enjoying the endless social

whirl with a newfound sense of confidence, there was ever present this sense of something missing. *Him*.

She would never talk happily with him at a dinner table, or stroll along a garden path on his arm. She would never dance with him under the magical lights of a ballroom.

Hating the discontent that claimed her, Lily forced her attention away from her inner turmoil. Her wishes and dreams were futile and only weighed her down with their depressive nature.

The Chadwicks stayed with Angelique until she found a place to sit among the other matrons and chaperones, and Emma took her place at her aunt's side.

Lily frowned at her older sister's constant dedication to the role she had chosen for herself as the responsible head of their little family. In struggling with her own yearning to express herself more honestly, Lily had become more and more frustrated by Emma's restraint. She wanted to suggest that her older sister mingle with the guests, dance a time or two, *something* to get her away from the wall. But Emma continued to insist that she was content with her lot as spinster and guardian to Lily and Portia.

Clearly, a falsehood. Lily was just not certain whether Emma lied only to them or to herself as well.

Once the music started, there was less opportunity for Lily to worry about her sisters or her own future. A distraction was exactly what she needed, and she did her best to make the most of it. Evenings went by much faster when she was engaged with other guests, doing what she could to enjoy the hours.

Unfortunately, Lord Fallbrook was in attendance.

Since the incident in Warwickshire, Lily had been very careful to avoid the man, but tonight, she could not completely escape his leering stare as he noticed her from a distance. The man positively made her skin crawl.

Her next dance was claimed by Mr. Campbell, and Lily went with him gladly. There was no fear, at least, of any inappropriate advances from him. Their conversation was easy and comfortable, reminding Lily how much she enjoyed his company.

Just as they positioned themselves for the start of a long country dance, Lily caught sight of someone familiar crossing the room.

Mr. Bentley.

As the bastard son of an earl and the proprietor of a gambling house, Bentley was barely tolerated by polite society. If not for the fact that his financial acumen had kept many of the gentlemen present tonight from going into debt with their lavish lifestyles, he may never have been invited to an event such as this.

That he was here now triggered a jolt of inspiration. Lily quickly glanced around for Portia.

"You are looking quite fresh and lovely this evening, Miss Chadwick."

Lily shifted her attention back to Mr. Campbell long enough to acknowledge his compliment. "Thank you, Mr. Campbell."

He smiled back, his perfectly trimmed beard curving around his mouth. His gaze was warm and kind as he stated, "I would like you to know how much I have come to appreciate our acquaintance. In fact, I hope you do not take it as too forward for me to say I believe we have become friends."

"I would be honored to count you as a friend, Mr. Campbell," Lily replied just as the steps of the dance drew them apart.

Curiosity had her attention shifting to find Mr. Bentley again as he strode through the crowd. Something in his manner struck Lily acutely.

He appeared distraught. His strides were long and purposeful, his head angled down, and his focus fixed on a doorway that led to a game room. Just before she lost sight of him, he turned to glance over his shoulder. The emotion revealed in his expression would have been obvious to anyone with a heart.

Lily followed the direction of his glance, though she already knew toward whom it had been directed. Emma stood at the other end of his tormented gaze, entirely unaware of his presence or his passionate regard.

Lily sighed. She wished her sister would do something. Heaven knew Emma deserved to be happy after all she had done for their family—taking care of their mother when she had been ill, then struggling to counter their father's destructive behavior, and taking a position at Bentley's club to fund Lily's and Portia's debuts.

But Mr. Bentley was not at all a proper match for a lady of high society. Even the whisper of a lady being involved with a man like Bentley had potential to cause a ruinous scandal, which certainly explained his distance. He clearly cared for her and would not damage her by association, and Emma would never risk her sisters' futures in such a way. Her loyalty and self-sacrifice were far too ingrained.

The basic unfairness of it simply infuriated Lily, as did her older sister's relentless adherence to propriety.

It was far past time for Emma to let go of her need to manage everything to death.

"Is everything all right, Miss Chadwick?"

Lily drew her focus back to Mr. Campbell as they made a turn about each other. Recovering her composure, she gave him a light smile. "Yes, I am sorry. I just saw someone unexpected. That is all."

She wondered if she should alert Emma to the fact that Mr. Bentley was here. It was not in Lily's nature to interfere in other people's personal business, but something in Mr. Bentley's expression, the torment in his gaze when he looked at Emma, sat heavily in Lily's heart. Something had to be done.

"If you do not mind, I would like to call on you tomorrow. I hope to speak also with Lady Chelmsworth and your elder sister."

"Yes," Lily replied, "we should be receiving callers at the usual time."

She took advantage of a turn in the dance to look back toward where Emma stood beside Angelique. Her sister deserved far more than what she had resigned herself to. Lily could no longer stand by while Emma refused to acknowledge the obvious connection that existed between her and her former employer.

"Excellent," Mr. Campbell said. The joyful relief in his tone and his wide grin finally caught Lily's full attention.

She had a feeling she may have missed something in their conversation. Not wanting to hurt his feelings by admitting she had barely been paying attention, she just smiled back at him.

The song ended some time later, and Lily was swept up by her next partner. A niggling concern continued to poke at the back of her mind in regard to Mr. Campbell, but she was forced to ignore it as the next dance required all of her attention. It was a waltz with the frightfully clumsy Lord Teshem.

Lily was turning precariously about the room, focusing all her effort on keeping her feet, despite Lord Teshem's seeming determination to send her flying, when a ripple went through the crowd around them. It was the kind of shock wave of gasps and twitters of nervous laughter that resulted only from an exceptionally scandalous occurrence. Lord Teshem twisted his head one way and then the other, apparently more interested in what had happened to cause such a reaction in the crowd than in keeping himself from smashing Lily's feet.

Lily bit her lip to keep from doing a little hop step as Lord Teshem came down on her tender toes a second time.

"What now?" he said under his breath just before he stopped dancing completely, leaving them both standing rather awkwardly in the middle of the room. "Is that…?" he began as he angled his squinted gaze across the dance floor. "Yes, I do believe that is Lady Chelmsworth."

Oh goodness. Lily turned to look. What on earth was Angelique up to?

What she saw caused a nervous laugh to bubble up from her chest, though if she was fully honest, there was a definite dose of delight in her humor as well.

Angelique was causing the greatest stir since…well, Lily wasn't sure exactly what past spectacle could compare to what she was witnessing.

The dowager countess—at an age when ladies were expected, no, practically *required* to sit demurely in their seats along the wall—was at that moment waltzing about the room on the arm of a young gentleman whose expression was formed into a perfect depiction of shock.

Shock, because Angelique was not just managing the vigorous steps of the waltz, she was mastering them with the grace and skill of a trained dancer.

"If you will excuse me, please," Lily muttered to her dance partner.

Lord Teshem merely grunted in response as Lily strode quickly from the dance floor to make her way around to where she had last seen Emma. If anyone knew what on earth had prompted such a fabulous display, it would be her.

She could see Emma up ahead. Her sister's mouth was actually open in stunned surprise as she watched Angelique.

"Isn't it just wonderful?" Portia said, coming up alongside Lily.

Lily turned to see her sister's face split into a grin that did nothing to conceal her glee.

"What on earth?" Lily muttered.

"I have no idea," Portia replied, "but I cannot wait to find out."

Emma did not even notice their approach. Nor did she budge when Lily and Portia took up their places on either side of her. All three sisters stood in silence for several minutes, watching Angelique swirl about the dance floor as though her feet had wings. Pure pleasure flashed from the lady's brown eyes, and her smile was more beautiful than anything Lily had seen in a long time.

"Do you think perhaps her many tales of being a ballerina in Paris prior to her marriage may not be imagined after all?" Lily whispered.

"And if *those* fantastical stories are true," Portia added, "what of all the others?"

Emma still could not seem to drag her gaze away from the dance floor. "It is amazing, isn't it?"

"Poor Lord Nicklethwaite," Lily offered with smothered amusement. "He seems a bit dazed."

"He appears to be holding on for dear life," Portia suggested boldly, not bothering to hide her own amusement.

"What could have prompted such a fantastic display?" Lily asked.

"She wanted to show me that everyone can dance," Emma replied in a dazed voice. Their staid and proper, always composed oldest sister was locked in shock.

"I believe she proved her point," Portia declared, and when Emma did not reply, she added smartly, "So, are you?"

"Am I what?" Emma asked, finally turning to look at Portia.

"Going to dance."

"No. Of course not."

"Why not?" Lily asked, readily taking Portia's cue.

"Because I am a spinster. I am not seeking suitors."

It was the same argument they had heard from Emma for months, but Lily knew something that might succeed in shaking her older sister out of her self-imposed little cage.

"What if Mr. Bentley was here?"

"Why would you mention him?" Emma asked lightly. Her expression and manner were so evasive it hurt to observe.

Empathy flooded her awareness. Lily suspected she knew at least a little bit of what her sister was feeling. "Because it is clear you miss him."

Portia leaned forward and, after briefly catching Lily's gaze to confirm agreement, got right to the crux of the matter. "You are obviously in love with the man."

"That is ridiculous. I am not in love with Mr. Bentley."

"You are a terrible liar, Emma," Portia said with a laugh. "If you could have seen what I saw that morning after you spent the night at his club, you would not bother to deny it."

"What did you see?"

Emma's question held a note of uncertainty Lily had never heard from her before. Her confident sister, the one who always knew what to do, who was always in charge, did not know how to manage matters of the heart any more than Lily did.

"He cares, Emma," Portia answered. "The whole time he stood in our parlor, he watched you. Every slight change in your expression caused him to tense. He strained at the bit in his effort not to go to you. It might have been amusing if it hadn't been so sad, since you barely acknowledged him until it was time to shoo him out the door. Do not try to deny how gloomy you have been since you stopped going to the club. Your mood has been quite depressing. It is obvious you have been heartsick over the man."

"That is ridic—" Emma began.

"It is not ridiculous." Frustration made Lily's voice harder than she intended. "Must you be so full of pride, Emma? The man loves you, and you love him. What exactly is the problem?"

"And don't you dare say it has anything to do with us," Portia added sharply.

After only a moment, Emma conceded. Perhaps she was tired of denying it. "You are right. About me, anyway. I do love him."

Portia asked pointedly, "And what are you going to do about it?"

"What can I do?" Emma asked, exasperation in her tone. "You both know his position in society. He is barely accepted in most circles and downright rejected from others."

Portia's expression tensed as she narrowed her gaze at their sister. "And? Tell me that is not your reason for denying your feelings for the man."

Emma sighed. "Of course not. I honestly could not care less about what ninety-nine percent of the people in this room think of me. But I do care what they think of the two of you. Such a thing could ruin both of your chances for a great match."

Lily could not allow that. Especially considering how greatly her circumstances had changed. She would not be the cause of Emma's continued unhappiness, even indirectly.

"Enough, Emma," she declared. "I know I speak for us both when I say none of that matters a whit to either of us. We will manage quite well with fewer invitations and a closer, more loyal group of friends."

Portia leaned in to add saucily, "Besides, we will still have Angelique, the great example of virtue and propriety that she is, as our sponsor."

With perfect timing, Angelique waltzed by at that very moment.

Lily studied Emma's face, willing her sister to take a chance. Silently begging her to claim her happiness. While she watched, Emma's expression shifted, and the tension she had been carrying for weeks seemed to simply slide away as she declared calmly, "I have to go back to the club. Right now. Tonight."

"Oh, I would not do that," Lily interjected quickly, holding back her smile as warmth spread through her heart.

"Why not?"

"Mr. Bentley is not there."

"How on earth could you know that?"

"I saw him enter the game room about an hour ago," Lily answered brightly. "I am quite certain he is still there."

Emma stared across the ballroom to the small antechamber. Lily could see the fear, uncertainty, and finally, resolution cross her sister's face. When Emma looked back to Lily and Portia, new life shone from her eyes.

"Would you girls mind having one more eccentric in the family?" she asked. "I am quite certain I am about to do something rather shocking. Scandalous even."

"Excellent." Portia was clearly thrilled.

Lily was more than that. She was… She honestly wasn't sure what emotion was swelling inside her so intensely, but she couldn't help adding, "Perhaps we shall become an entire family of eccentric women."

Emma narrowed her gaze at the cryptic statement, but Lily refused to say more.

As her older sister crossed through the crowd and out of sight, Lily's joy shifted unexpectedly into something dark and sad. A complex mixture of fear and yearning and loss swept through her.

What she wouldn't give for the same opportunity to risk it all for love.

As though she had conjured him from the pure force of her longing, Avenell crossed through her line of vision. Lily's heart seized with a sort of pleasure-pain. In an instant, everything within her stretched and expanded on a breath.

He walked as he usually did—his shoulders strong and forbidding, his gaze dark, and his manner cold.

But Lily felt the heat in his presence, the fire in his glance as it swept past her.

She stared after him as he continued through the main entrance, exiting the ballroom in long strides. Energy flooded Lily's bloodstream, infusing every corner of her awareness.

She hadn't expected to see him tonight. Was he there for her?

No, of course not. He had his own social responsibilities. It would be the height of foolishness to think he had chosen to attend this particular party because she was there. They had a plan to meet later that night—there was no reason for him to seek her out now.

Such was what the practical side of her brain explained. But the impractical side, the side ruled by instinct and emotion, simply acknowledged that the man she loved had just passed through her vicinity. And she was not content to stand still as he walked away.

"I have to, ah..." she stuttered, having started speaking before knowing what she was going to say. "I have to go..."

"Visit the necessary?" Portia offered dryly.

Lily accepted the excuse readily. "Yes, the necessary."

With a near-desperate breath of hope, Lily took off after the earl.

# *Twenty-five*

Avenell needed to get away.

The pressure of the crowded ballroom, the pressure in his chest, in his head, in his heart…

He couldn't take any more.

When he'd first arrived at the party, no more than thirty minutes earlier, his mood had been light with anticipation. His decision to attend had been based solely on his desire to be near Lily. Though they'd arranged to meet later in the night, he found it difficult to go so many hours without seeing her smile and feeling her presence.

He'd noticed her the moment he stepped into the ballroom.

She had told him once how she had grown accustomed to blending in and going unnoticed beside her sisters or in a crowd. He did not know how it was possible for anyone not to see the treasure that was Lily. Her unique and subtle brand of grace and charm accented her every movement and filled her expression with warmth. Men should be falling at her feet in hopes of gaining her favor.

Avenell found a place along the back wall of the ballroom where he was away from the flow of guests as they moved about. Though he nodded to passing acquaintances, he knew his expression likely warded off any inclinations to converse. He was not here to socialize. He was content to pass the time watching Lily dance, knowing he would have her in his arms before the night was through.

The evenings they had spent together over the previous week made him feel as though he existed in a dream. The physical pleasure stunned him, but not nearly as much as the quiet contentment that wound around him in the hours when they were not making love. The low tones of her voice soothed as they discussed everything from topics of great importance to casual observations of daily life. When she smiled, his chest would fill with something akin to joy, and in her eyes, he saw more depth and understanding than he had ever known before.

He hadn't realized how much that contentment terrified him until he stood in the ballroom, watching as Lily talked and smiled with her partner on the dance floor. She appeared so carefree, so at ease among the other swirling guests.

The lovely image she presented existed in stark contrast to the way Avenell stood stiffly on his own, his back nearly to the wall in an instinctive effort to avoid unintentional contact with people around him.

Fisting his hands at his sides, Avenell shifted his focus to Lily's dance partner, Mr. Arthur Campbell. At the sight of the other man's quiet confidence and staid air of self-possession, Avenell experienced a hot rush of jealousy. Though he'd never felt it before, he knew the emotion instantly by how it twisted his insides and made his blood pump heavy through his veins.

He had no right to such a reaction.

He extended his fingers, then fisted them again, even though the subtle movement was enough to send a series of prickling sensations up his arms. Avenell welcomed the reminder of his affliction, the reason he could not make his way out into the crowd to claim Lily as his own, to take her in his arms as he spun her about the dance floor.

He wanted to. Damn, how he wanted to be the man who took her hand in his to lead her to the center of the crowd. She would smile at him the way she smiled now at Campbell, confident and relaxed as they weaved in and out of the other couples. He would hold her close…

And there his vision ended.

He could not hold her close without flinching with pain. And then everyone would know. They would see his discomfort and his struggle, and Lily's joy would become overshadowed by pity and embarrassment.

Fury at the unfairness of it all flooded through him. Pricks of fire across his skin flared in his agitation, and he shifted on his feet, trying to ease the sensations, but succeeded only in making them worse.

Instinctively, his focus once again sought Lily through the shifting mass of dancers. In his distraction, he hadn't noticed when the song had changed to a waltz. He finally found her twirling about in the arms of a new partner. The sight of Lily's hand resting so casually on the other man's shoulder sent a spear of denial straight to Avenell's heart.

He could not be that man.

He could never be an equal partner to Lily.

Suddenly, his position at the back of the ballroom felt too closed off. He took a long breath in an attempt to calm his rising anxiety, but it remained present in the heightened sensitivity of his skin and the suffocating tightness of his throat.

It had been a mistake to come here. A mistake to think he could observe Lily in this environment without feeling too much.

He shifted his gaze to the exit, and with as much self-control as he could muster, he began to make his way around the outer edge of the ballroom.

But then something shifted in the crowd. There was a collective gasp followed by twittering murmurs as everyone around him made a push toward the dance floor. A group of young ladies excitedly pressed past him, giggling and craning their necks for a glimpse of whatever had caused the dramatic stir.

Panic spiked.

He couldn't breathe from the pressure and the pain caused by repeated contact with the guests moving around him like the rolling waves in a tide pool. His mind spun in his efforts to maintain some semblance of normalcy while his nerves rioted in a way they hadn't done since he was young. In the end, he could do nothing but push back away from the tightening crowd in a desperate attempt to get some space.

In his haste, Avenell did not see the footman with

his tray of champagne until he slammed into the fellow and a blast of fire spread across his back from the sudden contact. Crystal glasses crashed to the floor as the servant lost his balance.

Avenell froze. His muscles locked in position as he stared at the scene he'd caused, waiting for the jeers and sly glares of those around him. The fire raging across his skin was an intense contrast to the ball of ice that formed in his chest. It was his worst fear come to life. Now, everyone would see him for what he was.

A wreck.

An abomination.

Less than a man.

But when he chanced a glimpse around, he noted that although a few people glanced his way in curiosity, whatever had caused their initial swarm to the ballroom floor still held the attention of the majority.

He turned in place and made his way as directly as possible through the shifting crowd to the doorway, clenching his teeth at every brush of contact, refusing to meet the eyes of anyone he passed.

He had almost made his escape when he happened to see the gentle face and lovely form of the woman who had become far more precious to him than he deserved.

And she saw him.

Though he did not allow his attention to rest on her for even a moment as he passed by, he still soaked in the sight of her parted lips and widened eyes when she noticed his swift passing. His stomach clenched as tightly as his fists. God, how he wanted to go to her and draw her softness against his body in a desperate attempt to distract him from the pain he felt inside.

But Avenell kept going. He escaped the ballroom, but he could not escape the truth.

He pushed his tumultuous thoughts of Lily aside and concentrated solely on breathing. He forced air in and out of his lungs, feeling the expansion and contraction as he fisted and extended his hands in practiced synchronization.

He had no mind for where he was heading, only vaguely acknowledging his descent down the main stairs and an instinctive turn down a back hallway that led to a stretch of unoccupied rooms. He turned into the first one, a private study.

Stalking to the large desk set in front of a row of windows, Avenell braced his hands on the desktop. He stared down at his spread fingers and focused on the desk's smooth texture of stretched leather, willing himself to accept and then manage the rioting sensations coursing over his skin.

It took a few minutes to get his physical reaction under control. His emotional turmoil would take much longer to tame. Perhaps forever.

"My lord?"

Fire erupted again at the sound of Lily's voice, but this heat came from within.

He did not turn around, could not acknowledge her presence other than to straighten to his full height, bringing his hands to his sides and lifting his gaze to stare at the windows in front of him.

But then he saw her reflection in the glass.

The ache spreading through him was familiar. It

had been years since he had last felt its unbearable weight, and it carried far more strength now than it ever had in his youth.

She started toward him, and against every urging of self-preservation he possessed, Avenell turned to face her. It took tremendous self-control to shield her from the riot occurring inside him.

"I did not know you were going to be here tonight," she said.

"Neither did I," he replied, his tone abrupt, harsh.

She stopped in front of him. Her pale-green skirts floated against his ankles. He saw it all in her eyes. The longing. The desire. And so much more.

"Avenell." His name was a whisper, a sigh, a sacred vow on her lips.

The ache inside him deepened. He knew what she wanted. Somehow, he always knew. Despite the truth he had to acknowledge, he was unable to deny her.

He lowered his head to take the words from her, pressing his mouth to hers as her eyes fell closed. Lifting his hand, he cradled the side of her face, indulging in the smooth warmth of her cheek against his palm and the way her pulse fluttered where the pad of his little finger rested below her earlobe.

She tilted her head to deepen the kiss, and he responded with a sensual sweep of his tongue.

No matter how many times they had come together in the last couple of weeks, the heat never dissipated. The urgency and the passion seemed only to grow.

It was too much and yet would never be enough.

She began to lean into him, and though he tensed when she pressed against his chest, he did not stop her.

Nor did he object when her hands came up to rest on either side of his lower rib cage. He just breathed more deeply of her scent, allowing the essence that was Lily to overwhelm his senses.

After a few long minutes, he drew back to rest his forehead against hers. He could not resist the temptation of savoring that moment.

He wanted to believe it could always be like this, but he knew better.

She deserved a normal life with a normal man.

If Avenell released her now, she may still make a good match. Mr. Arthur Campbell, for example.

Jealousy raged hot again at the memory of how well suited the two had looked. The thought of another man taking her kisses—accepting her sweet-smelling embraces—filled him with furious regret for the loss of things he could never have.

But his anger, no matter how fierce, could not change what he was.

The stark reminder chilled the fire in his blood like a dousing of ice water, squeezing the breath from his lungs.

This was not going to be easy for either of them.

"Well, isn't this fortuitous."

Lily stiffened so sharply at the sound of Fallbrook's voice that Avenell felt the echoes of the movement through his body.

Looking to where the insolent lord lounged against the doorframe, Avenell acknowledged the utter loathing he had for the man. He released Lily and stepped around her, intentionally positioning himself as a barrier.

"Fallbrook." The hostility was clear in his tone. "You are intruding."

The other man chose to ignore his warning. His heavy-lidded gaze and the swaying motion of his body indicated that he had had too much to drink.

"I expected you to have tired of her by now, Harte. If I had known you would use her for so long," Fallbrook sneered, "I would have bid a little higher."

Rage unlike anything Avenell had ever felt rushed through him at the arrogant declaration. Fallbrook had just made an unforgivable mistake. The fool did not seem to notice.

"I should be incensed, considering all the time I put into her this Season for you to just sweep in and claim the prize." Fallbrook gave a dismissive wave of his hand. "I can be gracious, I suppose. Let me know once you have finished with her, Harte, so I may take my turn."

The furious energy seething through Avenell's body released like a flash of lightning as he lunged for Fallbrook and caught him by the front of his coat with one hand. With his other hand, he grasped the man's throat as he slammed him back against the doorframe. The crack of Fallbrook's head against the wood paneling was distinctly satisfying.

"You have made a vital error, Fallbrook," Avenell stated calmly through his teeth. "If you come within one hundred paces of this woman again, I will kill you."

Fallbrook's stunned eyes bulged as he clawed at Avenell's grip. His strangled sputters and gasps barely filtered through the sound of the blood rushing in Avenell's ears.

Only the shocking pressure of Lily's hand gently resting on the center of his back managed to draw him out of the blind rage.

"Leave him. Please," she whispered.

Avenell looked over his shoulder and saw the concern in her eyes, and the fear.

Dammit, he had not intended to scare her.

"This is not the way," she added.

He released Fallbrook instantly. The man fell to his knees as he coughed and drew long, ragged breaths into his lungs.

As soon as Avenell stepped back, she lowered her hand again. He reached toward her without taking his eyes off Fallbrook as the man struggled to regain his feet. She slipped her hand trustingly into his.

"If I hear you mutter a single breath about that night ever again, there will be nowhere safe for you to hide from the consequences."

Fallbrook pushed to his feet and made a show of brushing the wrinkles from his coat as he watched the earl from the corner of his eye. "I always suspected you were a bit mad, Harte."

"That may be true, for I find I rather enjoyed the feel of my hand around your throat." His voice lowered to a menacing calm. "If you value your dishonorable hide, you will stay away from this woman."

Fallbrook made the mistake of glancing toward Lily. It appeared as though he intended to say something, but the earl had had enough. He took a step forward, and though Lily couldn't see his face, whatever Fallbrook saw there must have been enough to convince him the earl's threat was real.

Fallbrook's eyes widened as he started inching along the wall toward the door, his hands raised in a show of surrender. "I'm done. I swear. No need for further warnings."

When the earl said nothing more, Fallbrook turned and rushed from the room.

As soon as he was gone, Avenell released Lily's hand. The loss of even such a minor connection to her suddenly took on a wealth of meaning. It didn't matter that he was the one who had imposed it.

"Please forget about him," she pleaded softly. "He was a nuisance long before Pendragon's. He has nothing to do with us."

The muscles along Avenell's jaw tensed as he ground his teeth. He could not bring himself to look at her.

"You should go back to the ball."

"I prefer to stay with you," she argued.

He tried to ignore the subtle note of desperation he heard in her voice.

"I was about to leave anyway."

"Take me with you."

"No."

There was a moment of silence following the vehemence of his denial. He could imagine how she must look at that moment. Her eyes soft and confused, her hands reaching.

He tensed from head to toe as she stepped around to stand in front of him, forcing him to look at her. "Tell me what is wrong, my lord. Your distress is obviously about far more than Fallbrook."

She had always seen too much.

He did not reply. He could feel the harshness of his own expression, the coldness in his eyes as he turned away and strode back toward the window. He needed distance.

"I love you."

He stopped instantly, the pain caused by her words making it impossible for him to take another step, another breath. He fisted his hands and somehow found the strength to mutter, "No, you don't."

"You asked me to always be honest with you, and I have. I love you. It is a simple truth."

He couldn't take it. He turned around to glare at her where she stood so quietly composed, her hands clasped in front of her, her smoky eyes trained on him, and her full lips displaying just the slightest quiver.

It was the quiver that convinced him his next words were necessary. Here was proof that this had gone too far. He had always known it could not last. As inevitable as it had been that they had come together, it was just as inevitable that their time would end.

"There is nothing simple about it," he growled fiercely, "and you are dreadfully naive to believe otherwise."

She tipped her head to the side. "Do you think I know nothing of my own heart?" she asked. "Do you think I do not comprehend the challenges inherent in loving you? I know—"

"You know only what I allow you to know," he sneered, his need to protect her making him cruel.

She took two steps toward him. He tensed so sharply that the muscles along his spine seized in a cramp. He welcomed the discomfort. It distracted him from his breaking heart.

"Then explain it me, Avenell. Tell me what happened to make you this way." Her voice was gentle, but a thread of steel ran through it.

It always amazed him how she could be commanding and imploring at once.

He stared at her, knowing he would forever be tormented by the image she presented in that moment. Calm, determined. Filled with compassion and a desire to understand. Filled with love.

He would rather remember her like this than with a look of pity and disappointment distorting her sweet features. That was inevitable. With him, it was always inevitable. He was not and could never be like other men. He could not give her the life she deserved, as his mistress…or wife.

He lowered his gaze.

"I tell you this only so you will see why this cannot go on any longer. Why I am no proper match for anyone."

Her chin lifted as though she wished to defy his statement, but she did not interrupt.

"When I was seven years old, I fell ill with a debilitating sickness. It began as an odd pain and tingling in the hands and feet. Within two weeks, the tingling became a weakness in the muscles that spread from the legs to the upper extremities and sent me to bed. By the third week, all I felt was pain from the back of my head down to the soles of my feet. In my muscles, every inch of my skin. I was terrified I would never be able to move again.

"I could barely swallow and couldn't move my eyes, so I kept them closed most of the time rather than stare constantly at the ceiling. Eventually, even breathing became a difficult endeavor. No one understood what illness had claimed me. Not the doctors, the nurses—certainly not my father. They often thought me asleep, and I would listen to them speak in hushed tones about how I was not expected to ever leave my bed again. Every night they anticipated that I would simply slip into death."

"What a terrifying thing for a child to experience." Her arms were wrapped around her middle, and silent tears rolled down her cheeks. "I am so sorry."

No. Not her pity.

"The odd paralysis went on for months," he continued roughly, anxious to finish, "though it felt like an eternity, when every day I had to fight for the breath to stay alive. Finally, even that turned against me when an infection invaded my lungs. The mindless fever was a relief. And then that too passed. Recovery was slow and painful. It took months—years—to regain my full strength. Some symptoms never went away. I still feel the million pinpricks of fire along my arms, my shoulders, and my chest from even the slightest stimulation. That pain will always be with me, though to this day no physician can tell me why."

She slowly approached him. "There may be a way to lessen the sensations. Perhaps I could—"

"Stop, Lily," he ordered harshly enough that it made her flinch. "There is nothing you can do. I have accepted what I am and what I can never be. I am not normal." He took a long breath through his nose before stating what needed to be said. "I cannot be loved by you."

Her expression tensed. "But you are, my lord. Nothing can stop me from feeling what I feel."

Avenell ground his teeth.

"What do you not understand, Lily? I do not *want* your love. This"—he sneered with a wave of his hand between them—"has always been about lust. You admitted that yourself when you offered yourself to me. It was never about anything more than that."

He threw the hard words at her, needing them to hurt her so she might accept the truth.

Instead, she straightened her spine and leveled him with a stare so open and direct it proved she was a far more courageous and noble human being than he could ever be.

"That is not true," she stated clearly. "It is so much more."

He wanted to believe her. But the reality of the situation could not be changed. *He* could not be changed.

"You are wrong. It is nothing to me," he said as he started for the door.

He needed to get out of there—get away from her before his facade slipped. The only way out of the room was to pass by her position. He schooled his features into a dark scowl and put as much cool disinterest into his voice as he could manage.

"I have no more patience for this conversation. Our relationship existed for one purpose, and that is now done. *We* are done."

From the corner of his eye, he saw her lower her gaze as he passed. Her lips trembled as she spoke one word.

"Avenell."

He directed his gaze forward and kept walking.

Turning down the hallway, he headed away from

the party, taking long, angry, desperate strides until he reached the next room. Slipping through the door, he closed it silently then pressed his forehead hard to the wood. His chest squeezed so tight it was reminiscent of being in the final throes of that illness he would never forget. He fought to deepen and even his breath, but he could do nothing for the savage beating of his heart.

And he welcomed the pain flowing through him. He embraced it as it seeped into every corner of his being, until after a while he grew numb. From the center of his soul to the farthest reach of his breath, he forced that numbness to take over. The deadness was far more comfortable than the tumult of emotion and passion he had experienced since he had spied a quietly bold young lady staring at him with eyes so soft and beckoning.

He did not shift from his spot, holding the door shut until he heard the soft rhythm of steps that had somehow become as precious to him as life itself.

He had chased her away.

He was glad to be rid of her.

As much pain as it caused to hurt her, it had to be done. He had reconciled himself to a lifetime of suffering, but her pain would be temporary. She would survive. She had the support and love of her family. She would move on and marry a noble gentleman and birth beautiful children. It was the life she was meant to have.

She was never intended to be mistress to a broken man.

If he didn't walk away now, she would eventually

realize her error, and the love he would have grown accustomed to, the love he would have started to rely on, would be yanked away. Avenell had survived such cruelty once.

He would not have survived it again. Not from Lily.

# Twenty-six

Lily curled up in her bed, but she did not sleep. Her body hurt from head to toe. Her head pounded with unshed tears, and her throat was tight. She could barely breathe past the emotion compressing her lungs.

She tried to steady her breath, tried to soak up warmth from the bedcovers to ease the ice in her blood. But she kept getting caught on involuntary sobs, and she was quite certain she would never be warm again.

Though the earl had spoken of his affliction in a monotone, devoid of emotion, his pain had been evident in his rigid stance and in everything left unsaid. She sensed the helplessness he could not admit to still carrying with him. Her very bones ached for how he had suffered.

His expression had been merciless when he had strode past her and out the door. She would have given anything in that moment for the freedom to reach out to him, to wrap her arms around him to keep him from leaving, so she could hold him to her breast until her love soothed away every lingering hurt.

But she couldn't. All she had been able to do was stand there with her hands clasped together so tightly her knuckles became bruised while her heart shattered.

He had refused her love. For all the trust she had put in him, he had not been able to trust her in return.

Understanding that was the most painful part. She believed everything she had said to him. She knew in her heart there existed a possibility for something amazing. But he needed to believe as well.

And hours later, she still lay huddled beneath her blankets. Dawn had long ago lightened her bedroom when a downstairs maid, the same who had delivered her perfume weeks ago, brought up a note.

Lily had not wanted to take it. Had not wanted to read the words she knew she would find in Avenell's strong, slanted script. But she also knew she would never accept the truth unless she saw it written out for her in his stark language.

*Though our arrangement has come to an end, the money in your account will remain available to you as long as you need it. I am sorry.*

She had hated him in that moment. Hated him with a fire that spread through her belly.

But it was a reactionary emotion and did not last. Eventually, she turned her anger back on herself.

Surely, there had to be something she could have done differently, something she should have done to inspire his trust. His affection.

His note was so final. So detached. Except for

those last words, and she clung to those words like a fragile lifeline.

He was sorry.

For what, she wondered. Sorry for all of it? Sorry he couldn't accept her love? Or sorry he had ever opened her up to the dream of what could have existed between them?

Everything in her rejected his claim that the only thing between them was lust and that their affair had simply run its course. Down in the depths of her marrow, she knew he was still holding something back.

She wanted so badly to return to him and beg him to take from her whatever he needed. If he felt only lust for her, then so be it. Her body, her love, and her passion were his, would always be his. She wanted that to be enough.

Very simply, it wasn't.

Not for him.

It was not enough for her either.

She squeezed her eyes shut in the quiet of her bedroom, trying to hold back the tears as she swallowed hard on the lump in her throat. Her heart was empty. The deep, hollow aching inside her had never been so gaping, so dark and relentless.

As painful as it was, she had to accept the truth.

Lily wanted more than to be his mistress, a woman who eased his lust but was not allowed to soothe his soul.

She deserved more.

And so, despite her heartache, she lay still and unmoving, wondering how she would go through that day, and the next, and the next, without him.

"Lily?"

The sound of Portia's voice pushed into Lily's awareness. She closed her eyes, craving solitude.

"Lily," her sister stated more firmly as she approached the bed.

Portia was not likely to go away until she accomplished what she was there for. Lily opened her eyes with a scowl.

"What do you want, Portia? I am trying to sleep."

Portia had come around to the side of the bed. She looked at Lily with an arched black brow as she planted her hands on her hips. "It is already past noon. You have never slept this late in your life. And you look horrid."

"I feel horrid." Lily emphasized her words by pulling the blankets over her head.

"What happened last night, Lily?" Portia's tone lowered empathetically. "I saw how distraught you were when you came back to the ballroom. I know it was not a sudden migraine that sent you home early. Please tell me. Perhaps I can help."

Lily wished she could open the floodgates and confess all to her sister. But she couldn't. It was still too raw, too deep.

"I am sorry, Portia. I just need to be alone. Please leave me be."

"I cannot," Portia replied.

She took hold of the bedcover and lifted it enough to slip in beside Lily before she drew it back over both their heads, enveloping them in a makeshift sanctuary.

The sisters lay facing each other under the privacy of the bedcovers.

"A caller has arrived for you," Portia said. "You must make an appearance downstairs."

"A caller?" Lily groaned. She could not imagine speaking with anyone today, or ever again.

"He is currently being entertained by Angelique, Emma, and Mr. Bentley, so you have a little time to ready yourself, but not much."

"Mr. Bentley?" That managed to prick Lily's curiosity.

Portia grinned a particularly naughty little grin. "In leaving early last night, you missed the delightful scandal that erupted, involving our very responsible and decorous sister."

"What happened?" Lily asked, grateful for the opportunity to be distracted from her despair. It suddenly felt dreadfully important that Emma managed to claim her happiness.

"I shall not tell you just now, but I do believe Mr. Bentley spent last night in Emma's bedroom."

Lily gasped. "You must be joking."

"They might have gotten away with no one becoming aware of it, but I happened to be awake to witness Emma sneaking the poor man out of the house just after dawn. He must have gone home to change clothes, then came right back again to join us for breakfast. Angelique is thrilled by his handsome company, as you can imagine." Portia laughed. "And you will not believe the change in Emma this morning. It is quite astonishing."

"Astonishing," Lily breathed.

"Now," Portia said sternly, her expression shifting to one of concern and determination. "It is time for you to get out of bed and join us. Mr. Campbell is anxiously awaiting your appearance."

Mr. Campbell.

"Oh no," Lily whispered as she recalled the bits of conversation they had had while dancing the night before. Something about him coming to call and wanting both Emma and Angelique to be present. Oh God! He was going to make an offer.

"Yes, I can see you understand," Portia said as she flipped back the covers, exposing them both. "Up with you, dear sister, your suitor awaits."

Though Lily did not move, she acknowledged that she would need to do as Portia had said. She would have to face Mr. Campbell and find some way to let the sweet man down nicely. She had no desire to hurt him, but she could not accept an offer from him.

She could not accept an offer from anyone.

Portia leaned forward again, drawing Lily's gaze. The younger woman's eyes held a wealth of empathy and reflected a maturity Lily had not witnessed in her sister before.

"I understand," Portia whispered. "You will need to put things to rights soon enough, but first you must deal with Mr. Campbell. Then you can focus on… the other."

Lily scowled in confusion. The gleam in Portia's eyes seemed far too knowing just then.

She couldn't possibly…

"Now, up," Portia said as she rolled gracefully to her feet. "I shall advise your dear Mr. Campbell that you will be down shortly. I would wager you have about twenty minutes before your delay will be perceived as quite rude."

If not for having had the night she just did, Lily would have considered her interview with Mr. Campbell to be the most difficult thing she would ever have to endure. Still, it was likely to be challenging in the extreme. Mainly because he was such a kind man and did not deserve the rejection Lily needed to deliver. If only she had been more aware, more thoughtful in her interactions with him, she might have found a way to dissuade him before it got to this point.

But she had been distracted in the last weeks. As was evidenced even more by the sight of Emma wearing a smile the likes of which Lily had never witnessed. Her older sister was nothing less than ecstatic, sitting beside a very relaxed and pleased-looking Mr. Bentley.

Lily expected Emma would have news of upcoming nuptials to impart to the family once their caller departed. The thought helped to put a smile on Lily's face as she greeted her suitor.

"A pleasure to see you, Mr. Campbell."

The older gentleman took her hand and bowed low.

Lily took a seat, and they all recommenced with small talk, but Lily could tell by Angelique's animated expression and Emma's speculative glances that Mr. Campbell may have already indicated to them the purpose of his visit. The mood in the room was far too anticipatory. Lily wished Portia had come down to the parlor with her. Her younger sister's exuberance surely would have added some needed distraction just then.

Lily's palms began to sweat. She really did not relish the idea of issuing a rejection.

But she could do nothing else.

Mr. Campbell turned to her with a smile. "Miss Lily, if you do not mind, I wonder if you would allow me a private moment of your time?"

Lily smiled in return, though her ears grew hot and her tongue sat thick in her mouth. "Of course, Mr. Campbell. That is, if my great-aunt does not object."

She turned to Angelique, who rose to her feet rather quickly. "Not at all, darling. Take all the time you need," she said with a grin before sashaying from the room.

Mr. Bentley offered his hand to Emma, who took it so naturally it was obvious how physically attuned the two were to each other. The sight was painful and beautiful at once.

Emma looked at her with a studied gaze as she said, "We shall be just a few minutes."

Lily nodded and watched as they left the room. Emma drew the door closed behind them, allowing at least a four-inch gap for the sake of propriety.

Lily had no idea what she was going to say and prayed the right words would come as needed. She dreaded such confrontations, and the subtle throbbing in her head started to make itself more known.

Mr. Campbell turned toward her on the sofa they shared and cleared his throat. His smile was easy, and his brown eyes met hers with open affection.

Lily felt a deep pulse of awareness for how different things could have turned out. If she had never spied Avenell across the ballroom… If she had never been abducted and taken to Pendragon's… If her father had never seen fit to take a loan from Hale…

So many ifs, yet one thing was certain—Lily's heart was inexorably claimed, whether the man who held it wanted it or not. She could not fathom promising herself to anyone when she had so fully given herself to another.

"Miss Chadwick, you must know I hold you in very high regard," Mr. Campbell was saying. "It has been a delight to count you as an acquaintance. As I mentioned last evening, I am very pleased by the way our friendship has developed over the course of this Season."

He paused then with a lifted brow, as though waiting for Lily's acknowledgment.

She nodded and took a breath to interrupt, but he continued, his words flowing as though they had been diligently rehearsed.

"I do not believe my purpose in calling on you today is likely to be much of a surprise."

"Mr. Campbell," Lily said, finally finding her voice.

"I have come to the conclusion that I am of an age when it is most appropriate for me to take a wife."

"Mr. Campbell," Lily said again, but he seemed not to hear her. She pressed her fingers to her temples as her headache became more pronounced.

"I have had in mind someone of demure and polite temperament. A lady with a moderate degree of prettiness who is also in possession of adequate intelligence so as to contribute to engaging conversation."

"Mr. Campbell, please allow me—"

"It was important that I find someone with the same mild nature as myself. I have no desire for theatrics or unnecessary passions in a life mate." He gave her a pleasant smile. "As I am sure you would agree, such things are tiresome."

Lily shook her head. What an awful match they would have made.

"Please, Mr. Campbell, I would ask that you go no further."

"But I must, my dear. You see, it would be my greatest pleasure if you would consider honoring me by accepting a position as my wife."

Lily clenched her teeth against the pounding in her skull. It had been said. He had offered for her hand. Now she had to turn him down in as delicate a way as she could manage.

"Mr. Campbell, I am quite flattered by your offer, but I am afraid I cannot accept it."

The poor man stared at her for a moment as though he wasn't certain he had heard her right. Then he blinked a few times.

"I do not understand. I was under the impression that you would welcome such a suit." His tone was filled with confusion and injured pride. "I assure you, I do not make my offer lightly."

"I am sorry, Mr. Campbell. It is difficult to explain."

"Perhaps you just need some time," he suggested. "I would be agreeable to a long engagement. There is no need to rush."

Lily shifted uncomfortably. This was proving to be more difficult than she had imagined. She did not want to hurt the man, but she could not accept him.

"Have I done something in particular to dissuade you?" he asked.

She shook her head. "No, please, it is not you, Mr. Campbell. It is just that..." Her tongue became hopelessly tangled.

"Is there something more I can offer you?"

"No, I—" She closed her eyes for a moment, but it only intensified the pain in her head.

"I would have thought my offer generous enough, considering your lack of dowry and your family's limited prospects. You should be grateful I considered you for such an important position," he declared before his expression turned disapproving. "This reticence is quite unattractive."

Lily had had enough. Her head felt like it intended to split in two, and her eyes had started to burn with the pain of it. She finally said the only words she knew would conclude the discussion immediately. "I am no maiden."

Oh no! Shock momentarily distracted her from the pounding in her head. What had she just said?

Campbell's eyes widened. He gave a short cough.

Lily had just a moment to acknowledge how much Portia would have loved to witness such a scene of collapsed etiquette before her ears burned red with embarrassment and she stumbled on in explanation.

"I am deeply sorry, Mr. Campbell, to confess something so indelicate and…shocking. It is just that I do value your friendship, and I think you are a wonderful man." Though his response to her refusal was starting to make her question that opinion. "I would not want you to believe my refusal of your *generous* proposal has anything to do with you when it is, in fact, due to my own actions."

He rose to his feet as she spoke and walked slowly around the sofa, as though taking some time to absorb what she had said. Lily waited with outward patience while inside, her nerves ran riotously. When he turned back to face her, she did her best not to cringe at the denunciation in his expression.

"Miss Chadwick, I admit I am rather taken aback by your confession." He grasped his hands behind his back and lifted his chin. "I had not expected you to reveal such a colossal moral failure. You disguise your perfidy well."

His words were meant to shame her, but Lily found herself growing angry instead. That a woman could be so swiftly and completely condemned for a behavior that men accepted as their right grated on her raw nerves.

"Mr. Campbell," she began, but stopped as she realized that defending herself would only succeed in exacerbating the situation. "I apologize for any distress or inconvenience I have caused you."

He acknowledged her apology with a nod. "I suppose I should be grateful for your honesty on the matter. Indeed, I shall count myself lucky. You may rest assured that I shall not spread tales of your sordid behavior. Such would be beneath me. Please do not bother to see me out." He offered an abbreviated bow before he turned and left without another word.

"Well, that was wretched," Lily muttered beneath her breath before she fell back against the couch and pressed her eyes closed against the burning behind her lids. Her headache was almost welcome in that moment, as it distracted from the pain in her heart.

At least it was over. Mr. Campbell would likely never speak to her again. She had never suspected him of being such a prude.

*Moral failure.*

Avenell had not considered her passion to be a moral failure.

Yet he too had walked away from her without a good-bye.

# Twenty-seven

"There is a woman here to see you, my lord."

The Earl of Harte did not bother to glance up from the dying coals glowing in the grate. His snuffbox rolled through his fingers in a constant pattern. In his other hand was a glass of warmed brandy—his second of the night. He had spent every night for more than a week in the comfortable shadows of his private study.

Though Keene's deportment was never anything but impeccably stoic, he heard the hint of censure in the way his butler said *woman*.

"I have no desire for company, Keene. Whoever it is, send her away."

"I am afraid I must insist upon an audience, my lord."

Avenell tensed at the familiar, sultry tones of Madam Pendragon, but he still did not look up from the flickering dance of glowing red against charred black.

"My lord?" Keene's question hung in the air.

"I know my presence here at your home is rather intrusive, but I promise I shall take only a few moments of your time," Pendragon added smoothly.

Avenell gave a nod. He heard Keene back from the room and then the rustle of bombazine and silk as the madam came forward. A gentleman would stand to greet her properly, but he remained where he was, sitting stiffly in the leather wingback chair, his feet braced on the floor, his gaze straight ahead.

If the woman expected courtesy when she invaded his private space uninvited, she would be waiting a long time.

"Do you mind if I join you for a drink, my lord?" There was amusement in her tone.

"As you wish."

A few moments later, the madam crossed in front of him, a snifter in hand. Rather than taking a seat, she walked to the fireplace where she turned to face him. He wondered briefly if she had remained standing to throw emphasis on his discourtesy or if she simply preferred the more dominant position.

He noted that she wore a long black pelisse over her gown, and a veiled hat sat perched jauntily on her blond head. The veil had been pushed back, and she stared at him with a curious glint in her green eyes.

"State your purpose, madam. I am not in the mood for extended company."

She smiled. "I can see that, my lord. My purpose in coming here tonight is to discover why."

Avenell frowned, not appreciating the cryptic response.

The madam arched a brow and sighed. "It has come to my attention that you have not visited your private suite in more than a week. Has the accommodation not been to your satisfaction?"

He shifted his attention back to the fire. Such an inquiry certainly did not warrant a personal visit. "The suite is fine. I have no further use for it."

"And the girl?"

He stiffened sharply at her audacity, the movement causing a prickle of fire across his skin.

Not waiting for him to respond, Pendragon made a graceful gesture with her brandy as she continued, "Forgive me for being so forward, my lord, but I have never been known for my subtleties. I feel the girl is somewhat my responsibility, since my actions put her into your hands. Have you discarded her so soon?"

Rising swiftly to his feet, Avenell slid his snuffbox into his pocket and downed the last of his brandy before striding to the side bar to pour himself another.

"You overstep, madam," he growled in reply.

"I think not."

Avenell turned to face her. Despite her languid posture, there was a hardness in her expression.

"Your concern is rather belated, don't you think?" he replied coldly. "The girl would have been far better served if she had never come under your influence."

The madam's eyes narrowed. "Perhaps, but circumstances beyond her control, or mine, placed her in my keeping. I did what I could to protect her from further harm and provide her with a possibility for future happiness. I believed in you to take care of the rest, my lord."

"Then you put your faith in the wrong man."

She smiled. "Again, I disagree."

Avenell's anger was too close to the surface to endure much more of Pendragon's conversation. "I do not give a damn," he snapped. "The truth cannot be changed. Whatever you had intended failed. The affair was doomed to disaster from the start."

Pendragon stalked toward him, an uncharacteristic frown marring her smooth brow. "You cannot possibly be so obtuse, my lord."

He ground his back teeth but said nothing.

"Tell me you did not spend all of those nights with her and never spread her thighs to claim your prize."

A growl of fury rumbled from his chest at the crudity in her words, but the sound did not seem to bother Pendragon one bit.

She actually laughed at his response. "Of course you did, my lord, as I knew you would. It was the final barrier you had yet to cross in your search for pleasure."

"It signifies nothing."

Her green eyes glittered. "It signifies everything."

The woman turned away from him and strode toward the chair he had recently vacated. With a swish of her skirts, she turned and lowered herself gracefully. Tipping her head, she looked at him with a superior little half smile.

"What did you feel when you took possession of your gentle maiden?"

Her words might have been mocking if not for her expression, which had settled into one of patient nonjudgment. It was the same way she had looked at him the first time he had gone to her.

"Think carefully. What did you feel?"

Avenell's gut tensed as he involuntarily recalled the sensations of being buried within Lily's warmth and softness. He relived in his mind the way their naked bodies moved together, heard her endless gasps and moans echo, felt the overwhelming heat, the pervading pleasure. Every time they came together it was intense and consuming, obliterating everything else in existence.

That was the problem. He always felt too much with her.

And despite that, he had never been able to shake his yearning for more.

"Was there pain, my lord?" Pendragon's question intruded into Avenell's thoughts.

He glanced up from where he had been staring with unseeing eyes at carpet beneath his feet.

"No," he answered roughly. His pain did not intrude while he made love to Lily.

It was only afterward that his nerves rebelled in force. Often leaving him shaken and breathless as he fought to regain control. That was when reality would return, and Avenell had not been able to escape the certainty that he would never have the kind of normalcy he craved. The pain that accompanied that conviction had gone beyond the physical and had been more debilitating than his affliction had ever been.

"And what does that tell you?" she pressed as though she were a governess intent upon drilling some incomprehensible lesson into her pupil's stubborn brain.

Avenell grew frustrated. Yes, he had felt true pleasure with Lily, the kind that he never expected to feel again. But there was far more at stake than sexual release.

"It tells me nothing to change the fact that she is better off without me."

"That may be true, my lord, or it may not. Such

is for the lady to decide, I would think." She rose gracefully to her feet and drained her snifter of the expensive brandy in one long swallow before sending him a flickering glance filled with meaning. "What you should be considering very carefully is whether or not you are better off without her."

After setting her empty glass aside, she lifted her hands to draw the veil down over her face once again, adding, "Though I do appreciate your business, my lord, I will completely understand if you choose not to visit my establishment in the future. I shall leave you to the rest of your evening."

Avenell barely acknowledged her departure. He remained frozen in place for a long time afterward.

Was he better off in this state of regret and constant longing?

Better off than what? The potential for loss? The fear of rejection? The frustration of never truly being like other men? The unflagging certainty that he would never be able to give her everything she deserved?

*She is better off without me.*

*Such is for the lady to decide, I would think.*

Details of the woman herself began to penetrate his thoughts. The generosity in her smile. Her gentle, open gaze. The way she had told him her secrets with trust and honesty, her compassion, and her quiet, understated courage.

And before he so effectively and willfully crushed it, he recalled the glimmer of hope she had inspired in him. The hope he had stripped away before it could settle too deeply in his being.

So many times, he had sensed in her a desire to push

their intimacy further. He had seen the yearning in her eyes and ignored it. He had witnessed the countless times she reached for him and then held back. He had been grateful for her restraint. He had been a coward.

He understood that she had known better all along. She had understood what was missing between them.

Rather than having the courage to explore those feelings—instead of trusting in her and her love—he had forced her away.

The truth was so clear.

From the very beginning, she had belonged to him, but not as a mistress belonged to her protector.

Lily was his as his soul was his. Just as he was hers.

She was a part of him. He was a part of her. He could not exist without her. And if he loved her, he *had* to trust that she had spoken the truth when she had said she wanted him, flaws and all.

He did. He *did* trust her.

He swept his gaze to the clock on the mantel.

It was not terribly late. She may still be at Lord Somersby's reception. He needed to speak with her immediately. Now that he understood, he could not allow another moment to pass without finding her and telling her every bit of what he had been keeping from her. He had to make up for his lack of trust.

He prayed she would give him that chance.

Dashing into the hall, he called for Keene to order his carriage.

When he had gone about acquiring a list of all the invitations the Chadwicks had accepted, it had been with the intention of ensuring he did not inadvertently encounter Lily. He needn't have bothered, since he had not left his house since the last time he had seen her.

But he was grateful for his foresight, since he knew exactly where to look for her.

Or at least he had thought he did.

Twenty minutes later, to his deep frustration and distress, he crossed from the Somersbys' drawing room to their conservatory in rushed strides, his gaze sweeping over every occupant. From there he explored each of the smaller individual parlor rooms and then the library, the billiard room, even the host's study in a desperate search for a glimpse of her rich, brown hair and generous smile. But every minute of searching only increased his anxiety and impatience as he found no evidence of Lily or the other members of her family anywhere. If she had been at the Somersby party at all, she had left early.

But just to be sure, he stayed at the reception another hour, making repeated rounds of every room.

Finally, dejected and angry for the wasted time, he realized he was not going to see her that night.

He would need to call on her at her home and somehow find a way to speak with her privately. He just hated that it would have to wait until tomorrow.

Morose but determined, he returned home. Keene greeted him at the door, taking his hat and overcoat as he always did. When Avenell would have started toward the stairs to retire in the quiet darkness of his bedroom, the butler cleared his throat.

"You have another caller, my lord. I told her you were not at home, but the young lady insisted upon waiting." The elderly servant pursed his long features. "She is in the library."

Just as Avenell had detected the unspoken information in Keene's introduction of Madam Pendragon, he understood what the butler did not say about this visitor, and he knew in a flash of certainty and elation that it was Lily.

She had come to him.

# Twenty-eight

Lily's stomach tightened with trepidation. She had not considered the possibility that the earl would not be at home when she had made the decision to speak with him.

His butler had given her an odd look when he had answered her knock. Though he had likely been roused from his bed, he appeared in perfect attire. When he informed her the earl was not home, she felt her courage trying to flee, but she caught it in time. This was far too important to turn tail at the slightest bit of conflict. She stood firm and insisted upon waiting.

With a disdainful nod, the butler let her in and led her to a handsome library and lit just enough candles to cast an uneven glow into the room.

Lily was too anxious to sit, so she stood where the butler left her, staring at the doorway, twisting her hands beneath her cloak. She had no idea what she would say. She knew only one thing—she was no longer content to allow life to happen around her. It was past time for her to claim some of her own momentum if she was to get what she desired most.

He had broken her heart. She had never felt the kind of devastation she had experienced when he had rejected the love she offered. But even that had not been as bad as contemplating his absence from the rest of her life.

She simply hadn't been able to do it.

The days without him had been unbearable, but she had gotten through them with the very basic belief that it could not possibly be over. Everything she had ever felt for him still thrived within her, had perhaps even grown stronger.

Tonight, she was determined to discover if any chance remained. She had to know if he could ever learn to trust her and want her in the way she wanted him. Completely. Forever.

It seemed like an age passed before she heard a sound in the hall. She stared at the door, half expecting to see the butler returning to show her out.

Instead, Avenell entered the room, carrying himself with purpose, his steps long and determined. His midnight eyes were locked upon her, as though she were the only thing in existence.

The intensity of his focus lit her body with thousands of tiny sparks. Her breath stopped. Her insides melted from just being in his presence, though her trepidation refused to ease.

For a moment, she feared she had conjured him from the heart of her deepest longing.

But longing alone could not account for the riot of emotions within her.

"You should not be here, Lily."

She was encouraged by his tone. He would not sound so harsh if he felt nothing.

"I do not think propriety need be an issue between us now. Not after what we have shared," she added in a quiet murmur. "I had to speak with you."

"What happened between us…" His eyes darkened to black. "I made a mistake—"

"No," Lily stated loudly, cutting him off. Her heart gave a heavy lurch. "Do not say that."

"It is the truth."

A chill ran through her at his matter-of-fact tone. Uncertainty threatened to take hold, but she forced it away. She could not risk anything less than her full conviction tonight.

Before she could find the words to deny his statement, he added, "I understand Arthur Campbell offered for your hand."

Lily stiffened at the abrupt change in topic. "How do you know of that?"

His brows furrowed. "Is it true?"

"I refused him."

"Because you had been my mistress," he stated bluntly.

"Yes." *And because I love you.* "It was an anticipated consequence. I accepted that I would never marry when I agreed to our arrangement."

"I should not have forced you to such a decision," he said, his eyes lowering briefly before meeting hers again. "I should have taken you straight home that night." There was more than regret in his voice as he added, "I never should have used you the way I did."

He seemed intent upon regret. She had to find a way to alter the direction of his focus.

Frustration made her reckless. Tilting her chin at

a mutinous angle, she held his gaze as she replied, "Do you forget? I offered myself to you. I practically begged you to take me."

He stood in silence as she spoke, all hard angles and stonelike strength. Rigid with control.

She slowly walked toward him. "I agreed to our affair willingly. Eagerly. I thought you did as well. Do not dare twist what happened between us into something ugly, Avenell. I will not allow it." Coming to a stop, she left enough space between them that she would be unable to reach for him if tempted. "I am worth more than that."

"Infinitely more." His voice was barely more than a raw whisper. His eyes were shadowed and deep beneath his furrowed brow.

"And so are you," Lily stated firmly, her heart beating fiercely against her ribs.

"Lily." He spoke her name with a deep resonance that went straight to her center. "You misunderstand."

"How do I misunderstand?" she asked, her voice intentionally challenging. "What am I not comprehending, Avenell?"

There was a long pause. The muscles in his jaw tensed, and his hands fisted at his sides. Lily ached for the strain she read in every line of his frame.

"I came looking for you tonight."

His words startled her. She wasn't sure what she had expected him to say, but it certainly hadn't been that. "You did? Why?"

Emotion seethed beneath his unyielding manner. Passion, fear, life, and love existed there. Everything she had ever wanted was within him—still out of reach.

"Tell me, Avenell. Trust me."

He shook his head, his eyes never leaving her face. "If you come with me, I will show you."

He held his hand out to her, and she did not hesitate. She only wished she had removed her gloves so she could feel his bare skin against hers.

He led her from the library and across the hall in long strides. It took a few seconds before her feet caught up with her heart, and she quickened her steps to match his frightfully determined pace.

Without a word, they ascended the stairs side by side. Lily flicked a glance at his profile and her belly fluttered with a wonderful sort of anticipation when she noted how tensely his jaw was clenched and how his gaze was fiercely trained forward. His sudden impatience roused the desire that never stayed below a simmer for long when he was near.

They continued down the hall and into his bedroom, where a low-banked fire warmed the room and cast dancing shadows against the walls.

Entering the room, Lily was struck by the changes that had been wrought since she had last been there on the night of her abduction. Though his massive four-poster bed remained, the coverings were now a mixture of midnight blue and a mysterious smoky gray. In fact, various shades of gray had been added throughout the room. The two heavy leather chairs had been beautifully reupholstered in a dove-gray damask, a plush rug in a light and misty color was laid before the fireplace, and on a delicate table between them stood a large vase of lilies, infusing the room with their delicate scent.

"Do you see?" the earl asked from behind her.

Once they entered the bedroom, he had released her hand to close the door, ensconcing them together in the private space. Lily turned to watch him walk toward one of the new chairs. He ran his fingers over the fabric.

"The color of your eyes when you are quiet and content," he stated in a low voice, then he crossed to the bed where he smoothed his palm over a velvet coverlet. "This is the darker shade your eyes become when you are aroused—with emotion or desire."

He looked at her, and Lily's world expanded on a sudden breath at what she saw in the depth of his gaze.

They both seemed rooted in place, standing in the center of his bedroom, staring at each other with their breaths coming fast and their focus locked upon each other, as though they were equally afraid the other might disappear.

"You exist in everything. You have become a part of me," he murmured thickly. "I cannot breathe without you."

Though her body trembled from head to toe with a raw welling of emotion, Lily remained where she was. She bit hard on her lower lip to temper her elation. Too much false hope had the potential to crush her.

"This cannot be like before," she said, amazed she managed to keep her composure when so much inside her was urgently demanding expression. "You hurt me."

The firm lines and familiar shadows of his face grew fiercer than she had ever seen. His gaze bored into her soul.

"I know, and I am sorry. I made so many mistakes with you. Give me a chance to make it right."

As he spoke, something in him shifted. Though his arms remained stiffly at his sides, Lily felt him reaching for her in silent, invisible yearning.

"Touch me, Lily." His voice was a raw, heavy whisper.

When she did not reply, the proud tilt of his head fell a notch, and he gave a weighted sigh. "I *need* you to touch me," he muttered, and in his tone was an essence of desperation she knew intimately.

Lily took several long breaths to calm the riot inside her. Slowly, she walked toward him. She stopped within a sigh of pressing her body to his. Holding his gaze, she lifted her hand first to his face and laid her palm gently along the rough texture of his jaw.

His eyes darkened, and his jaw tensed beneath her palm. But he said nothing.

"Are you sure this is what you want?" she asked softly.

"More than I have ever been sure of anything in my life." His voice was raw and bare. "Lily. Please..."

Dizzy with emotion, Lily swallowed past the thickness in her throat as she lifted her other hand to frame his face. Rising on her tiptoes, she was careful to keep from touching him anywhere else as she breathed a sigh across his lips.

Still looking into his eyes, she pressed her mouth to his.

Even there in his lips, she felt his rigidity. He wanted her to touch him, but it would not be easy for him. His fear and caution were long ingrained.

But she could be patient. She would not be deterred. She had every intention of showing him what was possible between them, even if it took all night. Or the rest of their lives.

Tilting her head, she fitted her lips more intimately with his. With infinite care, she enticed his lips to soften. She pressed sweet kisses to the corners of his mouth, then to the center of his full bottom lip. All the while, she looked into his eyes.

Heat flared inevitably between them. She focused on increasing it, expanding his reaction, encouraging him to trust her. Desire flickered brightly in the depths of his eyes. She coaxed it to greater life with a gentle, teasing flick of her tongue.

His lips parted for her. His breath mingled with hers. Lily deepened the kiss.

A harsh sound came from the back of his throat, and he slid his tongue forward to tangle with hers. Lily's breath came short, her insides melting with anticipation.

Despite the desperate longing tightening her chest, Lily drew back and dropped down onto her heels. With a fleeting brush of her thumb over his perfect lower lip, she lowered her hands. In slow, deliberate movements, she slid her fingers beneath the edges of his coat, pushing it back over his shoulders. She continued down along his arms until the coat slid free. She allowed it to fall unheeded to the floor at their feet.

Looking to his face, she saw his eyes were closed and his hands had curled into fists at his sides. His tension wrapped around her heart. She studied his features, the way the firelight accentuated the sharp angles and subtle curves she loved so much.

She removed his waistcoat and then his cravat, always acutely aware of keeping a certain distance between them. She intended to take this slow. Very slow. Moment by moment, she would show him, through every tender caress and patient breath, how a lover's touch should feel.

The muscles of his neck were tightly corded where they sloped to his shoulders. His pulse beat fast and heavy at the base of his throat. She wanted to press her hands to the heat of his skin, feel his thrumming pulse beneath her fingers.

But she restrained that urge for now.

Instead, with the neck of his shirt loosened, she grasped the fine silk at his sides to tug it free of his breeches. Before she could try to remove the garment herself, he broke from his frozen stance. He reached his hand back over his shoulder to crush a handful of the silk in his fist and dragged the shirt up over his head.

Lily paused on a ragged breath, admiring the sight of his bared chest and rippled abdomen. He was so strong, so tightly contained. Muscle and bone formed a rigid structure—a beautiful design of masculinity. It was hard to imagine the pain and vulnerability that had resided beneath such strength for so long.

After a few long breaths, she glanced up at his face.

He stared back at her, his gaze shielded and intense.

"Will you sit, please, my lord," she said gently.

He stepped back and lowered himself into one of the gray chairs.

Lily sank to her knees before him, keeping her head bowed as she removed his boots and stockings. She set them aside and lifted her eyes again to greedily soak in the sight of him.

His bare feet were planted firmly into the plush carpet. His legs were bent at the knees and were spread wide. She trailed her gaze over the surface of his strong thighs, curling her fingers into her palms, resisting the urge to test the taut muscles there. Above the waistband of his breeches, she noted the tightness of his abdomen and the way his short and fierce breaths expanded and contracted his rib cage.

The pull of his brows shadowed his eyes, which had narrowed to slits. The line of his jaw was harshly angled; his lips were slightly parted.

"I love you," she confessed in a quiet murmur. Something flickered deep in his eyes, and his hands gripped the arms of the chair, but he said nothing. "I have loved you from the moment I saw you through the crowd. My heart and soul already knew you. My body yearned for you. My whole life began in your arms." Emotion made her voice thick, and she paused to force breath around her resolute hope. "I would give anything for you to feel what I feel when I am with you. I would give anything for you to trust me…just long enough for me to show you how beautiful your passion is to me."

He rolled his lips in against the tip of his tongue, wetting them to speak. But when he took a breath, no words came out.

Lily rose to her feet. Holding his gaze, she took a step back.

Just as she had done numerous times before, she undressed for him.

Except tonight, she made use of all she had learned

since becoming his mistress. She knew he enjoyed the full thrust of her breasts, so she made sure to arch a bit more as she reached behind her for the buttons of her gown. When the dress fell away from her body, she allowed her fingers to drift over her bared skin, caressing the curve of her shoulders, trailing down her arms before smoothing over her hips.

The heat of his gaze touched every bit of flesh revealed, sought out every shadow, and burned through her thin shift. And then her shift too was dropped to the floor. Standing in just the stockings and garters he had bought her, she moved her hands over her thighs, up over her belly, and finally to her breasts. She lifted them, testing their weight and fullness, brushing her thumbs over the nipples until they puckered, sending delightful shocks of pleasure through her center.

He watched her, every bit of him tense and hard.

Then finally, she brought her hands up to release the pins from her hair. The silken tresses fell down her back, the wispy ends teasing the top curve of her buttocks as she stood proudly before him.

With swift, animalistic grace, he rose to his feet.

Lily held her breath. Her heart beat wild and unfettered. Her body hummed with desire—and more.

"You told me once that trust must be earned," he said in a gravelly tone thick with emotion, "yet you have given me yours from the start. You may not believe me, but you have mine as well. It is myself I am so unsure of."

"You do not have to be," Lily replied quickly. "Not with me."

She stepped toward him. Holding his gaze, she lifted her hands to rest them on either side of his lean waist. He did not start or flinch from her touch, and she smiled.

"Lily."

The murmur of her name slid into a swift inhale as she trailed the fingertips of one hand across his belly just above the band of his breeches. His lips parted, and his breath puffed in an irregular rhythm. Lily rested her fingers over the fastening of his breeches and paused. She tilted her head in a silent question. Without hesitation, he nodded, though the movement was jerky and stiff.

Lily was gentle but quick as she loosened his breeches and pushed them down past his hips, easing her hands over his tense buttocks. She watched him from beneath her lashes. He was aroused. That much was blatantly evident and overwhelmingly beautiful.

Heat curled potently in her loins, initiating a pulse of need more poignant than anything she had previously experienced.

Despite his physical desire, he was not relaxed. Tension still rode high through his body.

She appreciated the difficulty he had in allowing her such access. And she was determined to prove his trust was not misplaced.

She crouched before him to assist in removing the breeches completely.

When she straightened, they stood naked together. Facing each other before the warmth of the fire.

# Twenty-nine

Avenell had never felt so hot. Flames licked through his blood, seared his throat, and raged like an inferno through his head. It was desire, lust, the power of acceptance over resistance, the strength of the love he felt for the woman before him.

And fear.

But it was not the same fear that had emotionally crippled him for so long. He had gotten so comfortable in that place where no one could touch him, where no one was allowed to love him in case they should decide he was not worthy of it.

Lily had come into his life and forced him to feel again—hope, true desire, and a love that went far deeper than he could have ever expected. It was not physical pain that had been truly holding him back, but fear of feeling too much. Every time they were together, he felt his facade slip a bit more. The passion and yearning he possessed for Lily seemed to know no bounds.

He felt so foolish once he understood that. He had wasted so much time with this woman. He had no idea how to be this man. He had no idea how to show her what she made him feel, but he was willing to learn.

As he stood there acknowledging what was to come, it was not a fear of being touched that clenched his stomach so tightly he could barely breathe. It was the fear of not being touched. And yes, there in the deep, dark center of his heart, there was a thread of terror that Lily still might decide to walk away.

Life held no guarantees.

If he trusted her to touch him, he had to trust her to love him.

"My lord."

The lure of her voice, sultry and sweet, drew him out of his head, forced him to focus his gaze. Though she had stepped close to him, she had not put her hands on him again.

His breath hit the back of his teeth in short bursts. Every joint in his hands ached.

Finally, she lifted her fingertips to his mouth. With the gentlest touch, she ran the tip of her index finger across his lower lip. A tingling buzz of sensation followed her touch. Yearning to connect with her in that moment, he lifted his eyes to her face. The exquisite beauty in her expression stopped his breath.

Her gray eyes sparkled like silver mist, and a subtle smile curved her mouth as she observed the path of her fingertip. With a twitch at the corner of her mouth, she reached up to smooth her fingers over the crease between his brows, until the tension there eased away. Then she rested her palm against the ridge of his jaw and looked into his eyes.

He watched in amazement as her gaze darkened to smoke, swirling with depth and mystery. The quiet calm of her nature reached into his soul, exploring with gentle insistence, soothing long-buried wounds. She was all that was steady and true. Sensual, generous, and lovely. She was his, as he was hers.

He lowered his chin and turned his face into her palm.

Her lips tilted upwards in response to the gesture, and his heart gave a hard lurch.

Then she slid her hand down the side of his throat until her palm rested against his chest.

Avenell held his breath. Scorching, prickling heat scored his nerves.

He focused on her, on the love and desire that rushed in his blood, making his head heavy and his limbs weightless. His insides trembled with growing need. The conflicting desires to possess and to surrender.

In that moment, as his heart thudded heavily beneath her palm, he wanted nothing more than to know what it was like to give all of himself to her. He was tired of resisting, tired of enforcing a detachment that had never served him. He wanted to feel everything.

When her fingertip circled the flat disc of his nipple, a shock of sensation shot through him, making him suck in a swift breath. It was an odd combination of pleasure and pain.

She parted her lips on a sigh and circled his nipple again.

Avenell's stomach trembled. He forced back the growl rising from deep in his chest. Already he felt himself near to breaking under the strain of passivity.

Yet he knew this was only the beginning. He could see by the wicked flicker in her gaze that she had much more yet to show him.

Unable to watch the passing phases of wonder and delight as they flitted across her face without feeling every caress more intensely, Avenell closed his eyes. Within a split second, he realized his mistake but could not bring himself to alter course. With his eyes closed, he felt the warmth of her hand on his skin like magical torture. In his mind, he visualized sparkling ripples originating at her fingertips and extending outward through his body, soothing his damaged nerves, replacing pain with pleasure.

When she pressed both hands to his chest and smoothed them down over the plane of his stomach, he heard a soft hum issue from her lips. She stepped closer. Close enough that the fall of her hair tickled his skin in wispy sighs. Close enough that the tips of her toes touched his and her breath bathed his burning skin.

Instead of pressing herself to him as he expected—as he suddenly craved—she stepped around him, trailing her fingers across his belly, his side, until she was behind him. Her movements were reminiscent of their first night together at Pendragon's.

His body tightened at the first light brush of her fingertips on his back. Again, he knew the breath-stealing dance of pain and pleasure together. Every muscle clenched tight as he strained to release his hold on sensations that had ruled him for so long.

When she replaced her fingertips with the silken press of her lush lips, his body gave an involuntary jolt.

He did not realize just how tense he had become until her arms slid around his waist from behind and she pressed the length of her naked body to his.

"I love you," she whispered. The sound of her voice was a warm balm, soothing him from the inside, spreading through him in a gentle wave.

She held him like that, her cheek resting against the back of his shoulder, her breath fanning over his skin, her bare arms linked securely around him until the tautness of his frame eased by slow degrees.

Then she drew back and came around again to face him. She reached for his hands where they were fisted at his sides and eased her thumb into the hollow of his fist, forcing his fingers to uncurl. Then she lifted his hands to set them on her hips as she stepped into him. Her curves molded to his rigid form, and her arms slid around his back in a full embrace. Her warmth enveloped him.

It was soothing and arousing at once. And though his damaged nerves still reacted to the stimulation, when he allowed himself to relax and *trust*, the familiar pain faded into the background of all the other sensations she inspired.

Avenell curled his fingers into the lushness of her hips and clenched his teeth. Her soft belly pressed along his aching erection, making him throb from head to toe.

He opened his eyes to see her gazing up at him, her eyes lovely and mysterious. Rising up onto her tiptoes, she brought her mouth to his. The feel of her peaked nipples dragging over his chest, and the friction of her belly gliding over the length of his erection, released a piercing spear of need through his center.

Her lips were warm as they moved back and forth over his. Then her tongue, flicking gently at the corner of his mouth.

Avenell maintained a steady flow of breath as he accustomed himself to the feel of her limbs entwined around him, the roving attention of her hands, the desirous intention of her embrace. Just knowing how much she wanted this made him anxious to allow more.

She shifted against him and brought her mouth to the side of his throat. Her tongue glided hot and wet over his skin, giving rise to gooseflesh in its wake. Then she bowed her head and pressed her open mouth to his chest. His fingers grasped her more tightly as he fought to remain patient under her exploration.

But when her sweet tongue flicked out over his nipple, a rush of sexual poignancy so intricate and specific struck him like a bolt of lightning. In a split instant, it ignited every inch of his being.

There was no pain now. Only pleasure. Deep, piercing points of pleasure.

"Lily," he groaned.

She tipped her face to look up at him, and he wasted no time in claiming her wayward tongue and drawing it into his mouth. Their lips crushed against their teeth, and their tongues tangled with the increasing wildness of their mutual desire for more.

Avenell couldn't get enough of the sweet and heady taste of her mouth. Even when her arms came up to wind around his neck and her fingers delved through his hair to clutch at the back of his head, he did not pull back.

There was a time such a thing would have triggered

instant panic. But that had been before he had allowed himself to accept that he didn't have to guard himself every moment. Before this woman had convinced him that with her, he was safe.

Finally, he drew back, but only enough to where he could look into her eyes. Her yearning was palpable. Her love was like a drug that soothed and inflamed at once.

Very gently, she brought her hands to his chest, exerting just enough pressure to push him back a small step.

His lungs so tight he could barely breathe, Avenell did as she bade him.

As he lowered himself into the chair again, she dropped gracefully to her knees before him. Her hands eased up his legs and smoothed confidently over the tense surface of his thighs.

Nervousness and lust clawed at him in tandem, both fighting for the strongest grip as he balanced precariously between sexual delights and the darkness of his deeper passions. He did not think he could endure it. He gripped the arms of the chair so tightly, his forearms bulged with the effort to hold himself still.

Her full attention fell to the hard evidence of his need. She gazed at him with a look of bold hunger. Her hand lifted to hover over the pulsing length of him, and Avenell bit hard on his lip. But she hesitated. Before touching him, she slid her focus up along his reclining form, the appreciation in her gaze warming him further, until she reached his face.

"What are you feeling?" she asked.

Avenell shook his head, unable to find the words.

What *was* he feeling?

Everything.

His inability to respond brought a small frown to her forehead, and she rose up on her knees. Planting her hands on the surface of his thighs, she leaned forward against him, stretching her body along his. Her soft, smooth heat covered him, slid skin over skin from where her hips pressed against his inner thighs to her belly over his erection and the lush cushions of her breasts flattening on his chest.

She melted against him and lifted her hand to curl her fingers around the back of his neck. Looking intently into his eyes, she drew his mouth to hers.

With her kiss, she challenged him. She tilted her head and opened her mouth, coaxing his open as well. Her teeth scored his lower lip. Her tongue tangled with his, and her breath puffed into his mouth.

The purity of her passion, her need for him, was better than the most potent wine, and he savored it. He surrendered to the whirlwind she created inside him, barely realizing he had brought his arms around her back. He held her so tightly that her breath shortened, and a small laugh slid from her throat.

Drawing back, she smiled.

His short rush of response to her kiss had pleased her. He could see it shining in her eyes, making them sparkle.

"Someday you will have the words, my lord," she assured him.

She pushed at his shoulders until his arms loosened, and he relaxed back in the chair. With another flashing smile, she trailed brief, hot kisses across his chest where his nerves had long expressed only pain, but now sparked hot with new sensations. She did not stop there. She pressed more kisses across his abdomen while her hands smoothed over his thighs.

Avenell suspected her intention, and his muscles seized with bright and sudden anticipation. He was alarmed by how badly he wanted to feel her mouth on him. He could barely breathe for the bone-deep need inside him at that moment.

At his obvious tensing, Lily had ceased her exploration. She straightened her upper body, but she did not withdraw her attention entirely. She looked into his face with an expression of love so pure and unassuming it made his heart ache. Very gently, she slid her hands up along the surface of his thighs. Then, still holding his gaze, she took his erection in her hand.

"I want to feel you against my lips, Avenell," she murmured thickly, her eyes dark and needful. "I want to taste you with my tongue and take you into my mouth. I have read of this particular pleasure and would give anything to share it with you."

His muscles twitched as he forced them to relax by degrees. Her words shocked him and aroused him near to bursting. He did not think he would be able to maintain control through such delightful torment.

"Please, Avenell," she whispered, shifting her hand to close her fingers around him more securely. His breath stopped moving through his lungs.

Holding his gaze, she began to caress along the length of his erection. With drifting fingertips and gentle squeezes, she learned the shape and feel of him.

"Lily," he gasped, "I don't know if I can..."

"Trust me," she insisted.

Watching her expression closely, Avenell could see the pleasure it brought her as her lips parted with her breath and her eyelids grew heavy. He focused on that, drawing it into himself. Slowly, he sank into the sensations she roused in him with her loving attention.

Just as he began to absorb the intensity of her touch, she lowered her head and flicked her tongue against his tip.

He groaned and arched his neck.

She flicked her tongue again, then immediately circled it around the sensitive ridge in a luscious stroke that drew another groan from his tight throat.

She murmured soothing words as she gripped him securely at the base of his erection, then she slid her full lips down over him. Her mouth encompassed his hard, aching flesh in wet heat. He could not resist looking down at her as she knelt between his taut thighs. He had never known anything as erotic as the sight of her loving him with her mouth.

And when she looked up at him with a flutter of her lashes, the love inside him expanded. What little remained of his control was maintained with just a thin thread wound tight around his heart.

Shivers coursed through him, his chest grew tight, and the fire in his blood roared with an intensity that threatened the last fiber of his determination to remain submissive to her direction.

She moved over him. Drawing him deeply into her mouth with lovely, silken swirls of her tongue. A fierce and heavy throbbing initiated in his brain. His body buzzed from head to toe. A million pinpoints of pleasure rolled over one another until the brilliant physical sensation of her touch was all he knew.

His release was building. Roaring through his blood, chasing away all thought but one—he needed to be inside her. Now.

In a sudden burst of strength, he curled his spine toward her and fisted his hand in her hair. It took all available effort to gently ease her mouth up along the length of his erection. Her head fell back as he leaned over her. He plundered her mouth with his tongue, releasing the pent-up fury of his deepest need.

The sound of her throaty moan shot through him.

He tore his mouth away to mutter thickly, "I can take no more."

His hand fell away from her as she rose swiftly to her feet. Pressing her hand gently to his chest, she urged him back.

Avenell reclined in the chair as she came up over him, settling her knees on either side of his hips. She grasped him in her hands once again to position him between her thighs.

The heat of her core against him felt like heaven and hell at once. She was slick and ready. Avenell grasped her hips in his hands, but she held herself strong over him, allowing the tip of him to barely kiss the entrance of her body.

He loved seeing her command at that moment. Her body was that of a goddess, regal and strong, as she knelt over him. He could have used his superior strength to plunge into her, could have risen from the chair to drive her down onto the floor and claim her like a conqueror.

Instead, he submitted. He gave himself over to her desire, knowing he would reap all the benefits. He released his hands from her hips and returned his grip to the arms of the chair.

Accepting his surrender with a soft murmur, she rewarded him with a gentle roll of her hips. It was a small movement, but it allowed his erection to glide just a short way into her body.

A growl rumbled in his throat, and he arched his head back. How would he make it through this?

She rocked again.

He reached deeper.

Her chin lowered, and a visible shiver coursed through her body. Her breath shortened, and the rocking of her body became tighter, more confined. She teased him with the suggestion of taking him all the way in—then denied him.

Avenell yielded. His body became hers to mold; his senses were hers to command. He trusted her. As she took him bit by bit into her body, he offered himself up to her in every way possible. His body. His heart. His soul.

And her passion possessed him.

In the midst of a black haze of lust, Avenell acknowledged the beauty of giving himself over to this amazing woman. The realization was astounding.

But before he could explore it further, she leaned forward over him and gripped the top edge of the chair. Then she brought her weight down on him in one forceful move, taking him in completely.

He groaned and grasped her buttocks as her heat surrounded him in a luscious caress.

She lifted herself off him, then took him all the way again. A hot, plunging stroke. A mind-stealing arc of pleasure. The rhythm she chose was relentless and demanding. Avenell had never known anything so consuming. She swept them both along with an intensity that scared him and thrilled him.

And as he sensed her nearing her peak, he pushed up, wrapping his arms low around her hips, drawing her completely into his embrace. He pressed his open mouth to her throat, stunned by the deep pleasure he experienced as her legs clamped tight against his hips and her arms lifted to encircle his head and neck.

In those moments, they seemed to become one being. Melded. Complete.

As a heavy thickness rose in his throat, she stiffened and arched in his arms. Her inner muscles fluttered, and a strangled sound issued from her lips as her climax pulsed through her body.

Avenell stopped breathing.

He shook deep in his core as the world expanded. All at once, he experienced the deepest pleasure, entirely devoid of pain. It was everything. It was what he no longer feared and what he had always needed.

It was her.

A long time passed before either of them were ready to move again.

Keeping his arms wrapped around her, Avenell stood and lifted her. He crossed to the bed in long strides and carefully settled them beneath the covers.

He drew her against his side. She laid her hand gently over his belly, and he covered it with his own, keeping her there. Though the sensitivity of his nerves was returning by slow but inexorable degrees, it could not disrupt his desire to hold her. To feel her heartbeat against his rib cage and the waft of her breath over his skin.

"I love you, Lily." His low-spoken words blended seamlessly with the rhythm of their breathing, but he knew she had heard him when she pressed her lips to his skin.

"I did not want to love you," he continued, tightening his arm around her back when he felt her stiffen. "The last person I had loved could not accept the way I was after the illness. My father was not a man who cared to understand weakness of any kind. He expected his heir to display courage and strength. A boy who cried out in pain whenever someone brushed against him was an aberration. Something to be derided and belittled."

She shifted her hand to link her fingers between his but did not interrupt. Her quiet acceptance and gentle offer of support were enough to encourage him to continue.

"As I started to recover from the illness and felt the return of some small bit of strength to my muscles, I vowed to prove to him I was strong enough and brave enough to be an earl's son. I forced myself to walk every day, though extreme fatigue forced me to go slow in the beginning, and my muscles did not want to cooperate. Eventually, I regained my strength and full physical capabilities. But it was not enough. I was damaged. The pain I continued to experience belied my accomplishments. My father could not accept a child with such an affliction. A weakling who cowered in pain at the slightest touch.

"He left me in the country and never came back again."

A small sound slipped from Lily's lips, and she lifted her head from his shoulder to look into his face.

"He was the aberration, Avenell. Not you."

"He was not alone. The nurses who had been my comfort before the illness grew tired in dealing with the challenges I presented. Their patience ran thin as they began to believe I was just a spoiled child seeking attention. They could not understand why I might still be feeling pain so long after the illness had left my body."

"Were you ever seen by a doctor?"

"By many, in the beginning, but none of them knew what to make of my continued symptoms."

She lifted her hand to the side of his face. Her eyes were soft with emotion, and her lips quivered as she spoke. "I hate it that you went through that. You must have been so frightened, so hurt by your father's actions… I wish I could take all that pain away."

He took her hand in his and brought her fingertips to his lips. "You do, Lily. With every smile and every touch, you sweep it out of existence. I am sorry it took me so long to see that. I am sorry I hurt you before I understood."

She shook her head to stop him and rose up to press her lips sweetly to his. He would have allowed the kiss to deepen, but he had not finished all he wished to say. Curling his fingers around the back of her neck, he urged her to lift her head.

As her lips hovered a breath above his and her smoky gaze looked deep into his soul, he murmured, "I love you, Lily. Promise to love me forever, and I swear I will devote myself to your happiness. Marry me, Lily."

She smiled. "This promise will be far easier than the others you asked of me. Nothing would make me happier than to be your wife."

# *Epilogue*

*October 1817*

Lily stood at the window, gazing out at the sleepy city as the rising sun turned all that was black and gray to various shades of lavender and gold.

It was getting late. She should go before Angelique's household began to rise, but she didn't want to miss the transformation of night into day.

"It is strange," she mused out loud, "how different the sunrise seems when you view it after being up all night versus rising early."

"How so?" the earl asked from the bed behind her. His voice was warm and intimate.

Lily tipped her head and softened her gaze. "I am not sure I can explain it," she murmured.

She wrapped her arms around herself. She had dressed only in her shift after rising from bed, and the fire that had warmed the room had died down hours ago. A moment later, Avenell stepped up behind her to drape a cashmere shawl about her shoulders. It had been a gift from him. She kept it there in his bedroom to prevent her sisters from discovering it and wondering where it had come from.

Lily accepted his gesture with a smile and drew the wrap around her shoulders. Then she leaned back against him, craving the warmth of his body far more than what the swath of cloth could provide.

She felt his hesitation in the moment before he slid his arms around her waist, lowering his head to rest the side of his jaw against her temple. He still had some trouble with the more subtle gestures of intimacy, but Lily believed he would continue to relax over time—if she remained patient. Already, he seemed capable of tolerating so much more than he had in the past.

She knew it was because every prickle of discomfort was tempered by love.

"Tell me about the sunrise," he murmured against the curve of her ear.

She tilted her head, her gaze still soaking in the surreal beauty of the world shifting from dark to light. "I often used to rise before dawn, but I do not suppose I took the time to observe the awakening of the world around me. I started my day, trusting morning would come. And it did."

The brush of his lips across her temple sent a delightful thrill through her body. Lily sighed, feeling almost guilty for the wealth of happiness she had discovered with this man.

"I love the quiet beauty of the night sky," she continued thoughtfully, "filled with mystery and starlight, but there is something magical about the dawn. It is strange. When the sky begins to lighten and soft colors first appear, the transition is so gentle you hardly notice it. But if you are aware enough to observe, if you take the time to really be a part of the transformation, it feels…"

Her explanation trailed off. She found it difficult to find the words to properly describe the wonder she felt as she experienced the very common daily occurrence.

"It feels like it possesses all the possibilities of life," Avenell offered quietly.

Lily turned in place. She slipped her arms around his naked torso and tipped her head back to look into his face. Her smile was so wide her cheeks ached, but she did not hold back. Her joy in the past few months had grown by leaps and bounds, and only because of how much she had seen her happiness reflected in the man she loved.

Love flowed freely between them as he lowered his head to take her mouth in a kiss that was slow and deep.

"I should really be getting home." Lily sighed when he lifted his head, though she did nothing to remove herself from the circle of his arms.

A frown creased his brow. "Let me obtain a special license. We can be married by month's end."

Lily smiled. "No. You promised a long engagement, and I shall hold you to it."

A growl rumbled through his chest. "I want you as my wife."

"And you shall have me. After a public and lengthy courtship."

"You are killing me."

Lily slipped from his embrace. She crossed to her clothes and began to dress.

"I daresay you will survive the delay, Avenell," she answered through the smile she could not seem to wipe away.

As she sat and began to roll her stockings up her bare legs, she spared a swift glance at him from beneath her lashes. He had pulled on his breeches and stood beautiful and resolute against the lightening sky. His body, so firmly muscled, was not quite as rigid as it used to be, yet it still held all the strength and fortitude of his character.

"It is not as though you are being forced to abstain from all contact," she added cheekily. "I am simply not ready to share our relationship with the world."

He chuckled, and the sound warmed her heart. "Sweetheart, the world is well aware of my pursuit of you. How can they not be when I dance with you and only you at every ball and visit your great-aunt's house several times a week?"

Lily laughed as she stood to step into her gown. "Indeed, you are a very persistent suitor. Emma has nearly accepted the inevitable match."

Before she could reach around to try to fasten the buttons running up the back of her gown, he was there to assist. She turned to allow him access and was reminded of the first night she had found herself in this room, frightened and confused.

"The gossips are saying you have melted the ice of my heart," he said.

His voice was smooth and rich as he patiently worked the buttons on the back of her gown. She bit her lip to hold back the unexpected rush of desire through her system.

She shook her head. "Your heart was never frozen. In fact, it was the fire inside you that lured me." She smiled. "Like a moth to your flame."

He finished the last button and paused to brush his lips across the back of her neck.

"Marry me, Lily," he whispered. "Today."

"I will, but not yet," she replied, though her voice was unsteady. "I rather enjoy the excitement of sneaking off to be with my secret lover," she whispered in confession.

Turning in place, she met his gaze. "Soon you will become part of my family. You shall have to endure Emma's overbearing but well-intentioned nature, and Portia's irreverent impudence. Angelique will flirt even more shamelessly with you. The friendship I have noticed forming between you and Bentley will grow. But for now, you are only mine," she said a bit more fiercely than she had intended. "And I am not ready to share you with them all just yet."

His low laugh, which had been coming more easily lately, rolled freely from his throat as he brought her back into his arms.

"Yet, you force *me* to share *you*," he stated. "You realize that once we are married, I will be able to take you away on a grand honeymoon. It will be just the two of us. Not only for the darkest hours of night," he murmured suggestively as his hands began to roam up and down the length of her back, inciting delicious shivers. He lowered his head beside hers to tease the sensitive skin of her neck with his lips and breath. "But all day, as well. Through sunrise, midday, and dusk. Breakfast, lunch, and dinner."

Lily sighed, melting into him. Her hands reached around to grasp his buttocks, and she pressed her lips to his bare shoulder before asking, "Can we take all of our meals in bed?"

His laughter was deep, rolling, and infectious as he stepped away.

"I had better get you home, or I shall make another meal of *you*."

Lily's insides tingled as she watched him stride across the room to finish dressing. She had been well and truly liberated. The hollow ache that had resided in her center for so long had been completely eradicated.

Love had filled every empty space and continued to stretch out farther than she could have imagined.

Read on for a look at the next book in the Fallen Ladies Series

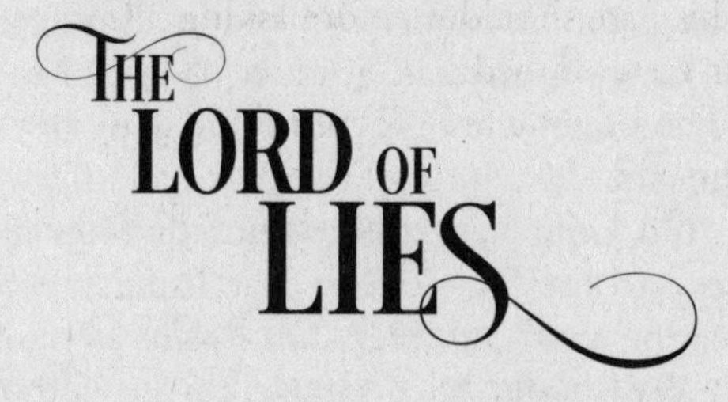


Coming soon from Sourcebooks Casablanca

# One

*London, June 1817*

Portia Chadwick was terrified. And furious.

And *terrified.*

Perched on the edge of her seat in the racing carriage, her legs braced for action, Portia clenched fistfuls of her skirts in a vain attempt to contain her panic.

Not twenty minutes ago, her sister, Lily, had been abducted right off the street in front of their great-aunt's house in Mayfair. They had just arrived home after an evening out when the assailant had come out of nowhere, knocking their driver to the ground with one blow and hauling Lily off her feet. Portia had scrambled from the carriage in time to see her sister being tossed into a waiting vehicle that took off as soon as the kidnapper climbed in after her.

Portia's immediate instinct had been to chase after the carriage with her skirts lifted to her knees, but Angelique had insisted there was another way.

And now here they were, driving at breakneck speed to the East End to search the streets for a boy wearing a red cap. Her aunt had clearly gone mad.

"We should have contacted the authorities," she said, fear making her combative.

"The authorities will do nothing but write up a report," Angelique replied. "Word of this will spread like a disease through the gossip mills. We need to save your sister, and quickly, but the authorities will be more harm than help."

Portia wasn't sure she agreed with the dowager countess's assessment, but she had followed Angelique's lead on impulse and now had no choice but to follow it through.

She hated feeling so ineffectual, so bloody useless.

"How in hell is a boy in a red cap going to help us?" Portia pressed.

"The boy knows how to get in touch with a man of great proficiency with this sort of thing," Angelique answered. "Trust me, darling. It is our very best chance to save your sister."

Portia's stomach twisted. "What kind of man?" she asked. "Who is he? How do you know he will help us?"

"He is known to do many things…for the proper incentive," Angelique replied evasively.

"Incentive?" Portia's anxiety spiked. "But we have little money."

"We have enough to bluff, *ma petite*. Now, stop arguing." The elderly lady leaned forward to peer out the window. "We are almost there. Keep your eyes alert for the boy. Remember to look for a red cap."

Portia shivered. From fear, anxiety, and the effort it took to suppress the urgent impulse to take action. She was desperate to be moving, running, talking. Something to produce progress. While they rolled through the narrow, twisting lanes, Lily was being taken farther away from them.

She focused all of her energy on scanning the streets through the window. Streetlamps were sparse, casting deep shadows through which anonymous figures moved about. It was near midnight and the East End was rife with activity.

Questionable activity.

The carriage slowed as they wound their way along the darkened lanes. Portia saw various characters moving about in the night. Men, women, and far more children than she would have expected, but not a single red cap.

And then, as they turned another corner—there!

A boy strolled casually with a chimney sweep's broom. One hand stuffed deep in the pocket of his oversize woolen trousers, a red cap sitting jauntily on his head.

"Is that him?" Portia asked, a flash of hope making her chest tight.

Her great-aunt leaned across Portia to peer out the window. "Let us hope so." She knocked on the roof, signaling for the carriage to stop. A moment later, Charles appeared in the doorway. A heavy bruise had already formed above his temple where he had been struck by Lily's attacker.

"Go fetch that boy there," Angelique said.

"Yes, m'lady."

While the loyal servant did as requested, the ladies waited in tense silence. Several moments later, the carriage door opened again.

"Wot do you fancy pieces want?"

The boy peered in through the open door of the carriage while Charles stood stiffly behind his shoulder. His young face was smeared with soot, making it hard to discern his age. But judging by his size, Portia guessed him to be about eleven or twelve. A bit old for a chimney sweep.

He stood warily, scanning the interior of the carriage, expertly assessing what danger they might represent. He dismissed Angelique quickly enough but took a few extra seconds studying Portia. When he gave her a jaunty little grin and tipped the brim of his hat, Portia realized with a touch of shock that the child was flirting with her.

"We are looking for nightshade." Angelique spoke in a dramatic whisper, though there was no one beyond Portia and the boy near enough to hear her.

The child snorted. "I ain't no apothecary," he said.

Angelique flashed a coin in the palm of her gloved hand. "You know who I seek, boy. We haven't the time for games and subterfuge."

A shadow of respect crossed the boy's face and he reached to take the coin, testing it between his teeth before shrugging his shoulders. "Can't take you to 'im. Not how it works. I deliver a message, an' his man'll contact you."

"No, please," Portia said, drawing the boy's eyes back to her. "We don't have time for messages." Based on the cryptic conversation, she finally had some hope her great-aunt had not led them astray and she was not going to let the opportunity slide away. "You must take us to this man directly. Immediately."

The boy narrowed his sharp gaze and flashed another grin. "Fer another coin an' a kiss, I may change me mind."

Angelique made a sound that could have been a scoff. But she reached back into her purse. "Here is your coin." She waved a hand toward Portia. "Give him a kiss so we can move this along."

The coin quickly disappeared into the child's pocket before he swept his hat off his head and turned his face to Portia. Feeling more than a little silly, Portia leaned forward to briefly brush her lips across the child's cheek.

He gave a quick whoop, then smashed his hat back on his head.

Turning to Charles, who still stood beside him, he said, "Head down the street a-ways, swing right after the butcher's place. Keep going till you pass the park. There'll be a row of houses that all look the same. Go to the one nearest the broken streetlamp. That's where you'll find Nightshade's man." He looked back to Portia and Angelique. "And I'd be grateful if you don't tell him it was me who sent ya. He'd have me hide fer not following the rules." The boy tossed a jaunty wink at Portia. "I like me hide."

The boy was ridiculously charming and Portia smiled despite her anxiety. "Thank you. We do appreciate your help."

The boy tipped the brim of his cap, then backed away. Charles quickly closed the carriage door, and a minute later, they were off again.

Portia stared across the carriage at her great-aunt with a dose of newfound respect. "Who is Nightshade?"

The lady's expression was vague as she replied, "No one knows, *ma petite chérie*."

"What do you mean?"

"He never meets his clients face-to-face." The old lady gestured toward the window. "There is a strict process to getting in touch with the man. We are fortunate your kiss is so highly regarded," she added with a sly glance.

Portia resisted the urge to roll her eyes. *Among young boys, maybe.* "Can this Nightshade be trusted?"

"He would not have gained the reputation he has if he were untrustworthy or incompetent. They say his insistence on remaining anonymous allows him to move through any environment undetected, that he is capable of infiltrating even the most elite social groups."

Portia leaned forward, captivated by the idea such a man existed. "How do you know of him?"

"Word gets around when there is someone willing to do what others cannot. Or will not." Angelique paused and looked down at the ring on her left hand. "A few years ago, I hired him to help me with a certain personal matter. If anyone can find Lily, it is Nightshade."

Portia fell silent, hoping her great-aunt was right. In spite of her ever-increasing worry for Lily, she couldn't help but wonder what the mysterious man had done for Angelique.

After several minutes, the carriage reached the area the boy had mentioned. It was a more residential neighborhood where both sides of the street were lined with brick row houses two stories high with narrow fronts and identical entrances. Portia peered through the window, straining to locate the broken streetlamp that would mark the correct house.

There. The moment she saw it, the carriage pulled to the side of the street. Charles must have seen it as well.

Portia took her great-aunt's arm in silence as they made their way up the walk to the darkened front door. She swept her gaze in all directions, trying to pierce the darkness surrounding them, alert for any threat. The shadows were deep in front of the house and no number marked the address. Two small windows bracketed the door, but no light shone from them. Portia tipped her head to look at the windows on the upper level. All was dark.

Blast. What if no one was home?

Angelique lifted the tarnished brass knocker and issued a loud echoing announcement of their presence.

Silence followed. And then a soft noise.

The door opened unexpectedly on well-oiled hinges, revealing a petite man in his later years with a smallish head and iron-gray hair worn back in an old-fashioned queue. Despite the man's diminutive height, he somehow managed to look at them down the length of a hawklike nose.

"Wot?"

His one word, uttered with none of the graces

assigned to even a poorly trained butler, threw Portia off. She stiffened in affront, then prepared to respond to the discourteous greeting with a bit of insolence herself.

Angelique saved her the trouble as the lady pushed through the door, past the little man who was helpless to stop her, and into the hall, saying as she went, "We have a matter of vital importance that requires Nightshade's immediate attention." She swung around to cast the little man a narrow-eyed look. "Where shall we wait?"

"Don't know who yer talking 'bout."

"Yes, you do. Now fetch your master or I will seek him out myself."

The little man pinched his face into a sour expression as he glanced toward the door, then back to Angelique as though debating the benefits of tossing them both back onto street. He cast a critical gaze over their appearances, seeming to take mental note of the quality in their clothing. Then he snorted and turned to amble into the shadows at the back of the hall.

Angelique turned to Portia. "Come. Let us find somewhere comfortable to wait."

The front hall was dark and narrow. Stairs rose up along the left side and three doors opened to the right. The hall itself contained nothing but a small table set near the door. Portia wandered toward the first door to peek into the room beyond.

It was a small parlor.

"This way," she said as she strode forward into the room.

The room was also quite dark, the only light being

a dim glow from the street outside, which did not reach far. But it was enough to see the outline of the furniture and a small candelabra set on a table near the sofa. Angelique took a seat in an armchair while Portia went directly to the cold fireplace looking for something to light the candles.

It felt good to finally have something to do. It kept her thoughts from flying in all sorts of wild directions. Once the candles were lit, she found herself unable to sit still. Though she tried several times to take a seat, she inevitably jumped to her feet again in a matter of minutes as fretful energy continued to rush unheeded through her body.

She began to pace.

# *Two*

It felt like they waited for hours in the dimly lit parlor. Angelique sat quietly, her eyelids dropping in the semidarkness. Portia almost envied the old woman her drowsiness as her own disquiet steadily grew. The longer they sat unattended, the harder it was going to be to track Lily down.

Portia wondered if perhaps the rude little butler had simply gone to bed rather than informing his master of his guests. After making her hundredth turn at the fireplace, she took off toward the door at the opposite end of the room with purposeful strides, determined to go in search of someone herself.

Just as she neared the door, a figure appeared in the darkened frame. The man made such a sudden and silent appearance that Portia was nearly startled from her skin. As it was, she barely managed to stop herself from colliding with the man by bracing her hand hard on the doorframe.

She looked at the newcomer sharply. Her worry and impatience coalesced into anger now that he had finally appeared.

He was a rather nondescript man in his later years, perhaps in his fifties somewhere, with light hair that was going to gray, a pale almost sickly complexion, a beard that had grown a bit bushy, and small wire-rimmed spectacles. He was dressed in a brown suit with matching waistcoat and stood with sloped shoulders, his hands stuffed into the front pockets of his coat.

Seemingly unconcerned with their near collision, he looked down at her from nearly a foot above her with an expression that could only be classified as annoyed.

The longer she stood there staring up at him, the more annoyed he became, as was evidenced by the lowering of his untamed brows and the pursing of his thin mouth.

And his annoyance annoyed Portia.

He was the one who had kept them waiting while her sister was dragged off to who knows where.

She pushed off from the doorframe and planted her hands on her hips.

"It is about time. Do you have any idea how long we have been waiting?"

The thick eyebrows shot up, reaching far above the top rim of his spectacles. "You have been waiting less than fifteen minutes," he replied in an entirely unhurried tone. "Do you have any idea what time of night it is?"

"I would say it is nearing one o'clock in the morning, which should signify that our issue is urgent and of such importance that it cannot wait until a more reasonable hour, which should in turn have pressed you to a hastier response."

The man made a sound in the back of his throat, a sort of abbreviated snort, then stared, saying nothing more. His lips pressed into such a tight line that they lost all hint of color and his eyes narrowed to a squint behind his spectacles.

"Portia, come sit. Allow the poor man into the room so we may conduct our business."

Portia realized then that her challenging stance essentially blocked the doorway, keeping the newcomer stranded on the threshold. Executing a little snort of her own, Portia turned with a whip of her skirts and strode to where her great-aunt was pushing herself a bit straighter in the armchair. Rather than sitting, which she knew wouldn't last long anyway, Portia took position beside the chair and waited for Nightshade's man to step forward and take control of the situation.

Taking control was not how Portia would describe the man's next actions.

After a slow glance at Angelique, he strolled into the room, keeping his hands in his pockets. He walked past the lit candelabra, his brows shooting upward again as if the fact that they had lit the room was more of an affront than their untimely barging into his household.

Portia studied him, irritated and curious.

*This* was the go-between for the highly skilled and ruthless Nightshade? He looked more like someone's daft uncle or a confused schoolteacher.

"Mr. Honeycutt," Angelique said, "we met once before, a few years ago…"

"Of course, Lady Chelmsworth," Honeycutt

interrupted without turning to face them as he wandered to the window overlooking the front street. "I recall our introduction. I assume tonight brings you here on another matter."

Portia bristled at the impatience obvious in his tone. The man was sorely lacking in manners.

"Indeed. This is my great-niece, Miss Chadwick," Angelique replied, waving an elegant hand toward Portia. "Her sister has been abducted tonight. Taken off the street and carried away. We need Nightshade to recover her."

Portia watched Mr. Honeycutt carefully, expecting some sort of reaction to the news of a young lady being kidnapped in such a way. But he gave no acknowledgment at all, just continued to stare out the window with his shoulders slouched and his chin tucked to his chest.

Portia couldn't stand any more of it.

"Mr. Honeycutt," she began in a sharp tone, but just as she spoke, he turned around again and pinned her with a stare that stopped the rest of her words.

Something in his manner, his gaze, his sudden focus managed to suck the dissent right out of her. Somewhere deep within the ugly brown coat and sloped posture she detected a strong thread of competence. She rolled her lips in between her teeth in a way she hadn't done since she was young and her mother would chastise her for her naughtiness, which had been often.

After waiting long enough to be assured she would not interrupt any further, Honeycutt shifted his attention back to Angelique. "Have you any idea who may have perpetrated the abduction or why?"

Angelique looked to Portia, giving her a nod.

During their drive across London, Portia had confessed to Angelique the truth about the mysterious loan and Hale's recent threats. The Chadwicks had initially decided to keep the full nature of their dire circumstances from the lady's knowledge rather than risk the possibility it might influence her decision to sponsor the younger sisters for the Season.

Portia straightened her spine and looked the man directly in the face. She realized it was vital he have all the information available if this Nightshade were to have any luck in tracking down where Lily had been taken, but it didn't make it any easier to admit her family's secrets to a stranger.

"Since my father's death several months ago, my oldest sister, Emma, had been receiving notes from someone named Mason Hale regarding an unpaid loan. Then last night, my sister Lily—the one who was just abducted—was personally threatened by Hale. He stated we had two days to repay him in full, with interest. He indicated he would have his money, one way or another." She paused, looking for some indication that Honeycutt was listening. He provided no reaction at all. After a bit, Portia realized he wasn't going to offer any and she continued. "Hale gave us until tomorrow to get the money to him. We had a plan to come up with the amount, but something must have changed. Hale must have decided not to wait."

Honeycutt was silent and unmoving for several minutes. Finally he asked, "Does anyone else have any cause to take your sister? Vengeance, lust, greed?"

"Not that I know of," Portia replied.

A sick rush of guilt settled in her stomach. She and Lily had not been talking as much as they used to. Portia had been so aggravated since she began her debut Season that she had not been very attentive to her sister.

"Do you know of Mason Hale? Where to find him?" Portia asked when Honeycutt remained silent longer than she was comfortable with.

He narrowed his gaze in irritation again and Portia stiffened. If he wasn't so bloody tight-lipped, she wouldn't be forced to press him.

"I will address the matter with my employer," Honeycutt finally replied.

The man turned his gaze to Angelique again. "As you may recall, his services require a partial payment up-front. The urgency of the matter will demand a substantial fee, my lady."

The dowager countess grunted in acceptance and reached into her reticule for a small sack of coins. She handed them to Portia, their eyes meeting briefly as she did so. The old lady lived on a limited allowance from the present earl and Portia certainly had no money.

This was the bluff her great-aunt had mentioned earlier.

Portia brought the sack of coins to Mr. Honeycutt, looking him directly in the eye as she came to stand before him.

"That is all I have on my person at the moment, Mr. Honeycutt," Angelique explained. "I did not waste time going for more funds but came directly here, you understand. I can promise the full fee once my niece is returned safely home."

Honeycutt glanced down at the small purse in Portia's hand, making no move to take it from her.

Portia's anxiety grew unbearable.

He had to accept it. Nightshade was their only option at this point. Precious time slid away with every second Honeycutt took to respond. Lily's image flashed through Portia's mind. Her sweet, gentle sister needed someone to take action.

Now.

Portia stepped toward Honeycutt, her anger over his obvious reticence forcing her hand. On fear and impulse, she grasped his wrist and yanked his hand out of his pocket. Before he could resist, she pressed the purse into his large palm. Holding it there with both of her hands, she looked up into his face, forcing him to meet her eyes.

"You have to accept," she said through a tight, aching throat. "Nightshade has to find my sister. There is no other option."

He glared at her with narrowed eyes. His affront at her boldness was clear.

Portia, full of fear and stubborn determination, refused to back down. She could feel the tension in his body, but it was more than annoyance, she realized. He possessed a sort of physical readiness she hadn't noticed before when his slow movements and careless posture had suggested a distinct lack of interest. His hand, enclosed in both of hers, felt stronger, more capable than she had expected. Standing close enough that she had to tip her head back to look into his face, she sensed something powerful emanating from him.

Something that forced a subtle shiver to course through her body.

She peered into his eyes. They were shadowed by his bushy brows and distorted by the glass of his spectacles, but she swore she saw something significant there. Tipping her head to the side, a frown creased her forehead as she focused her gaze—trying to discern just what it was that had caught her attention.

But then he curled his hand into a fist, claiming the purse before abruptly turning to walk away.

"I will get a message to my employer. I offer no guarantee." Honeycutt paused in the doorway. "Return home. Word of the investigation will be sent to you there."

"We will wait here for news," Portia replied.

"Impossible. There is no telling how long it will take for my employer to discover your sister's fate. It could be several hours. Or days."

Portia thought of going back to the house and awaiting word. She thought of Emma returning and having to be advised of Lily's abduction.

No. She could not go home without some solid results…even if she had to go out into the night and get them herself.

She folded her arms across her chest and squared her shoulders. "We will wait here."

Honeycutt stopped in the threshold to glare back at her over his sloped shoulder. "You cannot."

"We will," she insisted with an insolent lift of her eyebrows, "unless you intend to cause a scene by physically forcing two screaming females from your home." She smiled with false sweetness. "I received the impression you prefer to keep these dealings more discreet."

For a brief second, the man seemed at a loss on how to handle Portia's insistence. Then he gave a short grunt. "Do not expect any amenities," he muttered.

And then he was gone.

# Three

Portia stood there, apprehension coming back to the fore now that she and Angelique were alone again. She glanced back toward her great-aunt, whose eyes had grown heavy as her chin bobbed repeatedly toward her chest. The elderly lady would be asleep within minutes.

Portia made a swift decision. Picking up her skirts, she crossed the room in long strides, then paused at the door, peering into the hall. Everything was dark and silent.

Creeping forward, she strained her ears to hear any indication of where Honeycutt had gone. Had he left the house, gone to Nightshade already?

The floorboards above her gave a telltale creak.

Portia did not think twice as she made her way toward the narrow stairs leading up to the second floor. There was far too much at stake to worry about proper manners. Going excruciatingly slowly, she incorporated into her movements all of the little tricks she had developed as a child.

At the top of the stairs, Portia peered down a narrow

hallway, dark but for the light from one room seeping through the crack of a door barely left open. Portia crept forward, undeterred.

Nearing the lit room, Portia heard the low murmur of two distinct voices. But she could not make out what they said. The hallway was long and narrow and not at all conducive to hiding. There was not even a table to crouch behind.

Creeping forward, she got as close as she could, stopping in a deep shadow just beyond the pale beam of light extending across the floor. Pressing her back flat against the wall, she eased her breath into a slow, deep, silent rhythm as she had trained herself to do long ago.

Then she listened.

"This don't sound like somethin' Hale would do." Portia recognized the guttural tone of the rude little butler's voice coming from just inside the door. "He ain't no kidnapper."

"He never was before, but you and I know people can be pushed to do almost anything under the right circumstances."

Portia tensed.

This last was spoken by an unfamiliar voice. She had expected to hear Honeycutt, but this man spoke in a much lower tone and his words revealed the barest hint of cockney buried beneath the layers of finer intonation.

Breathing so slowly she could not even feel the air moving through her lungs, she waited. She had no idea what she would do if someone stepped into the hall and saw her skulking there. It was not in her nature to think so far ahead, preferring to rely on instinct and inspiration in such situations.

When, after a few minutes, no one came out of the room, she began to relax. She could still hear quite a bit of movement within and her curiosity won out over caution. Twisting her upper body, she leaned forward until she could take a quick peek through the crack in the door.

She saw the butler first. He stood with his back to her, thank God, as he riffled through the drawers of a tallboy dresser.

Beyond the butler, Honeycutt was only partially visible where he sat on a bench turned three-quarters away from her in front of a large mirror propped atop a table. Portia saw no one else in her limited view. It made her nervous, not being able to see where the third man may be.

But then her gaze swung back to Honeycutt as he grasped the bottom hem of his coat and drew it up over his head—along with the waistcoat beneath, the shirt, and the neckcloth.

It all came off in one attached piece.

Portia was pondering the reason for such a design when her attention was forcefully snared by what had been revealed by the sudden disrobing.

Honeycutt was not a man in his later years.

His upper body was sharply defined by hard, lean muscle beneath smooth, tawny skin. As he lifted his arms to clear the garment from his head, the dim candlelight rippled over the contours of his shoulders and back. There was not a bit of extra bulk or flab. Just taut, agile strength.

"Wot'll you do, Mr. Turner?"

Portia spun around to press her shoulders to the wall again, grasping her skirts in her hands to draw them in so as not to be seen from inside the room. She had forgotten herself for a few moments and had gotten frightfully close to tumbling right in. Chastising herself for such carelessness, she fought to regain control of her breath. But it was not so easy now that she had the surprising image of Honeycutt's strong masculine physique stamped indelibly in her mind.

"I'll pay Hale a visit. Find out if he knows anything about this girl. Even if he wasn't involved, Hale may have some information."

Honeycutt had talked with the intonation of the middle-class. This man spoke in a way that brought up impressions of back-alley dealings and midnight capers. There was a depth to his voice, a thread of danger in the low tenor that made Portia's skin tingle with alarm.

*What had the sour little butler called him? Mr. Turner?*

"Wot costume should I ready?"

*Costume?*

"Mr. Black, I think. And toss me the face cream, would you? I need to get this beard off."

Fury welled hot in Portia's stomach. She had been right to be suspicious. What kind of scam were they running? Had Angelique unwittingly walked them into a fleecing? They had already given Honeycutt—or was it Turner?—a significant purse.

No. They had been talking about Hale. There seemed to be some intention to investigate Lily's abduction.

There were several more moments of shuffling

movement as Portia contemplated the situation with rising trepidation. Then there was the distinct sound of water being poured into a basin, followed by the splashes of vigorous washing.

"Wot if Hale don't know nuthin'?" the butler asked.

Portia tensed. It was a question she had not allowed herself to consider in any depth. The abduction had to be connected with Hale. There was no other logical possibility. No other lead to follow if that were the case.

"Then we made a pretty purse for an hour's worth of work."

Portia's intention to remain hidden in the hall instantly disintegrated. Pushing off from the wall, she burst into the little room. "Like hell you did!"

The butler gave a start at her sudden intrusion. Portia ignored his shocked glare. All of her attention focused on the man who sat in front of the mirror with a towel draped over his head as he dried his hair. She fixed her furious gaze on his broad shoulders, the fire in her blood rising to an exponential degree.

"You have been hired to bring my sister home, and that is what you will do," she declared. "Am I clear, Mr. Honeycutt? Or is it Mr. Turner? Or should I just call you *Nightshade*?"

The butler took a swift and menacing step toward her. Portia did not acknowledge him, waiting instead for the other man to respond.

At first, Turner did nothing to acknowledge her presence, as though his strange toilet was often interrupted by angry young women. While she watched, waiting with her arms crossed indignantly over her chest, he finished drying his hair. The movements of his arms caused a fascinating bunching and releasing of the muscles across his shoulders and down his back. After a minute of this, as Portia's mouth went curiously dry, he stood from the bench and turned toward her.

Standing at full height, he grasped the ends of the towel with his large hands to keep it anchored over his face like the hood of a cloak. He was still bared to the waist and his woolen trousers rested low across lean hips. Portia's attention was immediately snared by the way muscles cut across his abdomen and angled past his hips in intriguing lines she hadn't known the human body possessed.

Her breath arrested quite forcefully on its way out of her lungs. Her knees locked, rooting her to the floor. And a frightening shiver skittered down her spine while another entirely unfamiliar sensation rippled through her insides.

There was something inherently dangerous in the man before her. Though his posture gave no indication of a threat, it was there anyway. In the subtle tightening of those angular muscles across his chest and abdomen and the way she could feel him staring at her, though she couldn't see his face beneath the deep shadow created by the towel.

Portia swallowed hard and lifted her chin.

She could not back down. Lily needed her to follow this through. No matter how intimidating the circumstances, it could not be close to what her sister was likely enduring.

"Wot should I do with her?"

Portia tensed.

"Nothing," he replied darkly. "I will handle her. Go ready the carriage."

The butler left the room and Portia squared her shoulders. "I am not leaving until you promise to do everything in your power to retrieve my sister."

"Then you delay me unnecessarily," he replied tersely. "I always do everything in my power, Miss Chadwick. Some things are beyond my reach." He turned and crossed to where a set of clothes had been laid out over a chair. With his back to her, he dropped the towel and bent to retrieve the clothing. She was so distracted by the sight of his woolen trousers tightening briefly over very firm masculine buttocks before he straightened again that she only just noticed his new clothing was sewn together as one piece in the same manner as Honeycutt's costume.

In the moment before he drew the garment over his head, Portia noted his hair was not the pale blond and gray it had been as Honeycutt. It appeared much darker, with some caramel-colored streaks, though that impression could have been a trick of the candlelight reflecting on the damp, tousled locks.

"If Hale is not behind your sister's abduction, what would you have me do? Young women disappear off the streets all the time and are most often never seen again."

"I do not accept that."

"You may have to."

"It has to be Hale," she insisted. "It is the only thing that even partially makes sense."

He grunted at that but did not reply as he walked back to take a seat before the mirror. She noticed that he was very careful to keep his face averted. From where she stood, all she saw in the mirror was the empty space over his shoulder.

"Take the old lady home so I can do what you hired me to do."

Portia's mind whirled as a strange resistance settled deep in her bones. She stood stiffly, watching as he reached for the towel again and draped it around his shoulders. Then he expertly applied a black, greasy substance to his hair, which had started to dry in a riotous mess. The grease smoothed his hair back along his skull, completely eliminating any suggestion of lighter streaks. After washing his hands in the water basin, he began applying something to his face. His movements were swift and competent, as though he had performed these same actions a thousand times.

Portia watched in silent fascination. Sidling farther into the room, she tried to get a better view, wondering why he donned his disguise so openly in front of her. By the time she got around to where she could see his face, she realized why he didn't bother to chase her off before beginning his ministrations.

He had become a different person.

Not quite as old as Honeycutt, this incarnation appeared perhaps thirty-five to forty, with black hair, a slightly swarthy skin tone, imposing black eyebrows, and a thin, black mustache. Put together with the simple white shirt, navy-blue coat, and the basic neckcloth he had donned, he looked like a man of the upper-middle class. A lawyer perhaps, or a banker.

She stared in amazement at how completely he had transformed from the forgettable Mr. Honeycutt to this strange man in a matter of minutes. And all while effectively preventing her from catching any discerning aspect of his natural self—aside from his bare upper body and a firm backside, which she was not likely to forget anytime soon.

Her amazement shifted in an instant to admiration and then determination.

"I am going with you," she declared.

# About the Author

Amy Sandas's love of romance began one summer when she stumbled across one of her mother's Barbara Cartland books. Her affinity for writing began with sappy preteen poems and led to a bachelor's degree with an emphasis on creative writing from the University of Minnesota Twin Cities. She lives with her husband and children in northern Wisconsin.